Michael Dibdin was born in 1947, and attended schools in Scotland and Ireland and universities in England and Canada. He is the author of the internationally bestselling Aurelio Zen series, which includes *Blood Rain*, *And Then You Die* and *Back to Bologna*. He died in 2007.

'This maestro of crime writing, deploying all his powers of caustic intelligence, grisly inventiveness and blisteringly entertaining evocation of place, goes out in coruscating style.' Peter Kemp, *Sunday Times* Books of the Year

'Dibdin's version of Italy is one that merits revisiting, his books as enriching in their own way as a stroll round the Uffizi.' Jake Kerridge, *Daily Telegraph* Books of the Year

'One of Dibdin's finest works . . . Wonderful.' Mark Sanderson, *Evening Standard*

'Ruth Rendell aside, no English writer has done more to expose the workings of the illusory barricade between crime fiction and literature.' Christopher Bray, *New Statesman*

———

'With his customary wit and wry insights into Italian life, Dibdin has sustained . . . one of the more distinguished of any recent crime series.' Simon Humphreys, *Mail on Sunday*

'One of the most memorable [creations] in crime fiction . . . Zen investigates with his inimitable mixture of world-weary insouciance, piercing insights into human souls, cunning, dodgy police tactics, and insubordinate behaviour.' Marcel Berlins, *The Times*

MICHAEL DIBDIN

End Games

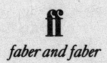

faber and faber

First published in 2007
by Faber and Faber Limited
3 Queen Square London WC1N 3AU
This paperback edition first published in 2008

Typeset by RefineCatch Limited, Bungay, Suffolk
Printed in the UK by CPI Bookmarque, Croydon, CR0 4TD

A CIP record for this book
is available from the British Library

ISBN 978-0-571-23617-6

2 4 6 8 10 9 7 5 3 1

The ferocious character of the Barbarians was displayed, in the funeral of a hero, whose valour, and fortune, they celebrated with mournful applause. By the labour of a captive multitude, they forcibly diverted the course of the Busentinus, a small river that washes the walls of Cosentia. The royal sepulchre, adorned with the splendid spoils, and trophies, of Rome, was constructed in the vacant bed; the waters were then restored to their natural channel; and the secret spot, where the remains of Alaric had been deposited, was for ever concealed by the inhuman massacre of the prisoners, who had been employed to execute the work.

Edward Gibbon, *The Decline and Fall of the Roman Empire*

The dead man parked his car at the edge of the town, beside a crumbling wall marking the bounds of a rock-gashed wasteland of crippled oaks and dusty scrub whose ownership had been the subject of litigation for over three decades, and which had gradually turned into an unofficial rubbish tip for the local population. The arrival of the gleaming, silver-grey Lancia was noted by several pairs of eyes, and soon known to everyone in the town, but despite the fact that the luxury saloon was left unguarded and unlocked, no attempt was made to interfere with it, because the driver was a dead man.

The only ones to see him close to were three boys, aged between five and ten, who had been acting out a boar hunt in the dense shrubbery under the cliff face. The five-year-old, who was the prey, had just been captured and was about to be dispatched when a man appeared on the path just a few metres away. He was in his fifties or early sixties, of medium stature, with pale skin and a shock of hair that was profuse and solidly black. He wore a black suit of some cheap synthetic fabric, and a wide collar, almost clerical, but matt and black, encircled his neck. From it, beneath the throat, hung a large metal crucifix. The man's chest and feet were bare. He trudged silently up the steep path towards the old town, looking down at the ground in front of him, and showed no sign of having seen the trio of onlookers.

As soon as he was out of sight the two younger boys were all for following him, scared but daring each other not to be. Sabatino, the eldest, put paid to that idea with a single jerk of the head. No one had confided in him about this event, but the community in which they all lived was a plangent sounding board when it came to news that might affect its members. Sabatino hadn't heard the primary note that must have been struck somewhere, but he had unconsciously absorbed the secondary vibrations resonating in other parts of that complex instrument. 'Danger!' they had whispered. 'Lie low, keep away, know nothing.' Discarding his role as the renowned and fearless hunter of wild boar for that of the responsible senior child, he rounded up his friend Francesco and the other boy and led them down a side path back to the safety of the town.

The sole witness to what happened next was a figure surveying the scene through binoculars from a ridge about a kilometre away on the other side of the valley. The dead man followed the track until it rose above the last remaining trees and ceased to be a rough line of beaten earth and scruffy grass, to become a stony ramp hewn out of the cliff face and deeply rutted by the abrasive force of ancient iron-rimmed cart wheels. By now *il morto* was clearly suffering, but he struggled on, pausing frequently to gasp for breath before tackling another stretch of the scorched rock on which the soles of his feet left bloody imprints. Above his bare head, the sun hovered like a hawk in the cloudless sky.

The isolated hill he was climbing was almost circular and had been eroded down to the underlying volcanic core and then quarried for building materials, so that in appearance it was almost flat, as though sheared off with a saw. When the dead man finally reached level ground, he collapsed and remained still for some time. The scene around him was one of utter desolation. The vestiges of a fortified gateway, whose blocks of stone had been too large and stubborn to remove, survived at the brink of the precipice where the crude thoroughfare had entered the former town, but looking towards the centre the only structures remaining above ground level were the ruins of houses, a small church, and opposite it an imposing fragment of walling framing an ornate doorway approached by five marble steps. All around lay heaps of rubble with weeds and small bushes growing out of them. The rounded paving stones of the main street were still clearly visible, however, and the dead man followed them, moaning with pain, until the cobbles opened out into a small piazza.

He then proceeded to the church, bowing his head and crossing himself on the threshold. Ten minutes passed before he emerged. He stopped for a moment to stare up at the massive remnants of stone frontage which dominated the square, then crossed over to the set of steps leading up to the gaping doorway, knelt down and slowly crawled up the steps on his knees, one by one, until he reached the uppermost. A wild fig tree had established itself in the charred wasteland within the former dwelling, feeding on some hidden source of water far below. The dead man bent over it and kissed one of its leaves, then bowed down until his forehead touched the slightly elevated doorstep.

The man watching from the ridge opposite put down his binoculars, lifted what looked like a bulky mobile phone off the dashboard of the Jeep Grand Cherokee beside him, extended the long recessed antenna and then pressed a button on the fascia. The resulting sound echoed about the walls of the valley for some time, but might easily have been mistaken for distant thunder.

A forkful of food stilled between the plate and his mouth, Zen sat watching the man at the next table. His gaunt, angular head looked as though it had been sculpted with a chainsaw from a knot-ridden baulk of lumber, but Zen was waiting for it to explode. Both men had ordered the *trattoria*'s dish of the day, but Zen's neighbour had then demanded *pepe*. This duly arrived, in the form of three fresh chilli peppers the size of rifle cartridges. He proceeded to chop them roughly and scatter the chunks over his pasta, seeds and all, before stirring the mass together and tucking in.

As so often since his transfer to Cosenza, Zen felt seriously foreign. He knew that if he had eaten even the smallest fragment of one of those peppers, he would have suffered not merely scorched taste-buds but also sweaty palpitations like those preceding a cardiac arrest, leaving him unable to eat, drink, talk or even think for at least fifteen minutes. His neighbour, on the other hand, chomped them down without the slightest change of expression. That grim countenance would never betray any emotion, but he appeared content with his lunch.

Zen toyed with his own food a bit longer, then pushed the plate away. Knobs of mutton knuckle protruded from the gloggy local pasta smothered in tomato sauce. Not for the first time, he asked himself how this bland yet cloying fruit had come to stand as the symbol of Italian cuisine worldwide, despite the fact that until a century or so ago very few Italians had even seen a tomato, never mind regarded them as a staple ingredient in every meal. As recently as his own childhood in Venice, they remained a rarity. His mother had never cooked them in her life. 'Roba del sud,' she would have said dismissively, 'southern stuff.'

Which, of course, was the answer to Zen's question. The Spanish had introduced the tomato from their American empire to their dominions in southern Italy, where it grew like a weed. The historic waves of Italian emigrants from the south had virtually subsisted on this cheap and abundant foodstuff, whose appearance conveniently recalled the images of the Sacred Heart of Jesus which hung on their walls, and on the bottled sauce that could be made from it to last year round. They had adopted it as a symbol of their cultural heritage and identity and then sold it to the credulous foreigners among whom they lived as the very essence of Italian cuisine.

Zen signalled the waiter. Obsession was an occupational hazard in Calabria, but obsessing about tomatoes was absurd. He paid over the agreed fee and responded with a brief nod to the waiter's thanks, nicely pitched as always in the grey area between grudging respect and overt truculence. The moment he emerged from the air-conditioned dining room into the sullen, stacked heat of the street, he felt his pores gaping open like the mouth of the goldfish he had kept as a child. He lit a cigarette and surveyed the visible slice of sky, an incandescent azure enlivened by puffy, faintly bruised clouds trailing translucent spumes of virga. The door behind him opened and Nicodemo, the owner of the restaurant, appeared and also lit up.

'You didn't like your meal?' he asked with a solicitous expression.

Zen chose his words carefully.

'It was very authentic.'

Nicodemo beamed. He had already told Zen, at some length, that he was *un immigrante*. Having spent almost thirty years as a construction worker in a Canadian city called Tronno, he had now retired to his native Calabria and opened a restaurant dedicated to preserving and reviving the genuine cuisine of his youth.

'My mother used to make that dish on very special occasions, starting at dawn,' he confided to Zen in reverential tones. 'The sauce takes hours to prepare, but the flavour of sheep from the bone and the fat is incomparable.'

'There is certainly very little to which it can be compared. I just don't have much appetite today.'

'You're not unwell, *dottore*?'

'No, no. Overwork, I expect.'

Nicodemo nodded sagely. He wouldn't of course dream of prying further – one didn't interrogate the local police chief – but a sympathetic word never went amiss.

'Ah, this terrible business.'

7

A silence fell, which the restaurateur perhaps broke to avoid the appearance of any possible indiscretion on his part.

'And to think that he came here once to eat!'

'Did he like the food?' Zen replied, with a trace of sarcasm that was entirely lost on the other man.

'But of course! He too was rediscovering his heritage, just like me when I first returned.'

Zen hurled his cigarette into the gutter.

'I'm sorry, I thought you were referring to the American lawyer.'

'I am! As soon as I saw the picture on television I recognised him.'

'Signor Newman ate here?'

He sounded no more than politely interested.

'Only once. It had come on to rain suddenly. He sheltered in the doorway for a while, then came inside when it didn't stop. He asked my advice about what to order and after he'd eaten we got chatting. First in Italian, then in dialect. The rough stuff, from up in the Sila mountains. He hadn't spoken that for years, but it gradually came back to him. Like discovering that you can still ride a bicycle, he said.'

Nicodemo shook his head.

'He seemed delighted to be home again, just like me. And now this happens! Calabria can be harsh to her sons.'

He grasped Zen's arm lightly. Zen did not care to be touched by strangers, but had come to recognise this as an accepted rhetorical gesture in the south and managed to control his instinct to recoil.

'I really shouldn't ask this, *dottore*, but do you think he'll be all right?'

Zen freed his arm by making another of the rhetorical gestures used to punctuate lengthy discourses between men in the street, an activity as normal, frequent and essential to civic life in Cosenza as it had been in the Athenian agora.

'In such matters, nothing is certain. But the victim's son is due to arrive shortly, so with any luck we should be able to begin serious negotiations soon.'

Nicodemo nodded obsequiously and seized Zen's hand.

'Thank you, thank you! Perhaps I shouldn't have asked, but even though we only met briefly, I liked the man. Besides, he is a fellow immigrant.'

Zen turned away.

'You're coming tomorrow?' the restaurateur called after him. 'I'm serving spaghetti with clams.'

Zen paused, struck by the innocent recipe like a familiar face sighted in a crowd. This was a dish he had grown up with, the soft clitoral gristle of the clams in their gaping porcelain shells, the hard, clean pasta soaked in the subtle juice, a nudge of garlic, a dab of oil, a splash of wine . . .

'I'm going to the coast to buy the clams fresh off the boats first thing tomorrow,' Nicodemo added encouragingly.

'Will they be cooked in tomato sauce?' queried Zen.

'*Ma certo!* Just like my mamma used to make.'

Zen inclined his head respectfully.

'May she rest in peace.'

At the corner of the block, he stopped in a café to erase the lingering taste of tomatoes stewed in mutton grease by drinking two coffees and crunching down half a tub of Tic Tacs. He was just starting his second espresso when everything became strange. The light dimmed as in an eclipse of the sun, a wind entered through the open doorway, the pages of a newspaper lying abandoned on a table turned over one by one, as though by the hand of an invisible reader. Outside in the street, someone cried out jaggedly above the seething sound that had insinuated itself into the laden silence. A fusillade of ice pellets erupted upwards from the pavement and then the sky broke, dropping waves of sound that shook the ground and made the water in Zen's glass ripple lightly. Next the initial fusillade of hail turned to a hard rain and within moments the sewers were gorged. The water backed up, deluging the street where people caught in the storm held up briefcases or newspapers to protect their heads and gazed across at the lights of the café on the other bank of the impassable torrent, while those safe inside cackled and jeered, savouring their sanctuary.

And then it was all over. The rain ceased, the flood subsided and the sun came out. By the time Zen had paid and left, the streets were already steaming themselves dry. The accumulated odours from the clogged drains combined with the water vapour to create a pale miasmal veil through which he made his way back up the hill to the Questura.

Nine and a half thousand kilometres away to the north-west, Jake Daniels awoke. Early light seeped through the hardwood venetians. Jake paused to check central processing performance and run a defrag, then rolled off the mattress and stood up. The barely audible breathing from the far side of the bed maintained its steady rhythm. He navigated the shallows of the bedroom and stepped out into the hall, closing the door behind him quietly. Madrona was great, but right now he needed his space.

He was fixing coffee and listening to the city's fabled all-girl band, the Westward Ho's, when his phone came to life. Inevitably, it was Martin. Martin was great too, except he didn't do down-time.

'Yo.'

'We need to dialogue, Jake.'

'Shoot.'

'Pete Newman, that lawyer who's been over in Europe providing logistical support on the movie angle? He's missing.'

'Missing what?'

'No, he disappeared three days ago, presumed kidnapped. So we need to progress alternative strategies to minimise how this incident might impact our mission.'

'Like when?'

'Right away. There are significant granularity issues that need to be addressed and the solutions migrated to the rest of our people here and then cascaded down to the folks we're teaming with at the location.'

'Huh?'

'Someone has to sweat the small stuff. I'm thinking I may need to go out there myself. You okay with lunch?'

'Whatever.'

Jake poured himself a mug of coffee, cradled his BlackBerry in the other hand and headed on out to the deck. The sun was just starting to show above the hills behind. Out towards the lake, a thick layer of gunge had toned down the pricey vista of stacked conifers and sloppy water to the kind of generic blur you only notice if it isn't there. Some dark agent in the guise of a crow hit the far end of the cedar planking in a clumsy clatter and then did the pimp roll over to a lump of wiener or marshmallow from last evening's cookout. Jake lay back in a colonial rocker, breathed in the salty air and took stock. All in all, he was cool with this latest development. A totally necessary feature of any killer game was that whenever you thought you were home and free, really weird shit happened. And seeing who was the gamemaster on this particular adventure, the surprises were always going to be world-class. Which was okay. Jake had a few surprises in store himself.

Gaming had pretty well been his whole life ever since he discovered the early classics like Mario and

Pac-Man at college. Crude and unsophisticated as those pioneering efforts had been in retrospect, they had spoken to him as nothing else before. The urge to add further levels and features to the games available, elegantly enough not to crash the Down's syndrome software on which the platform was built, had led him to switch majors from engineering to computer programming. He turned out to be a natural code warrior and a couple of years after graduating landed a job at the Redmond campus. Jake hadn't been one of the fabled Founding Fathers, but he was heavily vested and by the late 1990s his stock options, having split several times, amounted to a very sweet pile indeed. Then he got lucky, or maybe smart.

One day in the summer of 1998 he had been waiting to meet his stockbroker at a downtown restaurant that ran a sweepstake on what the Dow Jones industrial average would be at year's end. The bids were displayed on a board at the rear of the bar, and as Jake stared at the numbers he felt one of those familiar gut wobblies, like when you know that there's this monster fatal error lurking somewhere in the program you just wrote. So when his broker showed up he told her to dump his stock, thereby quite possibly contributing to the spectacular Nasdaq collapse a few weeks later. Then, instead of trying to reinvent himself as a vulture capitalist or pissing his capital away on some start-up dotcom company dedicated to revolutionising the way America buys toilet paper, he had put it all into real estate in time to clean up on the biggest property boom the city had ever seen. This had brought him an even bigger fortune, but best of all it had brought him Madrona, who had been working as a greeter for the firm that managed his portfolio of investments. Okay, he was forty-five and she was twenty-three, but so what? Ageing was an option and Jake had opted out.

It was only once they were married that he found out Madrona came from a fundamentalist Bible Belt family and believed that when the end times came, believers would be spirited up to heaven in the Rapture while Jesus and the Antichrist duked it out in the scorched wasteland below. Up until then, religion had been pretty much off the radar for Jake, but the more he heard about the coming Apocalypse – and Madrona had told him plenty, particularly back in the early days – the more interested he got. He hadn't bought into the sales talk and begging letters of the sleazy pastor out at the glass-and-plywood church where Madrona worshipped, but their promotional material plus some trawling on the web made the general scenario clear, and also that millions of other Americans, including the president, believed in it.

The God game was for sure the greatest total immersive reality challenge of all time, but these fundies were just hunkering down and trying to defend their corner instead of going out there and taking the initiative. That was always a losing strategy, and most of them were indeed losers, gambling on their free pass to eternity working when the time came. Maybe that was all they could do, but Jake was both rich and bored. To be honest, even the top-end, interactive, massively multiple role-playing stuff didn't really cut it for him any more. The stakes were too low and he was too good. Why piss around within the limits of the current technology when there was this persistent universe game that had been running for thousands of years, with killer graphics, no sharding or instancing and unlimited bandwidth? Not to mention an opponent who could come up with off-the-wall moves like targeting the lawyer Martin had sent out to work with the treasure hunters in Cosenza.

When he took his mug back to the kitchen for a refill, Madrona had emerged, wearing the retro baby-doll nightie Jake had given her for her birthday. It ended about an inch below her crotch and was pinkly transparent with appliquéd rabbits. It didn't matter what she wore, or what she didn't.

'Cuddle,' she said.

It was an imperative. The only problem with babes young enough to be your daughter was they had so much goddamn energy. Back when Jake was her age, he couldn't get laid to save his life. Now his problem was rationing the available supply to meet Madrona's demands. Still, the cost-per-fuck ratio was good, although Jake had an uneasy sense that it might develop a negative tilt some time in the future.

He tweaked his goatee and displayed an arc of perfect teeth.

'Are you Rapture-ready?' he said.

'Are you happy with the script?'

'It comes from the highest possible source.'

'Who is the screenwriter?'

'I was referring to the basic material, or Bible if you prefer. "Divinely inspired", some critics have been kind enough to say.'

'A bit long and rambling, though. Hitchcock said that to film a novel you first have to cut it down to a short story.'

'Which is where all novels started out and most should have stopped. And it was Truffaut, actually.'

Annalise Kirchner consulted her notes in a frigid fluster.

'Are you employing a theological consultant, *maestro*?'

'No pieces of silver have yet changed hands, but the subject naturally comes up when I meet one of my many friends in the Vatican.'

'How about alternative scenarios for the end of historical time? Do you plan to consult any scientists?'

'I simply can't be bothered. Atheists are such bores. They talk about God all the time.'

'Do you see this movie as making some sort of statement, and if so, what is it?'

Luciano Aldobrandini sighed. The young woman was quite decorative, if you liked that sort of thing, but clearly an idiot. It was time for him to take charge.

'Fräulein Kirchner, I have made many movies. Too many, some have said. Most of them were good, a few perhaps even great. But never have I faced a challenge such as this.'

The interviewer nodded empathetically. Behind her, the Austrian TV crew continued to monitor their equipment with disinterested concentration.

'Of course, the Holy Scriptures are hardly a new field for this medium,' Aldobrandini went on discursively. 'But most of the attempts that have been made, from De Mille to Mel, have taken as their subject the life and death of Christ, since that represents a human drama with which audiences can easily identify. Others have treated episodes from the Old Testament, which are also relatively straightforward to adapt for the screen since they portray aspects of the great human epic of the Jewish people.'

He puffed on his cigar.

'But neither the teachings and sufferings of Jesus, nor the trials and tribulations of the Jews, constitute in and of themselves the essence of the Biblical message. Like all great religions, Christianity has both a human and a superhuman – one might even say inhuman – face. Its mysteries are revealed in the natural world around us, but their *fons et origo* is supernatural and by definition passeth all understanding.'

'So how can such mysteries be transferred to the cinema screen?' asked the interviewer.

17

Luciano Aldobrandini did not like being interrupted when he was in full flight. He held up his hand like a traffic policeman.

'All in due course. As I was saying, previous cinematic treatments of the Bible have focused on its human aspects. The two great bookends of scripture, its alpha and omega, are of course Genesis and Revelations.'

He laughed reminiscently.

'As one of Dino's friends, I was involved in a minor way with John Huston's attempt to tackle the first of these back in the 1960s, and in my sentimental moments regret that I cannot be kinder about the result. But the second has never even been attempted, no doubt because parsing such a narrative for the lens has always appeared impossible.'

A young man appeared in the background, just behind the floodlights, waving frantically. The interviewer signalled the cameraman to pause the tape.

'Well?' demanded Aldobrandini curtly.

'Marcello's on the phone. He says it's urgent.'

'Tell him to wait.'

The young man disappeared and the interview recommenced.

'Saint John of Patmos has been variously described as an inspired visionary, a deranged drug addict and a delusional psychotic,' Aldobrandini continued smoothly. 'The work for which he is famous was only very narrowly accepted for inclusion in the biblical canon and has been the subject of controversy ever since. But the finer theological points do not concern me. What is incontrovertible is that in our post-9/11 world, the Book of Revelations touches many exposed cultural nerves. We all know that if terrorists gain access to nuclear or biological weapons, it will quite literally mean the end of the world. We also know that such a prospect would not give them a moment's pause, and that we are therefore potentially facing imminent extinction. That knowledge provides the necessary human element which now makes Saint John's eschatological ravings seem not merely relevant but even realistic.'

The young man reappeared.

'Marcello again, *maestro*. He says it's a matter of the highest priority and he must speak to you immediately.'

Luciano Aldobrandini slumped disgustedly.

'For the love of God, Pippo, I told you I wasn't to be disturbed! What do you think I pay you for? Oh well, I suppose we both know the answer to that. However, my agent works for me, not the other way round. Tell him I'll call him when I'm good and ready – and not to dare interrupt me again.'

He turned to camera again, but the incident had clearly unsettled him and he appeared to have lost the thread of his presentation.

'Nevertheless, it's hard to see how the actual content of the Book of Revelations can successfully be brought to the screen,' prompted the interviewer. 'The text reads more like a violent fantasy video game. One might perhaps be able to imagine a Japanese animé version, but I understand that your work is to be filmed on location in Calabria.'

'The raw material, yes. And some will remain raw. Other segments may be freeze-frame, slow motion or vastly speeded up. During the apocalyptic experience, as in Einsteinian physics, time and space become purely relative. The majority of the footage will be radically edited and post-processed using all the resources of modern computer graphics, and the results, I can assure you, will be something never before achieved, never even imagined or dreamt! Some envious individuals have been saying for years that I would never make another film, that I was burned out. Believe me, it's their eyeballs that will be burned out when they see this film, the ultimate and crowning work of my life!'

He paused motionless for a few seconds to allow for editing, then clapped his hands loudly, rose and announced, 'That's all the time I can spare, I'm afraid.'

He hastened off towards a door in the far wall of the vast room, the interviewer at his heels.

'Just one more thing!' she called. 'When does filming actually start?'

Aldobrandini ignored her. He locked the door behind him, then crossed the two antechambers leading to his private quarters at the far corner of the building. Once inside, he kicked off his shoes and collapsed supine on the sofa. Pippo appeared.

'Beulah, peel me a grape,' commanded his master. 'No, pour me a potent whisky and soda.'

'I've got Marcello on hold.'

20

Aldobrandini giggled.

'Well, don't squeeze him too tightly, *caro*, or he might spill all over you. God, I'm wrecked! Why do I even bother doing interviews?'

'Because it's in the contract that you have to, and because you're an applause whore.'

'Ah yes. And tomorrow?'

'Spanish, French, Swedish and Russian press, plus Fox, CNN, the BBC, some Japanese cable station and three highly influential media bloggers.'

'Dear Christ. All right, pass me Marcello. And that drink.'

Pippo handed over a portable phone and shimmied off towards the liquor cabinet.

'Marcello, how delightful to hear from you. What news on the Rialto?'

'Cut the crap, Luciano, this is serious. Jeremy's off the movie.'

Pippo returned with a brimming beaker, half of which Aldobrandini downed at one go.

'That's absurd. I spoke to him only the other day.'

'Yes, but what Jeremy didn't know then was that his agent had heard some bad buzz about the project and had decided to dig a little himself. He didn't like what he came up with and advised his client to pull, which he now has. It'll go public tomorrow, so you'll need to be prepared when you meet the media. Those Austrians hadn't heard, I hope?'

'They didn't mention it, but I've kept them hanging around the palazzo all day because I was simply too overwhelmed to talk to anyone.'

'Well, it's bound to come up. I suggest you spin it as a creative disagreement thing. Both you and Jeremy are great artists and can only achieve your full potential if you are in complete accord. Unfortunately on this occasion your views differed, and so with the greatest regret you have mutually decided that further collaboration would not be fruitful. You wish Jeremy all the best in the future and look forward to working with him again. Negotiations are in progress with a number of other big Hollywood stars, but it would be inappropriate to mention names at this stage.'

Aldobrandini sat drinking and thinking. This was a blow, no denying it. The author of Revelations played a key part in the high concept he had in mind for the film. Saint John had not only declared his work to be an account of a mystical experience, but had grounded this by locating it on the island of Patmos. That island could easily be invoked with some shots of Calabrian caves and shoreline, but the figure of the prophet himself was central. The idea was to leave the audience uncertain whether his visions had been an objective visitation or a subjective hallucination, but it was the visual image of John himself that must convince them that any of this was worth their attention. For that, the slim, saturnine and massively talented British actor had seemed perfect. Aldobrandini could just see his lugubrious yet oddly fragile frame hung with a simple cloak, while the inspired face, the expression pitched on the cusp between the ecstatic and the demonic, gazed up at the heavens. The El Greco look.

'So what did Jeremy's agent find out?' he asked Marcello.

'Well, that's the other thing we need to discuss. I have to say it's slightly disturbing. No more than that at this stage, but we need to tread carefully.'

'Cut the crap yourself, Marcello.'

'He didn't give me all the details, but basically it goes like this. He was in LA last week and of course mentioned our project. The response was, "It's great that Luciano's back in harness, but who's this Rapture Works outfit? No one's ever heard of them."'

'Neither have I.'

'They're the money behind the whole thing. Hollywood people always look at the bottom line. That's where the deep pockets are if you need to sue.'

'Why didn't you know this already, Marcello?'

'I did, but it didn't seem relevant. Our production company has an excellent reputation for making quirky, low-budget films that do very nicely with a largish niche audience worldwide. They get great reviews and have never ever lost money on a project. And frankly, Luciano, your career wasn't in the most sensational shape when this came up. It looked like a good deal all round.'

Aldobrandini sighed theatrically.

'All this business shit gives me a headache. You know that. That's what you get your cut to shield me from.'

'All right, I'll keep it brief. Jeremy's agent's people reported back that Rapture Works was incorporated just seven months ago and that its money seems to be channelled through a shell company in Bermuda. Now as I said, there may be nothing to worry about. You've had your upfront cut for vetting the shooting script and other advance work, and if it proves difficult to find a suitable replacement for Jeremy then you can do those scenes last. But after what I heard I reviewed the contract. Financially, everything's now in limbo until the first day of principal photography. I would advise you to bring that forward and start work as soon as possible.'

'What's the hurry? If they're going to default, they can do it any time.'

'Because it's just possible that this whole project is some sort of scam.'

'What?'

'Some clever tax dodge, or maybe money laundering. What I've heard is that the film may never get made. But there's a quick way to find out, which is to get the cameras rolling. On that day they are contractually obligated to move a significant sum out of escrow and into our account. If they don't, we'll start looking for alternative financing. If they do, you can forget all this and get down to crafting the great work of art that I know you still have it in you to make, Luciano, whatever your detractors may say. But my professional advice is to fast-track the shoot and force these people to get real or get out.'

Luciano Aldobrandini turned off the phone and hollered for Pippo.

'Another cocktail, darling.'

'The doctor said –'

'I know what the doctor said. I also know that I need to get drunk right now. Where's the *Narcisso*?'

'Last I heard, she was having her bottom scraped.'

'Don't be smutty, Pippo. Call the boatyard, tell them to get her seaworthy, then whistle up some matelots. I feel an urge for southern climes.'

'So you won't tell me what you discussed.'

'I don't remember every detail! In any case, it was all business matters relating to the film project. Nothing that could have the slightest bearing on this tragic event.'

Zen strolled to the window, looked out for some time, then lit a cigarette. The official ban on smoking in government buildings added a particular piquancy to this gesture, virtually making it part of the interrogation.

'What language did you speak?' he asked, turning back to face Nicola Mantega.

'Italian, of course.'

'Not Calabrian dialect?'

The witness hesitated just a moment before answering.

'Dialect? Signor Newman is an American lawyer. How could a man like that know the dialect?'

'Answer the question.'

'We spoke Italian.'

'Newman spoke it fluently?'

Mantega shrugged.

'For a foreigner.'

'So how did he learn Italian?'

'I have no idea.'

'You didn't discuss it?'

'Certainly not.'

'Didn't you think it unusual? And perhaps mention it? Some flattering comment . . .'

'I really didn't think about it. This wasn't a personal relationship! As I keep telling you, it was strictly business. Maybe he took lessons before coming out here. What do I know?'

Zen stared at him in silence for a moment.

'That's precisely what I'm trying to determine.'

Nicola Mantega's appearance was of a classic Calabrian type, with thick, lustrous black hair, a crumpled, oval face that barely contained all the troubles it had seen, a florid moustache and an expression of terminal depression.

'Let's just go back over that final phone call,' Zen said. 'You rang Signor Newman at ten thirty-two on the Tuesday morning . . .'

'It was some time that morning, yes.'

'It was at the time I stated. Newman hired a mobile phone and we have obtained a copy of the records. What we don't have is a transcript of what was said, but you have stated that you told him that some new factors had arisen regarding final arrangements for the film project, and that you needed to meet again. You then suggested that he come to dinner at your house at seven that evening, but he never turned up.'

'Exactly.'

'Nor did he return to his hotel that night. In short, he was almost certainly kidnapped on his way to that meeting at your villa, Signor Mantega. An arrangement which only he and you knew about.'

'He must have been followed. If the kidnappers are professionals, they would have had him under surveillance for days.'

'Perhaps, but how did they know that he was a suitable prospect? How did they know who he was and what he might be worth? For that matter, how did they know he was here at all?'

On the wall of Zen's office hung an elegantly designed notice proclaiming the vision statement of the new Italian police, thick with catchphrases such as *la nostra missione, i nostri valori, competenza professionale, integrità, creatività e innovazione*. As so often in the past, Zen decided to go for the last two.

'Acting on my orders, one of my officers interviewed your wife this morning while you were at work,' he said. 'She denied all knowledge of any guest having been invited for dinner on the evening in question.'

Mantega was staring at Zen with an expression of baffled indignation.

'I didn't tell her,' he said at last.

Zen nodded, as though this little misunderstanding had now been cleared up.

'Of course! You were planning to cook yourself. Some local delicacy, no doubt, to remind your guest of his origins. Stewed tripe in tomato sauce, perhaps.'

'What is the meaning of these insinuations?' Mantega demanded angrily. 'Signor Newman is an American. I wouldn't have dreamt of offering him one of our traditional Calabrian dishes. We are only too well aware that they are often unappreciated by foreigners.'

He glared pointedly at Zen.

'I didn't mention the occasion to my wife because I did not intend her to be present. As I keep trying to get you to understand, this was not a social event. The business that Signor Newman and I had to discuss was extremely confidential. I planned to receive him outside on the *terrazza*. It has a wonderful view of the city below, and there we could talk freely. As for food, there was some leftover *parmigiana di melanzane* in the fridge that I could warm up.'

Mantega was well into his stride by now.

'I did in fact tell my wife when I returned from work that night, but she may well not have been listening to me. Such is often the case. I'll remind her of what happened as soon as I get home. If it comes to her making a sworn testimony in the future, I'm sure that her story will tally with mine.'

'I'm sure it will,' said Zen drily. 'And she will probably deny ever having spoken to my subordinate. All right, you may go.'

Mantega frowned and stood up, shrugging awkwardly.

'I've told you everything I know,' he said in a defensive tone.

'You've been a model witness,' Zen returned. 'In fact I shall hold you up as an example to the people I have still to question, some of whom may be less helpful. "Why can't you be as co-operative as Signor

Mantega?" I shall say. "There's a man who's not afraid to tell me everything he knows." '

Mantega seemed about to say something for a moment, but then Natale Arnone came in and escorted him out. Zen went over to the window and stood looking down until the notary emerged on to the street. When Mantega was about ten metres off, one of the officers that Zen had detached from the elite Digos anti-terrorist squad got out of a parked car and started to follow. His companion started the car and drove ahead to take the point position.

Zen's pro tem transfer to his current post as chief of police for the province of Cosenza had come about purely as a matter of chance, and had not promised – still less delivered, until a few days ago – the slightest challenge to his professional skills. A new bureaucratic entity had appeared on the map of Italy: the *provincia di Crotone*, carved out of the neighbouring provinces of Cosenza and Catanzaro. It naturally demanded a fully staffed bureaucratic apparatus to run it, and this had to be constructed from scratch. One of the vacant positions was that of police chief, and Pasquale Rossi, the incumbent in Cosenza, had eventually been selected as someone professionally familiar with much of the territory concerned and thus in a position to bring his extensive experience to bear. His post had in turn gone to the deputy chief at Catanzaro, one Gaetano Monaco, but unfortunately the latter was unable to take up his duties since he had shot himself in the foot while cleaning his service pistol.

Once made, such appointments are very difficult to unmake, since the promotional ripple effect spreads far and wide and the suitability of each chosen candidate has to be vetted by all interested parties before approval. The Ministry in Rome had therefore opted for the expedient of a temporary replacement for the short period until the original appointee recovered from his self-inflicted injury, and their choice had fallen on Zen. He had been received politely enough by the questore and the other senior officers, but it had discreetly been made clear to him that he was a mere figurehead occupying the post in name only and need not concern himself too much with the day-to-day workings of the department. Which is exactly what he had been happy to do until the recent disappearance of an American lawyer which bore all the hallmarks of a professional kidnapping for ransom.

There was a knock at the door and Natale Arnone entered. He was in his late twenties, stockily built and with a shaven head, no neck and a generally thuggish manner accentuated by his unshaven jowls and bandit beard. After two months in Calabria, Zen was beginning to feel facially nude.

'This just arrived, sir,' Arnone said, laying a sheet of paper on the desk. It was a fax from the American consulate in Naples, which Zen had contacted immediately after lunch, and read as follows:

PETER NEWMAN

Passport # 733945610

Date of birth: 11/28/44

Place of birth: Spezzano della Sila, Italy

Remarks: Birth certified under name PIETRO OTTAVIO CALOPEZZATI. Name legally changed 5/30/69 at San Francisco. US citizenship acquired 4/19/68, sponsor Roberto Marcantonio Calopezzati, SBU//FOUO file reference 48294/AVP/0006

Attached were several official photographs of Newman and a digitalised scan of his fingerprints, taken when he received US citizenship. Zen handed Arnone the documents without comment. The young officer read them through and whistled quietly.

'Rather changes things, doesn't it?' Zen remarked.

The young officer erupted in a loutish, splurging laugh, instantly repressed.

'In more ways than one.'

Arnone tapped the sheet of paper.

'Until the land reform acts of the 1950s, the Calopezzati were the richest family in this province and far beyond. They owned half of Calabria.'

The two men eyed one another in silence.

'Drop whatever you're doing and get me a certified copy of that birth certificate,' said Zen.

When Arnone had gone, he rang the consulate in Naples and asked them to explain the significance of the letters SBU/FOUO preceding the file records of Peter Newman's naturalisation process.

'Sensitive but unclassified, for official use only,' came the reply.

'So I don't suppose there's any point in my asking for further details.'

'FOUO data will also be NOFORN. No foreign nationals. Distribution restricted to US citizens. Sorry we can't help you.'

'You already have,' Zen replied.

Jake and Martin met at SooChic, a Japanese-Peruvian fusion place with accents of the Deep South. The furnishings were 1950s Scandinavian, easy on the eye but hard on the ass. A waitperson showed up and dispensed some intense culinary talk therapy.

'So?' said Jake.

'Yeah,' said Martin.

Martin Nguyen's father had been one of the principal torturers for the Diem regime, and his son had inherited the plated face and sinkhole eyes that terrified the living shit out of you even before they cranked up the generator.

'Basically, we're solid,' said Martin. 'Newman is an independent contractor, totally ring-fenced off from Rapture Works. If he's been kidnapped, that's the family's problem. The son is on his way to Calabria now. Pete knew what he was getting himself into. He's from there, for Christ's sake.'

Food came. Jake speared a chunk of sushi and dipped it in the fiery corn porridge purée.

'Pete Newman?'

Martin nodded.

'Usual Ellis Island illiteracy, I guess. Pop was probably named Novemano or some damn thing.'

He chomped moodily on his chitterling tamale.

'I hate Italians.'

'Foreigners suck,' Jake remarked.

Martin looked at him sharply. Although he'd lived in the States most of his life, he still felt pretty foreign a lot of the time. Since getting hired by Jake as project manager for the Rapture Works venture, he'd learned how to decode and even speak the idiolect of the city's software community, where geeks married nerds and the incidence of autism was the highest in the country. Jake wasn't exactly autistic – mild Asperger's, maybe – although it had occurred to Martin that he might well fail the CAPTCHA test designed to distinguish between human and artificial intelligence, maybe in both categories. Too dumb to be human, too fucked up to be a machine. But the hard fact was that someone who walked and talked and looked and spoke like Jake was worth more money, right now, up front in cash, than anyone else in the restaurant would earn in his entire lifetime. Including Martin.

'I mean, to do business with,' he said. 'It's all "Sure, yeah, no problem, you got it" and then no delivery. And they don't even apologise, just act like you're a sucker for ever believing they meant what they said in the first place. You need me to go there, Jake. Aeroscan have concluded their installation and set-up and will be ready to roll at eleven this evening our time. The civil authorities have granted them unlimited clearance below a hundred metres.'

Jake gave him one of those looks.

'Three hundred feet,' said Martin. 'Newman said the

mayor practically creamed in her pants. Apparently Cosenza is one no-hope town and this is the biggest boost they've ever had. I mean, it would be if it was for real.'

He smiled hideously. Jake torqued his lips just a fraction, as if remembering a joke that had seemed funny at the time.

'So they bought the movie angle?'

Martin reassembled the shards of his face into an orderly pattern.

'Totally. There's another city down that way – Matera? An even smaller dump even further off the beaten track. Now it's jammed with tourist buses, hotels packed to the brim, restaurants gouging to the max, souvenir shops selling out by noon. Know why? Because Mel Gibson filmed *The Passion of the Christ* there.'

'Fuck,' murmured Jake contemplatively.

'So Pete Newman told the guys in Cosenza, if you think the Crucifixion was big, wait till you see the Apocalypse.'

More food arrived and they ordered another round of Diet Coke with sliced lime. Then the aisle was full of noises. The girl sitting at a table opposite reached for her mobile and started talking her boyfriend through the best route to the restaurant. Martin eyed her appreciatively. His line was that if they were legal they were over the hill. This one looked border-line.

'Babe,' he commented.

Jake dismissed her with a glance.

'Ringtone sucks. So how come you need to go out there?'

36

'Because if Aeroscan finds the treasure, we need to move fast. The movie cover is good for the search, but once we start digging it's a whole different ball game. Anything we turn up is legally the property of the Italian state. Cultural heritage bullshit. Just breaking ground will be a felony, so we're going to need a work crew who can be trusted not to talk later. I've got a plan for that, but now Pete's out of the picture I need to be there to head up the team in person. I also need clearance from you on the hired help angle.'

'What's the deal?'

'Contact of mine works for one of the big US contractors in Iraq. He's found me some able-bodied guys who've never left the country in their lives and arranged, for a consideration, to have them given passports and sent to Jordan. From Amman they'll fly into Italy on tourist visas and assemble at the site to carry out the excavation and transfer of the treasure to a storage facility rented by the film company. No Rapture Works footprint.'

Jake toyed with his peeled guinea pig in teriyaki sauce on a bed of collard greens.

'And after that?'

'We'll need to discuss details once I have a chance to perform an assessment at the mission location, but I can tell you right now that export/import is going to be a bitch. I mean, we're talking like drugs here.'

'I mean the Iraqi guys.'

'They go home.'

'And tell everyone about their excellent Italian adventure?'

A decisive headshake.

'They won't.'

'How can you be sure?'

'You don't need to know, Jake. Just trust me.'

'Quit bullshitting.'

Martin sighed.

'Okay. When the six of them get back, my contact invites them to dinner at some place in downtown Baghdad. He hands over some counterfeit cash with a few real bills on top, then fakes a phone call and says he has to run, business shit going down. The Iraqis couldn't care less. They've been paid and here's all this great Arab food they've been missing so much. Few minutes later a car draws up outside, the driver sprints away and . . . Well, you can figure out the rest yourself.'

He brushed away the service dude, who was trying to interest them in seaweed ice-cream made from llama's milk.

'You mean like permadeath?' said Jake. 'Man, that's heavy. Couldn't we just –'

Martin shook his head as decisively as before.

'No, Jake. If we go ahead on this one, we're going to need total deniability and cut-outs at every stage. That's the way it's got to be.'

'What about this contact of yours in Baghdad?'

'He doesn't know who I'm working for, never mind what we're doing, and he doesn't want to know.'

'But he knows we're setting it up to have those guys killed, right?'

'Yeah, plus whoever else is in the restaurant and on the street outside. Sure he knows. But he says the thing about working in Iraq is after a few months you quit worrying about that stuff.'

Jake put on a sick smile.

'I guess we're not in Kansas any more.'

'You can be back in Kansas any time you want,' Martin replied. 'I can pull the plug on all this right now and no one will ever be any the wiser. We'll tell the director the project's tanked, wind up Rapture Works and pay off Aeroscan. All you have to do is say the word. But if we hit pay dirt, which just could happen as early as tonight, then we'll be looking down the barrel at international arrest warrants and jail sentences in multiples of ten. So I need to do it my way.'

He sat back with a crinkly grin, regarding the other man with dispassionate intensity. The server approached.

'I also have a tomato and pimento sorbet! That comes with sweet potato and pumpkin fritters!'

'Well?' demanded Martin.

Jake finally met his tormentor's eyes and emitted a sound like a fledgling crow.

'Eeeh! Back when they hid the treasure, the guys who did the work got killed after. So it kind of makes sense.'

'You're authorising me to go ahead?'

Jake wriggled this way and that, but finally gave a lopsided shrug.

'How about coffee?' their server implored. 'I have an organic bean from a collective of farms in the San Ignacio valley that shows excellent brightness and acidity plus a funky edge that doesn't dominate the cup.'

'I'm good,' said Jake.

The flight from Milan was over an hour late due to a strike by baggage handlers earlier in the day and Tom had been seated in the very last row, next to the galley and the toilets, so by the time he finally emerged, the small airport of Lamezia Terme was almost deserted, public transport services had long since ceased and the last cab had driven away. An electronic display on the wall showed that the external temperature was a very pleasant twenty-three degrees, and after his overnight journey Tom was perfectly prepared to stretch out on a bench or underneath some shrubbery and go straight to sleep, but in the event this wasn't necessary. As he walked towards the baggage carousels, he was accosted by a paunchy, well-dressed, middle-aged man whose expression alternated rapidly between pleasure, sorrow, respect and encouragement.

'Signor Newman? I am Nicola Mantega. You called me from the United States a few days ago, if you remember. You said that your father had spoken of me.'

'Oh yes, right.'

'And you also mentioned that you would be arriving on the last flight from Milan tonight. Very pleased to meet you. I only wish that it could have been in happier circumstances.'

Having collected Tom's luggage, they proceeded outside. Neither noticed the young man who had been scanning the titles of the books in the window of the locked newsagent's stall and then followed them out, to be greeted effusively with a smacking kiss and a full embrace by the very attractive brunette standing beside a battered Fiat Panda. Tom's escort led him to an Alfa Romeo saloon parked in a lane designated for emergency vehicles only. He gestured the American inside, then returned to the driver's seat and started the engine.

'Has there been any news?' Tom Newman asked as the car sped away into the darkness beyond the airport perimeter lights. Mantega shook his head glumly.

'I'm sorry, nothing. But that is not surprising in a case like this. It is normal, even reassuring.'

The Alfa slowed slightly to take the sharp curve of the slip road and then they were on the *autostrada*, heading north to Cosenza.

'Reassuring?' Tom queried. 'I don't see why. Surely the kidnappers should have got in contact by now and made their ransom demand. The longer they delay, the more chance there is of the whole thing going wrong.'

Mantega smiled in a superior way.

'For them, the only things that can go wrong are the initial seizure and the ensuing payoff. The first apparently went without a hitch from their point of view. Now they are worried only about the second. They are going to take their time, extract every bit of information they can from their hostage . . .'

The victim's son looked at him in dismay.

'Oh, not by brutality,' Mantega continued in a discursive tone. 'They don't need that. Your father, like any kidnap victim, is utterly dependent on them for the basics of life. Food, water, sleep. They need only threaten to withhold some or all of those to get his complete co-operation. They will make their plans accordingly and then, and only then, will they risk contacting a third party, quite possibly me, to announce the conditions of his release.'

'But they are holding him somewhere, and I was told that the police have launched a massive investigation,' Tom Newman protested. 'Surely every day they delay increases the chances of his being found.'

By now, Mantega's smile was openly contemptuous.

'Your Italian is quite good, *signore*, although not quite as good as your father's, but I fear that you don't understand very well what you are talking about. The kidnapping took place on the road leading to my villa, just outside Cosenza. Twenty minutes later, the vehicle conveying your father would have been on this road, but heading the other way, towards Reggio. An hour after that, at the very most, he and his captors would be high up in the mountains of Aspromonte.'

He jerked his thumb towards the rear window.

'The government – be it the ancient Romans and Greeks, invading Normans, colonising Spanish or nationalistic Milanese – has tried again and again to make its laws hold sway in Aspromonte. On each occasion it has failed. That massif is a vast, shattered landscape, wild, barren, virtually impassable in many places, and riddled with caves and caverns. The people are primitive, ignorant, tough as nails, and speak the truth to no man save family members, and not to all of them. Naturally the police will make a show of strength, but to no effect other than saving their faces. I could hide all the people who just got off your flight from Milan up there for a year and no one would ever find them!'

Tom looked at him curiously.

'You could, Signor Mantega?'

Mantega hesitated a moment, then laughed lightly.

'As I mentioned, your Italian is not quite as good as your father's. What I meant was that all those people could be hidden up on Aspromonte, not that I personally could do it. An easy mistake for a foreigner. Our verbal forms are very complex.'

The *autostrada* was almost deserted at that time of night, and despite the long uphill gradient the Alfa was now touching two hundred k.p.h. Nevertheless, the modest, ageing Fiat containing the young couple who had apparently met back at the airport was able to keep pace with it, thanks to some expensive technical modifications, but a few kilometres back, where even its lights would be largely invisible to the target ahead on the winding, tunnel-ridden highway. The saloon belonging to Nicola Mantega had also been modified recently, although without the owner's knowledge or consent. The result was a mobile circle with inset cross on the flat screen visible within the opened glove compartment just in front of the woman's knees, on the basis of which information she told her colleague at

43

the wheel if he was breaching the agreed distance parameters.

'My father never spoke Italian to me,' Tom Newman declared.

'Indeed? Then how did you learn our beautiful language?'

'From my mother.'

'Ah! So she at least is Italian.'

'Was. She passed away four years ago.'

'My condolences.'

'Her family was from Puglia. Her parents were American citizens, but when she was five they decided to move back to Italy. My mother was brought up bilingually, and when she was eighteen she went to college in the States. That's where she met my father. He told me that he'd taken a course in Italian because he was in love and she liked to speak the language when they were alone together.'

A long silence followed this remark.

'Then there appears to be a discrepancy between what your father told you and what he told me, which was that he had been born here in Calabria.'

The young American stared at him sullenly, and then his eyes lit up.

'Then the man that you met can't have been my father! This must all have been a mistake. Some impostor must have taken his place and got kidnapped, and now he's –'

'I quite understand your natural grief and distress,' Mantega replied, 'but you must not delude yourself with puerile fantasies. Of course it was your father. He

44

showed me his passport at the outset just as I showed him my documents. The business we were discussing was extremely sensitive and confidential and it was essential that there should be absolute trust on both sides. There is no possibility that I could have been mistaken about his identity.'

Tom Newman was by now openly truculent.

'Yeah well, I've also seen my father's passport, Signor Mantega. If you had examined it more carefully, you would have noticed that the stated place of birth is the District of Columbia, USA.'

Mantega made the soft Italian gesture that turns away wrath.

'As it happens, I did notice that, and when he later told me he was Calabrian I naturally mentioned it.'

'What did he say?'

'That it was a long story. A very Calabrian reply. He clearly did not intend to discuss the matter. But he must have told you something about his origins. What did he say?'

'That he was an American,' Tom replied shortly.

Mantega smiled.

'A Red Indian?'

'Of course not! And we don't call them that any more.'

'Then where did he say that his family was from? All Americans are from somewhere else. Your country is only a couple of hundred years old.'

'That's quite a long time.'

Nicola Mantega's smile turned into a smug smirk.

'Long for you, short for us.'

'He told me that his family had been in the States for generations, and had intermarried so much that no one could figure out where anyone was from. Besides, he didn't care. "We're Americans and that's the end of it," he used to say. And I don't care about any of this either. All I want is to get my father back. Those bastards at the film company he was working for have disclaimed all responsibility on the grounds that he was an outside employee and his contract with them says nothing about liability for ransom demands. So the money's all going to have to come from my family.'

'Is it a large family?'

'No. I'm an only child and my father isn't particularly rich. I just hope the kidnappers realise that and are prepared to be reasonable.'

Nicola Mantega did not pursue this topic. By now they had crossed the col between the valleys of the Savuto and Craticello rivers, and were descending the long sweeping stretch of highway towards the lights of Cosenza nestled in the narrow plain below.

'You must be exhausted,' Mantega said. 'I've booked you into the Centrale. It's part of the Best Western chain – all-American comforts like air-conditioning and room service, and as the name suggests, right in the centre.'

'Was that where my father stayed?'

'No, he hired a car and needed to drive around, so for him I suggested a location out in a suburb called Rende, with easy access to the *autostrada*.'

The Alfa braked sharply as it entered the ramp off the *autostrada*. Fifteen minutes later, having seen Tom

46

Newman checked into his hotel and made an agreement to get in touch the next day, Mantega climbed back into his car and started to drive home. On the parallel street to the east, two young men on a MotoGuzzi kept pace. The man on the pillion talked incessantly into his mobile phone.

In Viale Trieste, the Alfa pulled up to a public phone booth. It was after midnight, and there was no one about except for a few derelicts. Mantega looked around, then fed a phone card into the machine. A couple of moments later, a white delivery van entered the square at the far end and came speeding round the corner. Mantega started to dial, then broke off at the squeal of tortured rubber and final crash and turned to look. It was quite clear what must have happened. A motorbike had turned into the square from a side-street just as the van hurtled past, and had been knocked to the ground. Luckily the two young men riding on it appeared to be uninjured. They picked themselves up, ran over to the van and started abusing the driver with a verbal violence that seemed likely to turn physical at any second. A stream of obscenity and blasphemy filled the air. Mantega grinned contemptuously and turned his attention back to the phone.

'Giorgio?' he said when the number answered. 'Nicola. He's arrived.'

'Too late. Tomorrow, the way we arranged.'

By now the altercation across the street had begun to wind down. The two bikers picked up their machine, revved up the engine and tested the brakes and lights. The van driver was intently scrutinising the front end of his vehicle, picking at the paintwork with his thumbnail. Meanwhile, in the back of the van the fourth member of the team lowered the directional microphone from the circle of plastic mesh forming the centre of one of the zeroes in the phone number emblazoned outside.

Nicola Mantega returned to his car and drove off just as a deafening blast from the MotoGuzzi's twin exhaust consigned all van drivers to the lowest circle of hell. But the motorcycle had also been modified, and when it doubled back to follow the Alfa up to Mantega's villa in the foothills above the city, its engine sounded no louder than a kitten's purr.

Ever since he arrived in Cosenza, Aurelio Zen had been sleeping badly. This was not the fault of the weather, although a few weeks earlier the thermometer had been nudging forty, nor of his accommodation, an efficient, soulless apartment maintained by the police for the use of visiting officers in one of the concrete blocks that disfigured the area around the Questura. It consisted of a sitting room and kitchenette with a dining area, two bedrooms, one of which Zen used as a study, and the best-equipped bathroom he had ever seen. A maid came once a week to clean the floor and change the bedding, and he had arranged for her to wash and iron his clothing as well. Apart from that, he was left entirely alone. The apartment was quiet, air-conditioned and just a few minutes' walk from his office.

Despite this, he had been sleeping badly, waking for no apparent reason and dreaming too much and far too vividly. Zen had never paid much attention to his dreams, but now they were thrusting themselves on his attention like a swarm of gypsy beggars, most of all in the intermediate state between sleep and waking when he was partly conscious but completely defenceless. As soon as he surfaced sufficiently to realise what was happening, he climbed out of bed, walked through to the state-of-the-art bathroom and took a cool shower before finishing off in a torrent of water as hot as he could bear. Standing naked in the well-equipped kitchen, he then filled the *caffetiera* and put it on the flame, lit his first cigarette of the day and phoned his wife in Lucca before she left home to open her pharmacy.

Zen had considered asking her to send him some sleeping pills, but he disliked admitting a weakness. Besides, he and Gemma had an unspoken agreement to keep their professional and personal lives separate as far as possible. In fact, he would have found it very difficult to say what they did talk about in these daily ten- to fifteen-minute conversations that seemed to flow along as effortlessly as a river and left him feeling calm, capable and ready to face the day. Having slurped down his muddy coffee, he then shaved, got dressed and left for work. Stepping out into the street was the final phase of his psychic detox ritual. Life in Calabria was by no means perfect, but the spectres and ghouls which tormented his nights could find no refuge in its merciless, crystalline light.

The next stop was a café and pastry shop called Dolci Idee. The display cases were laden with sugary iced cakes and buns of every description, but a sweet tooth was one item that didn't figure on Zen's sin list. He consumed a double espresso *amaro*, and then walked along one and a half blocks of the grid pattern on which the new city of Cosenza was constructed, past the church of Santa Teresa, a modern monstrosity with Romanesque pretensions, to the Questura. If the devotees of the saint had been making one sort of statement, those faithful to the cult of the state had made another, just as forceful and arguably more attractive, in the new provincial headquarters of the *Polizia di Stato*. This dated from the 1980s and was a wide, low building, windowless below the second storey and sheathed in ochre coloured metal sheets which were said to be bomb-proof.

The interior resembled the offices of a major business corporation rather than the grandiose follies of the Fascist era and the recycled baroque *palazzi* with which Zen was familiar. He tried to console himself with the thought that, as the proverb had it, everything had changed so that nothing would change, but something told him – was this the reason for those half-awake nightmares? – that something had indeed changed, and that there was no place for people like him in the new scheme of things. The basic design was open plan, with cubicles, a flat-screen computer monitor on every desk, bare walls, grey filing cabinets, corkboards stuck with memos, filtered lighting and furniture that might have been bought at Ikea. The building was nominally air-conditioned, but the system kept breaking down and none of the windows could be opened.

By virtue of his rank, Zen had an office all to himself, but with interior windows instead of walls as part of the force's new transparent ethos. These could be, and in Zen's case were, covered by slatted blinds which he always kept closed. On his desk that morning was a transcript of the recording made by the Digos team the night before of Nicola Mantega's phone call to someone named Giorgio. The interest of this was not so much what Mantega had said, although that sounded conspiratorially cryptic, as the manner in which contact had been established. An eminent *notaio* who drove an Alfa Romeo 159 Q4 and had three mobile phones and two land lines – Zen knew, since he had ordered interceptions on all of them – did not pull up at a public phone box after midnight to make a call unless he had something to hide. Mantega clearly suspected that his private and business phones might be tapped, but not that he was being followed. All of which fitted in nicely with Zen's view of him as a semi-competent provincial operator who knew far more than he had admitted about Newman's disappearance.

There was a discreet knock at the door.

'*Avanti!*'

Natale Arnone entered.

'Here's the material you requested, sir. And there's some foreigner down at the desk demanding to speak to the officer in charge of the Newman case. Claims to be the victim's son.'

'In what language?'

'Italian. He's pretty fluent, but comes across as a bit *rozzo*. Strident and pushy. Do you want me to deal with him?'

'I think an overwrought manner is forgivable under the circumstances. Send him up.'

Zen was looking through the paperwork which had accumulated overnight when Thomas Newman was shown in. After Arnone's warning, Zen had expected someone resembling the classic American football player: a thick cylindrical skull welded to massive shoulders, no neck, hairy piano-leg limbs and a voice like the brass section of a 1930s big band at full discordant climax. He was confronted instead by a lithe, energetic young man whose body made no exaggerated claims and was in any case trumped by the face of a mischievous but charming cherub with a mass of glossy black curls cut negligently long. Zen invited his visitor to be seated and gestured Arnone to leave. Newman eyed the crammed ashtray on Zen's desk.

'May I smoke? I thought it was illegal now.'

'It is.'

'But you are a policeman.'

'Exactly.'

They exchanged a glance, and Zen felt that subliminal clink of contact with another intelligence.

'What a splendid city!' exclaimed Newman. 'I woke early, because of the time difference, and then went out and just walked around for hours. The light, the landscape, the buildings, the people – it all seemed magical, yet somehow familiar.'

'You are too kind,' Zen replied smoothly. 'As it happens, I agree that Cosenza is the most attractive city in Calabria – not that the competition is exactly fierce. But you are of course biased in these matters, since your father is a native.'

Zen had had very few dealings with Americans, but the volatility with which Tom Newman's mood altered in a moment was completely familiar to him.

'You're the second person who's tried to get me to believe that bullshit!'

'Might the first have been Signor Nicola Mantega? I understand that he met you at the airport last night.'

'How did you know?'

Zen looked at him curiously.

'How do you know Signor Mantega?'

'My father mentioned the name to me when he called during his first week here. After the disappearance, I got Mantega's phone number from my father's office and then called him. He's been very helpful and supportive.'

'I'm sure he has,' Zen said drily. 'Apart from his personal legal situation regarding this matter, he may well turn out to be the intermediary once negotiations for your father's release get under way.'

'But why wouldn't the kidnappers deal directly with me? I can talk to them as well as Signor Mantega.'

'In such interactions they will want someone they know and trust. Besides, they may prefer to express themselves in dialect. It's a very different language from standard Italian and is incomprehensible even to me but preferred by many native Calabrians, particularly at moments of great intimacy or intensity. Which no doubt explains why your father had recourse to it during his stay here.'

Tom Newman flashed his deep hazel eyes at Zen in a way that was not at all cherubic.

'What is this crap? My father is one hundred per cent American! Is that clear?'

Zen picked his words carefully.

'It's clear that that is what you believe, *signore*, but the fact remains that during his stay in Cosenza your father has been heard speaking a variety of dialect distinctive to that mountain range over there.'

He gestured to the window, where the verdant flanks of the Sila plateau could be seen sloping down to the valley where the city lay. From the wide expanse of the flood plain came the persistent drone of the helicopter that an American film company had hired to scout out suitable locations for their next project. It was a noisy pest, but both the mayor and the prefect had given the enterprise their blessing and there was nothing to be done.

'I don't believe you,' Tom Newman said in a hard tone.

Zen shrugged.

'He would hardly have been the first Calabrian to have emigrated to *la Merica*. In fact he wouldn't even have been in the first hundred thousand. But as it happens you don't need to believe me.'

He leafed through some papers and then passed across the naturalisation details of Peter Newman supplied by the consulate in Naples together with an Italian birth certificate in the name of Pietro Ottavio Calopezzati.

'Are these official?' Tom asked after reading them.

'As official as can be. Your father assumed the name Peter Newman in 1969. Before that he was Pietro Calopezzati, born in the *comune* of Spezzano della Sila up in those mountains half an hour's drive from here. Are you telling me that you are completely ignorant of these facts?'

'Why would I lie to you?' Tom Newman snapped. 'I

didn't even know there was anything to lie about! Anyway, what's all this got to do with the kidnapping? That's what you're supposed to be investigating. Who cares if my father concealed his origins for some reason?'

'I care about everything that may be connected to the case, Signor Newman. One never knows what may turn out to be relevant. For instance, the Calopezzati were, until the political changes shortly after your father's birth, among the richest landowners in Italy. At this point I have no information about the present state of the family finances, but the kidnappers certainly will. That may well affect the amount of the ransom they demand. I take it you have a mobile phone.'

Newman stubbed out his cigarette.

'It doesn't work in Europe.'

'Then you'll basically be deaf and dumb over here, and as is often the case with those who suffer from those disabilities, people will take you for an idiot.'

'All right, I'll get one.'

'Pass the number on to me immediately. Once the kidnappers make their move, it's essential that we are able to react quickly. The gang will almost certainly set a timetable for further negotiations, and if they don't receive a prompt reply they may well break off contact. At that point things can rapidly get out of hand, with terrible results.'

Zen's face clouded over.

'Odd, your father deceiving you like that,' he murmured. 'I hope everything's going to be all right.'

The watcher outside Nicola Mantega's office on Corso Mazzini was getting bored. Thanks to his work with the Digos anti-terrorist squad, Benedetto was an old hand at stakeouts despite his relative youth, and knew that boredom was a surveillance operative's worst enemy. It eroded your concentration, imperceptibly but continually, and when something finally happened, your reflexes would be stiff and your reaction time sluggish. If the wait was long enough and the event sufficiently discreet, you might even miss it altogether.

The night before, Mantega had been followed back to his villa by the motorcyclists, who reported that he had gone straight to bed. In the morning, a fresh team had tailed him back to the city in what was seemingly one of the ubiquitous Ape three-wheeled vans used by smallholders and rural tradesmen, but in this case powered by a very quiet 1.5-litre engine mounted in the covered rear cargo space. The target had spent the entire time since then in his office, in which an assortment of listening devices had been installed in the course of a nocturnal visit by members of the technical support group. Later in the day, the motorcycle duo had relieved the Ape team at the rear of the office building, while Benedetto kept his eyes on the front door from the specially equipped delivery van, which had been repainted green and given a fresh logo overnight.

The end result of all this effort had been precisely zero. Mantega had left home and arrived at the office at the normal hour, and his phone calls had been entirely routine, relating to his work facilitating contracts, payments and legal issues for various nominally legitimate business enterprises. A total yawn, in short, and Benedetto was in fact yawning when Mantega emerged from the utilitarian 1960s office building shortly after noon. This was a perfectly reasonable hour for a *libera professionista* to begin winding down towards lunch, but two features of the situation immediately struck Benedetto. The first was that Mantega had changed out of the jacket, pullover and tie he had worn to work into decidedly unsmart jeans, an open-necked sweatshirt and work boots. The second was that instead of walking towards his favourite restaurant or driving off in the Alfa in which he had arrived, he got into a taxi which had drawn up near by a few minutes earlier. Benedetto started the van and radioed the others to get their MotoGuzzi going. The taxi headed east across the Crati river and then south, where the bikers overtook both the van and the taxi with breathtaking arrogance. A few minutes later, the front tail came through on the radio link.

'He paid off the cab in Casali and is now in a café opposite the station.'

'Understood. I'll take over.'

At one time, Casali had been a small and undistinguished village on the main road south from Cosenza, but that highway had long been superseded by the *autostrada* and the community itself subsumed into the suburbs of the city. Its centre was a modest piazza completely clogged with parked cars. Benedetto left the van a block further on and then doubled back, apparently talking non-stop on his mobile. In reality he was moving his lips silently while his colleague from the MotoGuzzi crew briefed him on the current situation. Mantega was still in the bar, drinking a cappuccino which he had already paid for, a slightly unusual thing to do in such a humble establishment. He had not apparently made contact with anybody.

After a brief glance inside, Benedetto took up position outside the bar, in the informal car park that the original *piazzetta*, a mere widening of the main road, had become. The bar was empty except for Mantega and three elderly men who looked as if they had been there since it opened. When Benedetto next looked – turning casually in the manner of a shiftless youth intent on his phone conversation – the target had emerged from the café and was now weaving his way rapidly through the ranks of parked cars, across the highway and into the station yard just as a diesel railcar emerged from the right and slowed to a halt. This was awkward. By the rule book, one of the others should have taken over at this point, but there was no time for that. Benedetto sprinted after him, narrowly avoiding an oncoming truck on the highway, and reached the platform just as the doors of the railcar were closing. He levered the rear one open and climbed aboard.

There were about a dozen other passengers. Benedetto slid on to a seat at the rear. Fortunately, Nicola Mantega had chosen to sit facing forward and gave no sign of having noticed Benedetto's presence. When the guard came round, both men bought tickets. In Mantega's case, this involved quite a lengthy discussion, but the roar of the engine as they climbed the steep gradient out of the valley made it impossible for Benedetto to hear what was said. He himself bought a single ticket all the way, then went to the lavatory and made a number of phone calls.

The back-up team at the Questura did their best, but it was an impossible task. There were twenty-six scheduled stops on the three and a half hour trip across the rugged interior of Calabria, twelve of which lay in the neighbouring province of Catanzaro and hence would require the co-operation of the authorities in that city, which was unlikely to be rapidly forthcoming at a time when most of their senior personnel would either be on the way home for lunch or at a restaurant. The metre-gauge railcar trundled along at no more than forty kilometres an hour, but on the winding, unimproved roads of that area even the MotoGuzzi would be hard pressed to maintain a better average speed. All Benedetto's instincts told him that Nicola Mantega was headed for a covert meeting with the kidnappers, the vital link in the chain of evidence that would bring the dormant investigation to life, and eventually to court. But there would be further feints, dodges and cut-outs at the other end, and he himself, alone and on foot, could do nothing.

In the end, it wouldn't have mattered anyway. In addition to the scheduled stations, the train also passed a number of *fermate facoltative*, unmanned halts where it could be stopped by request to the guard. It was at one of these, located at the head of a remote valley which the line looped languidly around, that Nicola Mantega descended. There was an abandoned station, its windows and doorways bricked up, and a disused siding and goods shed. Behind this, a heavily overgrown dirt track rose up the bare hillside, presumably leading to the village that had given the station its name, but there was no sign of it or of any other human presence in the scrubby landscape. The railcar revved up its engine in a cloud of diesel fumes and then sidled off. Benedetto headed for the solitude of the lavatory and switched on his mobile and radio, but he couldn't get a signal on the phone, the radio was out of range and anyway it was too late.

Nicola Mantega stood motionless until the railcar was out of sight, then started to walk slowly up the dirt track. After about a minute, a distant sound attracted his attention. A black Jeep was making its way down the hillside towards him, disdaining the levelled track. When it was about five metres away it swung around to face uphill and an electric window peeled down.

'*Salve*,' said Giorgio.

The rotor blades were whirling slowly to a halt as the three men stepped down from the Bell 412. To the west, just above the line of mountains that cradled the city, the sun was also powering down for the night, but on the ground the temperature was still over a hundred. Flanked by the pilot and technician, Phil Larson headed towards the metal box that Aeroscan had hired as a temporary office facility. It stood on the cracked concrete paving that also served as a landing pad, right alongside a skeletal concrete structure that had obviously been abandoned for years. It looked as though someone had set out to build a factory or a supermarket and then changed his mind or run out of money half-way through.

None of the men talked. They were all stupid from the heat, filthy from the dust kicked up by the backdraught, jittery from the continual noise and vibration of the helicopter and looking forward to stripping off their work clothes and getting back to the hotel as soon as possible. So Phil wasn't real happy when his phone started to ring. Even worse, the screen displayed *Anonimo* in place of the caller's name. He had learnt that this meant an out-of-area call, almost certainly international and probably from head office. The damnedest thing about operating in Europe was the time difference. Just as you crawled out of the galley after a hard day at the oars, the eager beavers back in the States were arriving at the office all caffeined up and keen to show their mettle.

'Phil Larson.'

'Phil? It's Martin Nguyen.'

'Hi, Mr Nguyen.'

'Phil? Phil? Are you there?'

'Sure I'm here.'

'I can't hear you, Phil! Can you hear me?'

'I can hear you fine, Mr Nguyen. Maybe there's a problem with the connection.'

'Phil? There must be a problem with the connection. I'll call you right back.'

Oh no you won't, thought Phil, speed-dialling another number.

'Hi, Phil.'

'Hi, Jason,' replied Phil, pushing open the door. Jason looked up at him in surprise and made to clam his cell.

'Leave it on!' Phil told him. 'I need to block an incoming while I unwind.'

After a quick rinse in what they called the sewer shower, Phil emerged wearing his street clothes. The others were all set to go. Phil told them that he'd be along later, retired to his office and scrolled down on the mobile till he hit 'Rapture Works'.

'Martin.'

'This is Phil, Mr Nguyen.'

'Finally! I've been trying to get you for almost half an hour. Where the fuck were you?'

Phil was not a serious student of human nature – too many variables – but Martin Nguyen had always struck him as being the nearest thing to the electrical circuitry that he loved and understood. Now he sounded like some goddamn chick. What was up?

'I had to take another call, Mr Nguyen. Our aviation fuel distributor didn't deliver on schedule and we've only got fifteen hours' supply left. Anyway, I've sorted it all out. The gasoline's going to arrive tomorrow, trucked in from . . .'

'I don't want to hear your goddamn life story, Larson. Report progress.'

'Well, we've been working twelve-hour shifts and getting through around a hundred kilometres each day.'

'But you haven't found anything.'

'You'd have heard if we had.'

'So how long is this going to take?'

'No way to tell, Mr Nguyen. We might find it first thing tomorrow, or it might be at the far end of our last beat.'

'How can we speed up the search?'

'We can't. The ultrasound waves require a given amount of time to penetrate down into the ground and reflect back up to the receiver. The duration of each wave bounce represents a physical constant. If the forward motion of the monitoring vehicle exceeds the envelope created by that constant, the information returned is worthless.'

Martin Nguyen's hiss echoed down the line.

'Then we need to grow our resources. Hire another helicopter.'

'Choppers are no use without the hardware.'

'Have extra units shipped over.'

'Well, you'd need to talk to head office about that, Mr Nguyen, but I think it might be a problem.'

'You mean a challenge?'

'No, I mean a problem. The scanner we're using was originally developed for military purposes, in high-flying planes or drones. The civilian variant, operable at low altitudes, is still in development, but Aeroscan was able to get hold of a beta release prototype for use on your project. It's a beauty, works just great, but as far as I know there aren't any more available right now.'

'Okay. You say you're working twelve hours a day. That's only a fifty per cent effort. Get your company to fly out more people, hire another pilot – maybe another gas supplier while you're at it – and keep going right around the clock.'

'I hate to tell you this, Mr Nguyen, but it can't be done. This is strictly visual navigation. We're flying at less than a hundred feet in a complex environment on the outskirts of a major city surrounded by mountains on three sides. We're working the flood plain now, but some of the side valleys on our survey chart are barely thirty feet across near the bottom. No aviation instruments could cope with that. The authorities have been pretty co-operative so far, but they'd never let us operate between civil dusk and dawn. Apart from anything else, we're supposed to be selecting prime locations for a movie shoot. How can you do that in the dark?'

That hiss again.

'So, worst-case scenario, when is the latest we'll know whether there's anything there?'

'About a month, if all goes well.'

'That's way too long.'

'I don't know what to tell you, Mr Nguyen. I didn't think this thing was time-dated.'

'The situation has changed. The director of the movie we're using as cover for the operation now wants to start shooting next week.'

'So? He won't bother us none.'

'No, but you'll bother him. He'll wonder what this helicopter is doing all day, patrolling up and down when he's trying to set up a scene. When he asks around, he'll be told that it's surveying locations for scenes in his movie. Bullshit, he'll say, I never asked for anything like that.'

'I'm sorry, Mr Nguyen, this is way beyond my area of competence.'

'All right, let's see how competent you are, Larson. You don't have a month any more. You have barely a week, so you'll have to prioritise.'

'On the basis of what criteria?'

'How do you mean?'

Phil sighed.

'Mr Nguyen, our project chart is posted right here on the wall of my office. I'm looking at it now. What I'm seeing is a large-scale map of the area divided into fifteen-metre-wide strips. Those that have been completed are shaded in – apart from today's, because I haven't had a chance yet. All the remaining strips look pretty well identical to me. I don't even know what we're looking for, except it's a man-made structure buried somewhere down beneath the river-bed. You're now asking me to favour some sections of the survey over others, so I'm asking you who are the good guys and who are the bad guys. They don't seem to be wearing their hats.'

'Don't get flippant with me, Larson!'

'Sorry, Mr Nguyen. The heat must be getting to me. Plus everything's a whole lot tougher since Newman went AWOL. Just yesterday this Italian guy comes around wanting to know what we're doing and where's our authorisation from the city. At least I think that's what he was saying, his English wasn't too good. I gave him the agreed cover story but he wanted to see the paperwork. I don't know where those permits are. Never even seen them. And I sure as hell can't deal effectively with people like that in a foreign language. That was what Pete Newman was for. I do electronics.'

Another, briefer silence.

'I'll be there tomorrow,' Martin Nguyen announced.

The isolated stone barn had evidently lain derelict for years, but still smelt strongly of sheep and manure, interwoven with more recent layers of rot, damp and mould. The floor was of beaten earth and the windows filled in with roughly mortared blocks of terracotta brick. Once Giorgio had closed and bolted the massive door, the darkness was broken only by peeps of light from the roof, whose flat stone slabs had shifted over the years. He turned on his torch and suspended it from a loop at the end of a length of rusty wire attached to the main roof-beam, so that it dangled down like a domestic light fixture, then he moved away into the shadowy depths at the fringes of the building.

It was only now that Mantega realised there was another odour present. It was the smell of fear, and the fear was his own. A couple of days after Peter Newman's kidnapping, an envelope had been deposited in the letter box of Mantega's villa. It was unstamped and addressed only with his name. The note inside, printed by a typewriter in block capitals, gave detailed instructions to be followed in the event that meeting in person proved to be necessary. Mantega had followed these to the letter, and Giorgio had duly shown up at the designated station on the secondary line to Catanzaro.

So far so good, but since then nothing had gone according to plan. Mantega had expected a warm welcome from his associate, a rapid update on the latest developments regarding both of them, followed by a discussion of the most appropriate means to bring their joint enterprise to fruition. None of that. Giorgio had remained silent and glacially cold throughout the twenty-minute drive to the ruin where they now were, and had offered absolutely no explanation for having insisted on the meeting in the first place.

'We'll talk once we get there,' was all he would say.

As he watched his host return, carrying two tumblers full of some colourless liquid, it occurred to Mantega that an important component of the primitive terror which had him in his grip was that Giorgio appeared physically different. He was still the same wiry weasel of a man, as thin and heavy as a sheet of beaten lead, but his movements had lost their fluidity, their *naturalezza*. He bristled with suppressed tension, and the hand that offered Mantega his glass of grappa might have been robotic.

'*Salute.*'

Neither man wanted to drink. Both did. Once this ceremony had been concluded, Mantega waited for Giorgio to get to the point. He felt sure that Peter Newman was being held near by, possibly even in the cellarage of the barn, and was anxious to discuss the ways and means for his release and their payment by the son. But Giorgio didn't seem to want to discuss anything. He just stood there, his back to the light, eyes focused on nothing within view, listening intently to the silence between them. Eventually Mantega could stand it no longer.

'I've been under a lot of pressure, you know!'

Giorgio moved his eyes, though not his head, and regarded him for a moment dispassionately.

'From the police, as a matter of fact,' Mantega continued with a hint of sarcastic emphasis. 'This outsider that they've brought in as a temporary replacement for Rossi seems determined to make his mark at my expense. He gave me a very unpleasant grilling yesterday, and seems to regard me as a probable accessory both before and after the fact.'

Still Giorgio said nothing.

'Rossi couldn't be bought, but he'd grown lazy,' Mantega went on. 'The new man has a quite different approach. He's given the case top priority, is heading the investigation in person and, since the victim is a prominent foreign citizen, he's getting full co-operation from his superiors and the judiciary. I therefore have to assume that all my phones, both at home and at work, are being tapped. I may even be under surveillance.'

'You are.'

Mantega's relief at having finally made the other man say something was undermined by what he had in fact said.

'How do you know?'

Giorgio put his glass in his pocket and lit a small cigar.

'Don't worry, it's all part of the price of doing business,' he replied.

'That's all very well for you to say! You're not under suspicion. How could you be when there's absolutely nothing to link you to the American? Anyway, as I told you last night, Newman's son has arrived, so let's get down to this business of yours. That call was from a public phone box, incidentally, with a tramp passed out in a doorway on one side of me and a violent outburst of road rage on the other. I don't want to live like this, Giorgio, so let's stop pissing around and get down to negotiating.'

Giorgio plucked the cigar from between his lips and exhaled a dense cloud of smoke. Then he smiled. When Giorgio smiled, you knew that the news was really, really bad.

'Negotiating what?'

Too late, Mantega sensed that he was on a steep, slippery slope with nothing left to do but slither down as best he could.

'For Christ's sake, Giorgio! The money angle. I don't know about you, but I'd like to see my share of the profits sooner rather than later.'

'For doing what?'

He can't be planning to stiff me, thought Mantega, but in his heart he knew that Giorgio could and that there wasn't a thing he could do about it.

'We had an agreement, Giorgio!'

'Have you a copy with you?'

'You gave me your word! We embraced and kissed!'

'And what did you do for me?'

Mantega flung his arms wide.

'What did I do?' he repeated dramatically. 'The whole thing was my idea! You would never even have known about this rich American if it hadn't been for me.'

'You told me he was Calabrian. A Calopezzati.'

'Who cares who he is? He's rich and he's here, totally out of his depth and all alone. I marked him down for you and arranged for him to visit me that evening so that you could take him. Without me, none of this would have been possible! You can't deny that.'

Giorgio bent down to stub out his cigar, then placed the butt carefully in his pocket.

'Let's have another drink,' he said.

'I don't want your damned drink, I want my money!'

But Giorgio had once again vanished into the dark recesses of the barn. A few moments later he returned, bottle in hand.

'Give me your glass,' he said.

'I don't want a drink!'

Giorgio stood quite still. He allowed the silence to reform and listened to it attentively for a while.

'Neither do I.'

In one motion, he swivelled round and hurled the bottle of grappa against the wall. Sensing that he was in great danger, Mantega did not move or speak. Giorgio reached into his jacket pocket and handed out a bundle of fifty-euro notes.

'What's this?' Mantega asked.

'Your fee.'

'My agreed fee was ten per cent of the ransom, Giorgio. We haven't even started negotiating yet. How can you possibly know how much the family will end up paying?'

'There won't be any negotiations. You get a kill fee of a thousand. Take it.'

'What do you mean, no negotiations? What's happened? What's going on?'

'At the back of the barn you'll find an old Vespa. Full tank, key in the ignition. Turn right when you reach the road, then left at the next junction. After that follow the signs for Cosenza. Dump the scooter in the outskirts and take a bus into town.'

There was a long silence.

'And Newman?' asked Mantega.

'He died.'

The two men stared at each other.

'What?' Mantega shouted. 'You let your hostage die and now you expect to buy me off with a lousy thousand euros? You must be crazy!'

Giorgio unhooked the torch from its support.

'Let me show you how crazy I am.'

He shone the stark beam up and to one side, coming to rest on one of the transverse timbers supporting the roof. Attached to the side of the joist was a silver box terminating in a glittering glass eye.

'Digital camcorder,' said Giorgio. 'I switched it on by remote control when I fetched the grappa and off again when I went back for the bottle. One of my *cumpagni* fixed it up for me, as well as the wire to hang up the torch that would draw you into its field of view.'

He shone the light straight into Mantega's face, blinding him.

'You have not only admitted your part in the kidnapping but claimed that the whole thing was your idea. Without you it wouldn't have been possible, you said. I kept my back to the camera all along, but I made sure that you were facing it. If I get arrested because you've blabbed, under duress or not, that video will end up in the hands of this new chief of police you're so scared of.'

He turned off the torch, leaving them both in the dark.

'Drive carefully, Nicoletta.'

'*I calabresi non sanno fare squadra. Tutto lì!* They can't play as a team and so they're condemned to remain ineffective whingers, always complaining that the state handouts they live on aren't generous enough.'

As if to illustrate his thesis, Giovanni Sforza attracted the waiter's attention with a loud *'Eh!'* and then stabbed his finger at the bread basket and the wine carafe. Moments later, both had been replenished.

'You see?' demanded Sforza. 'Bullying and beating is the only language they understand.'

'You sound like one of those racists who want to declare an independent Padania,' said Zen.

'I'm not a racist, I'm a realist,' Sforza returned mildly. 'A racist believes that a designated ethnic group can never function and compete effectively because of its innate deficiencies. I don't believe that. All I'm saying is that the Calabrians do not in fact function or compete effectively, despite having been given every opportunity to do so. Look at the Irish, by way of comparison. Their historical and economic circumstances were very similar for centuries, yet now their country is per capita one of the richest and most successful in Europe.'

Zen didn't want to talk about Ireland. In fact he didn't really want to talk at all, but Giovanni had invited him to lunch and it would have been churlish to refuse. Sforza was an overweight, melancholic individual from Bergamo who freely admitted that the only reason he had accepted his present posting as deputy questore in Cosenza was because it meant promotion. He and Zen saw eye to eye on almost everything that mattered, and tactfully agreed to differ on all the things that didn't.

'Anyway, I've ranted enough,' said Sforza, reminding Zen of why he liked him. 'How's the Newman case going?'

'No word yet from the kidnappers, but I've discovered one possibly significant fact. The victim's original name was not in fact Newman.'

Sforza made a visible effort to appear interested.

'Really? So what was it? Mickey Mouse? Arnold Schwarzenegger?'

'Pietro Ottavio Calopezzati. He was born here in the province of Cosenza.'

Sforza shrugged.

'In the two decades before the Great War, the south lost more men to emigration than the entire country lost fighting in that war.'

'The significance is threefold,' Zen replied. 'First of all, he lied about his identity, even to his son. Lying is always significant, since by nature we're truth tellers. Secondly, the documents relating to his American citizenship are held in a classified file marked "For Official Use Only". And finally, the Calopezzati family used to be the greatest landowners in these parts. Perhaps you've heard of them.'

Sforza shook his head.

'So what? The *latifondo* system is as obsolete as Russian serfdom. Far enough removed from us now, in fact, that we can even afford to indulge in a little nostalgia. If you ever drive over to the east coast, take a look around the Marchesato. You realise instantly that the only viable way to make any economic sense of that lunar landscape is intensive, centralised wheat farming on a massive scale with low labour costs.'

Zen laughed.

'You're sounding a little sentimental, Giovanni. Are you sure you're not secretly voting for the *Lega Nord*?'

Sforza erased that suggestion with a decisive swipe of his hand, but his eyes smiled.

'You know the old saying – once a Communist, always a Communist.'

'So you still believe in that line in the Marxist creed: "to each according to his needs"?'

'Devoutly.'

'Well, my needs presently include tracking down any surviving members of the Calopezzati clan and getting as much information as possible about their whereabouts and activities during the war years. Can you help?'

'Yes, but I need to smoke. Let's pay these swine and adjourn to a café.'

They found a suitable place a few doors away, with tables on the street where they could smoke. The coffee was tolerable, but Giovanni Sforza was incredible. He swung into action as one to the manner born, calling a dozen of his contacts and gouging the information he needed out of each until a complete network had come into being and formulated a result, which he then communicated to Zen.

'The man you need is Cataldo Antonacci. He curates the archives and local history section of the provincial museum. What he doesn't know about events around here for the last thousand years is not worth knowing. He's expecting you within the hour.'

'Did you explain the nature of my interest?'

'Naturally not. I merely said that the chief of police wished to consult him about a matter that he had not disclosed to me but which might quite possibly be legally privileged. He sounded very impressed.'

Twenty minutes later, Zen was in an elegant building on a quiet piazza high above the sterile grid of the modern city below, discussing the origins of the *latifondo* system in general and of the Calopezzati family in particular with Cataldo Antonacci. The historian's expression of benign bemusement suggested that Zen's visit possibly constituted a slight indelicacy, but one which he was too well bred to bring to his guest's attention. Nor, needless to say, did he enquire why such an eminent official as the *capo della polizia* for the province of Cosenza was so interested in a dry subject that most people had learned about at school and promptly forgotten.

With exquisite tact and a welcome gift for concise synthesis, he related the origins of the huge southern estates in land grants made by the Spanish viceroys of

Naples during the eighteenth century, and in their subsequent enlargement by shrewd purchases from adjoining landowners, often ancient noble families who had got into debt and needed cash fast. The key to success, the archivist explained, was to get possession of a property large enough to be virtually self-sufficient, to allow diversity of production involving economies of scale thus insulated from the vagaries of the market. The continuing integrity of the operation was then guaranteed by strict adherence to the primo-geniture system, under which the eldest son inherited everything, the other males being maintained on an allowance but forbidden to marry.

'To do that successfully over many generations requires good luck or good genes. The Calopezzati were gifted with both. They were of humble origins, small landowners from Cosenza, but they proved exceptionally astute and energetic in developing and managing their property, which eventually extended from the wheat plains around Crotone to the alpine forests and summer pastures of the Sila massif above us to the east. There was constant tension and occasional strife with the local peasantry, most usually over the encroachment and expropriation of smallholdings and common land bordering the Calopezzati domains, but in general the system worked fairly smoothly. By the mid-nineteenth century the family had been raised to baronial rank, was immensely wealthy and kept a splendid palace in Naples.'

'So where did it all go wrong?' Zen ventured to enquire.

'The short answer is after the Great War. By then the Calopezzati were powerful political players, and the baron thus spent most of his time at the centre of things in Rome, leaving the management of the estate to less able relatives or salaried underlings. In addition, socialist ideas about the rationalisation of land ownership had finally started to take root in the south, leading to demonstrations which often ended in bloodshed.'

Cataldo Antonacci shrugged.

'But in the end, it was their good luck that ran out. On the death of Baron Alfredo Calopezzati, the estate passed to his son Roberto, who was actively involved with the Fascist Mas X movement and later saw action in Ethiopia and the wider war that followed. He handed over administration of the estate to his sister Ottavia, who ruled over it with an iron hand from the old family stronghold at Altomonte, thirteen hundred metres up in the Sila mountains.'

'What was she like?'

'By all accounts, a stone-cold bitch. Her father Alfredo had been respected, if not exactly liked. Even her brother got some admiration for his courage and daring, although there were darker sides to his character. But to the best of my recollection I have never heard anyone say a positive thing about Ottavia. While the country fell apart and endured defeat and invasion, she remained shut up in that chilly fortress known locally as *la bastiglia*, surrounded by a retinue of loyal servants and armed guards. Then one winter night just before the end of the war, a fire broke out. It completely gutted the structure and killed the baroness, as Ottavia was called, although she had of course no claim to that title.'

'And what happened to the estate after the war?' asked Zen.

'It was broken up by the agrarian reforms of the 1950s and what remained to the family was sold off.'

'Did either Roberto or his sister have children?'

'Not so far as one knows, but the details of the war years remain murky. It's not even clear if Roberto survived, but Ottavia certainly died childless. She'd never married and was past childbearing age when the fire took her.'

'So the family is now extinct?'

'It may well be. That's the price you pay for voluntarily observing primogeniture even after it was made illegal. But surely in your position it would be possible to . . .'

Zen nodded his assent. Yes, he would certainly make further enquiries.

'As it happens, we're standing in a former possession of that family,' the archivist said as he saw his visitor to the door. 'This building was originally one of their many properties. When they came south from Naples for the summer, they would break their journey in Cosenza for a few days and wine and dine the local notables before making the long trek up into the mountains to Altomonte. Until a century ago there was no road beyond Spezzano. The baron and his entire retinue had to get out of their carriages and continue on muleback.'

Zen had taken a taxi to the offices of the museum, but he opted to return to the modern centre on foot, down the narrow curve of Corso Telesio, where renovated apartments awaited yuppies with enough money and stamina to gentrify the largely abandoned mediaeval maze, and across the Busento river, a mere trickle between islands of gravel and tall reeds at this time of year. For a moment he wondered if he had wasted his time by going to see Antonacci. What he had learned had been interesting, particularly the bits that didn't make sense, like Ottavia being past childbearing age when her son had been born. However, it remained doubtful how relevant any of it was to the task of getting Pietro Ottavio released as soon as possible by his kidnappers.

Jake and Madrona drove up into the mountains, pulled the bikes out of the back of the SUV and then cycled along an old railroad grade winding up above a dark, sinuous lake sheathed by forested slopes. Now they were sitting side by side on the timbers of a trestle overlooking the shimmering water below. The fresh, warm air was heady with the smell of pine sap and creosote.

'Tell me about the Rapture again,' he said.

Madrona smiled.

'Oh Jake, you're just like a baby, wanting to hear the same story over and over.'

She sighed wistfully.

'I've been thinking a lot about babies recently.'

'We'll have one, Madrona. Real soon. I just have to get this project finished first. As soon as that's done I'll switch to breeding mode, I promise.'

He grinned at her.

'The Lord has sworn and will not repent.'

'Huh?'

'Some hypertext link. I want to say someplace in the Bible, but I can't be bothered to Google it.'

'I never read that creepy Jewish stuff. They had their chance to accept Jesus as their personal saviour and they blew it.'

'But you told me that the end times can't happen without the Jewish state.'

'Oh sure. That's why we're in Iraq. Pastor Gary says that even though it turns out that Saddam didn't have any like missiles and was never a threat to us, he was a big threat to Israel. That's why the president had to send in the troops. The other stuff was just window dressing to keep the liberals quiet.'

Jake leant over and kissed her. God, he loved this woman. She wasn't maybe what you'd call really beautiful, but she was a total babe. A sweet smile, frizzy blonde hair, plus the guileless blue eyes of a child combined with that hot bod and a voice like wind-chimes colliding in a gale, harmonious but with a raucous edge. Above all, though, he loved Madrona for her mind. She was sublimely stupid.

This was a central processing issue, nothing to do with data storage, which for Jake was peripheral. Why overload your system with a bunch of mostly dormant read-only files when the internet could come up with anything you didn't know in like 0.18 seconds? Jake didn't know practically everything, but he wasn't stupid. You didn't rise like a rocket through the massed ranks of Microsofties without being able to spot a glitch invisible to other eyes, or figure out a more elegant route from A to B than detouring via Z. But Madrona was not only even more ignorant than him about every aspect of human knowledge, except maybe female grooming, she was also dumber than fuck. Jake found this adorable. It was like having some big, placid, playful dog around the place, only one you could have great sex with too.

'Yeah,' she said. 'Before the end times can happen, the Jews have to rebuild the Temple. Then Jesus and the Antichrist duke it out while we all watch from heaven. It's foretold in the Book of Revelations. God, I can't wait to see the movie!'

Jake sighed.

'Yeah, well, we're having some problems.'

'Really? Like what?'

'Oh, the director wanted to cast some English guy but he pulled out. Plus we're having some issues with the location shooting in Italy. I'm sending one of my people out there to try and fix things up.'

Madrona made her charming sideways moue.

'I've always wanted to go to Italy.'

'Chill, hon. I'll take you there for our babymoon.'

'But I don't get it. If those guys are being assholes, why don't you just make the movie here? Nevada or Utah or Arizona or someplace.'

Jake longed to tell her the truth, to bring her in on the whole delicious secret, but that would be too risky. The fact that Madrona had nothing to say didn't stop her talking incessantly, particularly when she got together with girlfriends like that turbo-bitch Crystl. The media had been sniffing around Rapture Works and its unique project for months. So far Martin Nguyen had managed to ensure that they gave big returns for small feeds, but as the commencement of shooting approached the predators were getting hungrier by the minute. If Madrona mentioned the truth to even one of the gals in her worship group or therapy workshop, somewhere along the line someone would figure out that there were big bucks to be made by breaking the story. At the same time, Jake couldn't lie to Madrona. It would be like stealing candy from a kid.

'No, it's got to be Italy. See, every game has a scenario, but only the players can make it all pan out by making the correct moves. By moving against Saddam, the guys in DC made a good blocking move. Right now I'm set to make an even better enabling move.'

'Wow,' said Madrona.

'Totally,' agreed Jake. 'Here's the thing. Okay, the Jews rebuild their temple. What about all the goodies they kept in there, the lost Ark and shit? You can't fake those. Plus a lot of people think they're not around any more.'

'How come?'

'It's like history. Way back, the Romans burned the Temple down and stole all that stuff.'

'That was the Jews' punishment for rejecting Jesus. But wouldn't they have melted them down and made it into jewellery? Hey, you know what! If you ever want to buy me something, I could really use some gold bracelets.'

Jake looked around at the jagged rocks and spiky conifers, then up at the vacant blue sky.

'Madrona, is God perfect?'

She laughed.

'Well, I could have used longer legs. But sure, of course he is.'

'Then everything he does must be perfect, right? So he wouldn't have designed a game which could never work out because one of the key items of loot is lost for ever.'

'I guess.'

'Okay. So if the Apocalypse is going to happen, all that treasure from the Temple must still be around somewhere. And I'm pretty sure I know where one chunk of it has been hidden all this time.'

Madrona looked totally awed.

'Really, hon? What are we talking about here?'

Her husband smiled artlessly.

'Like, a candlestick?'

At seven o'clock precisely, Claude Rousset awoke from plump, untroubled sleep, grasped the vacuum flask of coffee he had prepared before retiring the night before and stepped outside accompanied by Fifi, leaving his wife snoring contentedly in bed. The sun had not yet reached the side of the lake where their camper van was parked, but further out the water glinted prettily in a gentle breeze. The silence was absolute.

Fifi went off to urinate on selected features of the landscape while her master sipped his coffee and started planning the day's activities. Monsieur and Madame Rousset owned a furniture shop in Dijon. Every August they closed up the business and took to the road. Having thoroughly explored every region of France, many of them more than once, they had lately started to venture further afield. Switzerland and Spain had been first, then the Ligurian coast, Tuscany and the Amalfi peninsula. This year, feeling they were by now seasoned travellers, Claude had proposed to his wife that they tackle Sicily and *le Calabre sauvage*.

Sabine Rousset's response had at first been decidedly negative, but in the end her husband had prevailed. Fears of Mafia shoot-outs, larceny, theft, extreme poverty and casual violence were absurd and anachronistic, he had declared. Italy was a leading industrial nation and a founder member of the European Union, and that included the bits south of Naples. Sabine still had her doubts, but she had not held the marriage together for almost thirty years without learning to pick her battles.

When she finally emerged, the sun was up above the mountains, the temperature had climbed several degrees and her husband had made his plans. After leaving Crotone the previous day, they had visited San Severina and the Bosco del Gariglione, one of the few remaining patches of the primeval forest that had once covered these mountains – named *selva*, 'wild', by the Romans, later corrupted to Sila, as the extract from the Michelin guide read aloud at some length by Claude had explained.

Apart from the lake beside which they had spent the night, in a car park off a minor road, there appeared to be little more to detain them in the interior. After breakfast, they would therefore abandon these rugged heights and descend to Cosenza (*visite 3 heures environ*) and thence to the coast, where Claude had located a recommended camp site with good facilities close to shops and the beach. On the way he proposed a detour to the abandoned town of Altomonte, whose ruins were on a plateau now inaccessible to vehicles and required a stiff climb to reach, but which the guidebook described as *suggestif*, one of the highest terms of commendation in Monsieur Rousset's touristic lexicon.

They arrived shortly after ten o'clock. There were

two tracks leading up to the ruins, one of which left from the outskirts of the new town which had replaced its earlier namesake, but the guide made it clear that the other, accessible off a narrow and winding road with passing places, was the more suggestive. It was accordingly this route that Claude had chosen. The heat was still bearable and the small unpaved parking area was shaded by a grove of giant holm oaks. Having inspected the prospect with a beady eye, Madame Rousset professed herself perfectly content to remain in the camper while her husband explored this particular aspect of Calabrian savagery to his heart's content, just so long as they got to Cosenza in time for lunch. Her husband indicated gesturally that while he would not of course contest this decision, the loss was hers. Fifi, on the other hand, was clearly dying to stretch her legs and to stake a urinary claim on yet more virgin territory.

At first the path wound gently upwards through a dense undergrowth of scrub and spindly trees, but after a while the character of the landscape abruptly changed. The vegetation died out for want of soil and the way ahead became a series of steep and abrupt ramps quarried out of the crevices and gullies in the sheer rock face. The reasons given by the guidebook for both the construction and the abandonment of the original town at once became clear. In the centuries when marauding armies had processed through the area every few years – Greeks, Romans, the Goths led by Alaric, and later the French, the Spanish and Garibaldi's ragged army of liberation – this site had been a natural and virtually impregnable fortress, conveniently hidden from the invaders' view and, if discovered by chance, requiring infinitely more time and effort to conquer than it was worth.

It was only more recently that the disadvantages of the now unthreatened location had come to outweigh the benefits. Frigid winters with no shelter from the wind, sweltering summers with no shade from the sun, and a subsistence economy dependent on the male population leaving for months at a time to work on the great estates of the region. Once that population decided to emigrate en masse to America, Argentina and Australia, the town began its slow decline. The final blow had been an earthquake in the 1950s which demolished most of the houses, rendered two of the four original access paths unusable and persuaded the remaining waverers to move to a new settlement in the valley below. The original Altomonte was now completely uninhabited, although the townsfolk still returned once a year, on the feast day of their patron saint, to celebrate mass in the small twelfth-century church of their ancestors.

Claude Rousset was a devotee of *le footing* and liked to consider himself supremely fit for a man of his age, but by the time he had hauled himself up the final stretch of sun-baked rock and taken refuge in the shade of the shattered guard tower which rose beside the remains of a fortified arch at the brink of the cliff face, he was beginning to envy his wife, who was no doubt nibbling one of her mid-morning snacks in the verdant cool far below. Even Fifi looked momentarily disconsolate, but after a lot of loud lapping at the bowl her master produced from his backpack and filled from the litre of Evian he had also brought along, she quickly recovered and set off in search of adventure.

Claude took longer to recover, but he had also brought the guidebook and a camcorder, so as to be able to include this *curiosité* in the two-hour video presentation with accompanying commentary with which the Roussets regaled their friends during the winter months. He therefore set off towards the only two remaining structures of any size, taking panoramic shots of the general situation as he went. Twenty minutes should do it, he thought. They'd be on their way again by eleven-thirty, and down in Cosenza shortly after noon. Just time to find a parking spot, enjoy an aperitif in some pleasant café and then proceed to the restaurant which the Michelin had recommended for the typicality of its cuisine.

Somewhere out of sight, Fifi had started yapping loudly. If his wife had come along, she would be having hysterics, but Claude saw the poodle as a dog rather than a substitute grandchild. Dogs do what dogs do, and in this case Fifi had probably startled a hare or some other small mammal that lived virtually undisturbed in this wilderness. Well, let her have her fun. The sun was now significantly higher and hotter. He made his way over to the church and poked his head inside the unlocked door. 'Austere but of harmonious proportions', the guidebook said, which was on the generous side. Claude shot forty-five seconds, which he would later edit down by half, then did a slow pan of the former piazza. Unfortunately Fifi was still barking her head off, thereby ruining the impressive 'silence of desolation' audio angle that he'd had in mind. The next thing he knew, the little bitch was right there in front of him, yelping away and making runs towards the centre of the square, returning when he didn't follow.

Claude ignored her. The one remaining item on his clip list was the length of walling opposite. According to the guidebook, this had originally formed part of the façade of a fortified palace belonging to the Calopezzati, an illustrious family of the locality, which had burned down during the war. The remnants weren't much to look at, but Michelin had mentioned them so they had to be recorded. He set to work, panning slowly in to focus on the ornamented portal in the middle, the most impressive vestige of the original. It was only once Claude lowered the camera angle and zoomed in on the steps that he noticed the misshapen lump sprawled across them, and realised that the dark stains on the marble slabs were not in fact shadows cast by the contorted fig tree posed in the gaping doorway.

Aurelio Zen's journey to the crime scene was both more and less arduous. He was transferred by helicopter from the centre of Cosenza to the central square in Altomonte Vecchia in less than ten minutes, but he had been called in the middle of a horrible lunch and arrived both spiritually and literally nauseous.

Claude Rousset's original emergency call had been made minutes after his discovery of the body. Unfortunately a communications problem of a different kind had then delayed everything for over an hour. Monsieur and Madame Rousset had a clear division of labour when it came to the smattering of foreign languages necessary to maximise the value of their touristic experiences – he did German and English, she did Italian and Spanish, and there was no one in the police emergency call centre who spoke French.

Since Madame Rousset's phone was switched off, it was not until her husband had negotiated the even trickier and more tiring descent to the camper van that things started to happen. Twenty minutes after that a police patrol car arrived at the spot where the Roussets were parked. It took another twenty for the officers to climb to the top, assess the situation and call in by radio. Preliminary visual inspection appeared to suggest that they were dealing with a particularly brutal and premeditated homicide of a very unusual kind. The new chief of police had made it clear that he was to be summoned instantly in the event of anything out of the ordinary which might conceivably be related to the Newman disappearance, so he was duly hauled away from a plate of gristly meatballs in tomato sauce and deposited at the scene together with the forensic team. The latter were now kitted up and establishing secure perimeters. These were a bit vague, given that the body parts were spread over a wide area and the fact that Rousset and his damned dog had had a chance to wander about the place before they got there, so Zen felt that he wouldn't be compromising the science work too much by donning a pair of plastic galoshes and moving in for a closer look.

Human remains were nothing new to Zen and he rarely felt disturbed by them. The exceptions were where the injuries to the dead body indicated any suffering that the victim had undergone before death. There were no such indications here, but the scene was spectacularly gruesome just the same. Having disgraced himself on the brief helicopter ride, Zen was pleased to see one of the forensic men make a dash for the shrubbery beyond the perimeter, tearing off his antiseptic mask as he went. The body lay face down on the steps, except that it had no face, no head. The entire skull, as well as a deep chunk of the shoulders and upper torso, had been torn away and now lay in scattered fragments all over the surrounding cobbles. The trunk and limbs had subsequently received additional attention from birds and rodents.

The leader of the forensic team, who had been carefully searching the man's clothing, approached Zen.

'Nothing in his pockets, and it doesn't look like there are any identifying labels.'

'Approximate time of death?'

'At least forty-eight hours ago, but we'll need to get tests done.'

Zen was staring up at a *stemma* carved in the lintel of the doorway.

'What's that?' he asked, half to himself.

'Coat of arms of the Calopezzati family,' the forensic officer replied after a glance.

There was a silence.

'Local landowners, back in the day,' he added helpfully.

Zen nodded.

'Let me have your preliminary report at the very earliest opportunity, however basic it may be.'

'Very good, sir.'

'It must be damned hot in that biohazard gear.'

'It is.'

Aurelio Zen returned to the Questura in an unusually grim and resolute mood. What had gone before had been mere skirmishes. This was war, and as in any war the first priority was to secure one's base. He therefore headed first not to his own office but to that of the deputy questore. Giovanni Sforza had heard about the discovery of the body and Zen's trip to the scene, but his only allusion to this consisted of a slightly raised eyebrow.

'A bad one,' Zen told him. 'They blew his head off with something, a shotgun at very close range or maybe explosives. The killing occurred in situ, an abandoned village in the middle of nowhere.'

Giovanni nodded morosely, as though this merely confirmed his long-standing views about the awfulness of life in Calabria.

'Is it the American?' he asked.

'I don't know yet. It looks as though the victim was stripped and then dressed in a cheap suit like a corpse laid out for a traditional funeral. No form of identification. But the height and weight correspond with the data for Peter Newman.'

He paused, as though he had been about to add something and then changed his mind.

'I should have a definitive answer by this evening.'

Sforza gave him a heavily ironic smile.

'Just as well you're here, Aurelio. Otherwise the Ministry would have sent down some hotshot from Rome to boss us all around.'

By now, Zen was immune to the charms of irony. He swung round on the deputy questore.

'Well, since I am here, I plan to nail the bastards who did this! I'm sick to death of this romantic mystique of the south and the people's self-proclaimed status as eternal victims ground beneath the tyrant's boot throughout the ages. I'm particularly fed up with hearing how crime down here is ineradicable because it feeds off an unfathomable collective tradition of blood, honour and tragedy which we northerners can never presume to understand. To hell with that! It's time they all woke up and started taking responsibility for their actions, and I plan to be their alarm clock.'

Sforza nodded.

'A noble speech. Many of us have made it before, at least in our own minds.'

Zen waved his hands in a gesture of apology and lowered his voice.

'I'm sorry, Giovanni, but it was really horrific. It looked very much like a ritual killing, almost a pagan sacrifice, and it's somehow got under my skin. I have no idea how the investigation will play out, but I do know that it will be a constantly evolving situation and that timing will be of the essence. I may need to take extraordinary measures and make extraordinary demands on our available resources. So I'm asking you, in the name of the questore, to give me permission to do so in advance, sight unseen, using your name and rank as authorisation.'

Giovanni Sforza regarded him in silence.

'It is of course an insane request,' Zen added.

'There's nothing wrong with a little insanity,' said Sforza, 'as long as it's employed in the service of reason. Do what you like. But I warn you –'

He broke off.

'What?' asked Zen.

Sforza shook his head.

'Never mind. Those were brave words about the public perception of the south and the need for

Enlightenment values, but dare I say that they sounded ever so slightly callow? After all, just what are we doing with those values? Take the internet. Here's the most powerful intellectual tool in the history of the human race and we use it to write narcissistic online journals and to "have our say" like a swarm of squabbling starlings. Enlightenment values? We're playing hide-and-seek in the library of Alexandria.'

Zen's dismay must have shown in his expression. Sforza laughed.

'Oh, take it as a compliment, Aurelio! This case seems to have rejuvenated you. It's just that I have a different paradigm for the problems of policing the south. It's like arguing with a woman. You may win small victories, at a high cost, but afterwards everything goes on very much as it did before.'

He gestured self-deprecatingly.

'Take no notice of me. I'm just an old cynic.'

'You're a year younger than me, Giovanni,' Zen said acidly.

'Time in the south cannot be measured by the clock,' was the mock sententious reply.

Back in his office, Zen summoned Natale Arnone and briefed him on the situation.

'Right, here's my shopping list. The cadaver is on its way to the hospital for autopsy and further forensic tests. I want an immediate comparison of the dead man's fingerprints with those of the American sent to us by the consulate, and after that a DNA profile. I'll get on the phone and give the relevant orders, your job is to ensure that the people who promised me the earth don't try and fob me off with a handful of dirt. Got that?'

'Of course, sir.'

Arnone got up.

'I'm not finished yet,' Zen told him. 'I also want you to track down Thomas Newman, the American's son. He's staying at the Hotel Centrale. If he's not there now, leave a man in the lobby until he returns. Finally, I need to trace any surviving relatives of Ottavia Calopezzati as well as the man cited on that birth certificate as Pietro's father, Azzo whatever it was.'

Arnone looked mystified by this last request, but held his tongue.

'Is that all?' he asked.

'By no means all, but it should be enough to keep you busy until eight this evening. That's your deadline for delivery of all the foregoing items. *Buon coraggio.*'

When Arnone had gone, Zen lit a cigarette, then picked up the phone and dialled the extension of the officer in charge of operations.

'I am ordering a house-to-house search of the new town of Altomonte, beneath the hilltop where that corpse was discovered today. All road access and egress is to be sealed by personnel carriers with officers in battledress and armed with machine guns. Helicopters hovering low overhead to spot anyone who tries to escape on foot. Inside the net, every individual is to be questioned separately by plain-clothed officers concerning the arrival and killing of the victim, his identity and that of those responsible.

The level of duress is to exploit the legal limits to the maximum and slightly exceed them should the situation appear to warrant it. As with the discovery of the body, the whole operation is to be subject to a total media blackout until further notice. Authorisation for these orders has been given by the questore's office.'

The official coughed lightly.

'Very good, sir.'

He sounded doubtful.

'Is there a manning problem?' Zen demanded. 'Pull everyone off other jobs, cancel all –'

'It's not that.'

'Then what the hell is it?'

'Well, sir, I don't want to be critical or anything, only I know you're new to the area and I have to say that operations like this haven't proven very productive in the past. In fact, you might almost say that they've been counter-productive. People around here, the more you squeeze them, the harder they get.'

'Admirable attempt to save your colleagues from hours of irksome overtime,' Zen commented. 'Admirable, but doomed. I don't remotely expect any of the inhabitants of the place to talk. That isn't the object of the exercise. Execute the orders you have been given.'

Martin Nguyen held that one of the ways you distinguished winners from losers was by how many times they had to change planes to get to their destination. He had therefore been appalled to discover that to reach the godforsaken hole in the ground down which Rapture Works was pouring its millions, he needed to transfer not just in Los Angeles but also in Rome. On the up side, the transatlantic flight lasted almost ten hours and the time difference was in Martin's favour. He worked the twenty-dollar-a-minute credit-card phone in the armrest of his first-class seat to good effect, arranging to hire a European mobile – when was the rest of the world going to get over its hissy fit and switch to the US standard? – as well as a limo and driver, all to be delivered to him on arrival at Fiumicino airport.

The driver spoke extremely limited English, but he was there on time and proved to possess the skills, nerve and coolness of a Formula One professional. A little jaded after the long flight, Martin sat back in the rear of the Mercedes S-Class saloon and admired the Italian's amazing ability to overtake and undertake, using the hard shoulder or a notional third lane which he conjured into being for precisely the duration of opportunity required, as well as the shamelessly thuggish tactics he employed on slower vehicles, which in effect meant everything else on the road, accelerating towards them at well over a hundred m.p.h., braking at the very last moment to fetch up less than a metre from the victim's rear bumper and then repeatedly flashing his halogen high beams and sounding a series of aggressive and discordant horn blasts. The long section of single-lane working resulting from the reconstruction of the Salerno–Reggio *autostrada* proved almost excessively interesting, with plastic cones flying in all directions and at least one moment when Martin knew without a shadow of doubt that he was going to die.

In the end, they covered the five hundred kilometres from Rome to Cosenza in just under three hours, including a pit stop south of Naples. With the layover for the connection, flying would have taken four. Once the initial thrills of this crash course in extreme driving had worn off, Martin got busy with his rental phone. Okay, so this place was abroad. He knew what you did with broads. Someone fucks and someone gets fucked was the rule everywhere. Martin was sporting his Bluetooth, he was eager and armed. First up was the US consulate. They were as helpful as they had been during his earlier contacts with them, but apparently had nothing new to report on the Newman case.

'The officer in charge is called Aurelio Zen,' the consular official informed Martin. 'Let me spell that. Well, yeah, "aw-reely-oh" is how it might look to you, but "ow-raily-oh" is how they pronounce it here.

Anyway, I suggest that you get in contact with him tomorrow, if only for form's sake. It would just make everything go more smoothly. Do you have an interpreter? I can fix one up for you if you want.'

'An American?'

The official hesitated.

'I do know someone, but she's vacationing right now. But I have a whole list of Italians who speak English better than most Americans. Hey, only kidding! They're students, so they'd be glad to make some money.'

I'll bet, thought Martin. Students could be bought cheap, but there was no knowing who else might offer them a cut above the agreed rate to pass on details of the conversations they had been party to. You could trust Italians to drive cars, but much of what Martin would need to discuss came under the heading of highly sensitive and strictly confidential information. If any word of what Rapture Works was really up to in Calabria leaked out, the whole project would be blown sky high in no time, and Martin's job with it.

'Thanks, I'll think it over.'

'The other thing is Newman's son, Thomas. You'll probably want to meet with him too. He's at a hotel in the centre. Let me give you the number.'

Martin dialled it next. The desk clerk put him through to the room, where the phone rang and rang. Martin was about to hang up when a bleary voice answered.

'*Pronto*.'

Martin wondered what the hell the Lone Ranger had to do with it.

'Give me Tom Newman,' he stated crisply.

'That's me.'

'Oh, hi, Tom. My name is Martin. I'm a business associate of your father. All of us at the company are just shocked at what's happened, so I've been sent out from the States to see if we might be able to provide any help on the ground. I'll be arriving in Cosenza momentarily. I don't know how you're fixed for this evening, but I'd sure appreciate it if we could touch base at some point.'

Martin manufactured an embarrassed chuckle.

'I'm kind of like the new kid on the block here, so it would be real helpful to have someone who can bring me up to speed on the background and the current state of play. If you're free, that is.'

'Free as the wind,' the voice replied tonelessly.

'Well, how about dinner? I'm staying at a different hotel, but what say I swing by your place about six? Do you know somewhere that does good food?'

'Sure, but they don't really get going till eight.'

'They don't?'

'Nowhere does.'

'That late? Wow, this is seriously foreign. Still, when in Rome, I guess! Okay, how does a quarter of eight sound? Good speaking with you, Tom.'

Martin's next call, to Phil Larson, was pitched in a rather different register.

'Nguyen. I'll be there in a couple of hours. Anything new?'

105

'Not yet.'

'Any fresh ideas about narrowing the search area?'

'Not till someone firms up the variables in the equation for me, Mr Nguyen.'

'I've got a team doing that right now. They'll email me their conclusions by midnight tonight local time. When do you start work?'

'We get to the site at five-thirty and airborne around six.'

'Be there no later than five tomorrow. I need to brief you.'

The next call was the one that Martin had been dreading, but it had to be made. After ploughing through a security cordon of call-catchers, he finally got Luciano Aldobrandini on the line. At least the great director spoke excellent English.

'Good of you to take my call, *maestro*,' Martin gushed.

'I'd told Pippo that I was at home to nobody, but money doesn't speak, it shouts, as your famous *cantautore* put it. What can I do for you, Signor Nguyen?'

Martin gave out the warm guffaw of a door-to-door salesman working up to his pitch.

'Well, *maestro*, I just flew into Rome so I thought I'd give you a call.'

'You are in Rome now?'

Aldobrandini's tone was not welcoming.

'No, no, I'm on my way to Cosenza. As you know, our representative there has gone missing and I've been sent over to sort out the loose ends and get everything back on track. So I was kind of wondering if we might get together at some stage and hash out any outstanding issues.'

The film director's voice changed, perhaps consciously, to one of unctuous menace.

'No problem at all. A berth is in preparation.'

'A birth?'

'At Marina di Fuscaldo, for my yacht. It's the only place down that way to put up in season but parking's always a problem. I had to bounce out a couple of boaters who'd had the nerve to reserve months ago. One doesn't like to pull rank – a trifle vulgar, I always think – but sometimes it's the only way to get what one wants. The port is in a very nice position, with a splendid view of the precipitous coastline, and only twenty minutes or so from Cosenza. Why don't you drop by for cocktails one day, if you're not too busy? Among his many and varied talents, my assistant Pippo mixes the best martini this side of the Pillars of Hercules.'

The director's love of his own voice was his downfall. A moment before, Martin had been bemused, but by the time silence finally fell he was back on task.

'So when do you plan to start shooting, *maestro*?'

'We dock tomorrow afternoon and I propose to get down to work as soon as possible after that. I've spent months planning this project and have achieved as much as I can at the theoretical level. My creative juices don't really get flowing until the cameras start to turn, so I naturally want to move on to that stage as soon as possible.'

'I see,' replied Martin.

'I doubt it, but that's irrelevant. What I need from you is the money which you are contracted to pay to my agent on the first day of principal photography. I assume there will be no problem with that.'

'No, no. No, of course not.'

'Then I think we have nothing further to discuss at present. My cell phone has noted your number and I shall be in touch as soon as my ship comes in, so to speak.'

Martin Nguyen hung up and stared forwards through the windscreen. They had been sweeping up a long curve along the flank of a mountain range, but the magisterial progress of the Mercedes was now impeded by two articulated lorries engaged in a truckers' duel on the steep gradient. Clearly frustrated and humiliated at being able to go no faster than seventy, Martin's driver sent his vehicle darting to this side and that like a hummingbird, probing for an opening, then rammed his foot down and surged forward through a momentary gap between the two giant vehicles.

'Yeah, go for it!' Martin yelled. 'Stick it to him! Ram it up his ass till he bleeds! Fuck him, fuck him, fuck him!'

Natale Arnone reappeared in Zen's office two minutes before his deadline expired. He had phoned in earlier to report that the fingerprints of the corpse found at Altomonte matched those of Peter Newman and that the American's son had left his hotel at about two o'clock that afternoon but had not yet returned. The rest of Arnone's afternoon and early evening had been spent tracking down any surviving members of the Calopezzati family, as well as the individual named on Pietro Ottavio's birth certificate as the father. The latter had turned out to be a dead end.

'I checked with our central database in Rome as well as those for the civil authorities of every region in the country. The name Azzo Plecita does not appear in any of them. Only a fraction of the earlier paper archives have been digitalised, of course, but it did occur to me that *la baronessa* might just have made it all up.'

'Why would she do that?'

Arnone looked pleased by Zen's interest in his theory.

'Well, we know that she never married, so the child was evidently illegitimate. Ottavia's lawyer could easily have forged a document purporting to be a sworn declaration from the imaginary father to the effect that he wished his son to be named Calopezzati. That and a few bribes or threats to the clerk in Spezzano would have done it.'

A vague, dreamy look came over Zen's face. He was silent for a full thirty seconds, then slapped his palm on the desk so hard it made Arnone start.

'Azzo Plecita!' he cried. 'Calopezzati! It's an anagram of her own name. She wanted to produce a surrogate heir while keeping the whole thing in the family and excluding outsiders.'

'We can be a bit like that down here,' Arnone admitted.

'So what did you find out about the baronial bastard farmers?'

'That took longer, because I had to search the local paper trail as well. The net result is that the only surviving members with any relation to the Calopezzati are a stepdaughter last heard of thirty years ago and a half-cousin who may or may not have emigrated to Australia.'

'What about the brother, Roberto?'

'It appears that he had strong connections with the Fascist movement back in the 1930s and later went on to fight in the colonial wars, Greece, Albania and back here after the Allied invasion. After that his name disappears from the records. It may well be that he was killed but never identified.'

Zen dismissed his subordinate and then sat quite silent and still, staring at the wall, until Giovanni Sforza walked in and suggested that they repair to a bar.

'Why are you working overtime?' Zen asked him as they walked downstairs.

'It's all thanks to that excellent imitation of our allies in Iraq that your men put on earlier this evening. My phone's been ringing for the past three hours, everyone from the mayor down to the media wanting to know what the hell we think we're doing. It was evidently a very effective operation, Aurelio, but given that I've been covering for you until now, might I ask what it actually achieved?'

They crossed the street and entered the only decent drinking hole in the area, a clumsy, clunky attempt to clone steely Milanese chic in these inhospitable climes.

'I don't know yet,' Zen replied. 'It was a matter of tossing a large rock into the pond and seeing what rose to the surface. I certainly wasn't expecting any of the townspeople to talk, but as it happened someone did say something. A boy of nine, who on the day when the murder took place was playing with some friends close to the path that the victim must have taken.'

Zen ordered a beer, Sforza an expensive malt whisky. The barman poured him a scrupulously measly measure.

'Così poco?' thundered Sforza, in a tone that made Zen realise that there was another side to his friend, and one which quite possibly accounted for the fact that he had got where he was. The barman also took the hint and filled the glass close to the brim. The two men sat down at a marble-topped table in the arid interior, which at least had the advantage of not sporting any video game consoles, television screens or recorded music.

'So what did this boy of yours have to say?' asked Sforza, blatantly lighting a cigarette.

'At first he repeated the standard line about seeing and hearing nothing, but he hadn't quite mastered the knack of improvising innocuous details to support that during follow-up questioning. Corti and Caricato were in charge and it sounds as if they did a good job. They weren't rough with the kid, just listened to his story and elicited clarifying information. So Francesco and his friends had been playing up in the waste ground above the town? Yes. And they'd got there by the track which led up to Altomonte Vecchia? Yes. But they hadn't seen anyone else on the track? No. After some more innocuous questions about how long they spent playing and so on, and determining that they had returned home by the same path, Corti quite casually mentioned that in that case Francesco must have noticed the bright red luxury car that was parked just at the point where the path joined the road. The boy frowned. No, it was grey, he said.'

Zen laughed.

'Well, of course, they took him apart after that!'

Giovanni Sforza shook his head.

'Sorry, Aurelio, I'm not as bright as Corti. We already knew that Newman was there. Who cares what colour his car was?'

'Because it's the first tiny crack in the wall of silence. Obviously everyone in the town knew that the car had been there and that it was subsequently removed by the person or people who murdered Newman. Moreover, it indicates the modus operandi, which was a very odd one. It looks as if Newman arrived alone in the Lancia and then voluntarily walked up the long, arduous track to the spot where his body was found, barefoot and wearing the ritual garb of a corpse laid out for burial. And all this in plain view of the people in the town, even though an alternative and much more secluded route exists, the one taken by that French tourist. Doesn't that suggest anything to you?'

Sforza shrugged impatiently.

'Only that the people concerned were crazy. Kidnappers are in it for the money. It's just business to them. They may occasionally kill their hostage if negotiations break down or if the family tries to lure them into an ambush, but in this case they hadn't even tried to get in touch. Why would they destroy a potentially very profitable piece of merchandise without even putting it on the market?'

Zen nodded noncommittally and gathered up his things.

'Those are valid questions, Giovanni, but we shouldn't let them mesmerise us. I don't believe that whoever did this was crazy in the vulgar sense. The key to resolving these apparent oddities is to stop regarding them as odd, because the perpetrator almost certainly doesn't. It all makes complete sense to him, so it might be helpful to try to see the whole ghastly business in the same way that he sees it, as a deeply deliberate and meaningful performance. The question then becomes, what was the significance of this performance and for what audience was it intended?'

'Well, I'll leave all that to you, Aurelio. I haven't run a case in years. Out of training.'

He sipped his drink reflectively.

'To change the subject, how are you adjusting to life in Calabria?'

Zen waved vaguely.

'It depresses me. Not so much the gory details like this atrocity. It's more the sense of a generalised and ineradicable sadness about the place, despite its natural beauty. In fact, that just makes it worse. To tell you the truth, I'm surprised you can stick it here. I can't wait for whatever his name is to get healthy enough to take over the seat I'm keeping warm for him.'

'The word is that you may not have to wait very much longer,' Sforza commented. 'As for why I can stick it here, the reason is quite simply that I am ambitious. Not an attractive quality, perhaps, but I can't help it. I'm only too well aware of the thing you're talking about, that pervasive *tristezza*, but I'll be damned if I'm going to let it interfere with my career plans.'

He knocked back the rest of his whisky.

'Whereas you, Aurelio, if you will permit me to say so, haven't a gram of ambition in your body. Which is why I will be made questore in two or three years and you will be stuck on your current rung of the ladder until you retire. Shall we go and grab a bite to eat?'

'I'm not hungry. And I have work to do.'

Sforza looked shocked.

'At this hour? And with drink taken?'

Zen smiled weakly.

'Your diagnosis of my character may well be correct, Giovanni. But if I'm not as well endowed with ambition as you are, I at least have a goal, which is to track down the people who kidnapped that poor bastard, persuaded him to walk to the place of execution they had selected and then blew his head off. Until I've done that, I won't really have much interest even in a good meal, never mind the slop they serve here. *Buon appetito, però.*'

The old woman tossed and turned on the lumpy, sagging mattress, but sleep wouldn't take her. Maria lay waiting as though for a lover, but sleep didn't come. She was too old. Sleep just didn't want her any more.

The house was finally still once again, and the rest of the family asleep. The town too, save for the bleeping of a video game from the house across the alley, where Francesco Nicastro was playing the game he had been given for his ninth birthday. There was a lot of violence and bloodshed, but Francesco was enchanted by it. Apart from that, the town was superficially silent, but Maria could sense the whispers and rumours rustling through the streets and walls like rats, just as they had back at the beginning. Someone had been told then, and variously diluted and tainted versions had circulated through the community. The common denominator was that it was all the work of a certain person, and that no one was to interfere or intervene in any way. These stipulations had been observed. Various people had seen the dead man arrive, park his car and walk up the track leading to the old town. Some time later there had been a dull bang, its location impossible to place. Then night fell, and next day the parked car had gone. No one ever climbed up to the ruins above except on the feast of San Martino, and certainly no one had gone there now. In short, normal life had resumed as if the incident had never occurred, until this evening, when the police suddenly descended in force and invested the town, their horrible helicopters hovering overhead like vultures and their armoured vehicles sealing off all the exits.

Everyone agreed that nothing like it had been seen since the war, although Maria had longer and darker memories, of Fascist bullies descending on a town where the people had assembled for a rally to demand decent living wages and then shooting them down in cold blood. This time, however, she had not personally witnessed anything. For months now she had been bedridden with a flare-up of her arthritis, and had kept to her room. Some young policeman dressed like a soldier had had the nerve to open the door without knocking – she might easily have been in the altogether! – with his machine gun levelled. He'd had the grace to apologise and withdraw as soon as he understood the situation, but the rest of the family hadn't been so lucky. They'd all been herded into the living room, then taken out one by one and questioned by two extremely unpleasant men in suits not unlike that which had been worn by *il morto*. When each person's interrogation was over, they were taken to the kitchen and held there in isolation until the entire family had been individually questioned. Only then were they allowed to reassemble and exchange accounts of their experiences, at which point Maria had joined them.

Despite the pressure and threats – one of the thugs had demanded to see written authorisation for the illegal top floor of the house, which had been added to accommodate Maria when she couldn't manage for herself any more – no one had said anything. What was interesting was what the police had said. The car which had been parked at the edge of town, what make was it? What colour? What was the licence number? When had it arrived? When had it been removed and by whom? These were much tougher questions to evade, particularly when the cops gradually revealed that they already knew the answers. How could a luxury hire-car like that have been left abandoned on the outskirts of a *paese di merda* like this without being noticed, probably broken into and possibly stolen? All six members and two generations of the family had stonewalled them, insisting that they hadn't gone that way and had seen and heard nothing. But in all their minds, the same certainty had formed. No one outside the town except 'him' knew about the arrival and subsequent disappearance of the car. Now the police knew, so somebody must have talked.

Finally the helicopters had whirled away and the uniforms and suits had withdrawn, their show of power at an end. But this was not yet over, Maria sensed. Her seventy-eight years on earth had earned her many unwanted gifts, above all the dark secret she had carried intact for most of her life and would take with her to the tomb. So many years in this pitiless landscape, the only one she had ever known and which she loved beyond reason, had also given her a sixth sense for trouble. Despite the apparently baffled withdrawal of the forces of the state, she felt it very strongly now, which was perhaps why she was the only person in the household unable to sleep. To her finely tuned senses it was as obvious and irrefutable as an imminent storm is to birds. What she didn't know, any more than them, was when it would strike and from which direction. She herself would be safe, but Maria no longer cared about herself. She wanted her family to be safe, but the auguries were clear. She had tried to deny them, just as she always tried to deny the first twinge that signalled the onset of one of her arthritic attacks, and just as uselessly. Now she was in no further doubt. With immense difficulty, Maria got up out of bed and knelt, very slowly and carefully, before the image of her namesake on the wall, hoping as always that the pain this caused her might increase the efficacy of her prayers, said as always in the Latin liturgy of her youth. *Sancta Maria, ora pro nobis.*

Tom Newman stretched his legs luxuriously, crossed them at the ankle and settled back to watch the show. It was, in his opinion, pretty spectacular. Beyond the clustered tables, chairs and folded parasols of the café's enclave, the young beauties of the town were parading up and down the pavement in pairs, trios or larger groups, weaving their way past and through similar sets of young men. With a few rare exceptions, neither sex openly acknowledged the existence of its counterpart, but each was intensely aware of the other, as they were of everyone else on the street that night, including the young American sitting over a beer and a cigarette outside a café on the pedestrianised stretch of Corso Mazzini.

And for the most part, these beauties *were* beauties. Tom had already thrown everything he had ever heard about southern Italian women into the recycling bin. Two generations of proper nutrition and good medical care had worked wonders. Like their peers back home, they were showing a lot of midriff, but significantly more – from barely above the pubis to just below the undercurve of the breasts in some cases – and, at least in the mild ambient glow of the street lighting, significantly better. Best of all, Tom wasn't just an onlooker but an object of considerable interest. The squads of girls continually passing and repassing regarded him with lengthy, intense and startlingly candid stares. To an almost unnerving extent, they seemed to have an instinctive sense and acceptance of what they were here for and how long they had to make it happen, and weren't about to waste any opportunity of getting down to business. Tom didn't get looked at in the same way back in the States, that was for sure, like he was merchandise that was being checked out. The public street was as sweaty and dizzy with sex as any club.

All in all he was disgustingly happy, he thought, signalling the barman to bring another beer. He had spent most of the afternoon selecting and acquiring a mobile phone, and had then used it to call Martin Nguyen and change the arrangements for their meeting that evening. On reflection, he had realised that he didn't want to be stuck over dinner with some boring CEO type, so he had claimed a subsequent engagement related to his father's kidnapping and fixed up a ten o'clock rendezvous at this bar. Tom's Italian was still in recovery, but his efforts to speak it seemed to be both understood and appreciated. In short, if it hadn't been for the reason why he was there, this would have been the dream vacation. But although he could feel as happy as he liked, he couldn't show it, any more than he could approach one of the passing women – that one there, for instance, with stunning legs, a deep cleavage and the gaze of a lioness – and ask for her phone number. In a society as traditional as this, with the family at the centre of everything and the father its undisputed head, for someone in his position to go out trawling for dates would be the equivalent of pissing on the high altar.

Worse, this might go on for weeks, even months. Both Nicola Mantega and the local police chief had made that clear. Not that he was in any hurry to leave, he thought, scoping out a cutie who couldn't have been more than fifteen, with tits out to here under a T-shirt that read, in English, WILL FUCK FOR LOVE. All Tom wanted to do was to stay indefinitely and have a ball, but that was out of the question. 'How could you?' people would ask in shocked tones, and he didn't know what to answer, even to himself. For at least a decade, he and his father had led separate lives in separate cities on separate coasts. Visits were rare, limited to a couple of hours at some restaurant or show when his father came to New York on business, and phone calls were infrequent, brief and impersonal. When mamma was still alive, Tom had felt obliged to go back to San Francisco for the holidays, but after her death his father had moved into a condominium and pointedly converted the spare bedroom into an office.

That's how it had been for years, and although the matter was never discussed, Tom had every reason to suppose that his father found the arrangement as satisfactory as he did. He had certainly never seen any reason why it shouldn't go on in exactly the same way for the foreseeable future. But the kidnapping had changed everything. It wasn't enough to go on as he had always done. He was going to have to learn to play the part of a loving and devoted son traumatised by the ghastly fate that had overtaken his father, just when every nerve in his being was telling him that there was something vital for him in this city, a chance not to be missed.

Martin Nguyen arrived dead on time and cut straight to the chase.

'How long are you planning on staying?' he asked Tom.

'As long as it takes. Maybe longer. I kind of like it here.'

'What about your job?'

'I quit before coming out. I was going to anyway.'

'What were you doing?'

'Sous-chef in an upscale Manhattan restaurant. There was a change of ownership and the new manager really sucked. Plus my girlfriend had just dumped me, so when this business came up I took advantage to tell my boss where he could shove it.'

He bit his lip. 'When this business came up' was cold. He was going to have to be more careful.

'Glad to hear that there's a silver lining to this dark cloud,' Nguyen murmured silkily. 'But how are you managing for money? Europe's a total rip these days.'

'I've got some savings. When they run out, I'll head back and start over. There's always vacancies in the restaurant business. Too bad I can't work here, but you need an EU passport.'

A passer-by of about Tom's height, with one of those seasoned Italian faces that were as much about character as flesh, strode over to their table.

'I see that you're still enjoying life in Cosenza,' he said.

By now, Tom had recognised the intruder as the local police chief.

'Very much!' he returned. 'How about you?'

A moment later, he realised that the beer had been talking, but the other man appeared unfazed by the impertinence.

'I never feel at home in a city where you can't smell the sea,' he replied. 'I shall need to see you at the Questura tomorrow morning. How early can you be there?'

After a brief discussion as to times, Tom introduced Martin Nguyen, who had been listening to this exchange with some interest.

'Tell the *signore* that I wish to speak to him too,' said the man, before leaving them with a curt nod.

'Who was that guy?' demanded Martin Nguyen.

'The chief of police. He wants us both to meet with him tomorrow morning.'

'Why?'

'I don't know. To discuss the latest developments in my dad's kidnapping, maybe.'

'Has something happened?'

'I don't know.'

'Then why didn't you ask him?'

Tom bent forward with a slightly condescending look.

'Mr Nguyen, this is not the States. The police here are more like Homeland Security than your friendly local sheriff who's going to be running for re-election come the fall and needs your vote. If they want to tell you something, they will. If they don't, there's no point in asking.'

Nguyen was unappeased.

'But what have I got to do with it?'

'I told him you were a business associate of my dad's. I guess he thinks you have information about what he was doing here that might be significant.'

Martin Nguyen nodded vaguely.

'So you speak pretty good Italian, huh?'

Tom shrugged.

'My mom used to talk to me in Italian and it seems to be coming back. It's not that hard of a language once you know the basic rules. All I really need is more vocabulary, and I'm picking that up pretty fast.'

Nguyen digested this in silence for some moments.

'Well, I can offer you a job right here and now,' he finally said. 'It's only temporary, for as long as I have to stay here, but I'll pay five hundred dollars a day in cash.'

'To do what?'

'Act as my translator and general assistant.'

'Well, I don't know,' Tom said doubtfully. 'Pretty much the only thing I can think about right now is my dad, you know?'

'Okay, how about five hundred euros? That's over six hundred bucks at current exchange rates.'

Tom thought about this proposition for at least a couple of seconds. After Dawn did a fugue back to her mother in Idaho, citing irreconcilable differences and environmental issues, he discovered that her rosy fingers had previously used his cash card, whose PIN Tom had given her when he was too slammed to go to the machine, to remove all the money in his bank account. He'd had to leverage his Visa credit limit just to get here, but that wouldn't last for ever and there was no way of knowing how long he'd have to stay. He looked at Nguyen with what he hoped was the expression of a dutiful and disturbed son in a difficult situation.

'Gee, I don't know what to say! I could sure use the money, but it might look bad, you know? I mean, profiting from my father's ordeal.'

'Who's to know? You'll be paid in cash, either here or back in the States, whichever you prefer. And if someone does find out, so what? You were just helping out a family friend in a tough spot.'

Tom sighed deeply.

'Well, okay, I guess. Plus it might help take my mind off this nightmare.'

'But for that kind of money I expect you to be on call twenty-four seven, okay? I can't tell when something might come up where I need you. In fact, tomorrow you'd better move to the hotel where I'm staying. I'll comp you the room and all meals.'

He glanced at the tab and threw some money on the table.

'Okay, I'll be heading back. Don't stay up too late eye-balling the brood mares. We've got to make an early start. I'll pick you up around four-thirty, quarter to five.'

For the first time, Tom felt genuinely dismayed by Nguyen's job proposition.

'Heck, it'll hardly be light then!'

'We're headed for a facility where the shift starts at six, and I need to brief the personnel. Some of them speak English, some of them don't.'

He broke off and stared at Tom.

'How much did your dad tell you about what we're doing here?'

'Practically nothing. He never talked about his work.'

Or about anything else, he thought. My dad never talked to me. My dad never spoke Italian to me.

'Okay, I'll fill you in tomorrow,' said Nguyen. 'Be sure and get a good night's rest. I want you on deck and ready to roll when my car pulls up at your hotel.'

'Hell, you're the one who should worry about that, Mr Nguyen! Getting in from the States today and all. That jet-lag can kill you.'

From one of the many secret drawers artfully concealed in the lacquered cabinet of his skull, Martin Nguyen produced a lush smile of poisonous beauty.

'I've given up sleeping. My doctor said it was bad for me.'

Nicola Mantega was not a particularly stupid or careless man. His fatal weakness was that he was a creature of habit.

The massive police raid that afternoon and evening on the town of Altomonte Nuova had been widely reported on the local news, but without any reason being given. When interviewed, some of the townsfolk mentioned repeated flights by police helicopters during the day to the abandoned town perched high above its successor, but claimed to have no idea what this was all about. The police themselves were saying nothing and all access to the area had been cordoned off.

Superficially, none of this was of any obvious personal concern to Mantega himself. That was how a northerner would have argued, but Nicola knew better. The people of the south had been treated as a form of insect life for so long, he liked to argue, that they had evolved some of the faculties of insects. Almost powerless against the brute species that ruled the earth – although they could deliver a very nasty, even deadly, sting on occasion – they were hypersensitive to the most minute development in their immediate environment. And now Mantega's antennae were twitching uncontrollably. He had no idea why, but he knew that further information about this incident was needed, and urgently.

Mantega had spent the evening closeted in his office with one of those clients it was better that he should not be seen consorting with publicly. The subject under discussion was a tender submitted by the client in question for the contract to upgrade a thirty-kilometre section of the toll-free regional A3 motorway to the standard of the rest of the national network, with a view to charging the same kind of money for using it. Recent political changes both in Rome and at local level had made these kinds of negotiation more difficult than formerly, and potentially much more dangerous. This was all very tiresome, and the worst part of it for Mantega was persuading his client that such a change had in fact taken place, that tact and patience were now required to resolve any ensuing problems, and that neither he nor anyone else could smooth everything over by making a couple of phone calls, like in the good old days.

Mantega had done his best, but his mind had been occupied with other matters. His client must have noticed, because he had made a few very pointed comments about possibly 'needing to seek counsel elsewhere' before leaving via the fire exit at the rear of the building. Had the circumstances been different, Mantega would have been very concerned by this veiled threat, given the power base and range of contacts of the client in question. As it was, he really didn't give a damn. His meeting with Giorgio the day before, and now the news of the police raid on

Altomonte, made such issues seem relatively trivial. Estimates of the number of officers involved in the raid varied wildly, but the gist was that an operation on such a scale had not been seen in the region for years. And that was only its public face. If a hundred or more officers had been committed to the task of publicly putting the frighteners on the population of an isolated town, there would be an equal or even greater number working covertly behind the scenes. Something big was under way, that was for sure.

All of which brought Mantega's thoughts back to his relationship with Giorgio. They had attended the same school back in San Giovanni in Fiore, but Mantega had subsequently forgotten about Giorgio's existence until one day, years later, he popped up seeking help after being fired from his job as a security guard. As a gesture of friendship to an old classmate who had fallen on hard times, Mantega had arranged an introduction to a small-time gang in the city that did armed robberies, lorry hijacks, some drug imports and the odd minor kidnapping. All had gone well for a year or two, but in the end the gang had dumped Giorgio because, as their *capo* had put it, 'This guy's round the fucking twist.'

Giorgio had then started up in business on his own, exploiting the mainly barren and unclaimed territory between Cosenza and Crotone, but occasionally making forays into the outskirts of either city. Mantega's fable about Aspromonte to Tom Newman the other evening had of course been disinformational nonsense. Giorgio wouldn't dare show his face on

Aspromonte. But the *n'drangheta* was extremely territorial, and the clans took little or no interest in affairs outside their own borders. Giorgio had therefore been able to build up a modest but thriving trade on his home turf, to which Mantega acted as a general *consigliere* and fixer. So when an American named Peter Newman had hired him as a go-between with the local authorities over a film deal, Mantega immediately recognised the irresistible chance to at least quadruple the money on offer by suggesting to Giorgio that he would make an excellent kidnapping prospect.

It had all seemed to make sense at the time, but ever since that meeting in the abandoned barn Mantega had been deeply disturbed. Giorgio was by nature moody and violent, but Mantega had never felt himself personally threatened before. The manner in which the bundle of banknotes had been presented as a final, non-negotiable payment, coupled with the warning about reprisals in the event of his talking and the bald announcement that Newman was dead, had terrified him. The construction magnate he had dealt with that evening simply wanted to make a killing, but Giorgio was a killer.

Mantega placed various incriminating documents that had been lying on his desk into the safe, switched off the lights, locked the door and walked slowly downstairs, mulling over the problem which had preoccupied him all evening. As he reached the front door of the office block, the solution popped up. For all Mantega knew, he could be arrested the moment he left the office and interrogated by that hard-nosed bastard that they'd brought in to cover for Gaetano Monaco. It was all very well for Giorgio to say that he should say nothing even under duress, but that was a damn sight easier to do if you knew exactly what it was that you weren't supposed to say. Given today's developments, Mantega didn't have a clue, so the situation was sufficiently serious to justify his calling Giorgio.

He walked around the corner towards the phone booth that he had used the night before. Mantega was inclined to dismiss Giorgio's warning that he was being followed as a mere bluff, but nevertheless he paid extra attention to the action on the street before proceeding any further. A couple of vehicles passed, but the occupants paid him not the slightest attention. The only sign of life was from a young couple whose romantic evening had evidently turned out badly and were now having a vociferous row as they walked home along the other side of the street, the woman loudly proclaiming that if she was to be insulted like that then she would rather kill herself here and now and have done with it – and with you, you cold, heartless bastard!

Even if Mantega had been more alert, it was unlikely that he would have recognised the woman as the same one who had apparently been meeting someone off the flight that Tom Newman had arrived on two days earlier, or her partner as the driver of the delivery truck that had been involved in an accident at that very junction near the phone box the previous night. As it was, he barely noticed them. The last thing undercover agents did was to draw attention to themselves, while this couple were screaming their heads off and the centre of attention until a flash of stark, neutered light fixed the scene on the retina. A moment later the heavens resounded as though all the gods had farted at the same moment and hailstones the size of chickpeas started hitting the street, bouncing high in the air and battering Mantega's skull.

He sprinted for the shelter of the phone box and rang Giorgio's mobile. There was no reply, so he dialled the other number. Mantega didn't know which phone this rang. Giorgio told him never to use it except in a case of extreme emergency, and he never had.

'*Pronto?*'

Mantega didn't recognise the surly male voice, but it was hard to hear anything at all with the hail drumming on the metal roof.

'Giorgio?'

'Never heard of him,' the male voice said in the abrupt, no-nonsense tones of the dialect Mantega had grown up with, and which he had heard from the lips of that lawyer from San Francisco named Peter Newman. Giorgio had told him that Newman had died. What the hell was that supposed to mean?

'My name is Nicola Mantega. I'm a business contact of Giorgio's. I need to speak to him urgently.'

'Never heard of you either,' said the voice. 'You must have a wrong number.'

Mantega put down the phone in a state of profound anxiety. The number he had called was right there on the lighted display on the phone, and was identical with the one he had written down in his Filofax disguised with a string of random numerals. He looked out at the barren street, where the young couple were now engaged in a passionate clinch beneath the portico of a building opposite. There were no two ways around it, Giorgio had cut him off. He had been paid and dismissed, and would have to sort out any personal repercussions from the kidnapping he had arranged. In short, Nicola Mantega was in the most desperate situation in which any Italian can ever find himself. He was on his own.

The four men came to the Nicastro house just before three o'clock in the morning. A black Jeep Grand Cherokee, its numberplates removed, freewheeled silently down the main street, barely visible in the dim light of the sparse streetlamps hanging out on their brackets. Engine off and lights out, the vehicle came to a halt opposite the squat dwelling of concrete and terracotta brick infill faced with unpainted grout. It was a warm, windless night, the air fresh with scents awakened by the recent downpour, utterly quiet apart from the barking of a dog somewhere near by and the occasional rumble of thunder far away to the north over Monte Pollino.

One man remained with the vehicle. The other three, faceless in black ski masks, walked unhurriedly back to their destination. While one of them disabled the electricity and telephone connections running down the wall of the house, another picked the lock in the front door. In the event the door proved to be bolted as well, which annoyed the third man so much that he raised his voice to the others, telling them to get on with it and quickly. Then the creak of an opened shutter directed one of the men's attention to a top-floor window across the street, where an old woman was looking down at them.

'Back to bed, *nonna*!' he shouted.

Since the element of surprise had now been lost, the man who had cut the power and phone lines fixed three small charges of plastic explosive to the top, middle and bottom edge of the door on the side where the hinges were and wired them together to a fuse before joining his companions a short distance away. When the blast went off all three ran back, kicked the door open in reverse and rushed inside, wielding powerful torch beams that cut the darkness like scalpels.

In less than two minutes, they had searched every room in the house. The only inhabitant who tried to put up a fight was Antonio, the fifty-year-old head of the family. He was subdued by a pistol shot to his left kneecap and beaten unconscious. The operation then proceeded as planned and without further interruption. The mother and her eldest son and two daughters were locked up in one of the bedrooms, after which the intruders turned their attention to Francesco Nicastro. He had not made any attempt to protest or resist. Indeed, he still looked dozy and lost in his dreams. The man who had spoken angrily earlier felled him with a massive blow to the face, then picked him up like a sack of barley and threw him on to the bed. He prised his jaws open and wedged the teeth on either side with chunks of rubber cut from an old tractor tyre. One of the other men gripped the boy's tongue firmly with a pair of pliers while the leader sliced off a chunk of it with a razor blade. All three then clattered back down the stairs, got into the Jeep and drove away.

Across the street, Maria tried to block out the cacophony of screams emanating from the Nicastro house. The knowledge that her predictions had been validated brought no comfort. Her prayers had been powerless, she was powerless, they were all powerless. She walked in slow, painful steps down the stairs to the living room and the only phone in the house.

'Send an ambulance at once,' Maria told the emergency operator. 'There's been a terrible accident.'

Martin Nguyen's driver had been unbeatable when it came to getting maximum respect on the *autostrada* down from Rome, but faced with the task of finding his way around Cosenza it rapidly became clear that he didn't have a clue. The limo was much too good to give up – leather seats, tinted windows and a/c that really worked – but under the terms of the leasing agreement no one else was allowed to drive it. Martin's solution had been to call a cab to the Rende International Residence, then slip the guy enough cash to have him park his vehicle and act as navigator for the clueless *romano*.

They reached the Hotel Centrale at twenty to five. The air was mild and welcoming, but it was still dark. Tom Newman was waiting outside, and he and Martin proceeded to Aeroscan Surveying's base in the outlying southern suburbs of the city. Neither of the Americans had been able to get breakfast at their respective hotels before leaving, so Phil Larson instantly went up a notch in Martin's estimation by having brewed up a pot of coffee and bought some pastries from a bakery that opened early. Once Phil had got through giving them a long story about some break-in the previous night – 'Nothing missing, it looks

like, but you know how you feel kind of violated?' –
Martin opened his aluminium briefcase and passed a
thick sheaf of printed matter across the desk.

'That's the report of the team I've consulted,' he
said. 'You can read the small print later, but their
principal conclusions are clear and I want them
implemented *subito*.'

Larson looked at him curiously.

'I didn't know you spoke Italian, Mr Nguyen.'

'I was born in a country then called Indochina,
where the official language was French. Later I was
moved to the States, where I had to learn English, then
in high school I studied Spanish. Italian is pretty much
the same except for the make-up and the hairstyle.'

He went over to the map which took up most of one
wall.

'These are the areas you've done?' he queried,
indicating the shaded zones.

Phil Larson nodded.

'Okay, ignore the whole rest of this section and
concentrate on the upper valleys of the rivers off this
map to the south.'

Larson looked doubtful.

'Hell, we don't even have charts for that area. You
said to look at the confluence of the rivers and down in
the flood plain where we are now. That's what we've
been doing. Of course a lot of this terrain has been built
on in the last fifty years or so, like this place where we
are now. If the site we're looking for is underneath any
of that, we aren't going to find it anyway.'

'My consultants pointed that out. Plus that in a

sprawling flood plain like this the river-bed will have shifted around over the centuries, and that the deforestation of the surrounding mountains a century ago has completely screwed the hydrological aspects of the situation, the amount of water run-off and hence the height of the rivers. So a lot of their data is highly indeterminate. But there are other factors involved. One is that the men who originally constructed this thing were all killed afterwards to keep the location secret.'

Phil Larson grinned nervously.

'Not a company tradition, I hope?'

Martin ignored the comment.

'But if the site had been within view of the city of Cosenza, then to preserve the secret all the citizens would have had to be killed too, and there is no record of such a massacre.'

'We're pretty well out of sight of the city here,' Larson pointed out.

'Yeah, but back then the main road from Rome down to Sicily ran right along this side of the valley. Anyone using it would have spotted what was going on and maybe come back later to check it out. So bearing all this in mind, your brief is to look in the upper valleys of the rivers that splay out southwards from here.'

Larson frowned.

'But you said that we were looking for the foundations of a building. Why would anyone choose to build there? Here on the banks I can maybe see, but in the middle of a river? That's just crazy!'

Martin glanced at Tom, but he didn't appear to be paying any attention.

'It's a tomb,' he explained to Phil. 'The people who built it had this religious thing about the dead person resting undisturbed for ever, so beneath a river was perfect. No one except them knew where it was, so there was no way it was ever going to get dug up except by pure chance. Anyway, what do you care? You've been given your instructions.'

'Well, like I said, I don't have charts for that . . .'

'You've also said you're using visual navigation. Higher up, those rivers are hemmed in by the mountains, so their course can't have changed much. Start where they join up and follow each of them up to the five-hundred metre level. Does the pilot understand English?'

'Not so as you'd notice. I just point to the strips I want to cover every day.'

'Go and give him his new orders. My assistant will translate.'

Outside on the concrete forecourt, the pilot was checking his machine over with the meticulous attention of a man who knows that his life depends on it. Phil Larson briefed him on the new search plan, pausing from time to time for Tom to turn it into Italian. He added that the boss was visiting, so to make a good impression they should look busy and get going as soon as possible, then returned to the office where Martin Nguyen was waiting.

Tom stayed where he was. He'd been fascinated by planes ever since he was a boy, when a friend of his father's had taken him for a ride in a Cessna out over Marin County and done some freaky stuff that had scared him stiff and left an indelible memory. He half-hoped that this pilot might offer a repeat performance, but the Italian seemed preoccupied with other matters.

'I don't even have a chart of those valleys,' he complained to Tom. 'Not that it would help much. They're always stringing new electricity lines across them that aren't marked. And then there are the old pulleys they used to use to bring goods across to the far side from the road. They're abandoned, so they're not on the chart, but half of them are still there, sagging down just about exactly the altitude we'll be flying at.'

Tom nodded sympathetically.

'Anyway, the whole thing's pointless,' the pilot went on. 'If these Americans want to find the right scenery for this film they're making, they could do it much cheaper from the ground.'

Tom noted that the Italian's resentment and contempt were markedly increased by the idea that his employers were throwing their money away so stupidly.

'Apparently they're looking for something that's buried under the river,' he said, in an instinctive attempt to defend his compatriots. 'I guess they want to use it for a location in the movie.'

'Under the river? What kind of thing?'

Tom shrugged.

'Some tomb.'

The pilot continued to stare at him for so long that Tom began to think he must have offended him in some way. Then he smiled wearily.

'*Ma certo*,' he replied in a tone of contempt. '*La famosa tomba d'Alarico.*'

It was another perfect morning in Cosenza. Sunlight sidled in through the window, stripping away the acceptable surface of things to reveal the tawdry substance beneath. Seated at his desk, head in hands, Aurelio Zen sensed its intrusive presence as a glow between his fingers. He had been awake since shortly after four o'clock, following a phone call from the Questura under his standing instructions to be summoned at any hour of the day or night in the event of any significant development in the case. By then it was too late to do anything. What had happened had happened, and it was arguably all his fault. Police operations went wrong all the time, but this was different.

For years now, Zen had been living in a world where reality seemed to have been drained of all substance. Once upon a time, and he could still remember that time, authentic experience had been the default position, as unremarkable as gravity or the weather. Now, though, the authentic sounded a melancholy blue note as it receded, a Doppler effect induced by the speed of cultural change, as though sadly waving goodbye. There were, however, still exceptions to this general rule. Zen's experience was that for every ten kilometres you travelled between Rome and Cosenza, you moved back another year into the past, finally arriving in the mid-1950s. Authenticity was not as yet under serious threat here, and in some way that he couldn't have explained, that slewed the ethical equations too. What would have been good enough elsewhere simply wouldn't do here, back in the lost realm of the real.

The surgeons at Cosenza hospital were attempting to sew the severed portion of Francesco Nicastro's tongue back on to the root, but it was uncertain whether he would ever have any feeling or control over it. His father Antonio, the sole wage-earner, was awaiting his turn for an operation to restructure his knee, but it appeared unlikely that he would be able to work again. In short, whatever the outcome of the case, the family was ruined. Zen had spent an hour interrogating the two detectives who had questioned the boy in the first place, but both Corti and Caricato swore that Francesco had been interviewed alone and that neither of them had told anyone but their immediate superiors what the outcome had been. In the end, Zen believed them, but someone must have talked. Zen was privately inclined to think that Francesco's brother might have mentioned it to a friend – perhaps the third boy who had been playing near the path when *il morto* appeared – in all innocence, as a way of demonstrating what an idiot his sibling was and thereby bolstering his own status.

Natale Arnone entered with yet another coffee and some pastries. He also informed Zen that the two

Americans who had been instructed to appear that morning had arrived half an hour before, adding that the older one didn't seem too happy about being kept waiting.

'Oh, and Signor Mantega was on the phone again last night. Used the same public box as he did before, the one that's now tapped. Two calls. One was to a mobile phone, no reply. The other to a landline that's been traced to a house in San Giovanni in Fiore.'

Zen looked up wearily.

'And?'

'A man answered. Mantega asked to speak to someone called Giorgio. The man said he wasn't there. Mantega left instructions to have Giorgio contact him. I was just wondering if you wanted any immediate action taken.'

'Well, add both numbers to the intercept list, naturally.'

'That's already been done.'

'Who owns the property?'

'Dionisio Carduzzi, sixty-eight years old, retired carpenter, no criminal record.'

Zen sighed.

'All right. Have the place watched, but discreetly. See if the Digos boys can stage some sort of utility repair job requiring them to dig up the street near by. They're to note and if possible photograph everyone who comes and goes, take vehicle details and so on. But tell them to err on the side of caution. I don't want any more mutilation of innocents. Judging by what happened last night, this Giorgio is a ruthless sadist and evidently jumpy. After my press conference later this morning, he's going to be even jumpier.'

He pushed the mound of papers on his desk aside and made a brief phone call to the pathologist who had conducted the post-mortem examination on the corpse found the day before, then another to the Questura's press officer with instructions to set up a news conference for ten o'clock. After that, he told Arnone to bring on the Americans.

It was immediately clear when they entered that Arnone had been understating Martin Nguyen's mood. No sooner was he through the doorway than he launched into a barrage of protests and veiled threats, most of which Tom Newman chose to leave untranslated.

'I turn up here of my own free will for the meeting requested by you during our encounter last night,' Nguyen concluded, 'and you keep me waiting for over forty minutes! What time do you people get in to work, anyway?'

'I have been at work since four this morning.'

'Are you night shift? Let me speak to the day guy.'

'An incident has occurred which demanded my attention. I apologise for the inconvenience and am glad to say that I shall not detain you for long, Signor –'

He looked defeatedly at the name written on the folder he had opened.

'Nguyen,' Tom supplied.

'Precisely,' said Zen. 'You're staying at the Rende International Residence, I believe?'

'How do you know that?' demanded Nguyen.

'All hotels have to report the names and passport details of their guests to the police,' Tom muttered. 'It's standard procedure, nothing personal.'

Martin Nguyen sighed impatiently.

'Since you already know, why bother asking?'

'And you're planning to remain there?' Zen asked.

Nguyen shrugged.

'Perhaps.'

'For how long?'

'A week at least. Possibly longer. Why?'

'And what is the purpose of your visit to Cosenza?'

'Business.'

'Could you be a little more specific?'

'I'm executive-producing a significant property for a major-player American movie company. It's just about to go into production, and key scenes will be shot in and around this city. Luciano Aldobrandini, of whom you may perhaps have heard, is directing and he's on track to initiate shooting shortly. Up until his disappearance, Peter Newman was acting as our representative on the ground, liaising with the local contractors, getting the necessary permits and so on. Since his skill sets are no longer available to us, I have been tasked with the additional challenge of performing his role.'

Zen's face was as expressionless as the frescoed image of some minor saint who was being martyred in some unspeakable way but, thanks to his steadfast faith, remained at peace with himself.

'Signor Newman appears to have spent much of his time with a notary named Nicola Mantega. What was the subject under discussion when they met?'

'I couldn't say. Pete never mentioned the name, but that's normal. He was a self-starter, made his own contacts. We didn't expect detailed reports as long as he got results.'

Zen considered this in silence for a moment.

'And what about you, Signor, er –'

'Nguyen,' Tom interposed.

'What about me?' the other man demanded.

'Have you been in touch with Mantega since your arrival here?'

'No.'

'Do you plan to be?'

'What business is that of yours?'

Zen gazed for some time at the window, as though there was something of vital importance to be glimpsed through the luminous screening of the blinds.

'Signor Mantega is an interesting man,' he remarked blandly. 'He specialises in arranging deals between crooked businessmen and corrupt politicians. One therefore asks oneself why your company should have required his services.'

Nguyen's face hardened.

'Are you in fact asking yourself, or are you asking me?'

Zen pretended to consider this for a moment.

'Well, since you put it that way, I suppose I'm asking you.'

'Then I want a lawyer present,' Nguyen replied curtly.

Zen sighed in a weary way.

'I have no time for that nonsense. I've had a hard night, *signore*. I was simply hoping for your co-operation in providing some background to the case that concerns me now. But, to be honest, recent developments have rendered your status entirely peripheral and your resulting interest to me minimal. I therefore invite you to take your leave.'

After witnessing the initial confrontation, Arnone had remained standing in the corner of the room throughout. With a sweep of his hand, Zen signalled him to escort Martin Nguyen out, then turned to face Tom Newman.

'I'm afraid I have some bad news,' he said.

The spiny dorsal fin of the coast slipped past unnoticed beyond the vast expanse of glass shielding the saloon. Luciano Aldobrandini lay embedded in a winged leather recliner, naked except for a black thong, watching his personal recut for DVD of the film which had won him the silver at Venice back in the 1960s. It should have been the gold, but Visconti's people had packed the jury.

All things considered, it had held up pretty well, he thought. Artless and unsophisticated, of course, and given to crude over-emphasis at times. He would make it very differently now, but it was questionable whether the result would necessarily have been an improvement. Primitive though it was in many respects, the original had a raw, driven quality to it, a sense of energy to burn, amounting to sheer recklessness at times, that now felt very, very precious.

He switched off the DVD player and summoned Pippo.

'Bring me a Singapore Sling, darling.'

The lad frowned ominously.

'It's only ten to twelve.'

'Don't be a bore. In Singapore, it's cocktail time.'

His phone chirruped. Luciano glanced at the screen. It was Marcello.

'Where are you?' the agent asked, with a brittle tone and lack of the customary foreplay which suggested a state of some agitation.

'On board the *Narcisso*, southward bound to start preparations for the shoot,' his master replied. 'A calm sea and a prosperous voyage, since you haven't bothered to ask. At least, I trust it will prove to be prosperous. Some of my crew members are joining me in a few days and I intend to put on a show of having started principal photography by the end of the week, as per your instructions.'

Marcello grunted.

'From what I've heard, an advance crew is already in place and has been for several weeks.'

'Heard from whom?'

'Another client of mine.'

'Which specific talentless cunt are you referring to?'

'That's privileged information, Luciano. Anyway, you wouldn't be any the wiser if I told you. He's a rapper.'

'A what?'

'You see? Right now he's trekking on horseback along the edge of the Sila range above Cosenza. I called him about a business thing and asked how his holiday was going. "It would be blissful if it weren't for that damned helicopter that Luciano has hired," he said. It seems there's a lot of very noisy low-level flying going on. When my client asked what it was about, he was told it was preparatory location scouting for your movie.'

Aldobrandini straightened up abruptly.

'That's absurd! You know I never delegate that sort of work.'

'Exactly. So I engaged the services of an ex-spook who now works as a private eye in Reggio. Last night he raided the compound on the outskirts of Cosenza which this outfit uses as a base, and has just reported his findings. Briefly, the helicopter has been hired by an American company called Aeroscan Surveying. He broke into the machine and took a look inside. The entire cargo space is filled with electronic equipment and screens and seats for the operators. Further research on my part has revealed that Aeroscan is a specialised firm which uses ground-penetrating radar devices to locate objects concealed underground. Everything from unmapped sewage lines to military bunkers and archaeological remains. Are you planning to film underground, Luciano?'

'Not till they plant me there.'

Pippo returned with a brimming glass. His master downed the contents in one and commanded a refill.

'So this raises the question of why they are using your movie as the justification for their activities,' Marcello went on.

'And how they found out about the film project in the first place.'

'Fortunately, my employee also took a look inside the temporary office they've set up at the site. Tacked to the wall of one of the offices was a large-scale map of the whole area around Cosenza, stamped at the bottom with a form showing details of the surveying job. The box for the title of the relevant contract contained the words "Rapture Works".'

There was a long silence.

'It's beginning to look as if Jeremy's agent was right,' Marcello went on. 'I'm afraid we've been scammed.'

Luciano Aldobrandini accepted his second Singapore Sling without even noticing.

'But why would they do that?' he protested. 'All the money they've spent already, not to mention the risk of a lawsuit. We are going to sue, I take it?'

'Depends. We'd have to be able to prove intention to deceive and defraud.'

'But if all they wanted was to do an aerial survey, why drag me into it?'

'I have no idea. But don't forget that it was Rapture Works that insisted on the film being shot in Calabria. It's just possible that they may have two separate projects on the go and that they're being piggy-backed for some reason. As of now, we just don't know.'

'Well, I'm going to find out!'

Luciano scrolled through his address book to the name of Martin Nguyen, but the number was engaged and stayed that way for over five minutes. He finally succumbed to the robotic siren voice which intervened after ten rings and left a message. Then his eye was caught by the video screen, which had returned to muted TV mode. It showed a man on a podium speaking into a microphone. A window at the upper right read 'Breaking News' and the occasion appeared to be a press conference. Normally Luciano would have switched channels, but something about the tall, lean, angular figure struck him, the face particularly. It took another few moments to realise that shorn of the modern clothes – in some suitably fetching drapery, not too daring but seductively suggestive, and with longer, unkempt hair – this man, even more than the late lamented Jeremy, represented his ideal image of John of Patmos. The caption in the right-hand corner indicated that he was in fact the chief of police for the province of Cosenza. Luciano reached for the remote control and turned up the volume, just to hear if the man's voice was as good as his stunning physiognomy.

' . . . the remains of the American lawyer Peter Newman, who has subsequently been identified as a member of the Calopezzati family and hence of Calabrian origin. The victim's head had been blown off by a charge of plastic explosive detonated by remote control. Forensic tests have revealed that the explosive substance was identical to that used last night to force an entry into a house in the new town of Altomonte, located near by. The *capofamiglia*, Antonio Nicastro, was then shot while attempting to defend his nine-year-old son Francesco, whose tongue was subsequently severed with a razor blade. These events are clearly related and we urge anybody in possession of any information which might be relevant to come forward and –'

Luciano blanked the screen. Dear God, he thought, and this is where I was going to spend months making my masterpiece? 'We just don't know,' Marcello had said, but now he knew, with overwhelming and irrefutable conviction. There would be no movie. He, the great Aldobrandini, had been bought and sold like a rent boy to be used and then tossed away. Whatever happened now, his genius and his reputation, his entire career, had been besmirched for ever.

He stalked out on deck and up to the wheelhouse.

'I've changed my mind, Matteo,' he told the skipper. 'Alter course for Sardinia.'

Tom Newman felt angry. Normally a mild man, he was capable of spectacular outbursts of rage if he felt that others had taken advantage of his good nature. This was one such occasion. These people had pushed him too far. Fine, they'd soon find out what he was made of.

'*Ma cazzo, oh, dov'è 'sto beverragio?*' he shouted at the waiter.

The man paused in mid-stride, then flipped up his right forefinger in a gesture that read, 'Damn, I knew I'd forgotten something.'

'*Subito, signore!*'

Twenty seconds later, the waiter brought what looked like an innocent Campari Soda but in fact contained a shot of vodka – what the Italians called *un drink*, an alien name for an alien concept. Tom nodded graciously, settled back in his chair with a masterful smile and relaxed again, soaking up the sun and the scene around him. The sun was high in a blue sky flawless except for a few puffy white clouds spilling over the coastal chain of mountains from the Mediterranean to the west. Later on in the afternoon, they would bulk up, loom over the city like thugs and then unleash the mother of all thunderstorms, but for now they were merely decorative or maybe even symbolic, like in some Old Master's frescoed ceiling of strapping lads and overweight gals, signifiers of beneficence and plenty.

Since leaving the Questura after having received Aurelio Zen's bad news, he'd drifted at random through the streets, noticing everything with heightened awareness and interacting with whatever presented itself to his dazed consciousness. He'd bought some green peaches and fresh walnuts from one street vendor, and eaten them along with a chalky roundel of aged goat's cheese sold by another vendor, who looked a bit like a goat himself – skinny, neurotic and driven, like the gormless offspring of some Spanish noble family.

Then there had been the cheap clothing stores run by Chinese immigrants around the bus station, the bijou boutiques on the upscale streets selling pricey goods for wedding presents and the home beautiful, and odd places with English names like Daddy & Son and Miss Sixty – the latter, it turned out, catering not to geriatric spinsters but the adorable young women of the neighbourhood who wanted retro Carnaby Street gear to show off their amazing legs. Tom had listened to a bootleg CD of Calabrian folk music blaring from another street stall and with the help of the salesman had managed to pick out some of the words: *O sol, o sol, almo immortale, non t'asconder mai più, che certo veggio s'io non ti miro, non poss'aver peggio.* It was a hymn of praise to the sun, all about how when it is hidden from us we're screwed. Pure paganism, but he was feeling pretty pagan himself. It was in the air here, in the pitiless light, in the facial expressions and body language of the people all around. His father was dead, the police chief had told him. Like this was the first time in the history of the world that someone's father had died? The Greeks and Romans who'd run this place thousands of years ago would have understood that.

He'd bought the CD and felt it now in his pocket as he heard the melody again in his brain and looked at a passing woman, the fastenings of her bra standing out on her back under the tight top like widely spaced shoulder nipples. Then he saw a face he knew.

'Signor Mantega!'

Tom sprang to his feet and shook hands with the *notaio*.

'How have you been keeping?' Mantega asked distractedly.

'Pretty well, all things considered. What about you?'

Mantega looked startled, then made a large gesture and sighed deeply.

'Ah, you know! Work, always work.'

'Come and sit down,' Tom urged.

He was feeling lonely and, with two drinks inside him, expansive, but Mantega demurred.

'Actually, I'm in a bit of a hurry –'

'*Solo un momento*. I need to ask you something.'

Mantega hesitated, but finally joined Tom at his table. He waved away the waiter and stared at Tom.

'Well?' he said pointedly.

'It's just this expression I heard today and didn't understand, so I thought maybe it was dialect. *La tomba d'Alarico*. Does that mean anything to you?'

Mantega shrugged dismissively. He obviously couldn't have cared less about Tom's question, but couldn't resist the opportunity to hold forth all the same.

'But of course! Alaric was a barbarian chieftain who invaded Italy in the fifth century. He sacked Rome and then continued south, but died here in Cosenza and is believed to have been buried along with all the treasure he had plundered. There have been many attempts to find the tomb, all of them fruitless. When the Germans were in charge here during the war, they organised a particularly intensive search. The Goths were an important element in Nazi mythology. But even with all their resources, the results were once again negative.'

Tom shook his head in wonder.

'I'd never even heard of Alaric. So the treasure's still down there somewhere?'

Mantega shrugged impatiently. Now that he had said his piece, he had no further interest in this dusty subject.

'Who knows? From time to time some enthusiast comes along and tries again, but without success so far as anyone knows.'

He yawned, and then as a show of politeness added, 'Why are you interested in Alaric's tomb?'

Tom gave him a conspiratorial smile.

'You know that helicopter that's been prowling about? Turns out it's carrying some sort of electronic gear that can scan the subsoil. The company drew a blank down the main river-bed, so now they're going to try the valleys higher up. At least it should be a bit quieter around here.'

Mantega gave a perfunctory nod.

'Well, I must be going. Have you heard any further word from the police about negotiations for your father's release?'

It was only then that Tom realised Mantega hadn't heard the news yet. But he would eventually, and would find it very odd that Tom hadn't told him.

'He's dead.'

Mantega, who had started to get up, abruptly sat down again.

'What? How? When?'

'A couple of days ago. They've been keeping it quiet until they definitively identified the body. I only just heard the news myself, so the reality hasn't quite sunk in yet. I suppose I'm still in shock, you know?'

Mantega didn't seem concerned about this aspect of the situation.

'Is that your phone?' he asked, pointing to a shiny silver *telefonino* lying on the table.

'Got it just yesterday.'

'May I borrow it for a moment?' Mantega asked. 'I have to make an urgent call and my own mobile has gone dead. You know how it is. I must have forgotten to recharge it.'

'Help yourself,' said Tom.

Mantega smiled his thanks. As if finding the street too noisy, he got up and walked into the open doorway of the café. Tom watched him idly, in between exchanging glances with a stunning brunette who had sat down at a neighbouring table soon after Mantega arrived and was now smoking a cigarette and talking on her headset. Tom scribbled 'Lunch?' and his new phone number on a scrap of paper, then signalled the waiter and told him to take it over to the woman. While this transaction was in progress, he glanced over at Nicola Mantega, who was apparently having a furious argument with someone. The waiter handed the woman the note. They spoke briefly and he pointed over at Tom. The brunette looked over, and for a moment their eyes met again. Then Mantega reappeared. He handed back Tom's phone but did not sit down.

'Sorry, but I have to run,' he said, as breathlessly as though he already had been running. 'I'll be in touch shortly and in the meantime please accept my deepest sympathy for this shocking development. My poor boy! You must be devastated.'

Tom nodded vaguely.

'Yes, I must.'

'*A presto, allora.*'

Mantega trotted off rapidly.

'I'm not free for lunch,' a voice said.

Tom looked up to find the brunette standing above him.

'Oh, what a cute phone!' she exclaimed. She switched it on, pressed some of the miniature buttons and scanned the screen.

'You're pretty cute yourself.'

The woman took this coolly.

'You're an American?' she returned.

161

Tom smiled self-deprecatingly.

'I'm afraid so.'

'Oh, in Calabria, Americans are part of the family,' she replied with a nicely flirtatious edge. 'So many of our own people moved there.'

'Yes, I know. In fact, I may be from this area myself, or at least my father seems . . .'

He broke off in confusion, but the brunette was now intent on an incoming call on her earpiece. She turned to Tom.

'I must go.'

Tom gestured helplessly.

'Okay, how about dinner?'

But she was already out of earshot, hastening along in the direction taken by Nicola Mantega.

For someone whose religious beliefs, theologically considered, amounted to little more than pagan agnosticism, Maria was a good Catholic. It was true that her views on the Trinity, which she thought of as the executive steering committee at the core of any stable family – the father, the mother and the eldest son – probably wouldn't have passed muster with the Inquisition, had the Church still been taking a lively interest in the opinions of its dwindling flock instead of striving ever more desperately to maintain the ratio of bums to pews.

Maria accepted the existence of God in exactly the same way that she accepted the existence of the government, because you needed someone powerful to hate for not preventing, or at least mitigating, all the needless suffering that went on. She felt sorry for Jesus, having to take the blame for his father's mis-judgements, but it was hard to have much respect for a man who seemed to have spent his brief life preaching that if people were nicer to each other then the world would be a nicer place. As for the meaningless abstraction of the Holy Spirit, that had long been replaced in her mind by the warm, indulgent and eminently human person of the Madonna.

Maria conceived of the Blessed Virgin as possessing much the same range of limited and indirect, but often decisive, powers on the divine level as any mother worth her salt did here on earth. Sometimes she could help, sometimes not, but at least she could be counted on to listen sympathetically and to do her best. Her sphere of activity was of course strictly local. In the chapel dedicated to her in the old church up on the hilltop, she cured burns and eased the pains of childbirth, but if your feet or back were troubling you then you had to pay a visit to her shrines at Aprigliano or Cerenzia. It was like knowing where the different kinds of mushrooms grew or where to find the best wild asparagus.

Maria shared these unorthodox doctrinal views with just about every other elderly woman in the village, but like them she nevertheless attended mass every day. This was partly because someone had to do it, lest the family attract comment, and none of the others had the time or inclination, but largely because it got her out of the house and provided an opportunity to catch up on local gossip. On the day after the police raid on Altomonte and its horrifying sequel, almost all the other women in the community had evidently had the same idea, so the church was much more crowded than usual for evening mass. Sensing the prevailing mood, and perhaps impatient to hear the latest himself, the priest zipped through the service at a brisk pace, skipping the homily and keeping the readings brief.

The moment the congregation was dismissed, everyone got down to the real business. Many of them had already had a chance to take preliminary soundings in the course of their daily work, social calls and trips to the shops. Now the time had come to meet in committee, compare notes, sift the evidence and rough out the interim report which would later be delivered to their respective families. Lively discussion was going on both in the church itself and on the steps and street outside between small groups that constantly formed and reformed, relaying their findings to others for comparison and contrast. After about twenty minutes, a consensus gradually emerged.

Both the television news and the local paper had confirmed that the murdered man, despite having been reported following his earlier disappearance as being a visiting American, was in fact a member of the Calopezzati family which had ruled this part of Calabria like a feudal possession for almost two hundred years. The memory of their crimes and infamies was still fresh among the older generation, and there was general agreement that it was harsh but just for this Pietro Ottavio – evidently the illegitimate son of the *baronessa* Ottavia – to have been condemned to a symbolically ignominious death outside the family's former stronghold as retribution for the misdeeds of his forebears.

Where dissension emerged was over the punishment of Francesco Nicastro. There were those who held that he deserved it for giving information to the police. Rules were rules and they had to be enforced, brutally if necessary, if the community was to survive in the face of the even more brutal repression that had governed the region since time immemorial. Others argued that boys like Francesco were too modern to understand the old ways, adding that in any case no real harm had been done by his mentioning the victim's parked car, and above all that the penalty had been disproportionately severe. A few even dared to suggest that the incident was proof of the persistent rumours that 'he' had become addicted to the drugs in which he trafficked and had gone over the edge into madness, but the implications of this possibility were so disturbing that it was dismissed by the majority.

Both by nature and upbringing, Maria was a listener rather than a talker, particularly where the Calopezzati family was concerned. In fact, the name had not passed her lips for almost fifty years, and nothing in her speech or demeanour suggested that it meant anything more to her than to any of the other women present. She moved from group to group, nodding and shaking her head in turn, miming the appropriate righteous anger or resigned disapproval. Once she had gleaned all the facts, theories, rumours and opinions on offer, she slipped away home and shut herself up in her room. An hour later, when she emerged for dinner, she shocked the whole family by announcing that she was going into the city the next day. One of the women at church had told her about a new medication for arthritis that was now available, but you had to go to a certain doctor at the hospital to get it because the supply was strictly limited.

Maria's son offered to drive her, but she declared that she would rather take the bus. It was more relaxing and you didn't have to worry about parking.

Her daughter-in-law, who wore the trousers in the marriage, then tried to butt in but as usual went completely over the top, making it sound as though her *suocera* was a senile old fool who shouldn't be allowed out of the house, never mind turned loose in the dangerous streets of Cosenza. Maria waited until she had finished her tirade and then said, 'I'm going to the city tomorrow, I'm going alone, and that's all.'

Everyone knew that it was a waste of breath trying to argue with Maria when she used that tone of voice. Besides, the parents were more concerned about their son Sabatino, who had barely touched his food and sat staring blankly at the wall as if oblivious to everything about him. Francesco Nicastro was his best friend. They had played together in the stunted forest on the day when the dead man appeared. Maria rose and announced that she was going to bed early so as to get a good night's sleep.

Once in her room, she did indeed undress, but then lay down on top of the covers, glancing alternately at the sacred image on the wall and the looming abyss of the shadowy ceiling high above. The Virgin had been unable to help her in this matter, so Maria would have to help herself, and all of them. For herself she had no fears, but she knew how the kind of men who had inflicted these injuries on the community operated, particularly if there was any truth to the rumours that their leader was possessed by demons. Whatever happened, her son and his wife and Sabatino must be protected. She would have to take stringent precautions before, during and after her trip, keep her wits about her at all times and not carry anything that might identify her if things went wrong.

Above all, she had to decide what to say and how to say it. After so many years of a silence which she had always assumed would last until her death, it was almost impossible to imagine selecting the words and framing the sentences that would bring the whole matter to light for the first time. In addition, she might very well not be believed. The story she had to tell was just that, a story. She couldn't prove that it was true or produce any evidence or witnesses to support it. Maria had seen the new police chief on television and he looked like someone you could talk to, but that might just have been his public manner, assumed for the camera and the purposes of meeting the press. One to one, he could easily turn out to be the usual arrogant thug who would dismiss her statement as the ravings of a crazy old woman.

But none of this weakened her resolve, any more than the impenetrable silence of God, the futile gesture of his Son and the impotent anguish of the Madonna stopped her from praying or going to church. Both the gods and the police were as capricious and vindictive as any of the humans they lorded it over, but every once in a while you might be able to catch their attention and put in a good word for someone. But first you had to make that effort. It might not be sufficient, but if you had any sense of decency then it was necessary. You had to be prepared to ask, to beg, to plead, to grovel. That was all that could be done, and Maria was determined to do it.

When the papers landed on Zen's desk early that evening, his first reaction had not been to do with the contents but with the form they took. Written under the letterhead of the US consulate in Naples, the first instalment opened with a boilerplate statement to the effect that 'this communication contains potentially sensitive classified material' and hence was being sent in randomly sequenced segments via fax, since no 'mutually agreed encryption protocols' were in place between the agencies concerned and the use of email might therefore have constituted a 'bilateral security hazard'.

I remember when we first got fax machines at work, Zen thought. They were cutting edge then, a status marker. If you didn't have one, you weren't important. Now they were virtually obsolete and sat gathering dust in some unvisited corner of the building. I've witnessed the birth and decay of an entire technology, he thought, not just in my lifetime but within recent memory.

The communication in question was terse in the extreme. Sent in response to a phone call Zen had made the previous evening, it stated that Roberto Calopezzati had been resident in the United States from 1953 until 1965. The American consular official went on to express a disingenuously arch bewilderment at the fact that it had been necessary to contact him for this information. Surely it would have been more convenient for Zen to obtain it from his own internal sources, given that the said Calopezzati's twelve-year stay in the US had been under the auspices of the Italian government as a legal adviser at their embassy in Washington, DC.

Zen headed down the corridor to Giovanni Sforza's office. Livid clouds were hanging low above the city like clusters of poisonous fruit, but the storm wouldn't break. Inside the Questura, the atmosphere was as taut as overstretched sailcloth.

'I need your help again, Giovanni. There's an angle to the case that's been bothering me. It may not be relevant, but if so then it's a remarkable set of coincidences. According to the official records both here and in the United States, Peter Newman was born in the province of Cosenza under the name Pietro Ottavio Calopezzati. Later he became an American citizen, changed his name to Newman and as far as we know never returned to Italy until recently. In short, we appear to have a Calabrian who moves to the United States, styles himself Newman – *uomo nuovo* – and avoids any contact with his native country for over forty years. Then one fine day he returns, is kidnapped and is murdered in a highly theatrical way for no apparent motive whatsoever.'

Sforza nodded bureaucratically.

'And your point is?' he asked.

'To prove that he was indeed the person mentioned in the records. The Calopezzati family have proved very hard to trace, but I've learned an interesting fact about Roberto, who would be Pietro's uncle if the documents are correct. Our records contain no mention of him after the war, nor do any other related files. But I've learned from other sources that a person by that name worked at the Italian embassy in Washington for twelve years from 1953. I now need to know what became of him.'

'What post did he hold at the embassy?'

'Legal adviser.'

Giovanni Sforza evidently didn't know what resonance the name Calopezzati had in Calabria, but the term 'legal adviser' had its significance for him.

'Secret job,' he said. 'That would explain the security clearance level on that file you mentioned.'

Zen looked incredulous.

'The *servizi*?'

'Used to be their standard operating procedure. It wasn't usually covert work. To save everyone time and trouble, and foster good relations with a trusted ally, they were declared to the host government. But it complicates your task. Those people change their identities like we change our socks, only they don't wash the used ones, they throw them away. And they're very reluctant to divulge any information about their personnel, present or past. To anyone.'

Zen shrugged.

'Well, without it, this is all going to take a lot longer. And we don't have that much time. Now the news of

Newman's death is out, I'm under severe pressure. If I happen to mention in an unguarded moment that my investigation is being impeded by some secretive 007s in Rome, they'll be under a lot of pressure too. You might mention that in your sales pitch.'

'I can't promise anything, but I'll do my best.'

In the corridor, Zen was accosted by Natale Arnone, a stack of papers in his fist.

'The report from the Digos day team shadowing Nicola Mantega just came in,' he said. 'I know how busy you are, so I've filleted it for you.'

He handed over the sheaf of paperwork with a page containing heavy underlining uppermost.

'Mantega met Tom Newman by chance in a café around lunchtime. They made small talk for a while – some archaeological matter – and then Newman told Mantega that his father had been murdered. Mantega appeared perturbed by this news and immediately borrowed the American's mobile phone, presumably because he suspects his own is being tapped, to call that number in San Giovanni that we now have on intercept. There was no reply, but it switched over to an answering machine and Mantega left this message.'

His stubby forefinger, with its immaculately trimmed nail, indicated a transcribed passage on the page.

You crazy bastard! What do you think you're doing? Newman's son just told me that his father's dead. Well, that's the end of it as far as I'm concerned! I trusted you, Giorgio, and now I feel betrayed. It's all very well for you, lying low with your friends out of harm's way. I'm the one the cops are going to put through the mincer. If they do, and I still haven't heard from you, I'll tell them everything I know. Names, numbers, dates, times, places, the lot! And don't think you can blackmail me with that video. That was about a kidnapping. This is manslaughter at the very least, and probably murder. I had nothing to do with that and I'm sure as hell not taking the blame. I don't owe you anything and I shall take all necessary measures to protect my own position, so get in touch by tomorrow at the latest. If you don't, all bets are off, and you'll find out just what I'm –'

'The machine cut him off at that point,' Natale Arnone remarked when Zen had finished reading. 'Shall we take him? He's clearly been withholding evidence and would probably be ready to talk with a little persuasion.'

'True, but who knows how informative or conclusive his evidence would turn out to be? No, on balance I want to leave him loose a little while longer, along with the man whose phone he called. But he must be watched night and day and we must be prepared for him to try and slip off to another covert meeting with Giorgio at some point. If he does, we have to be ready to move in this time and close the trap. How's the surveillance operation on the house in San Giovanni going?'

'All in place. They're doubling up as a maintenance crew from the gas company during the day and a parked delivery truck overnight.'

A stunning guttural rumble that would have had any rap artist weeping in awe shook the city like a celestial earthquake.

'Young Newman also tried to pick up one of the female Digos agents. She took advantage of the situation to read the number Mantega had just called off the screen of his mobile, in case we didn't have an intercept in place.'

'What's the agent's name?'

'Mirella Kodra.'

'Tell her to get in touch with young Signor Newman, co-operate up to a certain point, find out whatever she can about what he's up to and report back.'

'Yes, sir.'

Zen heard his desk phone ringing and dashed into his office.

'I've found someone who is willing, subject to certain provisos, to talk to you about the subject we discussed,' Giovanni Sforza said, as though choosing his words carefully. 'I've got him on the line now and will put him through to you.'

'Who is he?'

'Don't ask. And don't ask him either.'

'Very well, I'll try to avoid the tough questions.'

'Avoid jokes too. These people take themselves very seriously indeed.'

After a number of fuzzy clicks, an unfamiliar voice spoke.

'*Buona sera, dottore.* I have been given to understand that you wish to contact a certain individual of my acquaintance. For the purposes of this conversation, we will refer to him simply as Roberto.'

'That is correct.'

'And that you wish to obtain a DNA sample from him. May I ask why?'

'To positively identify the victim of a murder I'm investigating. Circumstantial evidence appears to suggest that he was Roberto's nephew. Genetic profiling would instantly confirm or exclude that hypothesis, which in turn might well have a decisive effect on the progress of the case.'

There was a silence at the other end.

'So you don't wish to interview Roberto in person?' the other man said at length.

'Ideally, yes. He might well be able to supply other details relating to his family which are at present either vague or unknown. But I appreciate the sensitivities of your department, so if you insist I will settle for the DNA material. As you perhaps know, this isn't an invasive procedure. A mouth swab would suffice. What is crucial, however, is that there should be irrefutable evidence that the sample was indeed taken from the individual under discussion.'

'I can provide immaculate paperwork to support the authenticity of any sample, should Roberto consent to provide one.'

'I haven't the slightest doubt that you are in a position to provide any type of paperwork whatsoever,' Zen replied with a touch of steel in his voice. 'But should the case go to court, the person named in the documents you provided would be required to present himself before the judges in order to validate under oath the statements made therein. Do you really want to risk one of your agents being blown like that?'

A further silence ensued.

'As it happens, Roberto is willing to meet you in person, subject to stringent conditions.'

'Name them.'

'First, that the meeting be here in Rome. How do you propose to arrive?'

'Does it matter?'

'Yes.'

'When would this be?'

'Tomorrow at the earliest.'

'Then tomorrow. I'll take the night train.'

'Very well. Please ask Dottor Sforza to contact me with the estimated arrival time and other details in due course. You will be met at the station and conveyed to the meeting place. A medical orderly will be present to ensure that the correct procedures for taking the DNA samples are observed. Following that, you may speak to Roberto for a limited period, on condition that his refusal to respond to any given question is accepted as binding, and that no record of your conversation with him – whether written, electronic or in any other medium – is made. Do you agree?'

'I don't appear to have any option.'

'Correct. I hope the results of your visit prove helpful, *dottore*. *Buon lavoro*.'

Splayed out on the bed behind two layers of closed curtains, with CNN murmuring from the television, Martin Nguyen devoured the club sandwich that he'd ordered up from room service. It didn't look like a club sandwich, being layered on slices of a freshly baked roll, but it tasted better than any he'd ever had. Even the fries were great. They were nicely crisp but dense inside, and tasted earthily of potato. Martin had kind of forgotten that fries were made from potatoes, but when you had to chew on them a little the whole process became clear. *Al dente*, he thought.

He had been forced to listen to a lot of Italian since his arrival, and found that he understood it perfectly. Not so much the content, although he was picking up quite a bit of that too, but the form. This was atavistically familiar to him, unlike the incoherent lexis-free mumblings he had to deal with back on the West Coast, where the key point of the exchange often seemed to be the speaker's appeal to anyone present to give him a helping hand with the almost impossible task of articulating whatever banal thought had sparked and then immediately died in his brain. Every utterance ended up as a collaborative effort, like raising a barn. It was tough, backbreaking work, but it brought the community together. Italian, on the other hand, was a language much like Martin's own lost Vietnamese: pure, plain and declarative. In neither tongue was there even an approximate equivalent for such phrases as 'So I was, kind of, like, you know?'

Martin had necessarily learned to speak that dialect on demand, but he also had a number of other registers at his disposal when the need arose. He had been acutely aware of such a need many times that day, but all he had to fall back on were Tom Newman's translations. The loss of his verbal karate skills had been the greatest trial during an incredibly long working day which had left Martin feeling exhausted, baffled and all the more foreign for the apparent similarities to his own native culture. First there had been the crack-of-dawn meeting at the Aeroscan base, followed by an unpleasant encounter with the local police chief, who had turned out to be both tough and intelligent, qualities which Nguyen respected but preferred not to encounter in opponents in a position of power.

Then after lunch, during which Tom and the waiter had made the simple transaction of ordering a goddamn meal sound like the finale of some Three Tenors extravaganza, he had spent hours in a dingy, stifling office with the notary that Newman had hired as a fixer trying to figure out the current state of play plus how the hell anything got done in this Latino dump, if it ever did. Throughout, he had been dependent on Tom's translations of what was said on either side. The kid's English was way more sophisticated than Jake's, but Martin had no way of knowing what his Italian was like, and hence of how he, Martin Nguyen, was coming across.

To cap it all off, on the way back to the hotel Tom had blurted out the news that his father was dead. Here was cause for genuine grief. In Martin's view, there was a time and a place for homicide. Plumb in the middle of the stealth-bomber strategy he'd devised for this project, with the victim a declared Rapture Works contractor, was just totally inappropriate. He was furious that his hefty incentive bonus had been put at risk by a bunch of peasant *bandidos* with more balls than brains. This one was going to need heavy spin on it. It was essential that Aeroscan's operations continued as smoothly and invisibly as possible until the mission had been accomplished.

His mobile phone burbled into life. Martin didn't want to answer it, but he could no more ignore a ringtone than a mother could her crying baby.

'Yo.'

'Hi, Jake.'

'We've got issues, dude.'

'No fucking kidding!'

'The guy called you too?'

'What guy?'

'That big kahuna director we hired for the movie cover.'

'Aldobrandini? We spoke after I arrived here.'

'I mean real time. Like, you know, now.'

'I've been totally slammed, Jake. It's all swimming upstream here. What's new?'

'Aldo left a message. He somehow found out the whole thing is a scam. Said a lot of stuff about creative property rights and shit. Plus he's threatening to get on TV and expose us, then sue our asses. What a shitty break! If Newman doesn't get kidnapped, this never happens.'

Martin Nguyen took a moment to savour this, the longest discourse he had ever heard Jake pronounce. Then he turned his boss's habitual brevity against him.

'Newman's dead.'

'Huh?'

'Murdered. They dressed him up as a corpse, made him walk to an old village someplace, then blew his head off.'

'Fuck.'

After a long silence, Jake laughed.

'Well, I guess the game's hotting up.'

Like much of what Jake said, this didn't make any sense to Martin, so he decided to ignore it.

'I've refocused the search according to the parameters suggested by that team of consultants I told you about. The Aeroscan guy figures they can cover the area in three or four more days.'

'Yeah, but if Brandini goes on TV and tells everyone there isn't going to be any movie, we're screwed.'

'Chill, Jake. It's just the flying permits at risk. I can stall the authorities that long.'

'Okay, but if we get lucky, call me immediately. I've got a jet on standby.'

'Well, that's great, but it's going to take you half a day to get here and the time difference screws up the scheduling. Plus I don't know if you remember, but I just said that Pete Newman has been brutally murdered. That means that the cops here have a homicide investigation under way, and anyone associated with the victim – like me, for instance – is a potential witness, if not suspect. The police chief made that very clear to me today. So what with the threat of Aldobrandini going nuclear, I'm under a lot of pressure. Now Aeroscan might just come through tomorrow, in which case I'll have to move fast without you around or maybe even in touch, because it'll be the middle of the night over there. So it would help a lot if you told me what we're actually looking for.'

There was a long pause.

'It's kind of hard to explain over the phone, plus I've got to go. Let me shoot you a couple of URLs. Think you have problems? Madrona went out and bought this designer dog. It's like a total bitch.'

The line went dead. Martin felt rage coil up within him like a thwarted orgasm. For a moment he was tempted to hurl the phone at the wall, but in the end he tapped into his rage and used it to dissipate his earlier tiredness and sense of passive helplessness. He called room service and told them to remove his dirty dishes and bring a bottle of their best cognac, a soda siphon and a bucket of ice. Martin's father had started his career as a waiter at one of the most exclusive clubs in the French colony of Cochinchine, so he had been in a position to pass on to his son a few tips about the good things in life.

After leaving his office exceptionally late, Nicola Mantega drove up the *superstrada* to Spezzano Grande, a ragged stack of concrete boxes perched on the precipitous slopes of the Sila massif. The radio was tuned to the same local news channel he had listened to while driving to work, and as the Alfa Romeo skimmed round the long curving viaduct leading up to the Spezzano turn-off, Mantega was surprised to hear the familiar voice of the new police chief, Aurelio Zen.

' . . . where officers under my command discovered the remains of the American lawyer Peter Newman, who has subsequently been identified as a member of the Calopezzati family and hence of Calabrian origin. The victim's head had been blown off by a charge of plastic explosive detonated by remote control. Forensic tests have revealed that the explosive substance was identical to that used last night to force an entry into a house in the new town of Altomonte, located near by. The *capofamiglia*, Antonio Nicastro, was then shot while attempting to defend his nine-year-old son Francesco, whose tongue was subsequently severed . . .'

The exit for Spezzano angled sharply right, then left up a steep gradient, and at the speed Mantega took it a lesser car than the Alfa 159 Q4 might well have spun out of control. He stopped at the side of the road until his breathing had calmed down to something approaching normal, then nosed through the narrow streets and parked in front of a pizzeria. Gina and the boys were visiting her brother in Leipzig, where he had found work stripping Communist-era plumbing out of desirable nineteenth-century apartment buildings for rich Wessis, so on top of everything else Nicola couldn't get a home-cooked meal. The street was empty except for a kid who had been showing off his MotoGuzzi bike to his piece of arm-candy. She looked vaguely familiar, Mantega thought as he walked in and ordered. He'd definitely seen her before, maybe even that day, but where?

He sat down and gulped some beer. It wasn't surprising that his mind was going after what he'd been put through. He'd spent a miserable afternoon pretending to listen to the needs and demands of some Oriental who had flown in from America to represent the film company that Peter Newman had worked for, but his thoughts had been elsewhere. He already knew that the interim police chief didn't believe his story about the circumstances of Newman's disappearance, but hadn't had enough evidence to proceed against him when the case under investigation had merely been one of abduction. Now it was murder, and of the most atrocious kind. Crimes on that scale create their own judicial momentum, and Mantega knew that he would be one of its first victims. The only surprise was that they hadn't come for him already.

To prepare for that onslaught, he needed to be

briefed by Giorgio on what exactly had happened, and above all why, but any contact from that quarter now looked as unlikely as an intervention from the other quarter was inevitable. He had made his final pitch before lunch, borrowing Tom Newman's mobile on the grounds that it was new and therefore untapped. The only reply was from an answering machine, on which he had left a frenzied message whose tone he now regretted. In retrospect, his spontaneous reaction to Tom's news looked distinctly risky. Giorgio was not one to take kindly to threats and abuse. But what was he supposed to have done? The original deal they had struck was a straightforward business transaction, the victim returned a little poorer but otherwise unharmed and the perpetrators enriched by several million euros. A traditional Calabrian crime, with its roots in the immemorial banditry of the region. Nothing had ever been said about murder, still less a barbaric and apparently motiveless execution such as the one the police chief had described at his press conference.

He chomped his pizza down, then spent a little time flirting jokingly with the waitress, whose husband had been screwing the sister of the priest in Pedace ever since the difficult birth of their second child. The night outside was a still, solid block of oppressive heat. The storm that should have ripped it open, letting in the fresh air and a cooling downpour, had merely brooded over the area for a few hours and then shifted off to the east, leaving no resolution to the problems it had created. Mantega slipped gratefully into the air-conditioned zephyrs within the Alfa and drove up a tilted labyrinth of minor roads to his villa, where the electronic gates in the boundary fence automatically closed behind him. Tonight, there were no welcoming barks and plaintive whines to greet him. Attilio, his lively pit bull terrier, had come down with an acute intestinal ailment a few days earlier and was still in the care of the vet. Mantega unlocked the house, bolted the door behind him, reset the alarm system and then fetched a bottle of the local *digestivo* he favoured and watched an hour of mind-numbing television before going to bed.

He was awakened by stabbing pains and a sense of suffocation that induced muffled shrieks.

'Shut up!'

The low voice was also muffled, but Mantega had already recognised Giorgio's body odour. The gag over his mouth was removed.

'On your feet.'

The intruder twisted Mantega's right arm up behind his back and walked him through the dark topography of the house to the kitchen. Visibility was slightly better here, thanks to the security light on the patio. Giorgio sat his captive down on a chair beside the long table strewn with various incongruous artefacts purchased by Gina as part of her unending attempts to create a gracious home and stood over him, his back to the window, his face in shadow. He was wearing jeans, a black leather jacket and a dark woollen hat. His huge hands gleamed in the ambient light like dangling crabs.

'Keep your voice low,' Giorgio said. 'The house is under surveillance.'

'Who by?'

'The cops, of course. It took me almost two hours to get in. They're good, but I'm better.'

Mantega thought this over, then frowned.

'The burglar alarm?' prompted Giorgio. 'One of my friends disabled that on a previous visit, before things got hot. He's a wizard with wiring. The system looks like it's working, but it's just talking to itself. Or perhaps it was your dog you were thinking of? Another friend of mine tossed a chunk of poisoned meat over the fence after the cops outside had handed you off to the team that follows you around during the day.'

Mantega's eyes had adjusted by now, and his brain was more alert. The reason for the strange gleam on Giorgio's hands became obvious. He was wearing a pair of those skin-tight latex gloves used by doctors.

'It seems like this is all news to you,' Giorgio went on, 'which just confirms my feeling that you've become a liability rather than an asset. All these phone calls you've been making, whining and bitching away like some woman! That's not how a man conducts himself. I need men about me, Nicola, now more than ever. So I've decided that the time has come to sever our connection.'

One of the gleaming hands disappeared for a moment. Then it was back, holding a blade whose gleam was even more intense and much colder.

'No one saw me come and no one will see me go. I suppose you will be missed eventually, but not for many days. Those days are vital to us to make our plans without the fear of being betrayed by a scumbag like you. Your job for us is done, Nicola. All you can do now is harm.'

To his surprise, Mantega found that he was perfectly calm.

'You're right about one thing, Giorgio,' he said. 'There's plenty of harm that I can do, even from beyond the grave. Do you think it didn't occur to me that you might try this? The way you murdered Newman and mutilated that poor kid, it's clear that you've gone out of your mind. Well, I've been in this game long enough not to trust crazies, so a complete statement of all our dealings – not just about Newman, but everything, back from the very beginning – is in the hands of a third party and will be deposited with the authorities if anything happens to me. Names, locations, dates, ransom paid and all particulars of both you and your friends. Given that this latest exploit of yours is headline news, that would naturally result in the biggest manhunt this country has seen for years, with you as the star of the show.'

He held up his hand.

'Now, you may think that the whole community will form a circle and protect you faithfully whatever the cost. That would be a mistake. People round here have a healthy respect for power and patronage, but they don't have any more time for sadistic crackheads than I do. You'll be on your own and on the run, Giorgio. Even your friends may eventually start wondering how much your friendship is worth. Sooner or later there'll be a fire-fight at some ruined farmhouse where you've been holed up in misery for months like a kidnap hostage yourself, and you will come out of it either dead or facing a life sentence without parole in that high-security hostel in Terni.'

Giorgio gestured his boredom.

'This is just talk, Nicola. The plain fact is I don't need you any more.'

He approached, knife held out. It was then that Mantega had his supreme inspiration.

'Maybe not, but you do need money. And I'm talking about serious money, the kind that will buy friends and influence people or spirit you away abroad if things get too hot here. That's what you need, Giorgio, and I know where you can get it. Therefore you need me.'

Even Mantega didn't really believe that this last-minute appeal was going to work, but he felt he owed it to his reputation as a *notaio di fiducia* to give it a whirl. In the event, it stopped Giorgio in his tracks. He must be even more cash-strapped than I thought, Mantega reflected. This didn't entirely surprise him. Giorgio's eagerness when Mantega had suggested Peter Newman as a kidnapping prospect indicated that his finances had been at a low point. Since he had chosen to kill his hostage rather than ransom him, with the additional costs of the operation he might well be close to broke by now. Despite their operational efficiency and ruthless enforcement methods, Giorgio and his associates hadn't progressed much beyond the 'feast or famine' approach of the historical brigands. Whatever money they had, they spent, then looked around for more.

Mantega stood up and smiled widely.

'Put away that knife, Giorgio, and I'll tell you how you can make yourself a sackful of cash in a week or two, and at no risk whatsoever. Because the beauty of this scheme is that it isn't even illegal, strictly speaking.'

Giorgio attempted a contemptuous laugh.

'What kind of bullshit is this?'

'A very easy and lucrative kind,' Mantega returned with just the right professional polished ease. 'Draw up a chair, Giorgio. Let's get rich!'

Aurelio Zen stayed at his desk until ten o'clock that night, feeling more and more like the captain of a doomed vessel who is reluctantly observing the tradition of going down with his ship. Should he contact the investigating magistrate and advise the arrest of Nicola Mantega and Dionisio Carduzzi, both of them prima facie material witnesses and probable accessories to murder, the former before the fact and the latter after, as the call-catcher and go-between for the man known as Giorgio? Or should he hold off and wait for the even more opportune moment which all his instincts told him was not far off?

In the end he decided that he was too tired to make an effective decision. He walked back through the brooding darkness to his apartment, packed an overnight bag, then phoned the Questura's car pool and arranged for a vehicle to drive him first to the Cosenza Nord service station on the *autostrada*, where he bought a *panino* and a litre of mineral water, and then up the spectacular highway that snaked up out of the Crati flood plain before piercing the range of mountains in a series of tunnels and viaducts and twisting steeply down to the coast and the main north–south railway line.

It was a mild night, and Zen spent the hour or so he had to wait sitting outside on a station bench eating his ham and cheese roll, smelling the heady perfume of the sea breezes and listening to the distant hushing of waves on the beach. Leaving Cosenza felt like escaping from a locked room. By the time the *Conca d'Oro* night sleeper from Palermo pulled in at twenty to one in the morning, he was quite content to stretch out on his bed in a spacious Excelsior compartment and fall asleep for five and a half dreamless hours.

It was only when he was ejected from this sanctuary into the commuter rush hour at Rome that he realised to what extent he had become a provincial after just a few months in Calabria. He found it both physically difficult and emotionally repugnant to battle his way through the riptide of people coming at him from every direction, empty eyes trained like a gun on the personal zone immediately in front of them, attention absorbed by the loud songs or little voices in their heads, fingers fiddling with iPods and mobile phones, all oblivious of each other and their surroundings, marching relentlessly onwards like the ranks of the damned.

In the middle of the vast concourse of Termini station Zen gave up and came to a dazed halt. One of the zombies immediately approached. He automatically placed a cluster of small coins in its outstretched hand.

'This way, Dottor Zen,' it said.

'How did you recognise me?'

'We obtained a photograph.'

A Fiat saloon was illegally parked at the kerb. The man opened the rear door for Zen, then got into its equivalent on the far side.

'Your document, please,' he said as they drove away.

Zen handed over his police identification card.

'Where are we going?'

'To a house where you will meet the person you came to see. Our journey time will be approximately forty minutes, depending on the traffic. There will then be a short delay before the subject arrives.'

'For security reasons?'

'No, he wouldn't agree to an earlier meeting. He's an elderly man and doesn't like making an early start.'

They drove south-east out of the city along Via Tuscolana, across the ring road and up into the foothills of the Colli Albani. When they reached Frascati, Zen's escort announced that they were ahead of time and suggested stopping for a coffee. There were no parking spaces available on the edge of the main square, so the driver left their vehicle in the traffic lane of the main street outside the busiest and glossiest bar. One of the traffic wardens blew his whistle shrilly and came striding over, but the driver said a few words to him and the official slunk off. Frascati had been a playground for the rich and powerful since Etruscan times and the locals had learned a thing or two about dealing with such people.

Inside the bar, Zen was left to fend for himself. He ordered a cappuccino and an attractive-looking pastry and, having consumed both, eyed his minders with cold disdain. They stood at a distance, their mobile phones laid on the counter like pistols, apparently ignoring him although acutely aware of his presence. The driver, the younger and taller of the pair, was lean and hard, all prick and muscle. His superior was almost bald, with a superficially benign face, strongly featured and slightly inflated in appearance, like a wiser and sadder Mussolini.

Zen paid and walked outside to light his first cigarette of the day. As he smoked, he took in the scene all around with sharpened pleasure, eyeballing a sensational woman cradling a bottle of mineral water to her bosom like a baby. She gave him a lingering glance before moving on, the cheeks of her buttocks colluding furtively as she strolled away. Then he heard a familiar *squillo* and immediately reverted to his official self, striding up and down the pavement clutching his mobile phone like a life-support system.

'Arnone, sir. You ordered me to report any developments.'

'Go ahead.'

'The Digos crew watching that house in San Giovanni report that the owner, Dionisio Carduzzi, has left the house only twice. Last night he went to a local bar and drank wine with some friends. This morning he bought a paper, then went to the same bar and had a coffee. After that he went home and hasn't emerged since. His wife went to church yesterday and to the market this morning to buy vegetables and a chicken. That's all. No one else has entered or left the house.'

He's using *pizzini*, thought Zen, just like Bernardo Provenzano. Notes folded into a banknote and handed to the owner of the bar or the newsagent, or slipped under the table to one of those friends, or passed to a market vendor by his wife, or left in a missal at the church. The dilemma he had wrestled with the night before was now resolved. The only way to intercept such messages would be by mass arrests of essentially innocent people with no criminal history. That would be both clumsy and ineffective.

'Anything else?' he asked Arnone.

'Two things, sir. The phone interception team reported that when Carduzzi came back from his morning expedition, he called the offices of a construction firm down in Vibo Valentia and asked for someone named Aldo. He told him that their mutual friend required the immediate services of a mechanical digger on a low-loader, two heavy-duty trucks, a dozen first-rate stonemasons and twenty unskilled labourers. The equipment and personnel were to assemble in the parking area of the Rogliano service station south of Cosenza on the A3, where they would be met and led to the work site. Payment would be in the normal way.'

'Very well. Have someone at the meeting point and try and get photographs of the principals. Sounds like a classic abusive construction job. I can't see it's worth diverting manpower from ongoing assignments to follow them. Funny about them needing stonemasons, though. Cheap, poorly reinforced concrete is the mob's trademark.'

'Not if it's one of their own houses,' Arnone pointed out.

The two *servizi* thugs had now emerged from the bar. Mini-Mussolini walked over, touched Zen's arm and jerked his head impatiently towards the car. Zen ignored him.

'And the other thing?' he asked Arnone.

'Oh, just some crazy old woman here who insists on talking to you. Won't say what it's about and won't talk to anyone else.'

'Who is she?'

'Name's Maria Stefania Arrighi, resident in Altomonte Nuova. She got here at seven this morning and demanded to speak to the chief of police. She was told that you were out of town and wouldn't be back until late, but she said she would wait. Plonked herself down on the bench in the entrance hall and has been there ever since. Do you want us to throw her out?'

'Absolutely not, and if she leaves of her own accord, try to get a contact address and phone number.'

'I'll do my best, but basically she refuses to speak to anyone but you.'

Flanked by his two handlers, Zen got back into the car, which took a very steep minor road whose tight bends gave occasional views of the capital, the dome of St Peter's just visible through the flat pall of pollution that covered the surrounding *campagna*, a modern equivalent of the malarial miasma that had decimated the population for centuries.

When they finally reached their destination, Zen was reminded of Arnone's comment about the mob leaders' private dwellings. Not that there was anything ostentatious about this long, low villa set among ancient olive groves and vineyards. The connection was more subtle, based on the fact that a good three kilometres back they had passed a sign marking the beginning of the Castelli Romani regional park. The villa clearly post-dated the creation of this protected area where new construction was strictly forbidden, but the important and powerful figure who owned it was almost certainly a member not of the Mafia but of the government – an entirely different organisation, needless to say.

The room into which Zen was shown provided no obvious clue to the identity of this person beyond the fact that he could afford to indulge in the sort of bad taste that comes with an exorbitant price tag. There were several huge oil paintings in the blandly 'contemporary' style favoured by Arab collectors, featuring nude females and rearing stallions in a vaguely abstract wilderness. There were also a number of coffee-table art books on display, but any attempt to investigate further the ownership of the property was prevented by Zen's escort, who took up positions at opposite ends of the room. Twelve minutes passed before a passenger van drew up outside the house and a hydraulic lift deposited an elderly man seated in a wheelchair, which was pushed into the room by a formidable-looking woman in a starched uniform.

'This nurse will take the sample you require and return with it so that tests may be undertaken,' Mini-Mussolini announced.

'Take it from whom?' Zen demanded acidly.

'From the person you requested to meet.'

'And where is he?'

The man pointed to the occupant of the wheelchair, who sat mutely cradling a battered leather briefcase.

'I have your word for that?'

'You have my department's word for it.'

Zen levelled him with a look.

'I don't even know which department you're talking about, but if it's the one I think it is, then I hope for all our sakes that you're not the sharpest knife in their drawer. For my coming here to make any sense, I require documentary proof that the donor of the sample is Roberto Calopezzati. I further require to take possession of the sample and convey it personally to a police laboratory, where it will be entrusted to a technician of my choice. If you seek to impose any other solution, this has all been a complete waste of time.'

'Go away, Gino,' said the man in the wheelchair. 'You two as well. This experience is difficult enough for me without having you all standing around aimlessly like characters in some Pirandello play.'

The two minders and the nurse trooped meekly out.

'I apologise for this pantomime,' the man said to Zen. 'It was the idea of my successor as head of the agency you referred to. Not a bad fellow in many ways, but somewhat heavy-handed. Yes, I know you're listening, Rizzardo, but that happens to be my opinion, for what it's worth. Sit down, *signore*, sit down. I am Roberto Calopezzati, and I have brought the necessary documents to prove it. Before I present them, may I ask why I have the honour of being an object of attention to the police?'

Calopezzati was a bulky man with a strongly featured face set off by a white beard trimmed short and contrasted with jet-black cropped hair and two huge eyebrows of the same colour that lounged across his brow like furry caterpillars. His olive-green eyes were intense, direct and demanding, while his lips were thin but sensual. Only the lower half of his body, truncated at the knees, detracted from the general impression of vigour and power.

'I assumed that your successor would have explained that,' Zen replied.

'Well, I suppose we could always ask him. I don't actually know if he's listening in "real time", as they say these days – when did time stop being real, by the way? – but our conversation is certainly being recorded for quality-assurance purposes and for my protection. Anyway, all I have been told is that our meeting is with regard to the investigation of a murder in Cosenza.'

'You weren't informed of the identity of the victim?'

'No.'

'And you didn't see my press conference on television?'

'I don't have a television.'

'Ah well, in that case, *barone*, I'm afraid that I must be the bearer of bad news. All the prima facie evidence suggests that the victim was your nephew.'

Calopezzati sagged physically and looked his age for the first time.

'Pietro?' he whispered.

'That's what I've come here to ascertain. On the face of it, the victim was an American citizen travelling under the name of Peter Newman. When he disappeared some weeks ago while in Calabria on a business trip, the assumption was that he had been kidnapped for ransom. My investigations during that period suggested that his original identity was Pietro Ottavio Calopezzati, the son of your late sister Ottavia. The main reason why I've come here is to obtain a DNA sample from you which will confirm or rule out that hypothesis.'

Calopezzati sat silent and expressionless for over a minute, his body twitching violently at intervals as if stricken by a series of minor strokes. Zen let this process work itself out without comment.

'You'll get your sample,' the other man said at last, 'but it's redundant. The dead man was indeed my nephew.'

'Would you be prepared to comment on how Pietro Calopezzati became Peter Newman?'

'Possibly. But first things first.'

He opened the leather case and extracted a mass of papers.

'We'll go through these in chronological order, with one exception which I'll get to later.'

He passed the documents to Zen one by one.

'My birth certificate. Various photographs from my childhood and school years. A sequence of identity cards from the following period, up to the war years, then a different set dating from my work with the *servizi*, concluding with the one that is currently valid. I think you will agree that all the photographs show a marked likeness, qualified of course by the passage of time. However, I don't expect you to confirm my identity on that basis alone. As I said, I have withheld one document from the chronological order. It is this.'

He passed Zen a file card bearing the printed heading 'Partito Fascista Italiano'. The entries below indicated that Roberto Calopezzati was enrolled in the Cosenza section of the party with the rank of *caposquadrista*, the commander of a squad of Blackshirts. The attached photograph fitted into the now familiar pattern, but there was also a very clear thumbprint.

'And now for my last trick,' the man said.

From the leather bag, he produced an ink pad in a tin box and a blank sheet of paper. He opened the pad, rolled his right thumb in the ink and then printed the resulting image on the paper. Zen compared it to the print on the Fascist file card. They were identical.

'You are satisfied?' Calopezzati asked.

'Yes.'

'Then let us proceed to the sample you need. What exactly does that consist of?'

Zen paused for a moment.

'Correct me if I'm wrong, *barone*, but I have the impression that while the news of your nephew's death was a shock to you, it did not come as a complete surprise.'

'Only in the sense that I had no idea he'd returned home. For as long as we were in contact, I explicitly advised him never to do so, and in any event not to venture south of Rome. What on earth could have induced him to do such a thing?'

'I understand that he was employed by an American movie company to act as their *mediatore* during preparations for a production to be filmed there.'

Calopezzati waved his elegant hand dismissively. His feet must have been elegant too, thought Zen, wondering how they had been severed.

'That's just money! He could have found another job.'

'Perhaps he thought that the risks were by now minimal,' Zen murmured as though to himself. 'Perhaps after so many years he had grown nostalgic for his own country. You implied that you lost contact with Pietro at some point. When did that happen?'

'I don't recall exactly. At some point in the 1980s. He just stopped writing and phoning, or I did. He wasn't my child, after all.'

'But you were responsible for taking him to America?'

'After my sister died, I became his guardian. This was after the war, the whole country was in chaos. I moved Pietrino in with me in Rome and sent him to school there to learn Italian. He was a wild creature who had been brought up by Ottavia's entourage of servants, spoke only dialect and didn't respond well to discipline. Nevertheless, it was clearly my duty to protect him until he came of age, so when I entered the agency and was posted to the embassy in Washington I took him with me. Our ambassador at the time was a family friend and happened to be in a position to call in a favour from the US government in return for some help that we had provided for them. Thus it was arranged for Pietro Ottavio to become an American citizen. All in all, it seemed the best solution to the problem.'

'Which problem?'

'The problem of possible reprisals from my family's numerous enemies.'

'Were they really that dangerous?'

The man in the wheelchair made another fluent, fluid hand gesture.

'Who can estimate danger? One of my colleagues made clandestine trips to remote areas of our former colony of Eritrea during its war with Ethiopia and came back with nothing worse than a mild case of gonorrhoea. Another went to see a Washington Redskins game one evening and was beaten to death on his way home because the stupid bastard was too proud to give them his wallet.'

Roberto Calopezzati made his eloquent gesture again.

'Life is an acquired taste, Signor Zen, but death has mass-market appeal. Sooner or later, we all succumb to its charms. I tried to shield my nephew from them as best I could.'

What sounded like a peal of the thunder that Zen was by now habituated to – although not this early in the day – prevented any further conversation. It turned out to be the roar of a jet taking off from Ciampino, a few kilometres to the north, and obligingly faded away in a few moments.

'And it would have been an excellent solution,' Zen commented, 'if only he hadn't come back to Calabria and started talking to the locals in fluent dialect.'

'That marked him down as someone who had been born and raised in the area, but there are plenty of *calabresi* in the States, God knows. How did his killers discover his identity?'

'Speaking of that, do you know the identity of his father?'

Roberto sighed.

'My sister told me that it was a friend of ours named Carlo Sironi. He was a fighter pilot in the war, an utterly irresistible daredevil who was shot down while attacking an Allied bombing sortie over Salerno six months before Pietro was born. He and Ottavia had spent some time together in Naples shortly before, so it's just possible that she wasn't lying to me. The truth is that I don't know and don't really care. Whoever she might have screwed, Pietro was here and it was my duty to look after him to the best of my ability. Now will you answer my question, Signor Zen? Granted that Pietro was stupid enough to speak the dialect rather than just passing himself off as a dumb American, how could his killers have found out that he was a Calopezzati?'

Zen shot him a keen glance.

'Are you insulting my intelligence or your own, *barone*? There is only one possible answer, namely that he himself disclosed the information to someone, almost certainly the shady fixer he had employed to facilitate his business deals. Following your advice, Pietro had set out to become an American. Perhaps he had succeeded only too well. After forty years over there he simply couldn't conceive that anyone in a backwater like Calabria cared about what might or might not have happened in the years before he was born. But Americans care enormously about any provable antiquity and lineage in their family history, particularly if it involves a title. It's hardly surprising that he couldn't resist mentioning to his new acquaintance that he was a member of an Italian baronial family founded back in the mists of time before the first shipload of American pilgrims arrived.'

Calopezzati smiled pallidly.

'Actually, we're only late eighteenth century.'

Tom spent much of the morning watching television with Martin Nguyen. He'd been able to hold off moving hotels for twenty-four hours, on the grounds that the police wanted him to perform various legal functions connected with his father's death, but that morning Nguyen's limo had shown up to whisk him off to this flashy business location about two miles from the city centre, out in what Italians called the periphery. While he was in the car, Nicola Mantega had phoned to tell him that the world-famous film director Luciano Aldobrandini would be making a surprise appearance on the popular morning TV show *Ciao Italia!* and that there were rumours that what he was going to say might have a direct impact on the business interests of Tom's new employer. This news had been duly passed on and both men were now fixated on the screen, Tom's job being to translate Aldobrandini's words, in real time as far as possible, although Nguyen was burning a DVD as back-up.

Up to now the show had offered nothing but a succession of entry-level celebrities, burned-out celebrities, minor politicians and a footballer in drug rehab, but when the presenter finally announced the star whose name she had been teasingly trailing for almost an hour the results proved well worth the wait. Clad in a stunning cream linen suit over a blue silk shirt left largely open to reveal a perfectly judged tan, his mass of silver hair sculpted as though by some natural force, Aldobrandini looked youthful yet distinguished, strikingly virile and decisive but with vast inner reserves of gravitas.

He speedily got down to business, announcing that he had flown to Rome, 'interrupting my annual period of creative repose' on the Costa Smeralda, in order to break the dramatic news that he had withdrawn from the project to transfer the Book of Revelations to the screen – 'a work I hoped and believed would crown a long career dedicated solely to my art' – since he had lost all faith in the commitment and integrity of the American production company which had been financing it.

What followed was a presentation worthy of someone who had once played, very competently, various minor roles in post-war neo-realist films made on a shoestring budget by directors including Visconti and Fellini. Aldobrandini lamented the demise of that generation's values in favour of the cynical manipulations of market-driven accountants and middle managers, 'people without intelligence, without courage, without vision, without ideals, concerned only with maximising profits'. With a sad smile, he recounted his discovery that the backer of 'the intended masterwork of my late period, a funeral oration for the entire culture which formed and nourished me', was exploiting the project for reasons which had nothing to do with making the film.

Egged on by the eager but flustered hostess, who had obviously been primed with a list of helpful questions, Aldobrandini proceeded to disclose certain very specific details which had led him to suppose that the masterwork in question would never be made. His suspicions had been aroused, he said, by the withdrawal of the great British actor whom he had selected to play St John of Patmos. The reason given at the time had been that his agent had come to doubt the credibility of the project's backers. Until that moment, Aldobrandini proclaimed, he had 'never even thought of such a thing. I don't live in that world. For me it is all about the creative challenge *e basta!* When it comes to high finance and commercial skulduggery, I am an innocent abroad.' Nevertheless, this news led him to instigate certain enquiries, the results of which had appalled him.

'I am reliably informed that for several weeks now a helicopter has been operating in and around the city of Cosenza, supposedly carrying out a detailed survey of the terrain under the pretext of selecting suitable locations for the shooting of my film. *My* film!'

He appealed to his interviewer with a charming gesture.

'*Signorina*, you may or may not like my work . . . Well, that's very kind of you, but my point is that even my severest critics have never suggested that I am not *un autore*. Every single one of my films is handcrafted in every aspect and at every stage of its creation, from setting up to final editing. It is absurd to imagine that Luciano Aldobrandini would delegate the selection of locations to an outside contract! And needless to say he never did so. Nevertheless, these flights are taking place under the auspices of my American production company. Have you ever had occasion to hire a helicopter, *signorina*? I have, and believe me they don't come cheap. Since that money is clearly not being spent on preparations for my film, what is it being spent on? And where does that leave me and my dreams of making a final and lasting contribution to the glorious history of Italian cinema?'

Aldobrandini held up his palms in symbolic surrender.

'I don't know the answer to those questions, and until I do I can have no faith in those who suggested this project and promised to finance it. I am therefore, and with the greatest reluctance, severing all personal and professional connection with this whole sorry affair. It is a sad day for me, a sad day for art and a sad day for Italy.'

Martin Nguyen turned off the TV as the hostess thanked her guest and transitioned effortlessly to a commercial break.

'Holy fuck!' he said.

'Yeah, he was certainly in a hissy fit,' Tom replied casually. 'No one gives me 'nuff respec' now I'm over the hill stuff.'

'The guy's a genius,' said Martin in a tone of hushed reverence.

Tom gestured sceptically.

'Well, the jury's still pretty well out on that one. I like his early films, *Terra Bruciata* for example. That was one of my mom's favourites. She said it was just how people lived where she grew up.'

'I'm not talking about his fucking movies!' Martin yelled. 'He just killed us, live on national network TV! Next it'll be all over the –'

The phone in the room rang. Martin jerked his thumb.

'Take it.'

Tom did so. He listened for a long time, inserting the occasional *'Ho capito'*, *'Senz'altro'* and *'D'accordo, signore'*. Then he turned to Martin.

'That was the mayor's office. They want you to present yourself at ten o'clock tomorrow morning.'

'Present myself? What the fuck does that mean?'

'Sorry, I'm thinking in Italian. Go to city hall and meet with them.'

'Why?'

'It's about the permits your company was granted to operate those helicopter flights. Apparently they expire in forty-eight hours. Basically, they want to know if there's any truth in Aldobrandini's allegations. I don't want to sound alarmist, Mr Nguyen, but I think you should take this very seriously. Italy may seem all free and easy and spontaneous on the surface, but when the going gets rough you find out that it's basically a police state in many respects. This could just be one of those occasions.'

Martin Nguyen stared at the blank television screen.

'Holy fuck,' he repeated.

The convoy of vehicles came to rest at a remote spot on the banks of the Busento river a few kilometres south of Cosenza. The only access was by a dead-end dirt track leading steeply down from a minor road to the city from the village of Dipignano, which saw very little traffic now that there was a much faster route over the line of hills to the east connecting with the *autostrada*.

As a result, the guard who had been posted at the turn-off to deter intruders was only called upon to act once, when a farmer in a quad vehicle came along, trying to short-cut across the valley by fording the river and taking the equivalent track leading up on the western side. The guard simply shook his head and told the man that the road was *'chiusa per lavoro'*. What sort of work? Construction of a weir in the river-bed to improve flow levels and protect aquatic life. An environmental project. The farmer cackled cannily.

'Glad to hear someone's getting Rome's money!'

Say what you liked about Giorgio – and opinions on this subject were many and various, although rarely expressed – he knew how to organise and execute a project like this on time, under budget, with minimal risk and at the shortest possible notice. The last of these attributes was perhaps the most valuable, given the nature of his business. Opportunity tended to knock rarely and with no notice whatever, so to take advantage you needed to be able to think on your feet. He had spent the previous day scouting out a suitable site. Enquiries at the few neighbouring farms in the area Giorgio had eventually chosen revealed that no helicopters had been seen or heard in this valley as yet. This was crucial to the success of Mantega's scheme for instant riches, as was haste, since those searching for the location of the tomb might appear at any moment.

The first stage of the operation involved installing sandbags upstream to dam the flow of water – still minimal despite the recent rains, thanks to the absorption capacity of the baked hillsides all around – followed by the marking out of a circular area ten metres in diameter and the removal of the superficial rocks, gravel and vegetation. This was done by hand by the unskilled labourers, great care being taken not to mark the rocks with metal tools or to damage the various reeds and weeds that had taken root for the summer in muddy patches formed by the eddies of the stagnant stream but would be swept away once the winter floods arrived. A geotextile access path was then laid down to minimise any further disturbance to the surface and the big yellow mechanical digger unloaded from its transporter and brought up to excavate the site down to a level of about two metres.

While all this was going on, another phase of the job was taking place on the lower slopes of Monte Serratore to the south, where the stonemasons were dismantling a long-abandoned and roofless house of the type that abounded in the area and transferring the blocks of weathered basalt to the bed of a truck. These materials arrived at the construction site shortly after the team's lunch break, following which the masons started to install them in the excavated pit in the form of a circular wall five courses deep and nine hundred and forty-three centimetres in diameter. The masons protested that this was an irrational number, but Giorgio refused to be swayed. He had no idea what kind of linear measurement would have been used by the people who had supposedly built this structure, but it certainly wouldn't have been the standardised French import which even today wasn't in general use in certain parts of the region. Likewise, he had chosen the circular pattern on the basis of some very old earthwork mounds up in the mountains, which the schoolteacher had told the class were the graves of the Bruttii, the original inhabitants of Calabria. This information had caused general hilarity, since the deletion of the final letter gave a word meaning 'the uglies'. From that moment on, Giorgio's personal motto became *'Sugno brutto e mi 'nde vantu'*: ugly and proud of it.

The resulting structure, however, wasn't ugly at all. Indeed, as it gradually took shape, the stone blocks trimmed, laid and locked together with no visible mortar, Giorgio began to think for the first time that this scheme of Mantega's might actually work. Not that it would be any great loss to him if it didn't. His contact in Vibo Valentia owed him a couple of favours and had offered a very reasonable price for the equipment and wages. And if it did by any chance succeed, then there was no telling what kind of profits might be made on the operation. It was simply a question of what the purchaser wanted, how badly he wanted it and how much he could afford to pay. If Mantega was to be believed – and in cases offering the possibility of personal enrichment, he was – the answer to the last question was 'almost anything'.

Dusk had gathered by the time the walling was completed and the mechanical digger started to dump the rock and gravel excavated earlier into the resulting enclosure. Its claw would inevitably scar some of the stones in a potentially suspicious way, but the constraints of time and security had forced Giorgio to make various assumptions. One of these was that once it became apparent that the supposed tomb had already been opened, the treasure seekers would not bother to dig it out to a depth greater than the five courses of blocks that had been laid, and that they would use mechanical means to do so. Any marks on the rocks removed would therefore be attributed to their own equipment. And if by any chance they took a more painstaking approach, Giorgio had already worked out various ways to hurry them up. The work they imagined they were doing would of course be illegal, so it shouldn't take much to scare them off.

The final phases of the operation were undertaken after dark, lit by the headlights of the various trucks. The remaining stones from the demolished barn were tossed on top of the piled infill, suggesting elements of the vaulted roof which had been removed, then the surface rocks and vegetation were carefully replaced and the entire site cleared and swept by hand. Last of all, the dam of sandbags was removed, allowing the accumulated water to flow over the workings, obliterating the traces of human intervention. The construction convoy then snaked its way around the narrow country roads to the *autostrada* and headed south to their depot. As for Giorgio, he drove the black Jeep back up into the Sila mountains, heading home to his sister's apartment. At the former station of San Nicola, on a windswept plateau fifteen hundred metres above sea level, he pulled off the main road. Cowbells clanked intermittently in the far distance, but there was no other sound. This part of the railway had been abandoned, but the public payphone attached to the station building still worked and there was never anyone there.

Giorgio fed in some money and had started to dial when he heard a noise close behind him. He let the receiver drop and whirled around, his pistol in one hand and his torch in the other. A pair of hallucinogenic eyes stared back at him, a feral black cat out hunting for prey amidst the long grass that had grown up between the rusted rails. After a moment it disregarded him and moved away across the row of sleepers, balks of sun-spliced timber cut from the forests that had once clad this entire region, now aged and weathered like beams of the True Cross.

'*Pronto,*' Mantega's voice squeaked somewhere in the distance. '*Pronto, pronto?*'

Giorgio picked up the receiver.

'Signor Rossi?'

'He's gone out.'

Giorgio hung up and climbed back into the Jeep, well pleased with the way the day had gone. The coded message was to inform Nicola Mantega that the trap was ready. Once it was found and opened – self-evidently for the second time, the contents already looted – then the notary would initiate dealings with the disappointed tomb robbers. They would almost certainly demand to inspect a sample of the supposed treasure before proceeding any further. To guarantee the authenticity of the fakes that would subsequently be offered for purchase, some genuine sample of antique Roman gold work would have to be produced for verification. That was Giorgio's next task, and he had already decided on a way to accomplish it. This involved a kidnapping prospect he had had his eye on for some time, and would be put into effect the very next day.

Having been detained in Rome by work until early evening, Aurelio Zen decided to return to Calabria in the same way that he had arrived, rather than trekking all the way out to Fiumicino to catch a plane and then have to arrange for transport from the airport at the other end. He slept badly this time – possibly as the result of over-indulging at a restaurant near the Viminale, where he had eaten the first decent meal he had had for weeks and the only one in which tomatoes did not feature in any shape or form – and was then deposited at the junction for Cosenza shortly after four in the morning, almost an hour before the first connecting train.

By the time he got back to the city it was too late to go to bed and too early to go to work, so he killed time in the first bar he found open, drinking double espressos laced with a streak of milk, pondering his next move and generally feeling like hell. But the temperature was pleasantly mild and the air clean, with not a trace of the toxic pall that smothered the capital, dense enough to see as well as smell and taste. By the time he arrived at the Questura, he had formulated a suitable response to the demands of his superiors at the Ministry concerning his handling of the murder case which had gripped Italy and also, as they did not fail to remind him, had international implications.

Once in his office, he phoned the magistrate who had been appointed to oversee the investigation of the original presumed kidnapping and who was now so beside himself with delight at finding himself in charge of a gruesome, high-profile homicide that he had given Zen his mobile phone number. After the usual courtesies, Zen explained that he wished to file a request for an arrest warrant on one of the suspects, if the *signor giudice* could find a moment to receive him. The judge judiciously observed that there was no time like the present – or at least in an hour, when he would be at the Palace of Justice. Zen summoned Arnone.

'We're going to take Mantega,' he told his subordinate. 'It's a little sooner than I would ideally have liked, but I was put under a lot of pressure at headquarters yesterday. They badly want something they can feed to the media to show that we're on the job. It will also free up all the people who have been shadowing him. Given the way the situation appears to be evolving, I may well need them for other duties.'

'Very good.'

'Now listen, this is important. I want the arrest to be made as publicly as possible, for instance on the street or while he's at lunch, and I want you to handle it. If you can arrange for reporters and photographers from the local television and press to arrive fortuitously at about the same time, so much the better.'

'*Benissimo, capo.*'

'Oh, by the way, did anything come of that business about Giorgio ordering in a construction team from Vibo Valentia?'

'Following your instructions, an officer was dispatched to the assembly point on the *autostrada* to observe events and take photos, but I haven't debriefed her yet. I'll make enquiries and get back to you.'

'Let's take care of Mantega first. I'm off to get the warrant. After that it's up to you, but bear in mind what I said about it being a high-profile arrest. I want word of this to get around like a forest fire with a gale behind it. Understand?'

On his way out of the building, Zen caught sight of an old woman seated on the long, shiny and very hard bench placed in the entrance hall of the Questura for the use of supplicants seeking an official document or permit for one of the numerous activities for which such papers are mandatory. Zen was about to pass by, but then, recalling what Arnone had told him on the phone the day before, he stopped and went over to her.

'Are you being looked after, *signora*?'

The woman eyed him with an air of determination amounting to defiance. She looked as shrivelled as a raisin and as hard as a nut, and clearly wasn't going to be placated or put off her stride by anyone.

'I want to speak to the chief of police,' she said.

'I am he.'

The woman looked at him again, as if for the first time.

'Yes, I suppose you are,' she conceded grudgingly.

'And who are you, *signora*?'

'*Sono una creatura.* A person. My name is Maria Stefania Arrighi.'

'Ah, yes. You came here yesterday, didn't you?'

She nodded.

'They told me you were away.'

'I was. But why do you want to speak to me? I'm extremely busy this morning. If it's not an urgent matter . . .'

The woman shrugged.

'It may be urgent. It's certainly important. To me, at least.'

Zen weighed this up.

'I won't be free until after lunch, *signora*, but I promise to see you some time today.'

'Then I shall wait.'

'That bench looks very uncomfortable. Let's make an appointment for three o'clock. I'll leave instructions for you to be shown straight up to my office. In the meantime you can do a bit of shopping, have a bite to eat . . .'

His voice tailed away.

'I shall wait here,' the woman said.

It took Zen less than an hour to obtain the arrest warrant, which was well below par for that procedure. As he walked back to the Questura, his mobile rang. It was Lucio, the technician at the police laboratory in Rome whom he had selected to analyse Roberto Calopezzati's DNA sample, and then compare the results with those from the corpse of Pietro Ottavio Calopezzati, a.k.a. Peter Newman.

219

'I'm glad to see that you still have a lot of clout at the Ministry,' Lucio said, 'but next time around would you mind not using it to rough us up? Three of our best people got dragged in to work with me all night on these tests.'

'That's your answer. It wasn't my clout but panic on the top floor. This gaudy little murder, which would normally get buried away on the *Cronaca* pages, is suddenly front-page news. And it's not being handled as one of those condescending "Made in Calabria" stories but as a "What have we come to?" guilt piece. Anyway, do you have a positive result?'

'I wouldn't have phoned otherwise.'

'So there's a definite relationship?'

There was a pause at the other end.

'Between what?'

'For God's sake, Lucio! You may have been up all night, but I haven't had that much sleep either. Between the individual whose DNA sample I gave you yesterday and the other whose DNA profile you also have in your hands.'

'Oh. In that sense, no.'

'What do you mean, no?'

'I mean there is no correspondence at all.'

'But you said the results were positive!'

'Technically, they were. Sometimes matters are not so definitive, depending on the age of the sample, possible contamination and so on. But here there is no doubt whatsoever. The two subjects possess utterly different genetic profiles.'

'There is no possibility that one of them could be the son of the other's sister?'

'Absolutely not. They are quite definitely unrelated by blood in any way.'

There was a long silence.

'That was the result you were expecting, wasn't it?' Lucio put in at last.

It was a stiff test, but Zen rose to the occasion.

'Of course, Lucio! You've confirmed my hypothesis. Many thanks.'

He put the phone down and continued on his way, his eyes blank.

Enough was enough, thought Emanuele Pancrazi, gazing at the rapturous light streaming in through the bedroom window. Emanuele had just turned seventeen, his soul was gaping open like a mussel to filter every last drop of life on offer and only a few days remained before he would have to return home to school and everyday reality. It was time to assert himself.

Thus far, Emanuele had indulged the agenda lovingly crafted and managed by his father. This governed every aspect of their month together, mostly in the form of day trips to churches and castles, long treks in the mountains and painstaking guided tours of the supposed sites of ancient Greek cities which in practice had vanished almost entirely. The day before had been devoted to the dull and seemingly endless badlands of the Marchesato di Crotone, unenlivened as usual by his father's commentary on the historic system of sharecropping on the vast estates which had once covered the entire region, generating equally vast unearned profits for heartless absentee landlords such as the Calopezzati family.

In some dim way, prefiguring a wisdom that he didn't really want just yet, Emanuele realised that his visits to Cosenza were as difficult for his father as they were for him, if not more so. His parents had been separated for ten years, and he had long ago stopped wetting the bed and weeping in corners. He was young and tough and sanely egoistic, but he knew that his mother still suffered from the break-up, not because she missed his dad, as he once had, so badly, but because she felt guilty for the pain that they had both caused him. He had to assume that his father felt the same sense of culpability, and that his gruelling programme of educational experiences was not in fact a deliberate bid to wreck his son's visit but an attempt to provide a regime of constant activity, excluding any possibility of embarrassing hiatuses when the big dark questions that lurked in the background might assert themselves and demand to be addressed.

Nevertheless, the resulting experience was enough to make Emanuele feel as though he was back at school already. That had been just about acceptable when he was ten, or even fourteen, but time had now run out for this means of dealing with an event in the distant past which had changed his life for ever but wasn't really of much interest to him any more. Too bad if his parents couldn't get over it. Emanuele was on holiday in the deep south, almost a thousand kilometres from the apartment in Brescia where he lived with his mother. He wanted to relax, have fun and maybe even get a chance to chat up one of those juicy girls he had glimpsed from time to time through the car window as his father drove him home after another long day at the museum. Enough cultural uplift, enough history lessons. He programmed his mobile phone to ring, faked a brief conversation, then shuffled out to the living area of the spacious apartment facing Piazza del Duomo in the heart of the old city. His father was drinking coffee and consulting a map.

'Ah, Emanuele! I've been thinking about what we should do today. The Sila Piccola seems the obvious answer, with a diversion to Carlópoli to see the ruins of the monastery founded in the twelfth century by the Benedictines and later taken over by the Cistercians. This *complesso monastico* was the religious, economic and cultural centre of the region, its abbot at one time having been the illustrious Giocchino da Fiore, but it was later suppressed and then destroyed in an earthquake shortly after –'

'Actually, dad, a friend of mine from school just called. He's on holiday down here too, staying at a villa down on the beach. He says he's getting a bit bored with the sun and sand bit so he wants to come into Cosenza and have a look around.'

'Who is this boy?'

'Oh, just a friend. Anyway, we've arranged to meet in half an hour. We'll prowl around the streets a bit and then grab a bite to eat somewhere. So you can take the day off.'

'But when will you be back?' demanded his father in an almost panicky tone.

'Depends. I'll call you. Okay, I'd better go and put on some sharp clothes. You know how important personal appearance is down here. Don't want these southerners to get the idea that the rest of us are all slobs!'

Twenty minutes later, Emanuele emerged from the front door of the building and sauntered away down the main street. This initially provoked a moment of indecision in the two men sitting in a van parked outside the eighteenth-century palazzo on Via Giuseppe Campagna. Their instructions were to go to the Pancrazi apartment on the third floor, abduct the son and leave certain brutal verbal instructions with his father Achille, Professor of Ancient History at the local university. Now they faced a quandary.

On the one hand, Giorgio had made it quite clear – in one never-to-be-forgotten instance by a personally administered beating that had ended with his being pulled off the offender just in time – that he wouldn't tolerate his associates exercising any individual initiative in operational matters. On the other, taking the boy while he was alone would involve the two men and their boss in vastly less personal risk should anything go wrong. The normal course of action would have been to report in for further instructions, but the pair had been forbidden to make contact until the mission was complete. After a hasty discussion, they decided to go for it.

Their choice was validated almost immediately. If the kid had carried on the way he had set out, down the sinuous curves of Corso Telesio towards the bridge leading over the Busento river to the broad boulevards of the nineteenth- and twentieth-century city sprawled out below, it might have proved difficult to take him unchallenged. But Emanuele soon became intrigued by the network of alleys leading off to either side of the main street, and wandered away into the warren of mediaeval dwellings which formed an increasingly abandoned slum surrounding the gentrified core of the original centre. One of the two men Giorgio had selected for this job had grown up in just that part of town and knew his way around blindfold. He also knew that, despite his colleague's doubts, their van would fit into the alley that the boy had taken, and that there was an exit at the other end that would have them out of town in minutes, up on the *superstrada* into the mountains.

'We just won the lottery!' he said as they both pulled on their masks.

Tom Newman was seated up front in Nguyen's Mercedes, beside the driver. Nguyen sat alone in the back, furiously silent. The car gave Tom the creeps. It was like a hearse for the living. Maybe it was this thought that sparked his idea when Nicola Mantega rang him. He kept his responses down to the 'I'll be there right away' level. In theory his boss didn't understand Italian, but Tom had already been around Martin Nguyen long enough to know that it would always be dangerous to underestimate exactly how much he understood about anything.

'That was the police, Mr Nguyen,' he said when Mantega hung up. 'They want me to go to central headquarters right now. Some bureaucratic business involving my late father.'

He didn't even get a glance of sympathy in return.

'Get back to the hotel as soon as possible,' was the reply. 'These continuing distractions are a pain in the ass. If they continue, I'll be looking for a new interpreter.'

Tom didn't give a damn. He told the driver to pull over, stepped out into the balmy air and strutted off down the street as happy as a lord. Nicola Mantega wanted to talk to him in his office and then buy him lunch. This was very convenient, because Tom wanted to talk to *il notaio* about the big idea he'd had the evening before when he'd gone out to explore the dreary suburban streets of Rende, feeling lonely and disorientated for the first time since arriving, and in a weak moment had allowed himself to be seduced by an eatery named American's Dream. The brilliantly lit interior vaguely resembled a bad acid flashback to a classic 1950s diner, with grilles and hubcaps from autos of that era arrayed on the walls and a Beach Boys album playing at an unsubtle volume. Tom had ordered a cheeseburger and fries, *insalata Cesare* and a beer. It took twenty minutes to arrive and was horrible. The meat patty was thin and dry, the fries limp and tasteless, the Caesar a soggy mess made with the wrong kind of lettuce, prefabricated croutons and gloopy sauce out of a bottle. The bill came to almost twenty bucks.

Big deal, he'd thought as he retreated to his gaudy, sterile, whorehouse-minus-the-whores hotel. If you travel, you're going to have a bad meal once in a while. But while he was down at the *municipio* that morning, mindlessly offering Martin Nguyen a simplified version of the deputy mayor's pronouncements, so shaded with multiple layers of nuance that they often appeared to be meaningless, Tom had had his idea. The stuff that he had tried to eat the night before had all been simple American dishes that were easy to prepare and in their way delicious – not great cuisine, but satisfying and tasty when they were properly made and you were in the mood for them. And there was evidently a demand or how could the place stay in business?

The problem wasn't the concept, it was the execution. That was Tom's area of expertise, plus over here political correctness hadn't hit the table yet. Imagine being able to use raw egg in the Caesar, grind up nicely marbled chuck and foreshank fresh every day and soften hand-cut fries in pure beef dripping before crisping them at scorch temp. The concept felt solid, and in the changed financial circumstances following his father's decease he might well be able to realise it, but he was going to need insider assistance. There should be enough seed money there once the will was probated, but Tom had already been in Italy long enough to know that money was not enough for what he had in mind. You couldn't just rent a storefront property, kit it out with the necessary, turn on the neon sign and open the door for business. You needed some official paper or stamp to do almost anything – they even had one called the *certificato di esistenza in vita*, which officially affirmed that you were still alive, or at least had been when you applied for it – and while these were in theory available to any suitably qualified applicant on a first-come first-served basis, in practice the system didn't work quite like that. If you wanted results, above all if you wanted them fast, you needed a fixer who could cut corners and get the job done. Nicola Mantega was a perfect match.

Outside the building that housed Mantega's office, Tom noticed the stunning woman he had spoken to briefly at a café a couple of days ago and never heard from since. She was leaning up against some sort of maintenance truck, wearing a much more sluttish outfit than the last time, although she brought it off really well, and chatting animatedly to some handsome fuck in company overalls. Tom almost walked on, but then decided that if he was to make it in this town, he mustn't duck the first challenge that came along.

'*Salve!*' he shouted in the loud but unaggressive manner of the local people his age.

The woman looked at him blankly, then seemed to fake a smile.

'*Buon giorno.*'

She seemed preoccupied and made no move to approach him. An interesting person, thought Tom, and possibly some interest on her part too, but a lot else besides. A complex situation, in short, and not without a certain promise. He strolled over to where she was standing beside the electrician or whoever he was. God, she had fabulous eyes! Huge olive-green ovals filled with an intense but indefinable expression, like the women portrayed on Greek vases.

'You didn't call me,' he said.

'No.'

That didn't seem to leave Tom much to say, so after a long and meaningful look he turned and walked into the office building.

Given Mantega's reputation, he had expected his business premises to have an air of discreet luxury, with lots of potted plants and a brittle, babe-aceous receptionist displaying her cleavage and her boss's status. In the event it looked more like the back room of a failing used-car dealership, but Mantega's welcome couldn't have been more effusive.

'Tom, my friend! What terrible news about your father! I am devastated, destroyed, deranged! To think that this unspeakable crime should have happened here, and that I –'

Tom gestured negatively with his hand.

'I'd prefer not to speak of that just now.'

Mantega effortlessly flexed his features from a tragic mask to the devotional image of a saint's sorrowful but benign regard.

'Of course, of course! Tactless of me. I cannot apologise enough. Please sit down.'

He waved at a lime-green plastic bucket chair with stainless steel legs that had somehow survived, tawdrily intact, from the 1970s.

'You said you wanted to discuss something before we go to lunch,' Tom began. 'There's also something I want to ask you, but that can wait.'

'Yes, as it happens, there is something on my mind, something which would perhaps be better discussed in a secure environment. It's a rather delicate matter, if you take my meaning, but I see no reason why the two of us, working together, shouldn't be able to reach a mutually advantageous agreement.'

'About what?'

'Well, it concerns this American who arrived a few days ago.'

'Martin Nguyen?'

'I understand that you are working for him.'

Mantega laughed roguishly.

'Strictly illegal, you know! Non-EU citizens are not permitted to work here without signing their lives away after months of pleading with half a dozen different heads of the bureaucratic hydra for the right to do so. After all, you're taking bread out of the mouths of all our own poor Italian translators. I really ought to report you to the authorities!'

'What about my father? He was working here, before . . .'

Mantega instantly became solemn again.

'I managed to facilitate that on the basis that the work involved was of limited duration and scope and so *straordinario* that it could not be undertaken by anyone else. Your case is different. However, we'll overlook that.'

'I imagine that happens quite a bit here,' observed Tom.

'Of course, of course,' Mantega returned complacently. 'Otherwise we'd all be strangled by red tape and nothing would ever get done. Don't worry, your secret's safe with me. I won't breathe a word.'

Tom gave a guarded nod.

'So you want to reach an agreement with me concerning Signor Nguyen?'

'It's more to do with the people he is representing. You told me that under pretence of preparing to make a film here, they were in fact searching for the tomb of Alaric. As I told you yesterday, many others have tried in vain to locate that fabled hoard of treasure, and it may very well be that the latest arrivals will have no more luck. On the other hand, they no doubt have vastly superior technology at their disposal, so we can't rule out such a possibility. My point is this: if they do find the tomb, I need to know.'

'Why?'

Mantega raised his chin and looked at Tom with the air of someone doing his best to express an emotion he has read about but never experienced.

'Because I am a patriot,' he declared quietly. 'Not an Italian patriot, although I consider myself to be both an Italian and a European, in that order. But first and foremost I am a Calabrian!'

He bent forward and grasped Tom's arm so tightly it hurt.

'And so are you, my friend, despite your American passport. In our hearts, we are both Calabrians.'

Tom was by now feeling uncomfortable in all sorts of ways.

'What has all this to do with Rapture Works?' he replied.

'It's very simple. *La tomba d'Alarico* is a Calabrian heritage site of inestimable archaeological value which must contain a collection of priceless artefacts beside which even the Riace bronzes would pale in comparison. Now then, supposing your employers do find it, what are their intentions?'

'I have no idea.'

'Precisely. Of course, they may simply wish to have the glory of having made the discovery, and having done so will turn over future exploitation of the site to the appropriate authorities. In that case, I would have no quarrel with them. With a fat grant from Rome and the EU, we could build a superb extension to the Museo Civico in which to accommodate these treasures. People will fly in from all over the world to view them, bringing fame and prosperity to the city and the region. We might even consent to send some of them off to London, Paris and New York as one of those travelling museum shows you have to book tickets to get into. "The Treasures of the Tomb!" All well and good.'

His face darkened.

'But let us suppose that their intentions are different. Whoever is behind this search has clearly spent a lot of money, and may well be motivated by the prospect of financial gain. The treasure obviously couldn't be traded on the open market, but it wouldn't be impossible to locate some Russian billionaire who would pay almost anything to be in possession of such items. Then again, it might end up being scrapped for the intrinsic value of the gold and the precious stones, as has tragically happened so often in the past, thereby destroying this unique and irreplaceable archive of our mutual heritage. The fact is that we simply don't know what may happen in the event of this illegal search proving successful. I am therefore appealing to you, my friend, to inform me if that happens. Just phone me, at any hour of the day or night, and say, "The package has arrived." We'll then arrange a meeting at which you can give me the details. So tell me, Tommaso, are you prepared to perform your duty to the *madrepatria*?'

'Well . . . yes. I mean, I suppose so.'

'Wonderful! Now let's go to lunch, and then you can tell me what you want in return. There's a place just round the corner where I'm a regular.'

Tom had half-hoped that the brunette would still be outside the building, but there was no sign of her. They turned left into a side-street and entered a restaurant which kept such a low profile that Tom supposed that all the clientele must be regulars. This theory appeared to be supported by the number of people who greeted or were greeted by Nicola Mantega as he led the way to their table.

'So what can I do for you?' the older man said after rattling off some orders to the waiter in dialect.

'Well, Signor Mantega –'

'Call me Nicola.'

'The thing is this. I really like it here and I want to be able to stay, only not as a tourist. So I'd have to get one of those work permits. That would be one thing I'd need you for.'

Mantega appeared admirably unperturbed.

'What kind of work do you have in mind?'

Tom smiled bashfully.

'Well, this may sound like a crazy idea, but I think it just might work. I can't remember if I told you this, but I'm a trained chef. I've worked in a number of famous restaurants in New York and I've picked up a pretty good idea of how the business operates. So my idea is to open a place here, only – and this is maybe where it sounds a bit crazy – it would be an American restaurant. The idea would be to serve steaks, ribs, burgers, salads –'

He broke off, realising that Mantega wasn't listening. For a moment Tom was offended, then he noticed the general silence. All the other customers in the crowded restaurant had stopped talking and were gazing at something behind them. Turning, he saw a police officer in uniform accompanied by two others wearing combat fatigues and carrying machine guns. The trio walked down the aisle and stopped at their table.

'Nicola Mantega?' the officer asked.

'Yes.'

'You are under arrest. Come with us.'

For some reason, Tom expected Mantega to make a fuss, but he evidently understood and accepted the rules of the game.

'I'm so sorry about this nonsense,' he told Tom as he got up. 'Don't worry about the bill. It will all be taken care of.'

Three o'clock, the police chief had said. There was no clock on the wall, Maria didn't own a watch and she certainly wasn't going to stoop to asking the unmannerly lout manning the desk, who had been spying on her with a hard look and a contemptuous smirk throughout the many hours she had spent there. She rolled up the paper wrappings in which she had brought her frugal lunch and stuffed them back into her bag.

At least it didn't appear that she had been followed. This had been the aspect of returning a second day that had preoccupied her most. The family had of course made their usual futile fuss, but Maria had told them that the doctor she needed to see in order to get the new arthritis medicine had not been available the day before, so she was going to return and try again. This time her son had insisted on driving her, and in the end she'd given in. She wouldn't let him park outside the clinic and wait for her, though, claiming that it might well take hours. After she had assured herself that he had driven away, she had followed much the same routine as on the previous day, but using a different set of buses around the city centre before finally completing her journey to the Questura on foot, with many detours and false starts. One thing about living in a mountain village was that it kept you agile. Despite her seventy-eight years, Maria could still put on a better turn of speed than most of these languid city dwellers, and she hadn't noticed anyone hurrying to keep up with her.

In short, it seemed that her elaborate precautions had all been for nothing. Most likely her journey would prove to be too, even supposing that the police chief kept his word. Probably nothing that she had to tell him would seem relevant to what was happening now. It was, after all, ancient history, like the war itself. Bad things had happened but most people had survived, as they always did, and since then the world had moved on. 'You're living in the past, *nonna*!' was one of her daughter-in-law's favourite taunts. Maria knew that was true, but she couldn't help it. Where else was she to live? There was no other environment that would support virtually extinct life forms such as her own. But in the course of the time she had spent waiting yesterday and again today, she had finally worked out what she would tell this Aurelio Zen. It was a mixture of truth and falsehoods, but the falsehoods were of no concern except to the dead.

A clacking of heels presaged the appearance of a uniformed officer, who checked Maria's identity card and then told her that the chief of police was ready to receive her. They went up two flights in a lift and then down a long corridor into a smart modern office, the sort you saw on television, with incredibly brilliant bulbs embedded in the ceiling like so many tiny suns in heaven and furnishings that clearly hadn't been made either by or for human beings. The air was stuffy and blue with smoke, but Maria didn't mind. Her late husband had been a heavy smoker, which was why he was now late, and she still enjoyed the smell.

The chief of police rose politely as she entered, invited her to be seated and told her escort to leave. He was a handsome man with the appearance of a certain kind of priest: tall, lean, of indeterminate age, his aquiline features superficially severe but suggesting a basic bent towards such kindness and indulgence as he might be able to reconcile with the strict rules of his calling. Had she been fifty years younger, Maria would have fallen for him in a moment. As it was, she wanted to mother him, so utterly exhausted and depressed did he look, as though holding himself together only by a stubborn act of will, a quality she herself possessed and admired in others. For a moment she almost felt ashamed to be adding to his problems by demanding this audience. Then she reminded herself of their relative positions on the scale of power and hardened her heart.

'This has been a very busy day, *signora*,' Zen said crisply. 'I fear I can only spare you a few minutes. Unless, of course, what you have to tell me is of quite extraordinary value and relevance.'

Maria felt herself rising to the challenge thus presented.

'It is both.'

Zen unclasped his hands in a brief prayer-like gesture, implying that he would be the judge of that.

'Please proceed.'

'What I have to say concerns the man found dead up in the old town. On the television the other day, you said that he was a member of the Calopezzati family. That is untrue.'

Zen's gradually hardening stare seemed to indicate that Maria had already demonstrated the first of the two qualities he had named as essential to retain his interest.

'Have you any evidence to support this assertion?'

'I was there when it happened.'

The police chief said nothing, just sat there staring at her with those fascinating, implacable eyes. Not a priest, she thought, an inquisitor.

'It was just before the war ended. I was then in service at *la bastiglia* in the old town. Only in a lowly position, you understand. Washing and ironing the bed linen, dusting, sweeping and cleaning. The Calopezzati's personal attendants were all unmarried sons and daughters of impoverished local gentry, another class of people altogether. They treated us even worse than the baron, to speak the truth. Anyway, my family put me out to service, like I said, and it was hard, particularly at first. I knew they had to do it, because there were too many of us at home, but it was still hard.'

Zen laid his head in his hands and rubbed his eyes.

'*Mi scusate, signore,*' said Maria, scared. 'Here I am rambling on . . .'

Zen looked up at her with a bleary smile and then said something that utterly melted her heart.

'No, you must excuse me. It's just that I'm very tired. Talk as much as you want. If I may say so, you have a lovely voice. Like fish.'

'Fish?'

'Succulent, but with a strong backbone. I'm Venetian, and it was intended as a compliment. My time is no longer of any account. Just tell me, in your own words, whatever it is that you have come to say.'

Dear God, she thought, where were you when I wanted babies? It took a moment to compose herself and remember the story that she had decided to tell.

'I was lonely and frightened. I made friends with one of the other skivvies in that cold sepulchre, where in the first few months I sometimes got lost amongst all the corridors and stairs. Her name was Caterina Intrieri. I was fifteen years old, she was eighteen. After that we looked after each other. It made life a little easier for both of us. And then one day in the week after Pentecost, Caterina told me that she was with child. She wouldn't say who the father was. As far as I know, she told no one else but a *levatrice*, a wise woman who said that she would be brought to bed about Christmas. And so she would have, except for what happened.'

Maria clasped the battered bag she held on her knees like a chicken she was bringing to market and now feared might escape.

'What did happen?' prompted Zen.

'Caterina died, but the child survived and was taken by *la baronessa* as her own. What with the war and the constant changes of government, life was chaotic in those days. No one knew who was in charge, no one cared for anything but their own survival. With an unknown father and a dead mother, it was easy for

Signora Ottavia to claim Caterina's child as her own and have it registered with the authorities as Pietro Ottavio Calopezzati.'

'How did the boy's mother die?'

'In the usual way.'

'In childbirth?'

Maria did not respond to this question.

'The baby was given to a wet-nurse in Camigliatello,' she said. 'He was with her when the fire broke out.'

Zen coughed and then lit a cigarette.

'Tell me, what was it like, *la bastiglia*? I've never seen a photograph or a sketch. What did it look like? How did it strike the eye?'

Maria tried to remember. This was not a question she had expected to be asked, or even the same kind of question. But she was talking to the chief of police for the entire province. She wasn't sure of the answer, but she couldn't just sit there and say nothing. It was like being back in school.

'There were many storeys,' she began. 'Four in all, not counting the underground. But we were only allowed to visit three of them. The *piano nobile* on the first floor was only for the family and their personal attendants.'

'What else do you remember about it?' asked Zen sleepily.

There was a long silence.

'I remember the way the façade changed, depending on the time of day.'

'Go on.'

'It looked like something that had come from the heavens and been stuck down here like the heel of a boot. It faced west, so in the morning it was a blank wall, only with all those windows, like some insect's eyes! During the day, it was just there. At sunset all the windows gleamed and glinted red, and at night under the full moon it looked like a ghost with its arms raised up to scare you.'

Zen smiled faintly.

'What a pity it burned down. How did that come about, by the way?'

Maria preferred to lie as little as possible, but she had to see the matter through.

'It was a dark and stormy night. The most violent thunderstorm that's ever been seen in these parts. *La bastiglia* was by far the tallest building up in the old town. It was struck several times. Many fires broke out all at once. We servants did what we could, but all water had to be fetched one bucket at a time from the deep well that supplied the palace. It was a hopeless task.'

'And Ottavia Calopezzati was unable to escape in time?'

Maria nodded. Stunned by a blow from a fire-iron whilst she was sleeping and then trussed like a chicken with baling twine, the murderess had indeed been unable to escape the flames.

'So what became of her adopted child?'

'I have no idea. After the fire, the household broke up and returned to their families, if they could find them. As I said, everyone was looking out for themselves.'

Now the police chief seemed to be suffering from a headache, no doubt brought on by overwork. He leant forward, scowling, and pinched the bridge of his nose.

'I wonder how relevant all this is, *signora*. The motive for this murder is still unclear. Kidnappings go wrong for all kinds of reasons. For example, the victim may see or overhear something which would make his release perilous for the gang at any price. The question of whether or not he was the son of someone called Caterina Intrieri seems moot, to say the least.'

'No,' said Maria firmly. 'He was killed because they thought he was a Calopezzati, but they were wrong.'

'Who are "they"?'

'I don't know.'

'Then how can you know what they may or may not have thought?'

'I'm just telling you what everyone says.'

'Everyone is of no use to me. What I need is someone, a specific individual prepared to come forward and identify those responsible for this crime and for the atrocities that happened in your own town shortly afterwards. I had hoped that you might be that someone, *signora*. Why else would you have come here yesterday, and again today, and spent hours on end waiting to see me?'

'I wanted justice for Caterina. Her only child has been killed because it was tainted with the name of the family that made her life a misery, and the lives of everyone who lived around here then, if you could call it living.'

Zen glanced at his watch.

'Is that all you have to say?'

'It's all I know,' Maria replied stubbornly.

'I don't believe that for a moment, but I don't intend to press you. However, I may need to get in touch at some point in the future. Doing so in the normal way might cause difficulties for your family. Do you understand my meaning?'

Maria got a pen and a used bus ticket out of her handbag, wrote down a telephone number in large, plump numerals and handed the ticket to Zen.

'Call this number. If someone else answers, tell them that you work at the hospital and need to speak to me about the results of those tests I had. They'll fetch me and then we can talk.'

Zen stood up to indicate that the interview was over.

'You're an interesting person, Maria,' he said, using her name for the first time. 'What you've said is extremely interesting. What you haven't said might well be more interesting still. Do you know someone called Giorgio?'

Maria almost faltered then, dazzled by the feints setting up the knockout punch. But she too could hold herself together by sheer willpower.

'It's a very common name,' she replied.

The chief of police seemed to acknowledge her fortitude with an ironic smile.

'Excessively common, I'm inclined to think. The world would be a better place if there were fewer Giorgios in it. Or at least one fewer. I wish you a safe and speedy journey home.'

Since his son had made his own arrangements for the day, Professor Achille Pancrazi spent the afternoon working on a rather tricky review of a book by a former colleague at the University of Padua. He had initially been slightly taken aback by Emanuele's announcement that he was going to spend the day with an unnamed school friend, largely because even after years of separation he still lived in fear of his ex-wife and knew that he would be held to account if anything went wrong. But of course nothing would, and frankly an interval of free time in these welcome but somewhat tiring visits was always welcome.

Needless to say, he hadn't bothered to read Fraschetti's latest effusion. He was familiar with both the subject and the author, so a perusal of the introduction and table of contents sufficed as far as content went. As for style, a brief skim of a few paragraphs taken at random was enough to show that his rival's love affair with the jargon of the trade was by no means over. He was particularly amused by the constant references to 'desire', given that he knew for a fact that Fraschetti had never desired anyone of either sex in his life. But Pancrazi's real problem was how to pitch his critical response, which would be published in the *Cultura* insert of a national newspaper and read by just about everyone in the scholarly world for whom the subject matter was relevant. In other words, it wasn't so much a question of how he wanted to make his eminent – but well past his peak, despite his current fame – colleague look, but of how he wanted it to make *him* look. If he sounded too negative, then charges of professional envy could and would be brought, and not without a certain justification.

From way back in their far-off days together at Padua, Pancrazi had always considered Fraschetti his intellectual inferior. He didn't gloat about this any more than he did about the fact that he was the taller of the two, but in the event it was he who'd had to move all the way down the boot to the University of bloody Cosenza to get his professorship while Fraschetti had landed the post in Turin that they'd both applied for, and then gone on to be a media don into the bargain. And why? Because the half-smart bastard had more connections than a telephone exchange, plus a superficial talent for memorable soundbites and an easy-to-grasp high concept, in this case the idea that the early Romans, far from having any sense of manifest destiny or even a coherent culture, had simply muddled along from year to year, the results being cleaned up much later by Livy and others into a neat corporate history for imperial PR purposes.

Achille Pancrazi had written and revised four drafts of his review and was just starting a fifth, in a marginally more nuanced tone, when his phone rang. The screen showed that the caller was his son.

Despite the interruption, he answered with genuine pleasure.

'*Ciao, Manuele!*'

Emanuele, on the other hand, sounded preoccupied.

'There's something I want to show you, dad. Can you come right now?'

'Come where?'

'To the chapel of Santa Caterina on the back road to Mendicino.'

'Are you there now? I thought you and your friend were spending the day in town. Does he have a car?'

'Don't ask any more questions, dad, just come. Please!'

By now, Emanuele sounded desperate. Pancrazi considered that he knew the territory around Cosenza 'tolerably well', as he would have put it, but he was not familiar with that particular chapel, probably some devotional shrine of strictly local interest and no architectural merit. He had once joked to a colleague whose subject was the Early Modern period that he himself suffered from a professional version of Alzheimer's symptoms. 'I can remember the smallest details of everything that happened up to the fall of Constantinople, but the last five hundred years are just a blur.' What on earth could Emanuele and his friend have found there in such a place to justify his driving out there 'right now'? It was charming and flattering that they had even bothered to include him and his interests in their laddish day out together, but the whole thing still didn't quite make sense.

The evening rush hour was in full swing and it took him almost forty minutes to reach the rendezvous. It was a small building, squat and mean, set off beside the road in the middle of nowhere, not a house in sight. There was no sign of another vehicle either, which meant that there had either been a mistake about the location of the rendezvous or the two young men had got tired of waiting. Achille decided to take a look inside anyway, if the door was unlocked. It was. The interior was no improvement on the thinly plastered rough stone outside, a cramped space with a few rows of pews set before a small altar. The few ex votos about were old and illegible and the air smelt musty. The place was obviously no longer used on any regular basis. He was about to turn back when the door slammed shut behind him.

'Don't turn round, *professò*,' said a voice. 'Sit down facing the altar. Keep your hands in view at all times.'

A harsh laugh.

'Clasped in prayer, if you like.'

Achille Pancrazi knew immediately what had happened, but his first thought was for himself. God almighty, what would Reginella say when she heard? She had always despised and hated southerners, to the extent of initially refusing to allow her son to visit his father in Calabria. Achille and Emanuele had joined forces on that issue once he became old enough to take a stand on his rights and responsibilities, and they had prevailed, mocking her irrational fears, telling her that everything was different now, that it was time to wake up and stop behaving like a typical paranoid northern racist. They'd prevailed at the time, but now Reginella would exact a terrible revenge.

And why on earth was this happening to someone like him anyway? He knew that the gangs sometimes took relatively small fry, pharmacists or accountants, to keep their earnings up on a percentage basis, but it had never occurred to him that he might be on their list. All right, he was a university professor, but the pay was miserable even before the outrageous sums withheld under the divorce settlement that his ex-wife's butch lesbian lawyer had imposed. Just look at my bank statements, he felt like saying. I may have an impressive-sounding title, but the truth is that I'm just scraping by.

'It's not about money,' the man said, as though he had been reading Achille's thoughts. 'Just a little professional help. Things you can arrange quite easily and will cost you nothing but a little time. In return, I personally guarantee as a man of honour that you will get your son back, safe and unharmed.'

'When?'

'Once you have done what we ask.'

'Yes, of course, only . . . You see, he's due back at the weekend.'

'Back where?'

'To his mother. She'll kill me if he's still missing when she finds out what's happened.'

The man laughed again.

'Maybe we should have taken her as well!'

'Could you do that?' Achille found himself asking.

'I'm not interested in your domestic problems. But it's essential to our agreement that it remains private. If you or your wife or anyone else informs the authorities, then Emanuele will be returned to you one piece at a time, wrapped in plastic food bags. Do you understand?'

'I understand.'

'When we wish to contact you, we shall call your home number on your son's mobile. If I suspect that either number is being monitored by the police, out come the skinning and butchering knives. The same if you fail to follow our instructions to the letter and on time. Are you still following me?'

The man's patronising tone made Pancrazi really angry for the first time.

'I'm not stupid, you know!'

'I hope not. What we want is some old Roman treasure.'

'Treasure?' breathed Pancrazi faintly.

'Gold cups, diamond jewellery, what do I know? But it has to be genuine, the real thing, good enough to pass examination by an expert.'

'What period are we talking about here? Late republic? Early empire?'

'How the fuck should I know?' the man shouted.

'Of course,' murmured Pancrazi mildly. 'Not your area of competence.'

There followed a silence so long that Pancrazi began to think that the man had left as silently as he arrived, until he spoke again.

'Alaric.'

'What about him?'

'When did he live?'

'Late fourth to early fifth century, roughly. The exact dates are a matter of some dispute, but a recent paper by Schöndorf suggests that –'

'Okay, the stuff has to be older than that.'

'And where am I supposed to get it?'

'Not my problem, *professò*. But that's what you teach, isn't it? What you profess. The people who run the museums must give you a chance to handle the merchandise once in a while. Well, take that chance, use your wits and wait for me to call.'

'Then what happens?'

'We borrow the sample for a few days, then return it to you and you take it back to wherever you got it.'

'What guarantee do I have that you'll return it?'

The man laughed once more.

'None whatever. But if you don't deliver within the next forty-eight hours, your son will be returned to you in convenient bite-sized chunks. Simmer slowly in a good tomato sauce and you'll have yourself a meal. You might want to invite your ex-wife. There'll be plenty.'

Except for the looming presence of Natale Arnone, in full uniform and fingering the automatic pistol in the white holster attached to the diagonal strap across his ample chest, the scene of Zen's first interview with Nicola Mantega was identical to that of the previous one with Maria. The atmosphere, however, could not have been more different. The two principals had both removed their ties and unbuttoned their shirts. The air was a broth of smoke, spent breath and body odours, seasoned with fear.

'You've been a silly boy, Mantega,' Zen said quietly. 'It goes without saying that you're a total waste of space from a moral and legal point of view, but I have to deal with that every day in my job and by now I'm hardened to it. What I can't tolerate is sheer carelessness, perhaps because it calls into question my own reason for living. Evil is one thing, but a drunk driver who persistently takes blind corners on the wrong side of the road disturbs me.'

Mantega sat hunched in his chair like a resilient stuffed toy. He knew how this game was played. Zen gestured to Arnone.

'Again.'

The young inspector crossed the room to the bank of

electronic equipment and pressed a button. Mantega's voice issued from the loudspeakers attached to the computer terminal on Zen's desk, the recording of the call he had made on Tom Newman's mobile to the house in San Giovanni in Fiore where Giorgio's calls were received.

'You crazy bastard! What do you think you're doing? Newman's son just told me that his father's dead. Well, that's the end of it as far as I'm concerned! I trusted you, Giorgio, and now I feel betrayed. It's all very well for you, lying low with your friends out of harm's way. I'm the one the cops are going to put through the mincer. If they do, and I still haven't heard from you, I'll tell them everything I know. Names, numbers, dates, times, places, the lot! And don't think you can blackmail me with that video. That was about a kidnapping. This is manslaughter at the very least, and probably murder. I had nothing to do with that and I'm sure as hell not taking the blame. I don't owe you anything and I shall take all necessary measures to protect my own position, so get in touch by tomorrow at the latest. If you don't, all bets are off, and you'll find out just what I'm –'

Aurelio Zen came to stand directly over Nicola Mantega.

'So did he?'

Realising that silence and inertia would no longer do, that a move was required, Mantega glanced up at Zen with an expression of polite confusion.

'Did who do what?'

'Did Giorgio get in touch with you?'

'No.'

'I'm not surprised,' Zen commented. 'Giorgio is certainly evil and possibly mad, but he isn't stupid and doesn't want to be associated with imbeciles. And who shall blame him?'

Mantega hung his head and stayed silent.

'All right,' sighed Zen. 'As you so aptly put it, all bets are now off.'

'I have a right to legal representation.'

'You are a lawyer, Signor Mantega. Were, rather, as a result of that spectacular bit of silliness nine years ago, but no doubt the old skills are still there.'

'I want an independent witness present to represent my interests and to report any illegal pressure on your part. If you deny me my legal rights, the judges will throw the case out.'

Zen laughed flirtatiously.

'Who said anything about judges, Nicola? I'm not intending to waste the court's valuable time on a sleazy little go-between. Try and get it through your thick skull that this isn't all about you! The investigating magistrate is only interested in the men who kidnapped and murdered Peter Newman, and my only interest in you is as a link to them. You know who they are and quite possibly where. My instructions are to find a way to make you communicate that information.'

Zen turned away and gazed out of the window at the helicopter that had been tormenting the city for days.

'Arnone,' he murmured.

'Yes, sir?'

'At some point in the proceedings, I foresee that Signor Mantega may attempt to resist arrest and will have to be forcibly restrained.'

'I understand.'

Zen turned. Nicola Mantega had hunkered down again, preparing himself for the long haul ahead.

'What was the video you mentioned in your phone call?' Zen asked. 'The one you advised Giorgio not to try and blackmail you with.'

There was no reply. Zen clapped his hands loudly.

'All right, take him down and turn him over to Corti and Caricato. They are to begin conventionally, but step up the pressure if there's no valuable product after a couple of hours. Set up a shift rota for the night. No sleep for our guest, naturally. I may take a turn myself later on, depending on how things go.'

Martin Nguyen was hiding in his room. That wasn't how he'd put it to the front desk staff, of course. He'd told them that he would be teleconferencing until further notice and mustn't on any account be disturbed, but the truth was that he was hiding. He lay swathed in a robe of Thai silk on the brutally unyielding bed, wondering how he could have got it so wrong about these people. He'd assumed that on average Italians were about as dumb, lazy and street-level criminal as a certain racially challenged segment of the US population, only with better cuisine and cuter noses. He'd been prepared for that. What he hadn't been prepared for was to find them just as sharp and sophisticated as himself, if not more so.

It was just possible that this was the worst day that he'd ever had – apart from his childhood, which was *hors concours* in that respect. It had started with a disastrous meeting with the deputy mayor of Cosenza and two of his advisers at city hall. Panicked by the outcome, he had called Jake to consult, forgetting that it was the middle of the night over there, and then on top of everything else his fucking interpreter had gone off shift. At the same time, from a professional point of view Martin couldn't help appreciating the precise manner in which he had been shafted. He liked to think of himself as a top pro, able to take it and dish it out with the best of them, but he had to admit that on this occasion he'd been outplayed.

The Italians had home advantage, of course, but their game had been damn near perfect. After the curt, peremptory phone call the day before, summoning him to the meeting, Martin had expected a hostile reception. Nothing of the sort! He had been shown into an impressive and comfortable suite, offered coffee and even an alcoholic liqueur – something that would have caused a scandal resulting in instant dismissal had they been elected officials back in the States – and then plied with polite enquiries as to how he was enjoying his stay in Cosenza, and suggestions of pleasurable ways in which he might spend his spare time.

Once they got down to business, however, it became clear that he wasn't going to have much spare time. The tone might have been different from the brusque telephone call but the content remained the same: the permits which had been granted to the movie company to carry out low-level helicopter operations in the area were due to expire in a couple of days, and following Luciano Aldobrandini's public repudiation of the project and his statements casting doubt upon its viability, it would be impossible for the city to renew them without convincing evidence that the film was indeed going ahead and that the flights in question were essential to its production.

Martin had done the best he could under the circumstances. He had attempted – with some success, he thought – to get across the enormous difficulties of working with a proud, volatile genius such as Aldobrandini notoriously was. The slightest misunderstanding was perceived as a personal insult, a temporary setback regarded as a deliberate attempt by mean-minded businessmen who thought only of money to sabotage a great artist's crowning masterwork. There had indeed been a regrettable series of minor hitches resulting from the kidnapping of the company's representative Peter Newman, although he hoped the mayor appreciated that no attempt had been made to leverage this horrendous crime in a way that might have brought unwelcome publicity to the region. It had taken a few days to assemble an alternative leadership team, but now that it was in place all problems would shortly be resolved. He therefore hoped that a temporary extension to the flight permits might be granted, pending such a resolution.

It was a good pitch, if he did think so himself, but for all their exquisite civility and perfect manners, the opposition hadn't bought it. They explained that while they quite understood the dilemma in which Signor Nguyen found himself, they too, alas, were under pressure from sources located at various levels of the provincial, regional and even national government, sources whose continuing goodwill was a prerequisite for the successful outcome of many aspects of the city council's daily work. They must therefore reluctantly inform him that the expiration date of the permits in question would apply, unless and until a demonstrable commitment to the film project, backed by a suitable retraction from its prestigious celebrity director, was forthcoming. Thank you so much for coming, *signore*, a pleasure to have met you, *buona sera*, *arrivederla* and don't let the door hit you in the ass on your way out.

Martin hated feeling powerless, incompetent and outclassed, and hated still more others seeing him that way, but after a couple of hours hunkered down in his room he forced himself downstairs, both to avoid cabin fever and to prove that he still had it in the nuts. The open-plan bar and restaurant area was a classy venue, if you liked glittering mirror tiles, modernistic chandeliers made of concentric rings of clear plastic, lime-green walls, curved-back leatherette chairs in a deeper shade of the same colour, and tasteful classics like *Elvira Madigan* and the Barber weepie for strings subliminally audible throughout. His father's old pal President Van Thieu would have felt right at home, although he would have had the waiting staff shot after a lengthy and intensive Q&A with Nguyen senior.

When Martin finally got his drink, it was at least a good pour, and after negotiations with the bartender, he was brought a silver champagne bucket filled with slivers of slush to ice it down. Jake would be up by now. He wondered whether to call in with a progress report, but the only progress to date had been backwards. Still, the idea reminded him that he'd turned his mobile phone off when he retreated to his room. When he flipped it on again, there was a message from the Aeroscan guy asking him to call back. Martin sighed and took a long swig of his slurpee. Another slew of feeble excuses and hollow promises, he thought. But, as so many times that day, he was wrong.

'Keep it brief, Larson,' he rapped. 'I'm on hold in a three-way conference call.'

'Gee, I'm sorry, Mr Nguyen. I just thought I should let you know that we've found it.'

'Found what?'

'The data indicate a circular, non-ferrous structure approximately nine and a half metres in diameter buried a metre or so below the river rock up in the Busento valley about five kilometres south of the city. I guess it could have been a fish pool or a reservoir or something, but it's unquestionably man-made and very solidly constructed.'

Martin finished the rest of his drink in one.

'Get over here,' he told Larson. 'I want large-scale maps of the area and a full report.'

Back in his room, he called home over an encrypted Skype internet connection. It was twenty after noon where Jake was, which turned out to be his personal gym.

'Zup?' Jake said, gasping like a landed fish.

Martin let him sweat his heart rate down a few beats without an answer. He was no longer powerless and humiliated, and in no hurry to spread the excellent word.

'That exec jet you have on hold?' he said finally. 'What's the lead time on that baby?'

'Couple of hours? More, maybe. It's like in Fresno.'

'Get it warmed up, Jake.'

There was a pleased laugh the other end.

'How come?'

'The Aeroscan rep is swinging by momentarily to report in depth, but from what he just said on the phone it looks like we just struck gold. Literally.'

'Awesome!'

'How soon can you be here?'

'The leasing outfit said ten, eleven hours? What time do you have there?'

'Nine twenty-three.'

'In the morning?'

'In the evening.'

'Really?'

'Don't worry about that. Just get here as soon as you can. Call me from the plane when you're an hour out and I'll come meet you. It'll be good whatever because we can't move until after dark. Meanwhile I'll chase up our Iraqi expendables and get busy renting the machinery we'll need.'

A sudden thought struck him.

'Hey, Jake? You have got a passport, haven't you?'

'A password?'

'No, a passport. You know, a little blue booklet issued by the Feds with your name and picture inside? You'll need one when you arrive.'

'Bullshit. You just show them your driver's licence. I've been all over. Canada, Mexico –'

'That's just the attic and the basement, Jake. This is a different house. Believe me, you need a passport to get in.'

'Okay, I'll buy one online and have it overnighted.'

'The process doesn't work like that. It takes weeks.'

'Fuck, that's so totally twentieth century.'

'Yeah, but listen. Remember a couple years back you visited with Paul on that Caribbean island he owns a chunk of?'

'So?'

'So you had a passport then which will still be valid. And another thing. The candlestick you mentioned? I'm guessing that you'll want to export it. Could you give me a little more detail about the payload so I can start figuring out the logistics? Weight, dimensions, packaging requirements . . .'

'Not off the top of my head. It's like the Jewish national logo, only the real thing is solid gold. Let me get showered off and I'll shoot you an email attachment. Hey, this is great news, Martin! Maybe you deserve a bonus.'

'Maybe I do.'

Martin Nguyen sat back, a smile growing on his thin lips. It was not a pleasant smile, although Martin was in fact pleased. He Googled around a bit, then got on to eBay and typed 'temple menorah' in the Search box.

Nicola Mantega cracked shortly after four o'clock in the morning. It wasn't so much what the interrogators had done to him physically as their crushingly contemptuous, mean-spirited attitude. By then the original gorillas had been relieved by a fresh pair, who would in due course be relieved by another, and so on, on and on, world without end. But what really hurt was the chief of police calling him silly.

Mantega had always prided himself on being *furbissimo*, a *maestro* of cunning schemes and shady short-cuts to riches. To be called silly was far worse than the slaps in the face and kicks to the ankle administered by Zen's underlings when their verbal skills failed them. He, Nicola Mantega, silly? He'd show these bastards who was silly, and in the process extricate himself from this nightmare. Summoning up what remained of his dignity, he informed his tormentors that he was prepared to talk, but only to their superior. They appeared dubious, maybe even disappointed, but various phone calls were made and forty minutes later Aurelio Zen appeared in the basement interrogation room. He looked even more exhausted and dispirited than Mantega, which gave the latter hope.

'I want to make a deal,' he announced in a decisive

tone which suggested that the terms would be his, and slapped his right palm down hard on the battered desk which, with the stool on which he was perched, constituted the only furnishings in the small, stuffy room. Zen lit a cigarette, rubbed his eyes, coughed several times, then set the cigarette down on the back of Mantega's hand. When the latter's cries subsided and he had been forcibly reseated on the stool, Zen looked at him blearily.

'So sorry,' he said. 'I thought you were an ashtray.'

Mantega was still reeling from the pain, and the thought of what might yet lie in store for him.

'Why did you hurt me?' he demanded, his voice on the brink of breaking down.

'Why did your friends murder the American and mutilate that poor boy?'

'What are you talking about? They're not my –'

Zen sprang to his feet, grabbed Mantega's hair and tried to jerk his head back, but the fibres he was holding came away in his hand to reveal a gleaming bald pate.

'And you want to make a deal with me?' laughed Zen, tossing the toupee on the desk. 'Well, the product had better be good, because the salesman certainly doesn't impress much.'

'It's good, it's good,' mumbled Mantega. 'And it'll lead you to the people you really want.'

'I'm listening.'

Mantega took a deep breath.

'You know that helicopter that's been circling round the valley? Everyone thinks it's searching out locations for that film they're supposed to be making here. But I happen to know what it's really doing.'

'Which is?'

'Searching for buried treasure.'

'I'm not interested in treasure hunts.'

'Of course not, *signore*. Neither am I, and in any case it's very unlikely to succeed. Which is why I've convinced Giorgio –'

'Ah, so you do know him,' Zen murmured.

'Only by that name, which may well be false. I don't know his family name or where he's from and I've never seen his face.'

'What did you tell Giorgio?'

'I suggested to him . . .'

'When was this?'

'Two nights ago.'

'On the phone?'

'In person.'

'That's a certain lie. You've never been out of sight of my surveillance team, and they reported no such meeting.'

Mantega smiled archly. He had finally scored a point.

'Giorgio came to my house in the early hours of the morning. He knew that there was a police cordon there, but he managed to get through it without being seen. He grew up in the mountains hunting boar and wolves and told me that he can move more silently than a leaf falling from a tree.'

'You just said that you'd never seen his face.'

'He wore a mask.'

'Well, it was certainly kind of him to run such risks to drop in on an old friend,' Zen remarked sarcastically. 'What did he have to say?'

'He didn't want to talk. He came to kill me.'

'Why?'

'He said he'd decided that I was of no further use to him, and a possible risk.'

Zen laughed and lit another cigarette.

'Any chance of a coffee?' he asked one of the other officers.

The man hesitated.

'That place by the bus station,' the other prompted.

'Signor Mantega?' Zen enquired.

'*Un cappuccino scuro.* Lots of sugar.'

When the officer had left on his errand, Zen turned his eyes back to the prisoner, who was eyeing the glowing tip of his cigarette nervously.

'So Giorgio wanted to kill you. Good for him. Nevertheless, it's clear that he also failed in this admirable endeavour. How did you talk your way out of it?'

Invigorated by the mere thought of coffee, Mantega overlooked these gross insults.

'By offering him the chance to make a lot of money. Giorgio used to distribute drugs in this area, acting as an agent for one of the Reggio clans. Then he started using the product himself and the *reggiani* found themselves a new distributor. He had a costly habit to maintain, and whatever money he made on small local jobs went on crystal meth. That's why he needed the Newman kidnapping to replenish his funds.'

'But he didn't even try to bring that product to market,' Zen objected.

Mantega nodded dejectedly.

'I know. I can't understand it. Anyway, I knew he must be almost out of money, so I offered him the chance to co-operate on a hoax to prise a fortune out of these Americans who are searching for the tomb of Alaric. According to my sources, they are using a form of technology that can penetrate the surface of the earth to a certain depth and then analyse the results in order to reveal the presence of any structures or objects that may be buried there. So all we have to do, I told Giorgio – who was standing there with a knife in his hand, ready to cut my throat – is mock up something that will look to the radar like it might be a subterranean tomb. But when the Americans start digging, they'll find that the supposed tomb has already been opened and contains nothing but boulders and rubble from the Busento in its winter spate. *Che palle!* Someone got there before them. Which is when I get in touch. Yes, I say, the treasure of Alaric was indeed discovered just a few years ago, but those responsible are having great difficulty selling it, being just a little local firm. What would you like and how much are you prepared to pay?'

The officer who had left returned bearing a tray with their coffees. Both Zen and Mantega emptied their plastic cups in one go.

'And you expect them to believe you?' Zen asked.

Mantega laughed for the first time. He sensed that he was gaining the upper hand in the exchange, besides which the caffeine, on a painfully empty stomach, kicked in like a rugby full back.

'At the time, I was more worried about Giorgio believing me! Which he did, so at least I'd saved my life. But since you ask, *dottore*, I think that our story might very well be believed as long as it's properly presented, which task will be in my capable hands. Treasure hunters don't want to think that they've wasted years of their lives and millions of their money chasing the end of the rainbow, so they come pre-selected for a certain amount of credulity. Besides, what have we got to lose? If they don't bite, we can walk away.'

'And if they do bite?'

Mantega gestured largely.

'We'll offer them some decent fakes. It's been done before, you know.'

Zen let his head sink into his hands. He looked utterly defeated.

'All right, so that's how you're proposing to fool them,' he said. 'How are you proposing to fool me?'

This was the moment that Mantega had been waiting for.

'You called me silly,' he said, a little edge in his voice, 'but I'm not silly enough to try and fool a man like you. I may or may not succeed in fooling the treasure hunters, but that's just a sideshow, a means to an end, which is to fool Giorgio and hand him over to you.'

By now feeling fully empowered, Mantega allowed himself to crumple up and fold forward, his body language mirroring that of his opponent, always a good move in tough negotiations.

'Giorgio wanted to kill me!' he cried in an emphatic but muffled voice. 'He broke into my house in the middle of the night, woke me from sleep and threatened to cut my throat! Thank God my beloved wife and sons weren't there. But that man is a maniac, *dottore*. If he did it once, he may do it again. I won't sleep soundly until he is serving a life sentence without the possibility of parole for killing Pietro Calopezzati, and you are the only person who can achieve that. So what I'm proposing, Dottor Zen, is that you release me to act as the mediator between Giorgio and the Americans in the hoax that I've outlined. At some point in the ensuing negotiations, I will arrange a meeting at which Giorgio will be present and communicate the details of the time and place to you in advance, giving you plenty of time to prepare your men to move in and arrest him. What do you say?'

Shortly before noon the next day, Achille Pancrazi set off for Reggio di Calabria, seat of the regional government and of the Museo Archeologico Nazionale. He covered the two hundred kilometres in a little under an hour and a half, parked in a side-street near the museum and then killed the remaining time in a bar over a coffee and a shot of the local spirit flavoured with bergamot, the pungent, inedible citrus native to that part of Calabria. Professor Pancrazi did not normally drink before lunch, but today he felt a need to fortify himself.

At a quarter to two precisely he arrived at the museum and proceeded to the office of the assistant director he had spoken to earlier by phone.

'I apologise for being late,' he said once the ritual greetings and embraces had been concluded. 'Roadworks on the *autostrada*. I was stuck in a tailback for almost an hour.'

The director smiled wearily.

'After a while, you begin to wonder why the damn thing wasn't built properly in the first place.'

Pancrazi returned an equally weary glance, but no reply. Both men knew perfectly well why the A3, like most high-investment construction projects in the south funded by the Italian government, hadn't been built properly in the first place.

'Anyway, I do hope it's not too late,' Pancrazi added apologetically. 'You people must be wanting your lunch, but I can manage perfectly well on my own. As I said on the phone –'

'No, no! For you, professor, no problem at all. Please come with me.'

The director led him out into the main galleries, then down several flights of stairs and through various doors to the basement, which housed the museum's reserve collection and workshops. They traversed long lanes flanked by rows of tall metal shelving on which the artefacts were stored, eventually reaching a more brightly lit area where four men in blue overalls were chatting.

'Ready for lunch, boys?' the director said. 'Me too. Let me introduce Professor Achille Pancrazi from Cosenza University.'

There were polite murmurs and handshakes all round.

'What was it you wanted to inspect again, professor?' the director remarked. 'Those *pínakes* whose authenticity and origin are still in dispute, I believe.'

'Exactly,' said Pancrazi. He shrugged with a certain embarrassment. 'I've been asked to give a paper about that type of artefact in Stockholm next weekend and I realised yesterday that the topic of your recent find is almost certain to come up, so I'd better have another look to be sure I know what I'm talking about.'

'Of course, of course. Marco will show you where they're currently being stored. And then I'm afraid we're going to have to leave you to find your own way out. Shame you couldn't make it down here in time for lunch.'

One of the workmen led Pancrazi along the racks to a section where the thin terracotta votive tablets dedicated to the cult of Persephone in the Greek city of Locri were stored.

'Listen,' Pancrazi whispered conspiratorially. 'This may take some time, and of course smoking is not allowed in here. Is there somewhere I might go and have a puff if the need arises?'

'*Ma certo, professore!*'

The man led him over to a door in the outer wall. Above it was a lighted sign reading 'Fire Exit'.

'Just push the bar and you're standing in the loading dock area,' the workman said. 'Mind you hold the door open, though. Otherwise you'll have to go all the way round to the front to get back in.'

'But doesn't the alarm sound when the door's opened?' Pancrazi asked.

The caretaker gave him a knowing smile, as between two addicts.

'Supposed to, but we disable it during the day. As long as you don't let the door close behind you while you're out there, there'll be no problem.'

He returned to join his fellows, and the whole group started to move off in the direction of lunch. Achille Pancrazi tracked their voices across the open space of the basement until they dwindled away up the staircase. After that, it took him about fifteen minutes to search the storage area and locate the items he was seeking, and another five to pack the ones he selected to serve as a suitable ransom for his son Emanuele in layers of newspaper and a further layer of bubble-wrap. He slipped them into the large briefcase he had brought with him and left the premises through the door that the workman had pointed out to him.

By the time his modified 737 finally touched down at wherever the fuck it was, Jake felt pretty well bummed. It wasn't about the facilities. The Boeing Business Jet was a beauty, and having it all to himself was way cool. There was a regular king-size bed, a humungous TV with wrap-around sound, a flight attendant who wasn't Jake's type but was there when you needed her, plus satellite internet connection so he could keep up to speed with his online gaming. He'd even got to ride up front with the pilots for a while. But eleven hours was way too long to spend cooped up in a pressurised tube five miles above the ocean. Towards the end, Jake had found a leaflet that one of the cleaners must have left in a drawer of the desk in his living quarters. It was entitled *Rectal Carcinoma and God's Plan for You,* and by then he was so bored that he'd read the whole freaking thing from start to finish. Linear reading! In treeware format! It was just too weird.

Then there'd been Madrona. As soon as she heard where he was going, she was like, 'Iddly? I've always wanted to go to Iddly! It's so romantic! Can I come, Jake, can I, can I?' Luckily he'd been able to call her on the passport angle. Like three-quarters of her fellow citizens, Madrona didn't have one, but it was still tough to convince her that that meant she couldn't come along. Actually, Jake kind of agreed with her. The US was the only global superpower left in the game. If that didn't mean Americans could go anywhere they damn well chose, showing up with a wad of dollars and everyone pleased to see them, what was the point? As his plane taxied to a halt on a stand away from the terminal, he wondered how much it would cost to just *buy* Italy and then lease it back to the Italians as a franchised vacation facility. That would solve a lot of problems.

No sooner had the metal staircase docked with the plane than up rolled some classy European saloon from which Martin Nguyen emerged, looking even more desiccated and reptilian than usual.

'What's new, Jake?'

'Not much. Feeling kind of pixellated.'

Martin ushered him into the back of the car while the driver put his overnighter in the boot. Then they sped over to a gate in the perimeter fence, where the uniformed official barely glanced at the cover of Jake's passport before waving them through.

'How d'you manage that?' asked Jake wonderingly.

'VIP pull,' Martin returned in a tight, brisk tone. 'Getting back into the States is going to be a whole lot harder, but that's the price we pay for honouring freedom and keeping our homeland secure from terrorists.'

'I guess.'

A couple of minutes later, they were on the

autostrada. The airport had been built on an area of flat ground – as they so often were – but pretty soon the highway started to climb up into some spectacular scenery, different shades of green over some nice chunks of rock and not a building in sight. Jake just knew there had to be some great hiking, camping and off-road trails up in there. Plus this driver could really drive! Martin was yakking away in that clipped tone of his about how the Aeroscan data looked promising, there was definitely something in the Busento river-bed that couldn't be any kind of geological formation, he'd inspected the site that morning and it was really isolated, they should be able to get to work tonight without being observed, the machinery had been hired and the Iraqi labourers were good to go –

'Hey!' said Jake.

The monologue ceased.

'How long from here to the hotel?'

'Fifteen minutes?' said Nguyen. 'Twenty max, then at least six hours before we get moving. Get some sleep, Jake. You'll need it.'

'Bullshit. I've been stuck on that goddamn plane for what feels like my whole life. Now I'm here, I want to play. Tell this guy to get off the interstate, head up into the hills, and show me what this baby will do.'

'But Jake –'

'Hey, it's on my tab! Why can't I have a taste of what I bought?'

So Martin calls Tom Newman and passes on Jake's instructions, then Tom calls the driver and tells him what the guys in the back want, and the driver

277

confirms that several times just to make absolutely sure that whoever's nuts around here it's not him.

'Fast for fun?' he says in porno English.

Martin slips him a fifty-euro note.

'*Más rapido possibile.*'

'Huh?' says Jake.

'I'm a whore for languages.'

And then they're off the gentle gradients and cambered surface of the *autostrada*, plunging through dense thickets of chestnuts and oaks and maples and beeches on a narrow track that looks like it was built some time back in the Stone Age, rough-surfaced a century ago and then left to rot, up impossibly steep inclines and round reverse curves tight enough to fit in your pocket, using the whole road, horn blaring, astonishing views of the valley below and the mountains opposite snatched away in an instant, a controlled four-wheel skid every twenty seconds to position the car for yet another gut-wrenching acceleration, the engine finally getting into its stride after all that tootling around town, and Jake laughing like a maniac.

'Forget the goddamn treasure, this is worth the trip right here!'

And Martin goes to reply, only his mouth is filled with something he thinks is vomit and hopes isn't blood.

The Italian Republic – *res publica*, public stuff as distinct from family and personal concerns – may be compared to the planet upon a small portion of whose surface it is located. Superficially all is flux and flow, evolution and extinction, crisis and catastrophe, but this flashy biosphere amounts to no more than an infinitesimal fraction of the entire mass. People talk loosely about saving the earth, but that celestial body is at no more risk from the worst that man can do than is its metaphorical equivalent from the whims and wiles of whichever species currently occupies top spot in the political food chain. Immutable, inaccessible and to all intents and purposes eternal, the vast dead-weight of Italian bureaucracy goes spinning blindly on its way with utterly predictable momentum, indifferent to the weather outside.

In his private life, Aurelio Zen had often had cause to bemoan this fact, after being brought to the brink of tears or fury, or both, by the time and effort required to obtain – always in person at the *anagrafe* office of the local town council, and after a very long wait unless you had some strings to pull – the latest addition to the paper trail that follows every Italian from birth to death. Professionally, though, it was a godsend. This or that politician might currently be in or out, such and such a party reformed or deformed, the perpetual construction site of government landscaped with olive trees or houses of liberty, but the number of everyday events for which official documentation was required remained sufficiently large and various to provide the basis for a detailed biographical sketch of every citizen.

This had been even more true under the Fascist regime, and since Calabria was largely spared the bombardments that had destroyed archives in other parts of Italy and the post-war government had promptly rehired Mussolini's officially disgraced myrmidons to curate the surviving ones, unravelling the history of the Intrieri clan proved much less difficult than might have been the case elsewhere. Caterina had been born in February 1926 in San Giovanni in Fiore, the third of nine children, and her death from natural causes was certified by the authorities of Spezzano della Sila on the sixth of December 1944, eight days after the birth of Pietro Ottavio Calopezzati in the same *comune*. By the 1960s, the ranks of the Intrieri family in Calabria had been depleted both by death and by internal emigration to construction jobs created by the building boom in the north. Only three were still registered as resident in the province of Cosenza: two of them middle-aged women, the other a cousin of Caterina's who was now almost ninety.

So that trail was dead. Zen had never put much credence in it. He knew that Maria had told him the truth, but had also lied to him. What he didn't know was where the one blurred into the other, so the Intrieri story had to be followed up. The girl had indeed died 'of natural causes' when Maria had said, but there was no objective evidence whatsoever that the baby who had come into the world at the same time had been hers. Caterina had been the elder and probably the dominant of the two friends, and might well have made up a dramatic story to enliven their wretched lives in that cold, lifeless mansion. Besides, why should the Intrieri murder one of their own? Unless, of course, they hadn't known that he was. Zen had the sense of having strayed into the marshlands which infested the border between the *laguna morta* and *laguna viva* in his native Venice, a treacherous soup where you could neither stand nor sail, only be mired and dragged down.

He was saved, temporarily at least, by the appearance of the ever eager and confident Natale Arnone.

'Just an update on Signor Mantega,' he said, seeing the documents spread out on Zen's desk. 'It's not urgent. I'll come back.'

'No, let me have it,' Zen replied with a yawn. 'I've had enough of deciphering words written with steel nibs dipped into pots of condensed ink and then badly blotted. Is our friend the *notaio* behaving himself?''

Nicola Mantega had been released at ten o'clock that morning with very stringent conditions attached to his provisional liberty. He had been given a mobile phone whose outward appearance was identical to his own Nokia model, but whose innards had been stripped out and replaced with the basic telephonic equipment, minus the camera and other gadgets, the extra space being used to house a GPS chip and a spare battery. He was to keep the phone on his person at all times and to use it exclusively for all his communications, both personal and professional. Once a minute, the chip called in to report its location to police headquarters, while all calls to or from the phone were automatically monitored.

'He hasn't put a foot wrong so far,' Arnone reported. 'He drove straight home, then phoned his wife, who's on holiday in Germany, and told her to stay there until further notice. She didn't want to – something about she and the kids having outstayed their welcome with her sister-in-law – but the suspect told her to go to a hotel if she couldn't take it any more. Whatever happened, he was on no account to be disturbed at home until further notice.'

Zen smiled wanly. If he played his cards right, Mantega might yet get off with a short prison sentence for aiding and abetting Peter Newman's kidnappers, but his wife would never forget being ordered around in that high-handed manner.

'He spent the rest of the morning in his office making a number of calls to cancel meetings or delay deadlines on work that he apparently has in hand. Several of the men he called had obviously heard of his arrest, but he told them that it had all been a huge mistake and an embarrassment for the police which he had talked his way out of in no time.'

'No calls to Giorgio?' asked Zen.

'One, after lunch, to the house we have under surveillance in San Giovanni. Mantega left a brief message giving his new number, which he said was clean, and telling Giorgio to call him as soon as possible.'

'And has he?'

'Not so far. But he did get a call from young Signor Newman to say that some package had arrived. Mantega tried to set up a dinner appointment for tonight to discuss it, but Newman said he couldn't get away because he's working for that Oriental representing the American film company, I can't recall his name –'

'Neither can I, and I can't pronounce it either. Let's call him Fu Manchu.'

'Who?'

'Before your time. Carry on.'

'Well, Newman told him that Signor Manchu's boss had arrived from the United States and he couldn't get away, so they agreed to meet at Mantega's office tomorrow morning. That was a lie, however. In reality, our young American has a date with the Digos agent Kodra. She set that up as per your instructions, sir.'

Zen nodded vaguely.

'Good, good. She doesn't have to sleep with him of course, but . . . I have a feeling there's something going on here that I don't know about, never mind understand. Several things, in fact. Maybe even many.'

He looked up at the young officer.

'To tell the truth, Arnone, I don't have the faintest clue what's going on.'

'Yes, sir.'

'But of course I didn't say that.'

'No, sir. And I didn't hear it.'

'*Bravo.*'

Outside the unopenable pane of toughened glass, a continuous raft of cloud seemingly as solid as concrete stretched away featurelessly as far as the eye could see.

'It sounds suspiciously as though Mantega's co-operating,' Zen remarked finally. 'On the other hand, I wouldn't put it past him to try and do some private enterprise on the side. I also have a feeling that the thunderstorm is about to burst, and while my reasoning faculty may be falling apart I still trust my intuition, or experience, or whatever you want to call it. What else have I to count on?'

It was a rhetorical question, but Arnone answered it.

'Fear.'

Zen looked at him but did not reply. Arnone coughed in an embarrassed way.

'If you will permit the observation, sir, I think you underestimate yourself. My father always said, *"La paura guarda le vigne, non la siepe."* Fear guards the vineyard, not the hedge. And I know that you are feared.'

'Me?'

'Yes, sir. Because, with all due respect, you're not one of us. So no one knows what you might decide to do next. Sir.'

Zen nodded.

'That's logical. To be honest, there are times when I terrify myself.'

Given the constraints on Tom's time, his date had suggested a place in Rende. She'd also told him that her name was Mirella, but hadn't asked for his.

The initial call had come while Tom was stuck out on the fringes of town in the yard of a company that rented construction equipment, clarifying contractual details between the supercilious jerk in charge and an increasingly impatient Martin Nguyen. He couldn't talk right then, but had promised to call Mirella back as soon as possible.

'Who was that?' demanded Nguyen.

'Oh, just another bureaucratic thing they need me to do before they can release my dad's cadaver.'

'Bullshit,' Nguyen remarked succinctly, but didn't follow up the comment. He'd been looking kind of unwell ever since fetching his boss in from the airport, not nearly as feisty as usual and occasionally clutching his stomach and crunching down pills.

When they finally got back to the hotel, the head honcho – some Microsoft millionaire named Jake – was still sleeping off his jet lag. Nguyen went over to six short but brawny guys who were lounging around the lobby as if expecting to get thrown out any minute. They looked Italian but didn't speak it, so Tom's services were not required when Nguyen took them off to a conference room he'd booked for their briefing. Apparently one of them understood English and would pass on Nguyen's instructions to the others in their own language, which might as well have been Arabic for all that Tom could make any sense of it. Which left him free to call Mirella back.

The fact that she'd got in touch at all astonished him. He'd assumed that the striking young woman that he'd twice made a clumsy attempt to hit on had no interest in him whatsoever. She certainly hadn't provided him with the slightest encouragement on the occasions when they'd met, purely by chance, and he had more or less forgotten her, except he hadn't. And now here she was saying she could see him for a couple of hours that evening if he was free.

Strictly speaking, of course, he wasn't. Martin Nguyen had given him firm instructions to be on call and ready to leave at five minutes' notice, as a result of which he had already turned down Nicola Mantega's invitation to a working dinner that evening to discuss what Tom knew about the apparent discovery of Alaric's tomb. On the other hand, he'd gathered from Nguyen that the next stage of the operation wasn't going to happen until well after dark, and hadn't even been told what it was or whether his presence was required. So as long as he could get back to the hotel quickly if Nguyen summoned him, there was no reason to sit twiddling his thumbs in his room when he could be romancing – what a beautiful name! – Mirella.

They'd agreed to meet at seven-thirty, but Tom got there twenty minutes early to check the place out. A bank of thick thunderclouds squatted on the city like one of those unimaginably huge alien spaceships in that movie. A sense of oppression was thick on the ground. The venue turned out to be a garish pizzeria alongside an intersection just a few minutes' walk from the hotel. It looked borderline okay, and the alternatives were even more uninspiring, as indeed was the whole area. There were the vestiges of a straggling roadside town now bypassed by the *autostrada*, but it mostly consisted of dormitory apartment blocks whose commuting owners ate at home, and bars and fast food outlets for students from the 1970s university slab stretching away like the Great Wall of China across the line of hills to the west.

When Tom arrived, there were a dozen students there, hanging out rather than actually eating, their voices struggling to be heard above a barrage of rap music sweetened by Italian vowels. The décor was upscale public lavatory, only with bleached-out halogen lighting, mirrors just about everywhere except the floor, and clunky plastic tables and chairs in primary colours like a play-set for giant toddlers. That was okay. Tom had already figured out that there were few things to touch Italian taste at its best and none to equal it at its worst.

He ordered a beer and found himself wondering what Mirella was going to wear. The two outfits he had seen her in so far had been so different that they didn't provide much of a clue. In fact, thinking back, Tom realised that almost everything had been different on each occasion: the style of her hair, the make-up she wore, even her body language. It was almost as if the person he had seen on those two occasions had not in fact been the same but a pair of identical twins, structurally similar but each with a completely different personality. He smiled to himself at the absurd thought. Anyway, identical twins might just about be possible, but triplets would be pushing it, so pretty soon he'd get a take on who she really was – or rather, who she wanted him to think she was. Tom found this final insight rather disturbing. I'd never have had an idea like that back home, he thought. This place is complexing me. He wasn't sure whether he was entirely comfortable with that.

The answer to his question about her appearance proved to be yet another enigma, so different from either of her previous personae that Tom didn't even recognise her until she sat down at his table. Beneath a bulky blue padded coat she was wearing a prim suit in a clashing shade of muddy brown. No make-up, no jewellery, her hair drawn fiercely back and bunched in a tight bun. All in all, she looked like a small-town dental hygienist dolled up for a tough job interview in the big city. Guess I'm not going to get laid tonight, thought Tom, although under the circumstances there wouldn't have been any chance of that anyway.

'You seem surprised to see me,' Mirella said.

Tom didn't have a ready answer, so he just smiled.

'Now then,' she went on, 'you told me your name on the phone but I didn't understand it.'

'It's Tom. Thomas. Tommaso.'

'Tommaso.'

He loved the way she lingered on the double consonant, caressing it with her lips as though reluctant to let it go.

'*Un bel nome.*'

A surly servitor appeared at their table. Mirella ordered some kind of pizza. Tom said he would have the same.

'So you're staying out here?'

Tom nodded.

'Just around the corner. The Rende International Residence.'

'Oh, you must be rich! I've only been there once, when one of my friends got married. They held the wedding reception there. Isn't it very expensive?'

'Well, I'm not paying. I've been hired by a friend of my father's who's working for an American film company. They're planning to make a movie here, only he doesn't speak Italian so he needs me to translate for him. Not my normal line of work, but you know what they say – another day, another *dolore*. I mean *dollaro*.'

'Films! *Oddio, che bello!* I've always wanted to work in films.'

'Well, you've certainly got the looks for it!'

What a lame, pathetic, dumbfuck line, he thought, but she seemed pleased by the compliment.

'It isn't as glamorous as it sounds,' Tom went on quickly, with what he hoped was just the right touch of sophisticated world-weariness. 'But what about you? Do you work?'

Mirella responded with a light, airy explosion of breath and upward dab of her startling eyes that perfectly expressed disgust, contempt and fatalistic resignation.

'An office job with the provincial authorities. It's very secure, very boring and I know precisely how much I'll be earning when I reach retirement age.'

The food came.

'So what do you do?' Mirella asked after scarfing down two slabs of pizza with admirable greed and concentration.

'I'm a chef. Trained, qualified and with good references. I've worked at some celebrity restaurants in the United States and now I'm thinking of moving here and opening up my own place. This is where my roots are, after all.'

'So you said. What's your family name?'

Tom paused over a long swallow of beer. If he told her the truth, she would immediately make the connection to his murdered father, who had inflicted enough damage in years gone by. Tom did not intend to let him strangle this relationship at birth from beyond the grave.

'I'm not entirely sure,' he said. 'My father's family was certainly Calabrian, but they changed their name when they moved to America and I haven't had time to follow up that angle. These film people work you pretty hard! I'll need to do some research in the archives. Perhaps you could help with that, Mirella. Anyway, we can talk about that some other time. In the end, I'm more interested in my future than my past.'

'The essential is to keep them in balance.'

And so it went on. They continued to make pleasant small talk, but the conversation refused to get hot. The place itself didn't help – it had by now been invaded by a gang of languid adolescents wearing baggy jeans with the crotch down by their knees – but Tom also sensed an inner reticence in Mirella, a desire to avoid moving towards intimacy. That was typically Calabrian, of course, and for that matter he himself had been parsimonious with the truth, but it perhaps explained why he found himself being rather more frank than he had intended when she asked her next question, as if to show her the way, to demonstrate that he was prepared to risk trusting her.

'But I've also heard that this movie you're talking about is not going to happen. Didn't you see that interview on television with Luciano Aldobrandini? He claimed the whole thing was a fraud!'

Tom sighed theatrically.

'He may be right. Listen, Mirella. This is in the strictest confidence, but there's another project involved.'

By now she had finished eating, in her graceful, dedicated, methodical way, and was all attention.

'What's that?'

'They think they've found Alaric's tomb.'

She laughed then, for the first time.

'You're joking!'

Tom shrugged urbanely.

'I doubt that they are. There's a lot of money involved, and these people are heavyweights when it comes to business. The head of the whole outfit flew in today by private jet and they're planning to . . .'

He stopped himself just in time, and covered up by reaching for his cigarettes, then dolefully replacing them.

'I forgot, no smoking now!'

Mirella regarded him in a way he wished to prolong for the rest of his earthly existence.

'There's a bar next door,' she said. 'Let's have our coffees there and smoke outside.'

He was about to answer when his mobile woke like a colicky baby. It was Martin Nguyen and he didn't sound happy.

'Where the fuck are you? I called your room and there was no answer.'

'Slipped out to buy some cigarettes, Mr Nguyen. I'll be there in a few minutes.'

He threw much too much money on the table and, when they were both standing, grasped Mirella's arm for a moment, just above the elbow, and pulled her towards him.

'I'm so sorry,' he said. 'My boss wants me back right away. But listen . . .'

He tried to meet her eyes, but they were averted. It was then that, for the first time, he smelt her skin, a faint caprine odour like mild goat's cheese, earthy and creamy. But this smell wasn't about food.

'*Grazie per la bella serata,*' Mirella said, disentangling herself effortlessly.

'May I call you again?' Tom found himself saying.

She smiled vaguely, and was gone.

Jake was woken by a call from Madrona, wanting to know if he'd got there okay. She'd been worried about him, she said. Madrona worried about everything – getting pregnant, not getting pregnant, global warming, bird flu, you name it. It was one of the many things Jake found cute about her, although he sometimes kind of sensed, like a chill draught on the back of the neck, that it might turn out to be a real ball-buster later on.

He calmed her down and then jack-knifed out of bed. The clock said some crazy-ass time, but Jake had already figured that the way to handle this trip was like some gaming environment you're unfamiliar with. He knew he would need to accumulate a lot more experience points before he was fully up to speed, but one key factor was that the time on the clocks here was game time. Not real time, which Madrona had said was like midday, but the right time in the game. Same with everything else. This hotel Martin had booked him into wouldn't have made the cut as a second-class casino in Reno, but in the game scenario it was hot shit. That was okay. Jake could flex with the best.

He dug out his laptop, got online and slipped effortlessly into various roles, doing damage, saving the world, getting killed a couple of times. Then he checked out Madrona's blog – bunch of bitching about how she was having a really heavy period this month – sent a chatroom up in flames, cruised a few porno sites till he found one that rang his bells, jerked off, took a shower and got dressed. Round about ten, game time, he rode the marble-floored lift down to the lobby, feeling totally mellowed out. Martin Nguyen was in the bar nursing a glass of what looked like iced tea but probably wasn't. Jake was tempted to make an edgy remark about him needing something to settle his delicate stomach. He himself didn't either drink or smoke. Hell, he didn't even *smoke*.

'Dude,' said Jake.

Martin grunted. He still didn't look that hot, but Jake had to admire the way, when he'd got nauseous in the car on those bends, he'd just held the puke in his mouth and then swallowed it down again long enough to tell the driver to pull over.

'Where can I get a menu?'

Martin took another gulp of whisky.

'Kitchen's closed.'

'You're kidding.'

'Place is run like a mom and pop corner store. Dinner's seven till nine-thirty, then fuck you till breakfast.'

'Damn. I could really use some foie gras with PBJ.'

Martin grabbed his mouth real fast.

'Got invited to the opening of this new place in Belltown couple of days back,' Jake went on. 'That's their signature dish. Pan-seared foie gras with peanut butter and jelly. Awesome combo. What's the food like here?'

'Kind of an Italian feel,' Martin replied in a highly stressed tone. 'I'll have Tom get them to fix you a sandwich or something just as soon as the little shit shows up.'

'Tom?'

'Pete Newman's boy. I hired him to be my mouthpiece. He claims to be out buying smokes, but I heard him on the phone earlier schmoozing some bimbo. I'll fire him once we've figured out what the deal is on this tomb site.'

He signalled the waiter to freshen up his drink. Then he caught Jake's disapproving look.

'Inappropriate, huh? Yeah, I guess you're right. But what we're going to be doing later on tonight is even more inappropriate. Smashing our way into a world heritage site and stealing priceless historic artefacts which are government property?'

He waved largely at their bleak, bedazzled surroundings.

'You think Italian hotels suck? Imagine what their jails are like.'

'What's the deal with those Iraqis?'

'I'll call them in once we get there. My biggest challenge has been getting the equipment to the site. It's not like the towelheads don't know how to operate the machines. They're Halliburton trained, for God's sake. But the rules of the road over in Iraq are basically down to what size gun you carry, so I couldn't just turn them loose in the traffic over here. Apart from anything else, the poor fucks would be scared shitless. They still haven't gotten over being told that they can't even carry side arms. In the end, I fixed to have the hardware delivered by truck to a disused quarry near the site. Don't worry, it'll all come together just fine, unless –'

'Here I am, Mr Nguyen!'

It was Tom, breathless and superficially solicitous, but looking way more pleased with himself than the purchase of a pack of smokes warranted. Martin slipped him a fifty and told him to pass it on to the right people and get Jake fed.

'I read that material you emailed me,' Martin said to Jake when they were alone again. 'Let's just see if I've got the story straight. I mean, if we get arrested, then I want to know what it is I'm supposed to lie about.'

'You mean like talk me through it? Might challenge my attention span. Can't you do me a PowerPoint presentation?'

'I don't have the facilities for that, Jake. I'll try and keep it brief. Just listen up and tell me if I've got anything wrong.'

'Sure, Mart. You're the boss.'

Nguyen ignored this crack.

'The material you sent me, plus some follow-up research I did online, tells me that we're looking for the Great Menorah, one of the sacred vessels of the original temple in Jerusalem. It's of cast gold, hollow within, with a hexagonal base and seven branches representing the planets plus the sun, and weighs in at about one hundred pounds. It stood beside the Ark of the Covenant in the Temple and was captured by the

Romans when they sacked the city two thousand years ago.'

'Correct.'

'So the Romans take it back with them. We know that for sure because there's an image of Jewish slaves carrying it in the triumphal procession carved on the Arch of Titus, after which it was stashed away in one of their temples. Seems they really hated the Jews. It wasn't enough to beat them in battle, they had to steal their nutty one-god religion. Anyway, three and a half centuries later it's the Romans' turn to get conquered. Alaric cleans the city out, then heads south and ends up dying in this fleapit. His Goth homies bury him under the river with all the goodies he'd plundered, then do a total deniability with extreme prejudice operation on the work force.'

'You got it.'

Martin knocked back his drink.

'Let's go outside,' he told Jake. 'I need to smoke.'

They stepped out into the muscular embrace of the night air. Thunder rumbled and stumbled and then a fragmentation bomb exploded overhead, showering huge drops of water on the patio and the parched lawns, hedges and trees, raising a cool, sensuous freshness that reeked of growth and decay.

'Wow!' said Jake. 'They do like weather here too?'

'So if the story about Alaric is true,' Martin resumed, 'then there must be a ton of other valuable stuff in the tomb, worth probably billions, supposing you could find a buyer. But we're not interested in the money, just the menorah, right?'

'Right.'

'Why? Are you Jewish?'

Jake grinned.

'Are bears Catholic? Does the Pope shit in the woods?'

'Okay, okay! Sorry I asked. It's just that what we're going to be doing from here on in is very high-risk. Are you sure you want to be there tonight, Jake? If anything goes wrong, I might be able to talk my way out of it. I'm just an employee, but you're the *mandante*, as they say here. Might be smarter to stay here at the hotel and then cut back to your jet and get the hell out if the flares go up.'

'No way. I've been waiting over a year for this moment. Chickening out now would be like not showing up for your honeymoon.'

'Or your funeral.'

'Don't let that motion sickness thing get to you, Mart.'

Tom Newman sidled up to them.

'Sorry to intrude, guys, but your food's on the table. *Crostini rossi piccanti, caciocavallo ai ferri, zuppa di finocchi*. Best they could do at this hour.'

'Cool,' Jake replied cordially. 'I just love ethnic food.'

It was in the small hours of the morning, about ten past four, when Nicola Mantega finally heard from Giorgio. So did the police technicians who were monitoring the new phone that Mantega had been given, and as a result the call was immediately traced to a public phone in Cerenzia, about ten kilometres east of San Giovanni in Fiore but with easy access to the *superstrada*. When a police car arrived twenty minutes later there was no one about, and it was unlikely that anyone in the town had seen Giorgio come or go. Nevertheless, he had been terse.

'They moved in during the night with heavy equipment. Dug around a bit, took a look at the rocks inside, then left in a hurry.'

'How do you know?'

'I was watching. Oh, and I hear you got arrested and then released a few hours later. I hope you didn't make a deal.'

'Of course not! They simply had no evidence against me, so I –'

'I'll kill you if I have to, Nicoletta. Whether you're behind bars or walking the streets makes no difference. Remember that in the days to come and honour our agreement. If anything goes wrong, you're a dead man whatever happens to me.'

The phrase kept recurring to Mantega as he drove into Cosenza. *Sei un morto*. That was how the shattered trunk of the man he had known as Peter Newman was invariably described in the media: 'dressed like a corpse'. Giorgio might not be as powerful a figure as he liked to make out, but he was crazy. The thing about crazy people was that you never had the slightest idea what they were going to do next, any more than they did.

Tom Newman appeared at nine o'clock sharp. He looked terrible: pallid, exhausted and depressed. Since his father's death had been in Mantega's mind, it occurred to him that the boy might finally have realised the full horror of what had happened. But when he suggested that they adjourn to a bar for a restorative coffee and brioche, the next thing he knew Tom was standing in the street waving enthusiastically to an attractive young woman.

'Who's that?'

'Oh, just a friend,' Tom replied airily.

Over their coffees, Mantega elaborated at some length on what fools the police had made of themselves by arresting him the day before. It was vital to get this idea across to the *americani*. The last thing Mantega wanted was for them to suspect that they might be getting involved with someone complicit in criminal enterprises, especially since they were. Tom made sympathetic noises, but his attention was evidently wandering off in directions that Mantega couldn't identify.

'So, I understand that the package has arrived,' he said once they were back in his office. 'Am I to understand that your employers have succeeded where so many previous efforts have failed? Have they indeed located the site where Alaric the Goth was buried?'

His tone was studiously jocular if not ironical, but the young man's response was an abrupt return to his earlier mood of sullen gloom.

'Hell exists, but it may be empty,' he said.

'*Scusami?*'

'They've found what they think is Alaric's tomb, only when they dug it out, all that was there was a circle of stone walling filled with river rock. So now they're thinking it must have been discovered earlier and all the stuff looted and they're packing up to leave on their private jet this afternoon. The only question is whether I go with them.'

'Why would you want to do that?' murmured Mantega. 'Judging by the encounter I just witnessed in the street, you seem to be doing quite nicely back in your ancestral home. My congratulations! The only problem now is to find a way in which you can support yourself here and enjoy to the full the ripe fruit of our soaring peaks and fertile valleys, so to speak. I know that you have ideas about opening a restaurant, but that sort of venture requires a lot of money to be done successfully.'

He leant forward and gazed at Tom intently.

'Luckily for you, I have an idea. Some three or four years ago, I was approached by a certain party with a very unusual proposition.'

Mantega broke off and looked around cautiously.

'You understand that I am speaking now in the strictest confidence,' he went on in a conspiratorial undertone. 'Nothing of what I say must be repeated beyond the four walls of this room. Agreed?'

Tom jerked his body in a spasm combining a shrug and a nod.

'The individual's name need not concern us,' Mantega continued. 'Suffice it to say that his story was so incredible that I didn't even bother hearing him out to the end. On the contrary, I laughed in his face, told him in no uncertain terms not to bother me with such nonsense again and showed him the door.'

Mantega leant still nearer to Tom.

'But after what you have just told me, I'm now asking myself if that wasn't perhaps the biggest mistake that I've ever made in my life!'

He straightened up again, brisk and businesslike, marshalling the facts in his mind before proceeding.

'This man claimed that by using advanced technological equipment called ground-penetrating radar, mounted on the back of a four-wheel-drive vehicle during the dry season when there's no more than a trickle of water in the Busento, he and his associates had located the tomb of Alaric and then returned with mechanical diggers, cracked the vault and plundered the contents.'

He paused to let this sensational statement sink in. Tom Newman's reaction was minimal, but at least he appeared to be listening.

'The reason this person approached me, according to him, was that having got his hands on those untold treasures, he had belatedly realised that they were almost impossible to dispose of at a profit. None of the items concerned could be sold legally without a validated provenance and the necessary documentation. On the other hand, he was understandably reluctant to melt them down and sell them for the value of the raw materials. He therefore hoped that I could either arrange the necessary paperwork, or help him locate a potential purchaser who would overlook such tedious details.'

Mantega shot his visitor a glance. Tom was still listening, but he didn't seem particularly interested.

'So you're saying that there's someone around here who has the stuff that my guys were looking for stashed away in his basement or something?'

Mantega wiped the air with his hands forcefully.

'I absolutely do not say that! Apart from anything else, I have had no contact with the man in question since that occasion several years ago. Even supposing his claims to have been true, there is no telling what he may have decided to do with the treasure in the meantime. But since, according to your account, the tomb has indeed been opened and cleaned out by someone at some stage, there is just a possibility that the artefacts it contained are still in existence, located not far from where we are now sitting, and in the hands of someone whom I can contact at any moment with one phone call. That's all.'

He got up and strode to the window, where he stood for a moment looking pensively down at the street.

'So?' Tom demanded.

Mantega turned back to him with a loud laugh.

'Quite right! Your *bella ignota* seems to be awaiting you below, so let us by all means wrap this up speedily.'

He started to walk back, then stopped and clutched his forehead.

'Here, my friend, we move into the realm of the purely hypothetical,' he pronounced, in a manner suggesting that he was perfectly at home in this abstruse sphere. 'But since I note with pleasure that your grasp of the subjunctive has improved markedly since our initial meeting, let us suppose, purely for the sake of argument, that the person whom I mentioned earlier were still in possession of Alaric's fabled treasure in its original form. Let us further suppose that certain other persons might wish to acquire one or more items for an agreed price, having of course inspected samples of the merchandise and had them authenticated by an independent expert of their own choice. Should any or all of this prove to be the case, then given the language problem and the need for absolute confidentiality, you –'

He flung out a dramatic digit in Tom's direction.

'– would in effect be the necessary and sole mediator between the interested parties. As such, you should in my professional opinion both expect and demand a percentage of the sale price.'

Tom got to his feet and walked over to the window, positioning himself where his host had stood earlier.

'It is her, isn't it?' remarked Mantega. 'I hope she's waiting for you. Rather than for me, I mean.'

'I don't understand,' Tom said earnestly, turning back to face him. 'Last I heard, you wanted me to collaborate on this business because you had ethical issues with this priceless Calabrian heritage site being despoiled and the contents exported by my employers. Now you're telling me that I can make a lot of money on the side by facilitating the sale of some or all of the treasure to those very same people. Is it just me, or is there something here that doesn't quite add up?'

Mantega smiled broadly.

'Ah, Signor Tommaso! Your grasp of the verbal subjunctive may have improved, but you evidently haven't yet understood that in Calabria life itself is subjunctive. Reality here has always been so harsh that we have by necessity learnt to content ourselves with the possible, the desirable and the purely imaginary.'

He went over to Tom and grasped his arm. The young man flinched, a startled look in his distant eyes. Too bad, thought Mantega. It was about time for young Tommasino to forget the American culture of crisp deals and binding handshakes and learn the intricate round-dance of male power courtship here in the south.

'Everything I said the other day was utterly sincere,' he declared. 'Supposing that Alaric's horde of treasure has indeed been found, my principal object is to secure whatever may be secured for the public good of this province, and indeed the whole nation.'

He released his grip on the other man's arm in favour of a more flexible choreography, punctuating his remarks with intense rhetorical gestures like someone signing for the deaf.

'But how can that be achieved? I know for a fact that the man who came to see me cares nothing for such selfless aspirations. He wants money, only money, and unless he gets it the historic artefacts from that burial site will without doubt be dispersed if not destroyed. It's like a kidnapping! Only he knows where they are, which is certainly not in his house, or anywhere associated with him. But if your employers can be persuaded to ransom one of the items that he has seized at a sufficiently high price, it is possible that I may be able to convince him, by a mixture of cajolery and threats, that his interests are best served by taking the money on offer and handing over the rest of the loot to the authorities, rather than having me denounce him to the police.'

Breaking his tense pose, he relaxed with a fluid gesture of his right hand.

'There will undoubtedly be some personal danger involved. I know this man to be both violent and unpredictable. Nevertheless, I ask nothing for myself but the satisfaction of having served my people. You, on the other hand, are a returning fellow-countryman, *un immigrante*, and it is only right that your return fare should be paid by those who neither know nor care about these matters so dear to us.'

He waved helplessly.

'All this may well come to nothing, of course. But we owe it to ourselves and to our common heritage to try. Please, return to your employers and tell them what I have told you. Emphasise that samples of the merchandise will be provided for validation under whatever circumstances they may demand. If they show the slightest interest, then I'll get in touch with my contact as soon as I hear from you. After that, matters should move very quickly.'

Mantega grinned broadly, as though mocking his own fervour.

'But not a word to your girlfriend, mind. Poor women! They only have one thing to sell, but for us the possibilities are endless.'

A terrible thing had occurred. For the first time in his life that he could recall, rare periods of illness aside, Aurelio Zen couldn't face the prospect of lunch.

Until now, this quasi-sacred Italian rite had been the high point of his working day, the central pillar that supported the whole edifice. Zen was not greedy, but given that he had to eat anyway he preferred to do so as well as possible. In every single one of his numerous postings all over the country down the years he had always succeeded, after a few days, in tracking down a restaurant or *trattoria* that satisfied his needs. But not in Cosenza, and the reason was clear. The city was so small that most people went home for lunch, and so far off the tourist trail that there was little or no passing trade. Good restaurants did exist, but they only served dinner and Sunday lunch. Moreover, Natale Arnone's remark about his being feared had given Zen an uneasy feeling that if he returned to one of his usual haunts the food would not only be unpalatable but one of the staff might have spat in the tomato sauce curdling in his dish of pasta.

Nevertheless, he was hungry and the day was not too hot, so he decided to take advantage of the power which had created that fear to do something that he hadn't done for years. He called up a car from the pool and had himself driven to the finest *gastronomia* in town, where he ordered a varied selection of picnic foods, and then to the densely wooded gardens of the Villa Communale up in the old city. He told the driver to return in one hour precisely and wandered off along the path beneath massive chestnut and ilex trees until he found a suitable bench in a patch of sunlight mitigated by the canopy of verdure above, with a glorious panoramic view across the valley of the Crati river to the western slopes of the Sila massif.

For the next half-hour he sat there in perfect solitude, savouring a selection of antipasti, air-cured ham and salami from the mountains before him, a sharp sheep's cheese, chunks of crusty wholewheat bread baked in a wood-fired oven, and half a bottle of a very tolerable rosé. Apart from birdsong, the only sounds were distant honks and hoots from the valley far below him. When his hunger was assuaged, he lit a cigarette – another plus for this establishment – and finished the wine along with the remaining dried tomatoes *sott'olio*, chewy russet roundels delivering an intensity of flavour which forced Zen to concede that this Aztec import might be good for something after all.

When he had finished, he packed up all the rubbish and deposited it in one of the bins provided by the progressive, centre-left city council, retaining only the plastic beaker he had been given for the wine. This he took to a fountain set in the sheer cliff behind and filled several times with water issuing from a metal tube embedded in the lips of a sculpted Triton, gulping it down with the greatest pleasure. The mythological frieze suggested a blow job gone horribly wrong, but a plaque above it proclaimed that the water was channelled from a natural source inside the peak on which the original Bruttii had founded their city. It was startlingly pure and stone-cold, even at this time of year, and had been issuing forth for countless centuries before that gang of Gothic military tourists had shown up to bury their dead leader somewhere beneath the mingled rivers into which it flowed.

This innocent, even lyrical, thought took the edge off his blissful mood by reminding him of work. The scene was still very pleasant, but it was as if the sun had gone behind a veil of high cirrus, although in point of fact it hadn't. Earlier that morning, Zen had listened in to the conversation between Tom Newman and Nicola Mantega – courtesy of the electronic devices installed in the latter's office – concerning the whereabouts of the treasure that had been buried with that Gothic chieftain. Mantega had performed very much as Zen had expected, which is to say in the manner of a third-rate tenor in a provincial opera house. He had neither the range nor the volume, not to mention the subtlety, to tackle really big roles in Rome or Milan, but he could certainly ham it up and belt it out. It remained to be seen whether anything would come of his plan for drawing Giorgio into a trap, but Zen's only real criticism of it, having nothing better to suggest himself at present, was that it left him feeling trapped too. He longed to take action, but any move he made might ruin everything. There seemed to be nothing to do but wait and then react to events, and this was depressing him enormously.

He was summoned from his reverie by the police driver, who had not only returned at the agreed time but had come on foot to find Zen, who had forgotten all about their arrangement. He got up unwillingly and took a last, long look at the hulking plateau opposite, the perched towns and villages appearing at this distance like quarries slashed into its wooded flanks, the elegant curves of the *superstrada* striding insolently across the landscape on its stilted viaducts. That thought in turn suggested one action that he could take, and as soon as he returned to the Questura he summoned Natale Arnone.

'Do I have an accent?' he asked the young officer.

Arnone looked shifty.

'Sir?'

'When I speak, are you conscious of an accent? In other words, could you tell that I wasn't from around here if you didn't already know?'

'Well, sir, the thing is that –'

'A simple yes or no will suffice, Arnone.'

'Then yes. Sir.'

'Right. I want you to call this number and ask for Signora Maria Arrighi. If she answers, pass the phone to me and get out. If someone else answers, and asks who's calling, tell him or her that you are a doctor at the hospital and that you need to discuss the results of the *signora*'s tests with her. If she's not at home, find out when she will be. Do not leave a number for her to call back. Got that?'

'Yes, sir.'

Zen did not listen to the ensuing phone call. He walked over to the window and looked out at the mass of the Sila mountains looming over the city to the east. He was now convinced that the origins of the case he was investigating lay there, and perhaps also the solution.

'*Un momento solo,*' he heard Arnone say behind him.

Zen put his hand over the mouthpiece of the held-out phone.

'Pull Mirella Kodra off the front-line surveillance on Mantega. It sounds as though he's starting to have doubts about her.'

Arnone nodded. Zen removed his hand and put the receiver to his ear.

'Signora Arrighi, this is Aurelio Zen speaking. I need to see you tomorrow.'

'Ah, that's difficult!'

Zen tried to visualise the room that Maria was in, a squalid cube lit by a shrill bare bulb beneath which a swarm of flies circled endlessly, and whose walls had even better ears than those installed in Nicola Mantega's office.

'One of my friends died last night and I'm helping with the arrangements,' Maria went on. 'I can't just drop all that now and say I have to go into the city to see my doctor. It would surprise the people here and cause comment. Do you understand, *dottore*?'

'Perfectly. And please allow me to offer my condolences. When is the funeral?'

'In a few days. Benedicta had relatives abroad. They will need time to get here.'

Zen grunted.

'Obviously I have no wish to intrude at such a painful moment, but if you were prepared to meet me tomorrow morning, I have an idea to make such a meeting possible.'

'Which is?'

'That you announce that you intend to make a pilgrimage on foot to the church in Altomonte Vecchia in order to pray for your friend. You might say that it is your belief that prayers sent from the old church are more powerful than those that originate in the new. And also that you wish to go alone, at – shall we say? – eleven o'clock in the morning, and be undisturbed. If you agree, I should then join you there, having ascended from the other side of the hill with some of my men, who will seal off all entrances to the old city to everyone except you.'

There was silence at the other end.

'You are proposing an assignation?' Maria said at last.

'Well, yes,' Zen said after a moment. 'Yes, I suppose I am.'

'Why?'

At first he didn't know how to reply, and then all the answers came at once.

'Because you're the only person I've met here whom I trust. Because you remind me of my mother, may God grant her peace. Because not long from now you will be as your friend Benedicta is, and I believe that there are things you have never told anyone which might compromise your bureaucratic status *in vitam venturi saeculi.*'

A long silence followed, then the acoustic at the far end of the line altered. There were background noises and a mumbly voice somewhere offstage.

'I'm speaking to my doctor,' Maria muttered. Then into the phone, very distinctly: 'Tomorrow at eleven? *Eh no, dottore! Mi dispiace, ma non posso veramente.* I have to make a personal pilgrimage, all alone, to the church in the old town up on the hill here to pray for my dear friend Benedicta. She was a good person at heart, but the manner in which she died meant that she had no time to confess her sins and I can't help worrying about the status of her immortal soul. So I shall be there at that time, not at the hospital. But thank you so much for having the kindness to call me. I shall not forget it.'

'Car leaves in thirty minutes,' Martin Nguyen snapped when Tom appeared back at the hotel. 'You want a ride home, get your ass in gear. I've cancelled your room.'

Martin's own room had been gutted and his impedimenta reduced to two armoured and combination-locked suitcases which stood beside the unmade bed. It had been a morning from hell. First the Iraqi work crew had had to be shipped off home, blissfully unaware that their death sentences had been revoked. Martin had got a break on the price from his Baghdad contact over that aspect of the deal, but he wasn't about to pass this bit of good news on to Jake – not that he could have got through anyway. Jake's site was down. He was offline. All you could get out of him was error messages and access denied.

'Mantega says he knows the people who found Alaric's treasure.'

For a moment, Martin thought that Tom was speaking Italian. He heard the words clearly but couldn't make any sense of them.

'Mantega?' he queried.

'The notary who was –'

'Notary!' Martin screamed. 'Who cares about fucking notaries? If they were any good they'd be lawyers. A goddamn fortune has just gone down the drain and you're talking to me about notaries! Are you out of your mind? Letting crazies board a plane is against FAA regs. Buy your own ticket home!'

Tom stood his ground. On the way back to Rende that morning, he'd called Mirella and suggested dinner. She'd said she'd check her diary and would get back, but she'd taken his call and she hadn't said no. Tom wasn't afraid of Martin Nguyen.

'Mantega is willing to get in touch with them and ask them to hand over samples for you to have verified as genuine by an independent expert of your choosing. If you're satisfied that they're authentic, further pieces would be available for purchase on an item by item basis.'

Martin speared Tom with a look.

'How did Mantega know that we were looking for that treasure? What happened to our film location cover story?'

'Well, there was that Aldobrandini interview. After that, knowing Mantega, he probably asked around. Quizzed the pilot or the ground staff. What do I know? It's hard to keep an operation of that size secret in a place like this.'

That made a kind of sense, plus it was what Martin wanted to hear.

'Okay, tell your friend the notary that we'll give him twenty-four hours. That's firm and non-negotiable. He has to get the samples to us for evaluation within that window.'

He tossed Tom out and started calculating time,

money, ways and means. Martin had always been boss at multitasking, but he'd never had a chance to do it for such high stakes before. There was a certain drop-dead parcel of land above the Da Rang river that he'd had his eyes on for years. He'd often dreamt of wintering there, maybe even retiring and going home one of these days. The country was opening up more and more with every year that passed, even for the sons of former torturers. Most of the population was under forty and had only the vaguest memories of those times. Besides, the Vietnamese had by necessity always been pragmatists. They might still pay lip service to the party line, but all they really wanted was your money. Martin decided that it was time to assert his ethnic and cultural origins, to reassume his *indochinité*.

He logged on to an internet research site that employed brainy, underfunded college kids and golden-age retirees who knew everything there was to know about just one thing, and within twenty minutes had a list of a dozen possibles which he whittled down on the phone to six, then three, before selecting the curator of antiquities at a museum in Bucharest. Martin had always associated Romanians with campy vampires and taxi drivers who couldn't find their ass in the dark without a flashlight and a map, but it turned out that the Romans had been there way back when and had left behind a ton of stuff on which this Gheorghe Alecsandri was a recognised world-class expert. Add in that the guy was cheap, available and spoke way better English than Jake and it was a no-brainer. Martin fixed for him to arrive that evening, evaluate the samples, return a thousand euros richer the next day, ask no questions and tell no tales. He then spent a half-hour online arranging for the overnight transport to the local airport of a product he had recently bought on eBay, before heading to the top floor to try and get Jake onside.

This wasn't easy. Just getting Jake to unlock his door wasn't easy. Getting Jake to respond to this new development really wasn't easy, but if that sweet chunk of real estate was ever to be his then it had to be done. Jake never talked much, but now he wouldn't talk at all. It took twenty minutes to elicit even the occasional 'Eeeh', but Martin doggedly kept going, repeating the gist of the story over and over again in different words. An eternity seemed to pass before he finally got Jake warmed up to a mental age of around three or four, at which point, just like a toddler, he wouldn't shut up. Martin then had to listen to a rambling, incoherent monologue about how Jake had been totally scammed and suckered. By the rules of the game the menorah had to have been there, only it wasn't, so the game itself must be screwed and that was like just such a total bummer, nothing made sense any more, what use was money if you couldn't buy what you wanted . . .

'Jake? Hello, Jake!'

'Eeeh.'

'Listen to me, Jake. Here's something I haven't told you. These guys mentioned some of the stuff they stole from the tomb when they opened it. One was a solid gold seven-branched candlestick. Mantega said it really impressed them because it was so big and an absolute bitch to haul away. Are you hearing me, Jake? The menorah was there, it's safe in their hands and they're willing to cut a deal. This ain't over yet, so don't go quitting on me now.'

'Eeeh!'

'Put the jet on hold. I've arranged for an expert to get here tonight, the director of a major European museum. He'll look over the pieces that we're being offered for evaluation purposes. If he says they're genuine, that means their whole story and the rest of the treasure must also be genuine. In which case we get back to the other party and tell them that all we're interested in buying is that big candlestick. After that, it's just down to money.'

Jake scowled and slouched around a bit longer, but in the end he seemed to see the logic of this.

'Yeah, well, like, whatever, I guess.'

The call that Nicola Mantega had been expecting came shortly after four that afternoon.

'Check your mailbox,' said Giorgio. 'Collect the goods and take them to the buyers for assessment. Keep them in view at all times and bring them with you when you leave, then take them back to where you got them, put the receipt in an envelope and deliver it by hand to the address written on the paper enclosed. These items are not for sale.'

Mantega ran downstairs to the bleak entrance hall of the building and unlocked his slot in the metal bin on the wall. Alongside the usual pile of junk and bills lay a plain brown envelope, unstamped and unaddressed. Inside was a left-luggage ticket headed Fratelli Girimonti and an address near the bus station. That day's date had been stamped below, along with the handwritten time of deposit, about five hours before. There was also a scrap of paper with an address up in the old city painfully written in block capitals.

Mantega decided to walk the length of Corso Mazzini to his destination and take a taxi back. The exercise would do him good and help calm his spirits, which were understandably in a state of some turbulence. He would also have a much better chance of spotting young Tommaso's girlfriend or any other visible tail. At the end of the gun-barrel vista that the long straight boulevard afforded, a massive white thunderhead was visibly expanding in the thinner air high above, burgeoning out like the blast of dust and debris from a slow-motion explosion. Down in the street, every surface was denuded by the caustic sunlight whose brutal candour taught every Calabrian that what you saw was what you got and all you would ever get, thus making life easier for such people as himself, who traded in appearances that weren't always quite so candid. He processed down Corso Mazzini, acknowledging the greetings of male acquaintances and the pointed glances of women young enough to be his daughter, telling him that while he might be a bit portly he was still powerful. They knew where the oil to cook their eggs came from. Mantega felt himself relaxing with every step he took. As long as he stayed here, in his own territory, surrounded by his people, nothing really bad could ever happen to him.

Fratelli Girimonti turned out to be an old-fashioned ironmonger's shop, opposite the square hollowed out of the hillside where the country bus routes terminated. It sold nails and screws and nuts and bolts and washers of every size and type, drills and chisels, hatchets and hammers, nippers and clippers, not to mention the cast-iron cooking pans, barbecues and patio furniture suspended on hooks from the ceiling. For your ferrous metal needs, this was clearly the place to come. The left-luggage facility was a minor aspect of the services available there, a remnant of an earlier era when peasants and travelling salesmen arrived by bus and needed a place to deposit their baggage until they moved on or found lodgings. Nicola Mantega handed over the ticket, paid the miniscule fee due and took possession of a large and surprisingly heavy cardboard box.

He went outside and looked around for a taxi. There were always a few of them hanging around the bus station.

'Prego.'

It took Mantega a moment to adjust his sightline to focus on the saloon double-parked outside the ironmonger's. It took him another to recognise the face of the new police chief staring at him through an opened slit in the tinted rear window.

'No really, thanks so much, very kind of you but I'd really rather take a taxi,' he blurted out.

'I'm not being kind,' Zen returned. 'Get in.'

Feeling horribly conspicuous, Mantega elbowed his way through the mobile mass of street people, students, African pedlars, gypsy beggars and bargain seekers.

'How do you know Giorgio's people didn't see this?' he demanded angrily of Zen as the car pulled away.

'Why should Giorgio expose his people to stake out a perfectly routine transaction? Besides, the surveillance team that followed you here didn't report the presence of any competition, so I decided to take a chance. Cosenza is starting to bore me and I want to force the pace a little. Let's have a look at the goods.'

With the aid of a nasty-looking knife supplied by

Zen's driver Mantega slit open the plastic strip sealing the cardboard box perched on his knees, revealing multiple layers of faded newsprint. Like children opening Christmas presents, both men started pulling out the packaging and flinging it on to the floor. Mantega got there first, and lifted out the most beautiful object that he had ever handled in his life. It was a beaten gold plate engraved with patterns of intertwined curling vines in relief. Zen had meanwhile found the other item, a shallow dish with intaglio designs of nymphs and satyrs. The gold glowed with all the intensity, depth and provocation of human flesh. Mantega felt himself caressing it as he would a woman's body. He was not given to feelings of awe and had no precedent for the ones that overwhelmed him now. Somehow the objects that had emerged from their tawdry wrappings in a reused cardboard box seemed more alive than he was.

'Where in God's name did Giorgio get these?' Zen asked.

'I have no idea. He wants me to take them back to that ironmonger's and deliver the receipt to an address up by the cathedral. He said they were not for sale. But of course you already know that.'

'Yes, but I don't have the address. Show me that note.'

Mantega handed it over with a sigh.

'Please be discreet in the manner in which you handle this aspect of the operation, *dottore*. If Giorgio begins to suspect that I have betrayed him, he will come to me and kill me! You understand?'

For a moment he had forgotten himself, and immediately feared that the chief of police might take offence. But Zen ignored not only his remarks but the entire subject.

'So now you have to show these little beauties to the American treasure hunters in order to demonstrate the *genuinità del prodotto*.'

'That's right.'

'Well, get busy. Things are moving more and more quickly, Signor Mantega. We must adjust to their rhythm if we don't want to be left behind.'

'I'll do it as soon as I return to my office.'

'You fool! I'll be listening in anyway. Do it now.'

It was an order. Mantega got out his phone.

'How are you, Tommaso? Good, good. Listen, I have a message for your boss. The samples we discussed are now in my hands and I can bring them to your hotel at half an hour's notice. But they are extremely valuable and I have been given strict orders not to let them out of my sight at any time. I therefore feel that on balance it might be best not to proceed until the person who is to examine them has arrived. Could you therefore let me know as soon as that occurs, whatever hour of the day or night it may be? I'll expect your call.'

He closed the phone and glanced at Zen. They were on the *superstrada*, near Carabinieri headquarters and the new railway station. He could pick up a cab there.

'Can I go now?' he asked.

There was no reply. Zen's silences felt far more menacing than anything he said, so Mantega was relieved when he finally spoke.

'Let's suppose that these samples are indeed certified as genuine. How do you propose to supply the merchandise for sale?'

Mantega had given a considerable amount of thought to this.

'I shall handle that part of the negotiations. Obviously we can't invite them to view the assembled treasure and then pick and choose what they want, since we don't have anything to show them. But such a sale would have to be shrouded in secrecy, for the protection of the buyer just as much as the vendor, and even the richest man on earth wouldn't be able to afford the whole hoard. When the time comes, I shall play on that aspect of the matter and try to elicit from the Americans what sort of objects they are interested in.'

Zen picked up the gold plate, whose essence seemed to hover fascinatingly between the soft glow apparent to the eye and the substantial weight of the mass beneath.

'All right, suppose that they say that they really fancy this dinner service, only they'd like the whole eighteen-piece set.'

Mantega smiled complacently.

'We have a long tradition of artisan work in Calabria. The lute and guitar makers of Bisignano are famous all over the world. Their ancestors were brought here from Naples centuries ago by the Calopezzati family. Isolated from all subsequent developments, they went on making their instruments just as they always had. When the use of those old instruments was rediscovered, they were the only craftsmen in the world with an unbroken tradition. It's as if the heirs of the great Cremona violin makers were still turning out seventeenth-century fiddles. What's true for them is true for many other trades, including goldsmiths. You may consider us ignorant provincials, *dottore*, but our isolation has served us well in that respect. Once we discover what it is exactly that these people want, a suitable replica can be discreetly crafted at very short notice.'

'Very well, but Giorgio is only likely to appear when the money is handed over. How and when exactly will that take place?'

'I shall follow a variant of the procedures for a kidnapping ransom.'

Zen eyed Mantega in a way that instantly deflated his earlier pride.

'Ah! I've suspected all along that you were familiar with such matters.'

Mantega swallowed that down.

'The case is of course not identical. With a kidnapping, the sentiment of the family is a major factor. On occasion, they will even pay without seeing the hostage first. That doesn't apply here. Clearly the payment and the handover of the goods must be simultaneous, giving both parties a chance to ensure that all is in order. I shall suggest my villa as a suitable location, and I guarantee that Giorgio will be present. When it comes to large amounts of money, he doesn't trust anyone but himself.'

Appropriately enough, they were now crossing the Ponte Alarico back into the city, within easy walking distance of Mantega's office. Zen told the driver to pull over and let his passenger out.

'You've got forty-eight hours to set up a meeting with Giorgio,' he said. 'After that, I'll take you back into custody and proceed by other means. And don't dream of betraying me in the smallest degree. You are complicit in the kidnapping and murder of an American citizen. Giorgio might kill you, but I'll call my contacts at the United States consulate in Naples and have you renditioned off to wherever they're outsourcing their torture these days.'

Gheorghe Alecsandri arrived shortly after nine that evening on a flight from Rome. When the passengers emerged, Martin Nguyen was waiting in the foyer beside his driver, who was holding up a sign with the Romanian's name printed in block capitals. Martin had vaguely been expecting an exotic creature from the Caucasian steppes – embroidered linen blouse, floppy black pants, knee-length boots – but his hireling turned out to be indistinguishable from all the Calabrians pouring off the plane after a busy day in the capital.

Once they were in the car, Martin produced an envelope and handed it over.

'Your fee, Doctor Alecsandri.'

The academic then made what would have been his first mistake had he been attempting to pass for one of those local commuters. He smiled, broadly, warmly and with apparent sincerity.

'Please call me George,' he said in impeccable English.

Martin noted approvingly that he immediately opened the envelope, extracted the sheaf of hundred-euro bills and counted them. Nguyen respected caution.

'So, you wish me to deliver an opinion on some antiquities,' Alecsandri said. 'May I enquire as to their provenance?'

'No.'

'Ah. And neither, I assume, about your interest in them, Mr –'

'That's right.'

Alecsandri looked away. It occurred to Martin that he might have sounded a bit curt, a shade too American. Business was business and the guy had already been paid, for Christ's sake. On the other hand, Martin knew that Europeans could be awful sensitive about their precious proprieties, and he needed to keep this guy sweet for now.

'The fact of the matter, George, is that I'm acting on behalf of a friend,' he said, with as expansive a gesture as it was in his nature to make. 'The items in question have been offered for sale by a third party. My friend is interested, but naturally wishes to ensure that they are genuine. Others are interested too, so we need to keep the whole enterprise absolutely secret for the moment.'

'Of course, of course,' the Romanian murmured. 'You can count on my discretion.'

Martin phoned Tom Newman.

'He's on the ground. Get Mantega round with the samples. We'll be there in forty minutes, max.'

In the end, it took twenty-five. At one point, Alecsandri pointed to the driver and whispered, 'This man's a maniac!'

'*Un romano,*' replied Martin.

Alecsandri tossed his head lightly, as if that explained everything.

The conference began an hour later in the sitting room that formed part of the suite which Jake occupied. It had been delayed by Alecsandri's desire to shower and change, and the length of time it took Martin to prise Jake away from his online game and Tom Newman away from his mobile phone, on which he had been making arrangements to meet some girl called Mirella at the Antica Osteria dell'Arenella for dinner the following evening. Tom had been speaking Italian, but Martin's passive command of the language was increasing by leaps and bounds. Too bad his ability to speak it lagged behind, otherwise he could dispense with his translator altogether. But he had plans for doing so just as soon as a deal was struck, so he didn't comment on Tom's evident intention of taking tomorrow night off. In fact, it rather suited his purposes.

He finally got all the players assembled. Martin himself was wearing his usual Islamic fundamentalist outfit: a black lightweight woollen suit over a grey clerical-style shirt tightly buttoned at the collar and tiny, highly polished slip-on shoes. Jake sported a baseball cap turned backwards on his shaven skull, a T-shirt that read 'AWGTHTGTTSA???', faded jeans artfully torn at the knee and thigh, and basketball shoes that must have cost more than Martin's whole ensemble. Tom had gone native in pigskin loafers, khaki cords, check shirt open half-way down his chest, a yellow lambs-wool pullover draped off his shoulders like a scarf, and aviator shades perched way up in the nest of blue-black curls above his broad and unfurrowed brow. Only Mantega and Alecsandri could have passed unremarked anywhere. Well, almost anywhere, because the Italian was clearly strapped, an automatic pistol peeking out of the shoulder holster he had left just sufficiently visible for his purposes.

Martin gestured to Nicola Mantega, who proceeded to unpack a large golden plate and dish from the cardboard box he had brought with him and lay them down on the long table of some faux wood. Everyone clustered around, but there weren't enough chairs for them all to sit down.

'You go here,' Martin told Jake. 'George, over there please.'

He himself remained standing, as did Mantega and Tom. Jake picked up the plate and tilted it this way and that.

'Tableware,' he said. 'You ever meet Rob?'

The question was directed at Martin.

'We worked together on NT?' Jake went on. 'He bought his dishes at Costco, like in a crate, hundred a time, then threw them in the garbage when he'd done. Said it was cheaper than running the dishwasher.'

'And more environmentally friendly, no doubt.'

Martin felt furious at Jake for revealing to these foreigners that he, Martin Nguyen, worked for a moron.

'What do those letters on your shirt mean?' he snapped.

Jake returned one of his unfathomably shallow glances.

'Are we going to have to go through this shit again?'

Martin realised he'd screwed up.

'Hey, Jake, I'm sorry! Didn't know I'd asked you before.'

'You didn't. That's what it means.'

He stretched the T-shirt out tightly, his nipples poking through the cotton in a pubescently girlish manner, grinned hugely at the assembled company, then resumed fingering his wispy goatee. Gheorghe Alecsandri had meanwhile been studying the two artefacts on the table with the aid of various instruments which he took out of the bulky overnight bag he had brought up with him from the sales rep's cubicle into which he had been checked for the night. He examined each at considerable length, first by the naked eye, then under a series of furled magnifying glasses, and finally a small microscope that fitted away neatly into a leather case. He entirely ignored the massive silence which had formed in the room since Jake's exchange with Martin. He replaced the two pieces on the table, sat back in his chair and sighed deeply.

'Yes,' he said.

'They're the real McCoy?' prompted Martin.

The Romanian gave him a look that he understood better than Jake's, but definitely didn't appreciate. It was time to make enough money to buy his way out of being looked at like that, the same way you could buy your way out of living in a walkup by the freeway, if you won the lottery.

'I can't see what Scotch whisky has to do with the matter,' Alecsandri replied.

'Answer the question!' rapped Martin.

'They are quite certainly genuine, probably executed by a Greek artisan, or one familiar with that tradition, for a Roman patron.'

Martin looked at Jake, but he was staring at the blank screen of the TV and didn't appear to be listening.

'You're sure of that?' he insisted.

'It is impossible to be absolutely sure. Gold is a metallic element. It cannot be carbon-dated unless it contains organic impurities, which I doubt very much is the case here.'

'When were they made?'

'That is conjectural. On stylistic evidence, my best guess would be the second century after Christ. Certainly no later than the third.'

He began to pack away his instruments.

'I might add, if this aspect of the situation is of any interest to you, that they are exquisite and show very little sign of wear. It is probable that they were used for display purposes, the actual food being consumed from cheap oven-fired dishes which were eventually discarded in the manner of your friend's colleague Rob in one of those landfill sites that have proved so useful to archaeologists in the past, as they doubtless will to those who investigate our quaint social customs in the future.'

He took one last look at the two golden objects and then stood up.

'Quite unique and inexpressibly precious,' he said. 'Were they offered for sale to the institution for which I work, I shouldn't have the slightest hesitation in advising the directors to proceed with the acquisition.'

He looked at Martin and grinned coldly.

'But I am not such a fool as to imagine that there is any chance of that happening.'

'Nice doing business with you, George!' Martin replied. 'Run along and get some sleep. My driver will take you back to the airport in time for your flight home tomorrow. Thanks for coming. We sure appreciate your input.'

When the door had closed and been locked behind the Romanian, Martin turned to Nicola Mantega.

'Okay, this stuff's good. What else you got?'

After listening to Tom's translation, Nicola Mantega gave an oddly feminine shrug.

'I'm just the negotiator. They haven't shown me any more than what's on the table now. But if there's anything in particular that you're interested in . . .'

'There is. Just one, in fact. If your friends are unable to supply it, then no deal.'

'They are not my friends, *signore*, but I can certainly make enquiries. Discreetly, of course, given the highly sensitive nature of the transaction. Please provide further details of the item in question.'

Jake shot Martin a Greta Garbo look and shambled off into the bedroom, mumbling to himself in Leetspeak. Taking the hint, Martin Nguyen slapped the startled Mantega on the back.

'Hey, it's past midnight! Let's all get some sleep and then talk it through over lunch tomorrow.'

The three of them trooped out and headed for the lifts. Tomorrow, thought Martin, it was going to be time to try out his rudimentary Italian on Nicola Mantega. He didn't trust himself to handle the detailed negotiations involved in the purchase and handover of the menorah, but there was another matter that he had to communicate privately to this sleazy notary public. One of Martin's principles in life was never to leave his personal security in pawn to third parties with everything to gain and nothing to lose by revealing – or threatening to reveal – the truth. So Tom would have to be disposed of. Calabria struck Martin as a suitable place for this to happen, and Nicola Mantega as the kind of operator who might well know someone prepared, for the going rate, to take care of this chore.

A hawk was being harassed by a pack of crows. To gain altitude, they beat their wings like drowning swimmers thrashing about, then swivelled and dived as if to ram their opponent, squawking madly but always deliberately missing their target. At each feigned assault, the hawk adjusted the angle of its outstretched wings and glided on, surfing the currents of hot air rising from the rock and scrub beneath. It could easily have turned on its tormentors and gutted them with its great claws, but killing on the wing was alien to its species. For their part, the mob of crows might have attacked this competitor on their territory in earnest, flustering it enough to give one of them an opening to drive its spiky beak into the intruder's body, but neither was such behaviour programmed into their genetic code. It was thus a confrontation that neither protagonist could win decisively, and would go on and on until one or the other tired of the game and gave up.

Aurelio Zen had never paid much attention to birds, but the stealthy approach of death had made him more attentive to any form of life. He was sitting on the top step of the burnt-out *bastiglia*, on the very spot where Pietro Ottavio had been explosively decapitated, looking alternately up at this dumb show in the sky and down at the tapestry of plants and shrubs that had established themselves among the charred blocks of stone in the years since the baronial residence had been consumed by fire one winter night.

The most striking specimen was a fig tree whose roots must, with their seemingly intuitive attraction to proximate water, have found out the ancient well which had once supplied the needs of the Calopezzati family and its retinue of servants, clerks, managers and armed guards. There was also a young almond on whose leaves a beetle resembling a piece of jewellery was crawling about, its carapace a brilliant green flecked with gold and black. Eventually it took to the air with a low droning noise like a clockwork toy and was snaffled up by a passing golden oriole. Zen consoled himself for its loss by turning his attention back to the aerial scrimmage. He knew the idea to be absurd, but it was difficult to believe that hawks didn't enjoy flying for its own sake.

In this context, the electronic whining of his mobile phone came as a double shock. How he hated these attention-seeking pests to which everyone was shamelessly addicted! He recalled a dinner party in Lucca where half the guests had spent the evening yammering away to people who weren't there while ignoring those who were. When he'd complained on the way home afterwards, Gemma had told him that that was the way it was these days. He should adapt, she'd said, but he couldn't. It was in his nature, just as the behaviour of hawks and crows was in theirs.

'Old woman attempted to approach up the path,' Arnone's voice said. 'I've stopped her and sent you her photograph.'

Natale Arnone was guarding the exit from the track leading up to the abandoned town from the new settlement of Altomonte. On the other side of the hill, Luigi Caricato was performing a similar duty at the only other point of access, which Zen and the two officers had used earlier, leaving their unmarked car in the deserted car park below. Zen pressed the necessary minuscule buttons and Maria's face appeared on the screen of his phone.

'Let her in,' he told Arnone. 'Then lock the front door until further notice. Tell Caricato to do the same with the rear entrance.'

A dark pall of thunderclouds hung over the coastal mountain range to the west, but here on the heights of the Sila massif the sun shone harshly down, except in the quadrant of shadow cast by the remaining walls of the Calopezzati stronghold. Zen had arrived deliberately early for his appointment with Maria, but now the outcome of their meeting seemed almost irrelevant. It was enough to be here, in the pleasantly warm and very fresh air, surrounded by a host of plants and creatures which Zen was unable to name. A diminutive, rotund figure appeared in the distance, making its way steadily up the former main street of the town past the ruined walls stripped of all reusable material, the cellars now stocked only with rubble, and the foundations marking the outline of vanished houses where vanished people had enjoyed or suffered the finite and largely predictable selection of experiences that life affords.

When Maria reached the *piazzetta*, Zen got to his feet and walked over to her. They exchanged restrained greetings.

'Are you sure you weren't followed, *signora*?' Zen asked.

He was enjoying his morning off work, but Giorgio had demonstrated his capacity of swift and merciless retribution and Zen was concerned for Maria's safety.

'Who would bother following an old woman like me? Besides, I took a side path which joins the main track well out of sight of the town, then stopped in the woods to see if anyone came. There's no need for concern.'

'You must be tired. It's a stiff climb.'

Maria made a dismissive swishing sound.

'I've done it so many times that my legs don't even notice. I could do it on a moonless night by starlight.'

Up here in the mountains the stars would still be a luminous presence, Zen realised. It had used to be like that everywhere, but within his lifetime that celestial array had been erased like a mediaeval fresco gaudily overpainted in a more enlightened era.

'Come and sit in the shade,' he said. 'It's deliciously cool over there.'

He pointed to the steps where he had been sitting. Maria shook her head with finality.

'Not there,' she said.

It took Zen a moment to understand.

'Ah, of course. Because of the murder.'

'What murder?' Maria demanded.

'Why, the American lawyer. The son of Caterina Intrieri, according to you.'

Now Maria looked confused.

'There's a bench beside the church,' she said. 'It'll be just as shady there and we'll get the breeze from Monte Botte Donato. It's very healthy, scented with resin. At least it used to be, before the railway came and they cut all the trees down. My father worked for the company that bought the rights. He said that felling those enormous pines was like chopping off your own limbs. But we needed the money.'

Zen noted her agitation, and the chatter with which she had tried to conceal it, but made no comment.

'So, what is it you want from me?' Maria said, when they had taken their places on the stone bench.

'I want you to tell me everything you know, have heard or can guess about the man called Giorgio,' he said with an earnest edge quite as revealing in its way as Maria's babble. 'You won't give me that, of course, but I beg you to give me something, anything. This man is not only evil but quite possibly mad. He dressed up Caterina's son as a corpse and made him walk up that path you have taken so many times, then pressed the button of a remote control, like changing channels on TV, and blew his head off. He personally cut off the tip of Francesco Nicastro's tongue. You heard the screams. The boy may never be able to talk or eat normally again. I realise that it's difficult for you to tell me what I know you know, because I am who I am and you are who you are. But your friend Benedicta has just died, *signora*. Your own death, may God forbid, cannot be long delayed. Do you want to go to your grave knowing that you protected a sadistic murderer, a threat to the community of which you are a part, because you were too proud to talk to the one person who could prevent him from doing any more harm? Deliberately and wilfully indulged, *signora*, pride is a mortal sin. Even the blessed sacraments may not suffice to ensure the salvation of your soul.'

Maria listened to this speech in silence.

'Did your mother want you to be a priest rather than a policeman?' she asked at last.

Zen smiled meekly.

'She never got over it. But I had no vocation.'

'Well, you certainly put our local priest to shame. A little too emphatic, perhaps, but that's to be expected in someone so young.'

But I do have a vocation, Zen thought. It's this stupid, meaningless, utterly compromised job that I try to do as well as I can.

'Were the origins of the child baptised Pietro Ottavio Calopezzati ever questioned?' he asked.

'Only once. Some Fascist bureaucrat from the north with ideas above his station asked *la baronessa* to confirm that the baby was indeed her natural child.'

'And what did she reply?'

'"I solemnly swear that this child was born of no other woman." Which was literally true.'

'And Giorgio?' prompted Zen.

341

Maria considered this for some time, her head tilted askew like a bird's, her eyes focused on nothing apparent.

'I know for certain only that he calls himself that. The rest is hearsay. I have heard that his family name is Fardella or Fardeja. I have heard that he sells foreign drugs to our young people, that he has become addicted to them himself and that he lives in San Giovanni in Fiore. But he won't be there now.'

'Where will he be?'

Maria looked at him as though this question were too ingenuous to bother answering.

'In the mountains, of course. *Si è dato al brigantaggio.* That's what our men have done for centuries when the authorities hunted them down. They hide away in the forest, then watch and wait their chance.'

'You said there were no forests left.'

'Not like before, but there are places which were too far away from the railway to be worth logging. That's where Giorgio will be. You could send a regiment to search those crags and they'd never find him!'

The last sentence was uttered as a defiant taunt. Zen glanced up at the lid of cloud sliding over the sky. The avian duel aloft had ended with the hawk being seen off by its pack of opponents, which now sat crowing harshly atop the burned-out shell of the huge mansion.

'But why did Giorgio kill his kidnapping hostage as soon as he found out that he was a member of the Calopezzati family?' Zen murmured, as if talking to himself aloud.

Maria appeared to be appraising the appearance of her shoes.

'I have heard two stories,' she replied at last in an equally neutral tone. 'Some people say that over a century ago, before the Great War, the Calopezzati stole a piece of land belonging to Giorgio's great-grandmother. They used to do that all the time, to even out the borders of their estate. They would simply seize land that didn't belong to them, put up fences and send their guards to patrol the territory. The wronged family could seek redress in court, but the judgement wouldn't be handed down for decades, most people couldn't afford the legal fees and everyone knew that the Calopezzati had the judges in their pockets. So Giorgio's great-grandfather did what a man was expected to do. He took his shotgun and lay in wait for the baron one day, only he was discovered and killed by the guards. It was officially declared to be a hunting accident and no one was ever punished.'

'And the other?'

'That happened later. Everyone here worked for the Calopezzati, so the baron could pay as low a wage as he liked. During the Depression, things got so bad that families who didn't have a relative in America to send them money were starving, so they organised a demonstration in San Giovanni to get a decent living wage. That was all. No attempt to take back the land that the Calopezzati had stolen, no demands for the estate to be broken up and returned to the people, and certainly no violence. They assembled in the piazza in front of the cathedral, as they did every Sunday after mass, as much as anything simply to be together, to feel that they weren't alone in their misery. The police were present but made no attempt to intervene. What no one knew was that a squad of armed Blackshirts had climbed the bell-tower earlier that morning. Their leader was Roberto Calopezzati, the baron's son. At his signal, they began firing live rounds into the crowd. Amongst those killed was Giorgio's great-aunt.'

One of Aurelio Zen's strengths was knowing when to shut up. He did so now.

'One or both of those stories may explain why he did what he did,' Maria concluded dreamily. 'Of course he was mistaken about the identity of his victim. In any case, due punishment had already been inflicted.'

Her odd, oblique, glassy gaze went everywhere except for the vast ruin across the *piazzetta*. Never once did she glance in that direction.

'Punishment,' Zen echoed vaguely.

'The fire!'

A long silence intervened. At length Zen nodded.

'Of course. That terrible accident . . .'

And then, finally, Maria turned her alienated eyes on him and the blackened palace behind.

'It wasn't an accident.'

Zen nodded again, as though assessing a mundane fact which had just come to light.

'Why did you kill her?'

Maria laughed then, a rasping cackle that seemed to come from the ground.

'*Perché? Perché!* Because when I was a little girl my mother taught me how to lay and light a fire. Because every morning until I was sent away into service my duty was to rise before anyone else in the household, before it was light, and bring flames to life in the hearth. Because to make sure I woke in time I drank three cups of water before going to bed and my bladder never failed me. Because I stole a jerrican of petrol from the stores and spread it throughout the house and up the stairs to show the fire which way to go. Because *la baronessa* managed to clean up most of the blood but the smell hung in the air for days and the stains never faded. Because Caterina appeared to me night after night, her womb gaping open like an oven. Because I was lonely and terrified yet unafraid. Because to this day I don't know where they buried her. Because of the baby. Because.'

Zen considered this for some time.

'You said that when Ottavia Calopezzati informed the authorities that the child she was claiming as her own had been born of no other woman, that statement was true.'

'She strangled Caterina and did a Caesarian on her corpse with one of the kitchen knives. Miraculously, the boy survived.'

She turned to Zen and scrutinised him.

'There, *pretino mio*, I have made my confession. I swear to you, before God and as an honest woman, that everything I have told you is true. Are you going to absolve me or arrest me? Not that I care. This world is nothing to me now and the world to come will be far, far worse. But at least I have achieved something in my life. Yes, I'll go to hell, but I sent that bitch there first.

And not just in the after-life but on this earth, in her flesh, with all her sins on her head, unshriven and unblessed, and me standing out here in the piazza listening to her howls.'

Unable to sustain her gaze, Zen looked away.

'So now it's your turn,' said Maria. 'Giorgio's great-grandfather knew what he had to do when the Calopezzati seized his property. I knew what I must do when Ottavia Calopezzati murdered my friend and stole her baby. And you know what you must do.'

Zen got to his feet.

'I'm just a lone hawk, *signora*. Here in Calabria, it seems that the crows always win.'

He turned and walked away, leaving her alone in that desolate landscape.

'. . . unfortunately, but there are many other artefacts, inestimably rare, beautiful and precious, which we would be happy to offer for sale. It will take a little time to remove them from their secure place of storage and transport them to a suitable site for inspection, but assuming that your client's interest in the merchandise is genuine and that he has sufficient funds . . .'

'So you don't have the candlestick?'

Nicola Mantega would have put a slow loris to shame in the languidity of the gesture with which he indicated the pain, humiliation and infinite regret it cost him to confirm that, no, the sacred menorah from the Temple of Jerusalem, alas, did not figure among the items that his contacts had recovered from Alaric's tomb.

'Sure you do,' Martin Nguyen replied.

'He just said they don't,' Tom Newman interjected.

'Shut up and translate, kid.'

The setting was a fish restaurant down on the coast. Mantega had wanted to make a big-deal lunch out of it, but Martin had nixed that idea. He'd spent the morning at the airport, almost three hours wasted trying to get the replica menorah out of the hands of a bunch of customs thugs who seemed to think they worked for the KGB, and was in no mood for another lavish foodie-opera production with no surtitles. They ended up with a fish fry and salad. There were no other customers seated in the annexe at the back of the place, and the waiters, as if sensing the nature of the situation, kept their distance.

'Okay,' Martin continued weightily. 'Before we go any further I need a verbal undertaking from both of you that nothing mentioned here today or resulting from it later will be disclosed to any other parties. Do you agree?'

Tom Newman nodded and muttered something in Italian to Nicola Mantega. After a pensive pause, he nodded too. Martin Nguyen flashed them his horrifying smile.

'You may wonder why your agreement to this condition is necessary. The answer is that the scheme which I'm about to propose will mean laying ourselves open to charges of fraud, conspiracy and, at least in my case, tax evasion.'

He paused for the Italian translation – Tom seemed to have some trouble with the legal terminology – and then Mantega's reaction. Everything seemed to be going smoothly so far, so he was amazed when Tom expressed an opinion.

'I guess you can count me out, Mr Nguyen.'

Martin laid down his knife and fork, sipped his glass of sparkling mineral water and stared out at the lazy waves breaking on a beach that seemed both endless and pointless.

'I have to get back home, anyway. The police called me this morning. They're all set to release my father's body for burial, so I'll have to see to all that, contact the relatives, fix the funeral, get the will probated . . .'

His eyes clashed briefly with Martin's as he speared a calamari ring.

'Plus I don't want to be involved in any criminal activities.'

Not the least of Martin's talents was an instinctive understanding of the odds at any given juncture and a willingness to obey them.

'I completely understand. You must of course see that poor Peter is appropriately laid to rest. But I'm not asking you to commit any crime. All I need is for you to translate my conversation with Signor Mantega and keep quiet about it afterwards. Once we have reached agreement, I will give you the balance of your wages due plus a bonus of one thousand euros towards the expenses of repatriating your father's body. What do you say?'

The kid eventually settled for fifteen hundred, and Martin got down to business. He kept it brief and vague, partly because he suspected that Tom's Italian wasn't that great when it came to technical stuff, but mostly because he didn't want him to know any more than the essential minimum even for the short period he had left to live.

'The menorah which my employer wishes to buy is in fact in my possession,' he announced. 'However, it requires some work done before you, Signor Mantega, present it to the buyer at our agreed handover point. This process must take no longer than twenty-four hours.'

349

Mantega looked wary.

'What kind of work?'

'Ageing. Distressing.'

He caught Tom's panicked glance and amplified his terms.

'Making it look like it's been around for ever and buried in a damp vault for the last fifteen hundred years.'

Mantega digested this.

'So it's a –' he began.

'It's whatever my client believes it to be,' Martin interrupted with a significant glance.

Mantega thought some more, then nodded.

'We can do this. But why do you need me?'

'To clinch the sale, Signor Mantega. My client must believe in the provenance of the menorah that he will be offered for purchase. He must believe that it originally formed part of the treasure hoard in the tomb allegedly discovered by your clients. *Capito?*'

'*Ho capito.*'

'Excellent. Then I think we can dispense with our translator's services.'

He turned to Tom.

'Run along and keep my chauffeur company. There's a couple of matters I need to discuss privately with Signor Mantega.'

'But you don't speak Italian, Mr Nguyen.'

'*Hablo il denaro.* I speak money, kid. It's a universal language. Beat it.'

Once they were alone, he and Mantega got along famously. It even turned out that the pudgy wop spoke some English. They concluded the deal in twenty minutes, after which Martin went off to the washroom for a lengthy pee during which he called Jake.

'It's down to the price and delivery,' he said.

'No way!'

'So they say. We'll find out tomorrow. Only I'm worried about the price, Jake. I mean strictly speaking this stuff is priceless.'

'It's worthless?'

'It's invaluable.'

'It has no value?'

'No, like no one knows what the market price is because there's never been any market. I'll jew them down as much as I can, but from what I'm hearing it looks like we're talking seven figures. Maybe one and a half, two?'

'Wow, you don't know what this means to me!'

Martin Nguyen adjusted his dress before leaving.

'I think I've got a pretty good idea what it's going to mean to you,' he said.

'Congratulations on your demotion!' Giovanni Sforza cried as Zen passed him in the corridor on the way back to his office.

'What demotion?'

'My spies tell me that the word in the bazaars and coffee houses is that Gaetano's foot has been declassified from the list of species at risk of extinction. He'll be taking over here on Monday, so prepare to be forcibly retired to your home in Tuscany. *Beato te!* Only wish I had your luck.'

'Who's Gaetano?'

'Why, the man you've been standing in for! The silly ass who blew one of his toes off while fiddling around with the service revolver he hadn't used in thirty years. Sometime chief of police in Catanzaro and now appointed Supreme Czar of all the Cosenzas, in which position he will no doubt wield the knout with a vengeance. Gaetano will wrap up that murder case that's been baffling you in a matter of days. No disgrace for you, Aurelio. Down here it's not who you are that counts, it's who you know.'

With a twinkly smile, the *bergamasco* vanished into his office while Zen stomped back to his. As he crossed the open-plan area in the centre of the building, Natale Arnone emerged from one of the cubicles.

'Ah, there you are, sir! It looks as though things are finally starting to move. Instead of going straight to his office this morning, Nicola Mantega drove to the square by the bus station and took a large cardboard box into Fratelli Girimonti. He was inside just a few minutes, then proceeded to a residential building facing Piazza del Duomo up in the old centre, where he delivered an envelope to the mailbox of an apartment owned by Achille Pancrazi, Professor of Ancient History at the university. Further enquiries revealed that Professor Pancrazi left yesterday on a flight for Milan, accompanied by his teenage son Emanuele, and has not yet returned.'

Zen lit a cigarette, as much for the symbolic warmth it represented as for the nicotine it contained. The Questura's air-conditioning system had now been raised from the dead, so instead of his office being as sweatily airless as one of those containers in which illegal immigrants were found from time to time, it resembled the cold hold in a frozen-vegetable factory.

'We'll need to have a word with the professor at some point,' Zen remarked, 'but there's no hurry. What did our Nicola do after that?'

'He phoned the Americans and proposed lunch in a restaurant at San Lùcido, on the coast just outside Paola.'

'He used the phone we gave him?'

'Yes. He appears to be co-operating in that respect.'

353

'"Appears" may well be the operative word, Arnone.'

'He and the two Americans, Signor Manchu and young Tommaso, proceeded to the restaurant, where they remained for approximately ninety minutes. Unfortunately the nature of the situation was such that it proved impossible for our surveillance team to record the conversation without the risk of disclosing their own presence.'

'But Mantega presumably called in to report on these developments, as per the terms of his conditional release.'

'No, sir.'

A bomb exploded overhead, leaving their ears ringing and Zen's office sunk in near-darkness as the electricity went out.

'*Gesù Giuseppe e Maria cacciati a jettatura e ra casa mia*,' muttered Natale Arnone, making not the sign of the cross but the two-fingered gesture to ward off evil.

'What did Mantega do next?' Zen asked casually.

'He . . . he, er, proceeded . . .'

'Can't you just say "went", Arnone? You're not in court, you know.'

'Sorry, sir. He went to a village called Grimaldi, about twenty kilometres south of here, where he visited a famous goldsmith, Michele Biafora. His work has been displayed in Naples, even in Rome. *Madonna, che pioggia!* It never used to rain like this.'

'Why did he go there?'

'We don't know. Mantega hasn't reported in, and once again our people couldn't get close enough to observe the encounter. But we could easily pull Biafora in and question him directly.'

'No, no. This is not an operation that can be performed incrementally. When the time comes, it will be all or nothing. Afterwards we can pick up the pieces, such as *il professore* and this goldsmith, at our leisure.'

They stood in silence for a moment, during which a dim, sickly, fuddled light made itself apparent in the room.

'Ah, they've got the emergency generator working!' Arnone cried with some pride.

'Sort of,' Zen replied. 'Where's Mantega now?'

'Back at his office. Oh, one more thing. He also called young Newman, but not on his dedicated phone. He stopped at a service station on the *autostrada* and used a payphone. We picked up the intercept on Newman's phone.'

Another series of spectacular rumbles stunned their ears, as if the remaining weakened masonry from the shattered dam were now tumbling down into the flooded valley below.

'He asked what Tommaso was doing this evening,' Arnone added.

'Did he say why?'

'No, and the American didn't ask. He told Mantega that he would be spending the evening with his girlfriend. That's the Digos agent you assigned to that task, Mirella Kodra.'

Zen noted the look on Arnone's face.

'Are you jealous?' he enquired with a hint of malice.

355

'No, no! Those Digos girls turn up their noses at ordinary cops like me. Besides, with a name like that she must be from one of the Albanian communities here. Those people are weird. It would never work out.'

He stifled a laugh.

'Apparently that guy she teams up with when they need a young couple is openly gay. I heard he stuck his tongue in her mouth during one of their fake clinches. Mirella spat in his face and told him to go and ram a gerbil up his boyfriend's arse!'

Arnone burst into further laughter, from the belly this time, then froze.

'Sorry, sir. Don't know what came over me.'

Zen had a pretty good idea, but did not comment on this aspect of the matter.

'Very good, Arnone. Now then, I need to trace all persons by the name of Fardella or some dialect version thereof who were either born or have ever been resident in San Giovanni in Fiore. Check our own records, then get on to the town council. But discreetly. Make it sound like a routine bureaucratic enquiry of some urgency but no real significance. Report back as soon as possible.'

'*Subito, signore!*'

Once Arnone had left, Zen called his wife.

'It looks as though I'll be home soon,' he said.

'Shall I put on the pasta?' Gemma asked.

'Not that soon, silly. But I've been reliably informed that my temporary posting here has just about reached the end of its shelf life.'

'Good. I've been rather missing you. You're an awful person to have around, Aurelio, but when you aren't here life seems a bit boring.'

'Accidie is a mortal sin, my child, a wilful failure to delight in God's creation.'

'On second thoughts, can't you get transferred somewhere else? Maybe Iraq.'

'I imagine that one of the few things the Iraqis don't have to worry about at present is feeling bored.'

'What kind of sauce do you want on the pasta?'

'Anything you like, my love, as long as no tomatoes are involved.'

Mirella and Tom were walking up an inclined alley in the old town when the attack occurred. The evening had been a success so far, in Tom's opinion, and he was looking forward to the rest of it. Mirella had suggested a restaurant he hadn't known about, in the cellars of an ancient building in a mediaeval suburb called Arenella, outside the original city walls on the far side of the river. As soon as they entered the wide, low vaulted space, Tom realised that this was where he should have been eating all along.

How does one tell, he thought as they were shown to a table at the centre of the action, yet just far enough away from the glowing bed of hardwood embers covered by a wrought-iron grill where gigantic steaks were sizzling. In some indefinable way everything just felt and smelt right. There was an air of seriousness about both the diners and the waiters, although neither were in any obvious sense taking themselves seriously. Whatever that quality was, it was as much taken for granted on both sides as the silverware and glasses on the tables, or indeed the vaccination scar on Mirella's arm. Her hair was loose and frizzy this evening, and she was wearing a sleeveless black satin top which displayed her bosom and those magnificent arms, on one of which, high up, appeared a tiny pale star that would never tan: shiny, almost translucent, infinitely touching and lovely.

No sooner were they seated than cuts of air-cured ham and other antipasti appeared on the table, together with freshly baked breadsticks and a carafe of water 'from my own spring in the mountains', the owner proclaimed with just the right air of arrogant nonchalance. He then announced that today he had managed to procure a supply of early mushrooms brought on by the recent unseasonable rain in the beech forests all around, and proposed a salad of *òvali* and *rositi* – 'the finest for flavour' – followed by pasta with more mushrooms and then a shared *fiorentina* steak, 'since you are a couple, so young, so handsome and with such healthy appetites!' His virtual commands having been approved, the owner bustled off to boss some other guests around while Tom and Mirella ate their way through shaved raw white and pink mushrooms sprinkled with oil and lemon juice, ribbons of home-made egg pasta overlaid with chunks of unctuous *porcini*, the best beef Tom had ever tasted, a fabulous salad, aged ewe's-milk cheese and the slabs of Amedei dark chocolate – 'seventy per cent pure cocoa' the owner informed them – that came with their coffees.

It was all fabulous and shockingly nude, each course explicitly and proudly just what it was, no messing about. Tom was personally ecstatic and professionally envious. The restaurants where he had worked were capable of good things, but there was always a tendency to go that little bit too far, so as not to be left behind by other gastro-brothels in town that went way, way too far. These people had more dignity. The food they served not only tasted good, it was in good taste.

But Tom's abiding memory of that evening, the one he knew would linger long after all else was forgotten, had nothing to do with their meal. The thunderstorm that had rocked the city that afternoon had been brief but extremely violent, and it had seemed reasonable to assume that the wrath of whichever vengeful gods ruled the region had been assuaged for that day. In Calabria, however, it was not always wise to let reason be your guide. Mirella and Tom were in the middle of their pasta course when the 'Tuba mirum' from Verdi's *Requiem* resonated thrillingly through the tomb-like cavern of the restaurant. There was a flutter of nervous laughs all around and then everyone started eating again, but a moment later all the lights went out for the second time that day. In a brief harangue from the darkness, the owner informed his customers that alternative illumination would be provided immediately.

And so it was. By the light of the huge bed of glowing embers under the grill, the waiters carried candles to every table until little by little the place came to life again, but a finer, gentler, subtler life, more intimate and complicit than before.

'Beeswax,' remarked Mirella, leaning over to sniff and touch the honey-coloured column with its oval tip of flame.

Tom didn't reply. He'd just realised that the hackneyed phrase 'falling in love' means precisely what it says. It felt just like falling, a blissful abandonment edged with shame and panic. God, she was beautiful! But it wasn't about that. He felt an instinctive revulsion – what the Italians called *pudore* – at the idea of enumerating and rating her physical attributes, even to himself. Yeah, she had good stuff, but so did lots of other women. What they didn't have was the mantle that surrounded Mirella like a saint's halo. Tom had never understood that musty old artistic convention, but he realised now that it was simply a means of expressing the fact that the person portrayed was exceptional in some way which we can neither define nor deny. He also realised that he was nuts, and maybe a little bit drunk.

'I hate the smell of those cheap paraffin candles,' Mirella said. 'The light they give is cheap too, thin and soulless. *Luce industriale.*'

She laughed at her own joke. Maybe she's a little drunk too, thought Tom. Maybe this might be going someplace. So when Mirella said that she'd heard of a good club in the perched city looming over them, one of the new *locali* which had opened in an attempt to restore some life to what was increasingly a ghost town, he enthusiastically endorsed the idea. They crossed the river on a narrow planked bridge, then proceeded across the road that ran along the right bank of the Crati and up several flights of very steep steps which brought them out at the end of a dimly lit, reeking alley that led up the hillside between two rows of unremarkable buildings that seemed to lean slightly towards each other, like old people seeking moral if not physical support.

When the man appeared from a doorway just ahead and dashed straight at them, Tom assumed that he must be late for an urgent appointment. Like the well-brought-up West Coast boy he was, he turned aside to let the other man pass and so the knife merely gashed his lower ribs rather than puncturing his bowels. In fact he was only aware of it when he touched his shirt to make sure it had not been disarranged by the encounter and his hand came away sticky red. Even then it took him some time to realise whose blood it was, largely because he was watching, with some dismay, what his date was doing to the poor man who had inadvertently bumped into him and had now turned back, no doubt to apologise for his clumsiness.

With a series of snarls and grunts that didn't even sound human, never mind female, Mirella pushed the man's outstretched arm aside, broke his nose with the heel of her hand, skewered him in the eyes with the long, delicately rounded fingernails that Tom had admired earlier, kneed him hard between the legs and then, when he bent over shrieking, in the face. Something fell to the cobblestones with a metallic ring. A hunting knife, it looked like. Gee, thought Tom, where did that come from?

'Police!' Mirella shouted. 'You're under arrest.'

She took a canister from her handbag and handed it to Tom.

'I need to call in. Give him a dose of this if he shows any signs of activity. Eyes, nose, mouth. Oh my God! Are you all right?'

'Sure, no problem.'

She tore his shirt apart and examined his flesh, exploring the region with intricate, intimate palpations, then got on her mobile and started talking in a way Tom had never heard her do: curt, concise and commanding. He couldn't make out much of what she said, she was talking so fast, but she sounded like she was in the military or something. No, police she had said. Police?

Tom might not have been able to understand what Mirella was saying, but it had an invigorating effect on the man, who had been exploring the alley on his hands and knees but now started staring around muzzily and trying to stagger to his feet. Tom administered a dose of the pepper spray, but he was standing downwind and even the mild whiff he got just about knocked him out. The assailant, who had taken it straight in the eyes, started howling and clawing at his face. And then there were sirens, winding up through the streets from the new city. Within a minute the alley was full of uniforms and paramedics in green who gave Tom a check-up on the spot before stretchering him into the back of an ambulance that had somehow managed to reverse down the narrow alley without fouling any of the police cars which had arrived earlier. Italians always seemed to know where they were in space, Tom reflected as the ambulance drove off, siren beeping in a loud, cartoonish way. Maybe that was why they were so good at art.

Sitting out on the patio of his villa the next morning, savouring a cup of Earl Grey tea and a slice of bread smeared with apricot jam, soaking up the sun and admiring the magnificent view, Nicola Mantega couldn't help but admit that he had been rather clever, if he did say so himself. It crossed his mind for a moment that he might have been a bit *too* clever, but after reviewing his plans time and time again he still hadn't found any serious flaw.

The deal he had made with Martin Nguyen, negotiated in a mishmash of his own small stock of English and Nguyen's crude but comprehensible Italian, was a thing of beauty. The American had apparently bought a full-scale replica of the menorah from an artisan in Israel and had it air-freighted to Calabria. The thing was constructed out of hollow steel with a gilt patina to a plausible approximation of the original design and dimensions, part of the beauty of the scheme being that no one knew for sure what these were. Nguyen intended to pass this off to his employer as the genuine article, supposedly looted by the tomb robbers who had first located Alaric's resting place. To do so successfully, he needed Mantega to have some cosmetic work done on the too-perfect replica and then present it to the purchaser in a suitably convincing way. Oh, and one other thing. For these services, he would pay Mantega a quarter of a million euros in cash.

But the real beauty of this new arrangement was that it cut Giorgio completely out of the picture. Of course, Mantega would need to lure him to a meeting where the police would be lying in wait to arrest him, but that could be done later as a quite separate operation. Or not. The word on the streets was that Gaetano Monaco would be returning shortly from sick leave to take over the position of police chief from this northern intruder who had substituted for him during his recovery from a serious injury to his foot, incurred during a heroic personal intervention in one of the cases he was dealing with. Nicola Mantega had never had any dealings with Monaco during the latter's previous posting to the neighbouring province of Catanzaro, but on the basis of what he had been told by various contacts who had, he was likely to be a much more approachable proposition than this Aurelio Zen. It wasn't that he was overtly corrupt, rather that he understood the infinite nuances necessary to the facilitation of all business in Calabria and was prepared to play within that set of rules.

Mantega checked his watch. No problem, there was still almost an hour before the charade got under way. He was slightly surprised not to have heard from Rocco Battista, the Cosenza low-life he had employed to execute the 'one other thing' that Signor Nguyen needed done. Mantega hadn't wanted to be a party to this, but Nguyen had been both insistent and persuasive. 'All he needs to do is walk up to my boss and say, "I think there's something you ought to know," and we're both looking at jail time.' At least Mantega had been able to talk him out of having the young man killed, pointing out that the violent death of two generations of the Newman family would be bound to produce huge publicity and a massive police intervention, neither of which was in their joint interests. Mantega's real reasons had been moral. Killing someone who had betrayed you was honourable; killing someone because you feared that he might betray you was not. On the contrary, it suggested weakness and was therefore despicable. Besides, Mantega quite liked Tom Newman. But the Chinese or Japanese or whatever brand of Oriental Nguyen was wouldn't be capable of understanding the finer points of Calabrian ethics, so he'd stuck to the practicalities of the matter. In the end Nguyen had settled for a serious but non-fatal wound that would look like a mugging gone wrong and put the kid in hospital until the deal was complete and the money laundered.

After their lunch down on the coast, Mantega had returned to Cosenza and done the round of various bars until he tracked down a suitable individual for this operation. Rocco Battista was a low-level thug with an equine member, a heart of gilt and the brains of a quail who was employed as a hired *spacciatore* to sell the illegal drugs that Giorgio imported and distributed. From Giorgio's point of view, Rocco was the cut-out, the fall guy. He had expendable written all over his tattooed, metal-pierced, razor-chop-side-burned face, and as far as Mantega was concerned the sooner he was expended the better. But given that he was still around, he had hired the little scumbag to do the necessary to Tom Newman, who would be dining that night at that fancy restaurant in Arenella with some hottie he'd picked up. Rocco was to call him from a payphone once the job was done with a coded message signifying that all had gone according to plan, and then he would be paid. But Rocco hadn't called, which was odd. He was such a greedy, needy little fuck that normally he would have called even if he'd screwed it up. *Ma pazienza!* Life was full of anomalies. The important thing was to keep your eye on the ball, and in that respect Mantega felt himself to be way ahead of the game.

He checked his watch again and reluctantly got to his feet. When it came to appointments, Americans were notoriously *terribili*: they always arrived on time. He went back into the house, showered, shaved, dressed soberly to impress and then descended to the basement garage. With some trepidation, he turned on the overhead lighting, fearing to be shocked by what met his eyes. But instead of shock, he was almost tempted to go down on his knees, although he wasn't sure that was what Jews did and as far as he was aware he hadn't a drop of Jewish blood in him, but who knew? No, it was a purely aesthetic response to an amazing artefact, taller than he was, glowing as though from within and branching out like a well-pruned tree, or an orrery at that fateful moment when all the planets are aligned.

After engaging the services of Rocco Battista the day before, Mantega had hired a local man who did small haulage jobs around the area to pick up the freight shipment that Martin Nguyen had cleared through customs and bring it to Mantega's villa. There it was unloaded, the wooden frame levered off, the plastic bubble-wrap removed and the candelabrum erected on its two-tiered hexagonal stand. At that point the gold-plated replica had looked impressive, finely detailed but rather raw and new. Mantega had also secured the services of a renowned goldsmith whose artisanal skills were unquestioned but who had fallen foul of the law some time ago over a delicate issue involving the precise provenance of the gold that he used to create his masterpieces. Mantega had been able to help Michele Biafora extricate himself from that self-inflicted injury, and in return for that and a thousand-euro sweetener, Biafora had agreed to come to the villa late the previous evening with one of his apprentices and spend the entire night treating the replica menorah to various toxic chemical substances and a terrifying variety of pointed and edged tools that reminded Mantega of youthful visits to the dentist.

All was now in readiness for the inspection by Nguyen and his boss. The local carrier's van was parked in the forecourt, and his two brawny sons were skulking about looking exactly like members of the gang that had supplied the goods. But there was one final refinement to add. He set the three oil lamps that Gina used to create 'atmosphere' for their outdoor dinner parties down on the concrete floor of the garage, fired them into life and then threw the breaker on the fuse box supplying the basement. In the lambent, uncertain radiance of the lanterns, the menorah looked even better. In fact it looked perfect.

The two Americans arrived at precisely one minute before the appointed hour. Mantega had already seen the one that Nguyen referred to as his employer, although he found this hard to believe. He had privately dubbed him 'the ape', and felt almost aggrieved on behalf of his employee. Mantega didn't like Martin Nguyen, much less trust him, but he respected him as a type of man he recognised, someone who knew how to get things done. So why was he working for the creature that now slouched in wearing a T-shirt that displayed his beefy tattooed forearms, a pair of torn jeans and some garish orange sports shoes? His gait, manners, expression and communication skills suggested that he was the lost sibling of the two haulage kids outside, but Nguyen had assured him that the ape was good for the one point eight million they had agreed to stick him for.

The fact that Tom Newman wasn't present confirmed that although Rocco Battista hadn't been in touch, he had done the business. Unfortunately it also meant that Mantega's carefully prepared speech in Italian about the power being out – one of those storms last night must have hit a pylon somewhere, happens all the time out here in the country, we'll just have to make do with these old-fashioned lamps I found – went for nothing. It didn't matter. Whatever Mantega's doubts about the ape, the latter evidently had none whatsoever about the merchandise being offered for sale. The visit was less of an inspection than an adoration. Mantega was reminded of a *nonna* venerating the miracle-working statue of some saint which was displayed once a year on his feast day, except that such devout elderly women would never disport themselves like this. Casting a huge hunched shadow in the wavering lamplight, the ape danced triumphantly about the golden trophy, uttering inarticulate cries and ejaculations and running his paws over the various knobs and curves as though he wanted to have sex with it right there and then.

In the end Nguyen managed to drag him away, but not before handing Mantega a note containing instructions regarding the place and time for the final handover and pay-off, and adding that he would need help to lift the wrapped and repackaged menorah into a waiting helicopter. Mantega was naturally bursting with questions, but Nguyen had made it clear that he wasn't going to answer any of them. Still, a quarter of a million was a quarter of a million. What had he to lose?

Rocco Battista had only made one mistake. Well, two really, but the second could be forgiven. Rocco had had no way of knowing that the girlfriend his target was escorting was a member of an elite anti-terrorist squad, well able to look after herself and her less capable companion even without her gun once she'd kicked her dress shoes off. And Rocco's first mistake could also be forgiven. He had stripped his person of all identifying marks and documents, but naturally he had taken his mobile phone along. Rocco was in his early twenties, and would no more think of leaving the house without his phone than without his trousers. And if it hadn't been for the intervention of Tom's companion, no harm would have been done. As it was, though, Rocco's defiant refusal to tell the (expletive deleted) cops the (expletive deleted) time by the (expletive deleted) clock on the (expletive deleted) wall became entirely irrelevant. The magnitude and resilience of Rocco Battista's balls was in no doubt, but his phone proved to be as forthcoming as a logorrhoeic teenager. *Un vero cacasentenze.*

The cache of names and numbers that Rocco's mobile yielded would however have meant little if Natale Arnone had not completed the assignment given him by Zen the day before. This had been to track down anyone by the name of Fardella who was connected by birth or residence with Giorgio's presumed home town of San Giovanni in Fiore. There were five in all, two of whom had moved elsewhere and one who was in a hospice. There were also Silvia Fardella, resident in Via del Serpente 13, and her brother Giorgio of the same address, born in 1968 and a butcher by occupation. All of which made a very satisfying click when Silvia Fardella's telephone number turned out to be present in the directory of Rocco's mobile. Her name, however, didn't. The script beside the number consisted of just three letters. *Lui.* Him.

Aurelio Zen was unable to attend immediately to the implications of this, since he had to deal with the appearance of the female Digos agent who had spent all night at the hospital with the victim she had been accompanying, on his orders, at the time of the attack. Mirella Kodra was extraordinarily lovely, he realised, in the abstracted way in which he thought of much younger women these days. Good legs, great *cioccie*, a fleece of fluffy hair atop an ovoid face that held its past experiences in perfect balance while eagerly looking forward to more.

'How is Signor Newman?' Zen asked.

'Stable and in no danger. He managed to avoid the main thrust of the knife. The resulting injury was a clean flesh incision about a centimetre deep with no organ trauma. The wound was cleaned, sutured and dressed. He has been told to rest, avoid physical exertion but stay mobile and return tomorrow to have the dressing changed and the stitches examined. After that he will be free to go home to arrange for his father's funeral. The doctors plan to discharge him this afternoon.'

'Very good. Unfortunately his attacker *sta faccendo il duro* and we've barely been able to get a word out of him. We must therefore assume that young Newman was targeted for the same reason as his father – because the criminals involved believe that he is the last living representative of the Calopezzati family. Since the initial attack was unsuccessful, we must further assume that it may be repeated. I am therefore transferring you with immediate effect from surveillance duties on Nicola Mantega to bodyguard duties on the potential victim. It would be unwise for him to return to his hotel in Rende, as those concerned almost certainly know that he was staying there. I want you to find somewhere else for him to stay and to ensure his personal safety until further notice. I have a major operation in preparation and I don't want it screwed up by some sideshow involving American tourists. Is that clear?'

The Digos agent came abruptly to attention.

'*Sissignore!*' she hissed.

She knows that I lied to her, thought Zen as Mirella Kodra stalked out. A major operation in preparation? Ha! He'd said that to sweeten the pill of taking this elite operative off active duties and relegating her to the status of a nursemaid. Judging by her expression and tone of voice, the pill had still tasted very bitter.

And what a fatuous, obvious lie. With only two days left before being replaced by Gaetano Monaco, Zen was in no position to mount any major operations, and everyone in the building, including Mirella Kodra, knew that.

Only what if they were wrong?

Aurelio Zen didn't think of himself as a gambler. He didn't buy lottery tickets or even play the Totocalcio football pools. Passing the famous casino in Venice as a small child, he had asked his father what went on in there and his father had explained. Aurelio was accustomed to his father explaining things. The procedure could sometimes be a bit boring, but he valued it as one of the few links between them. Asked about some aspect of the operations of the railway he worked for, for example, his father would always deliver a lucid, detailed and convincing answer. When it came to what went on behind the imposing portal of the *casinò*, Angelo Zen's tone remained calm and authoritative, but the content was reduced to the gibbering of an idiot.

'It's for rich people. They pay a lot of money to wager a lot more on a certain number or the cards they hold. Then they wait and see what happens.'

'And what does happen?' Aurelio had asked, clutching his father's hand as they walked along the redolent alley leading to the station.

'The right number or card either comes up or it doesn't. If it does, those rich bastards get even richer.'

'And if it doesn't?'

'Then they lose everything.'

At the time, Zen hadn't understood why anyone would want to take risks like that, entirely dependent on forces beyond one's control, an opinion that was confirmed when his father disappeared shortly afterwards. He'd lost everything without even being conscious of placing the bet, and had never thought to do so again. But life has a way of mocking such resolutions, and he now decided – instantly and without reflection – to stake everything on one spin of the wheel. He therefore summoned Natale Arnone and instructed him to fetch Rocco Battista up from his holding cell in the basement.

The prisoner was an unprepossessing specimen, vaguely resembling a genetic cross between a wild boar and a stockfish. It is no doubt true that the triumphs of art cannot redeem the defects of nature, but the various forms of mutilation that Rocco had inflicted on his features provided conclusive evidence that there is always room for disimprovement. He shuffled into the room and was about to sit down on the chair facing Zen's desk, when Natale Arnone adroitly removed it.

'Stand up straight before the chief of police, you scum!'

Battista stumbled back to his feet and stood looking around dully, but probably no more dully than usual. Zen had already been told that since his initial defiant statement of intent, the prisoner had not once responded by word or gesture to any of the questions and comments of the interrogating officers. He was also acutely aware that the success of the plan he had in mind depended on his eliciting not just a response but the one he needed, so he left Battista standing there, hanging his head and staring down at the floor in a manner which suggested, in a pathetically inadequate way, that while the cops could break his bones they would never break his will.

Zen lounged back in his chair and stared unblinkingly at the individual with whom he had to deal, taking him in, sizing him up, getting his measure. After an intolerable and seemingly interminable silence had fully matured, he leant forward like a doctor who has concluded his diagnosis, and spoke.

'In my opinion, Rocco, the root of the problem is that you are stupid. That's not your fault. Men can no more control the degree of intelligence they were born with than they can the size of their *membro virile*.'

A satisfied smirk appeared on Rocco Battista's lips.

'They can however control what they do with the equipment that nature has provided,' Zen went on. 'You were observed speaking to Nicola Mantega yesterday. When I broke him early this morning, I told him that he'd been silly. In your case, the appropriate word is stupid. I therefore suggest that we take stock of the situation in which you find yourself. The only witnesses to the attack were you, the victim and his lady friend. One, two, three. When this case comes to trial, any testimony you may give in your own defence will of course be discounted as worthless. As for the victim, he appears to have gone into shock immediately after you knifed him and has only the vaguest and most confused ideas about what happened. In other words, the only credible witness – the person who will in effect decide your fate – is the woman who was accompanying him.

'As you learned to your cost last night, she is also a police officer. Unless she wishes to relinquish that career, she will tell the magistrates simply and solely what I order her to tell them. If she testifies that your intentions were clearly homicidal, and thwarted only by the victim's agility and alertness, you will be convicted of attempted murder. If on the other hand she deposes that, far from being flustered and off balance, you knew exactly what you were doing – inflicting a painful but non-life-threatening injury, a little lesson for Signor Newman with the implied threat that he might not get off so lightly next time – then you will go down for assault occasioning minor bodily harm.

'Now there's a big difference between an assault and a botched homicide, Rocco. At least ten years and possibly a lot more, depending on whether the judge's piles are playing up. But at the bare minimum, a whole decade when instead of eating, drinking, fighting, fucking and indulging in whatever other pastimes console you for your destined role in life as a dickhead, you'll be locked up for twenty-two hours a day with five other dickheads in a cell designed to accommodate two, under the beady eyes of the uniformed dickheads who run the house of punishment according to their own tried and trusted methods, and take particular pleasure in denying their charges the tempting option of suicide by slow strangulation from a knotted bedsheet tied to the window bars.

'That's the choice facing you now, Rocco. Do you want to spend your next ten to fifteen years eating shitty pizza, stomping whichever of your cretinous crew is marginally more fucked up than you that night and contributing to the alarming incidence of sexually transmitted disease, or would you prefer to escape from these horrors and settle down to a quiet life at the taxpayers' expense? I appreciate that this is a difficult decision, particularly for someone whose head starts throbbing intolerably when the waiter says *"Acqua gassata o naturale?"* But I'm afraid that you do have to make it. Now. Specifically, in the next five minutes. If you do what I want, your prison spell will be so brief that you may barely have time to find out the hard way who gets to bugger whom in the particular wing of the facility to which you have been committed, since I doubt very much that you would be anyone's first choice. If not, you'll be offered virtually unlimited opportunities to suck your wife's cock.'

Another minute passed in silence. Then Rocco Battista spoke for the first time.

'What do you want me to do?'

'To phone Giorgio Fardella using the number registered to his sister Silvia in San Giovanni in Fiore and listed in the directory of your mobile phone under the name *Lui*. Your mobile carrier has informed us that you called this number three times in the last two years, which suggests that you are known to Giorgio but not one of his close associates. I'm guessing here, but it seems probable that he employed you from time to time, no doubt on minor jobs requiring neither intelligence nor skill but involving a risk to which he was unwilling to expose the more valuable members of his organisation. Three minutes.'

Once again, Rocco achieved speech.

'What do I say?'

'Giorgio almost certainly will not be at his sister's apartment in Via del Serpente, but someone will. You are to say that you have an urgent message which must be passed on without delay. The message is that Nicola Mantega is cheating Giorgio over their plan to sell fake antiquities to an American buyer. You have discovered that Mantega has made arrangements with a third party to supply the desired merchandise, thereby cutting Giorgio out of the picture and out of the profits. You will add that the deal will be concluded very shortly and that Giorgio, or someone speaking for him, should therefore summon Nicola Mantega to a personal meeting at the very earliest opportunity, preferably no later than tonight. Ninety seconds.'

In the event, it was almost half an hour before Rocco speed-dialled the number on the mobile that Zen had restored to him. It went completely against his nature to do the sensible thing, but the police chief had somehow talked him into it. What tipped the balance was that line about the bitch who had so royally kicked his arse the night before testifying that he, Rocco Battista, far from being flustered and off balance, had known exactly what he was doing. No one had ever suggested that Rocco had even the vaguest idea what he was doing. The prospect of being denounced as competent in open court, before all the judges and *avvocati* in their finery, quite turned his head. It might even get reported on television! 'According to the prosecution's leading witness, an experienced policewoman of impeccable character, Rocco Battista knew exactly what he was doing.' Making a hoax phone call to Giorgio, who had always treated him like shit anyway, was a small price to pay for a glowing public testimonial which would change his status on the street for ever.

The helicopter ride was maybe the sweetest moment in Jake's life. Okay, it had cost a shitload of money, but it wasn't every day that you got to stick it to your real-time opponent in such a satisfying way.

Phil Larson was still working on the logistics of getting the Aeroscan equipment back to the States, so Jake had fixed for him to hire a sky crane from the company he'd worked with on the survey. The idea was to fly out over the ocean, something to do with the movie, plus there'd be some bulky filming gear so they would need plenty of cargo capacity. After that it all flowed like well-written code. The pilot's English was barely comprehensible, but he turned out to be a real hot-dogger once they got airborne, plus the truck containing the payload showed up right on time. The only problem was that Martin Nguyen showed up with it, so Jake kind of had to invite him along. It would have been cooler to do it alone, but Nguyen's muscles and body weight might well prove useful when the time came, even with the grid of rollers that covered the floor of the hold. Jake told the pilot to drive out over the water a couple of miles or kilos or whatever they called them here, then get down real close to the surface and pull over so they could open the cargo door. The guy seemed to understand, and had given Jake and Martin harnesses and restraint lines to prevent them falling out of the open door, plus headsets so they could talk over the noise of the engine and Jake could give him instructions without coming up into the cockpit.

'We haven't interfaced on this, Jake!' said Martin's hollow voice over the intercom as the bear in the air ran up the tree. 'How can I project-manage the process without a data dump? Where are we headed? What's the deal?'

'Ninja looting.'

Martin started yapping again, so Jake turned the speakers off. Be great to have a set of those when Madrona started getting ballsy about babies. The helicopter flew over the wooded range of mountains that ran parallel to the coast, then out over the ocean, whatever the fuck they called it here. Who cared what they called it? It was all one big Pacific. At this point Jake realised that the pilot might need to rap with him about suitable locations for the next phase of the operation, so he turned his headset back on and guess what? In a total validation of everything Jake believed in – no, knew! – the pilot came on a moment later and said, 'Is good?' And it was. The helicopter circled round, dipped down and started running back the way they'd come. Jake slid back the cargo door and clipped it open. A hundred feet below, the water lay as crisply rumpled as a length of silk pulled off the bolt for the buyer's approval.

'Let's go!' he shouted to Martin.

It took maybe five minutes to get the crate positioned correctly and partially out of the doorway.

Way before then Martin had started yapping again, so Jake switched him off and started just pointing and pushing. After another few minutes of slewing and shoving they succeeded in manoeuvring the crate's centre of gravity over the sill of the helicopter's deck, after which everything happened of its own accord. The inner end of the laden box shot violently into the air, slapping Martin upside the head, then the whole thing flipped out and fell away – splosh! Jake watched it sink, unlatched the door, slammed it shut and told the pilot to drive home. He ripped off his safety harness and pranced around the cargo space, slipping on the metal rollers and falling hard, then holding up his hand and flipping a finger at the roof.

'End times, my fucking ass!'

You couldn't win the God game, but he had just stalled the inevitable outcome for a century or two. Life felt good and Jake aimed to enjoy it and Madrona and maybe even their goddamn kids, but it had sure been fun playing.

It wasn't till they were back over the coast that he noticed Martin Nguyen was still lying splayed out on the floor where he'd fallen, his head wrenched round at an angle you just knew had to be impossible except maybe for owls. As Jake gradually figured out what must have happened, all of his feelings for this man – who he'd known for like a while, and was pretty sure had screwed him over the purchase price for the menorah – came together in an impassioned outburst of raw, primal whatever.

'Dude!' he cried.

Tom lay on the bed staring up at an intricate pattern of cracks on the ceiling. They resembled a river delta seen from space, a satellite photograph of somewhere he'd never been, some remote place where the people had retained their traditional customs and cuisine, a lost heartland where life made sense the way it was supposed to.

The room to which he was confined was slightly larger than Rocco Battista's cell, but not much cheerier or better furnished. There was a narrow bed, a chest of drawers and some bare shelving. The window was locked, the shutters closed and the conditioned air chilly and synthetic-smelling. Outside the door, which was also locked, stood an armed policeman who admitted nurses and doctors as necessary, gave Tom his meals, accompanied him to the toilet and then locked him up again. He responded to the patient's Italian as though it were Japanese, occasionally shaking his head or shrugging his shoulders, but never uttered a word.

The exact time of day or night has little significance in a hospital, and it was not until a doctor came, examined the wound, checked Tom's pulse and blood pressure, gave him a tub of painkillers and pronounced him fit to depart that he discovered that it was in fact four o'clock in the afternoon. His clothing was returned and the taciturn policeman escorted him to a car parked in a quiet courtyard within the hospital complex. They drove north to an apartment block between Piazza Loreto and Piazza Europa, in the unprepossessing modern suburbs of the city. Tom asked several times where they were going, but the policeman either ignored him or just shook his head in the contemptuous and utterly final Calabrian manner.

They parked outside a charmless structure dating from the 1970s or 1980s and remained in the car for at least five minutes while Tom's escort scrutinised the comings and goings on the street. When he was finally satisfied, he got out, flung open Tom's door and scurried him inside the apartment block like a movie star's minder dodging the paparazzi. The scene within, however, was not a luxurious night-club or glittering awards ceremony but a dingy foyer with bad lighting, bad paint and seriously bad smells. The policeman spent another nervous minute while the lift trundled lethargically back to the ground floor and then conveyed them, equally lethargically, to the seventh. By the time his escort unlocked one of the doors in the corridor, Tom's wound had started to ache quite painfully.

Behind the door was a narrow passage lined with coats and books and umbrellas. The policeman looked inside one of the rooms to the left and gestured sharply to Tom that he should enter it. It was almost a replica of the one he had just left at the hospital, only with more dust and lots of cardboard boxes filled with files and papers scattered all over the floor. The only decoration was a large rectangular photograph of uniformed men and women standing in three neatly aligned ranks in ascending levels. Some graduation ceremony, it looked like. He had to move some of the boxes aside to get to the bed, and on top of the pile of documents in one of them he noticed a certificate from a police academy stating that Mirella Kodra had excelled in the firearms training course she had taken two years previously.

So this must be the spare bedroom in her apartment. No unmarried Calabrian woman would dream of letting it be known that she had allowed a man to spend the night in her home. Therefore Tom was not categorised as a man by Mirella. He was a problem, a job, a parcel that had to be passed around like in that kid's game. He was not a guest, still less a potential lover, just a displaced person who must grudgingly be housed and fed until he got well enough to do everyone a favour by pissing off back to where he came from. He slumped down on the bed, feeling utterly lonely and exhausted and bereft. What a fool he'd been, with his big ideas of rediscovering his Calabrian roots and opening *una vera trattoria americana autentica*! It wasn't so much what he didn't know. Given time, he could learn that. It was about what he did know and would never be able to forget, stuff that was inappropriate here, behaviour and habits and ideas that were alien, maybe even offensive.

But how could he pretend to be ignorant of those things? How could a person ever unknow anything? He swallowed two of the capsules he'd been given – without water, to avoid appealing to his swinish guard – then lay down again, gasping at the pain, drew his knees up into a foetal crouch and went to sleep.

He was awoken by voices he couldn't recognise or understand, a man and a woman, perhaps arguing. The room was in complete darkness. At length the voices fell silent and a door slammed somewhere. Footsteps came and went gently for some time, and then the door to his room opened and a figure in silhouette broke the rectangular panel of light. Mirella. .

'How are you feeling?'

'I'm feeling fine. You know why? Because I'm homeward bound, homeward bound. Do you know that song?'

'You told me the other evening that this was your home.'

'I was misinformed.'

'Not by me.'

Tom shifted position on the bed. Those painkillers really mellowed you out. Once his eyes had adjusted, he could just about make out Mirella's face.

'And how are you, *signorina*?' he asked with some asperity and using the third person mode of address.

'Tired. There's a big operation in progress. They're hoping to arrest the man who killed your father. They needed help with setting it up but don't want me there when it happens. That's why I'm late, and tired. When it comes to the crunch, it's pretty much boys only. That tires you, after a while.'

Silence fell.

'Why are you addressing me formally?' she said.

'Just trying to be polite. I know almost nothing about you, and most of what I thought I knew turns out to be false. You told me you were a pen-pusher and call-catcher for the local government, but apparently you work for the police.'

Mirella sighed.

'I'm sorry, Tommaso.'

He didn't reply.

'I'll make us something to eat,' she said.

'I'm not hungry.'

'You must eat.'

'Forget it! I'm not accepting charity from some soup kitchen set up to save immigrants like me from starving to death and making you guys look bad.'

In the doorway, strongly shadowed, Mirella turned.

'I am also an immigrant.'

'Oh sure.'

'It's true. I'm *arbëreshe*. Five hundred years ago, when the Turks conquered our country and burned our cities, my ancestors emigrated from Albania to a town just north of here, San Demetrio Corone. In our language, Shën Mitër.'

'Whatever you say, *signorina*,' Tom replied coldly.

The next thing he knew, she was leaning over him and shouting angrily.

'I wouldn't do this for just anyone, you know! You could be shut up at the men's barracks with a truckle bed and food fetched in from the canteen. I invited you here out of the kindness of my heart and you treat me as disdainfully as you would a whore!'

Her fury astonished him.

'I've never been with a whore,' was all he could find to say.

'You're impossible!' she cried and stormed out, slamming the door behind her.

Pots clanked and thudded, water ran, there was the crinkle of a plastic bag. Tom got painfully to his feet. Stay mobile, the doctor had told him. Don't bend or stretch or lift anything, but keep moving as much as you can. Just normal movements. He walked through to the kitchen. Mirella wasn't there. He leant back against the doorpost exploring the messages that his body was sending him. The first twenty-four hours will be the worst, the doctor had said. Pleasure is a fleeting illusion but pain never lets you down. It's the real deal. On pain, you can always count.

'Excuse me, please.'

Mirella brushed past him. She had showered and changed into a crisp white blouse and black pants.

'What are you making?'

'A pasta sauce. I also bought a roast chicken and some salad.'

'Sounds great.'

'No, only adequate. My mother is a wonderful cook. I take after my father.'

He watched her fingers working on the wooden chopping board, the spreading stain of the onion's white blood.

'Italian-Americans are always bragging about how great their mother's pasta sauce is.'

'Then it's good that you're homeward bound. Over there you can live your dream of Italy. Here we have to live with the reality. My father would kill me if he knew that you were spending the night here. But you can forget the idea of talking your way on to that business jet with your employers. One is dead, the other has fled the country.'

'What? How?'

She streamed pasta into the boiling water.

'They were dumping a crate at sea from a helicopter and something went wrong. Never mind, there are plenty of commercial flights from Rome. Go! Leave! The people who return don't fit in. They're an embarrassment, like house guests who've outstayed their welcome. They think they're family here, but they're just another kind of tourist. *Chine cangia a via vecchia ppe'la nova, trivuli lassa e malanova trova.*'

'What does that mean?'

'You see? You don't even speak the language! It means that changing your old way of life for a new one removes minor problems only to create newer and bigger ones. You have to have been born and raised here to be Calabrian, but these people think they've inherited the title like some baron in the old days. A friend of my father who lived abroad for many years said that America nourishes your body but eats your soul. Maybe it eats your brain as well.'

She added chunks of raw, lumpy, hunchbacked tomato to the simmering onions.

'And you accused me of being cold,' Tom said.

'I'm simply a realist. You Americans are idealists, and when reality doesn't measure up to your expectations you turn brutal. You invented your own country and think that gives you the right to invent everyone else's, even though you know nothing about their history or traditions. Why should you bother? History and traditions are the consolations of the poor. Rich people like you don't need them.'

She turned away from the stove and started to lay the table.

'I apologise. I invited you into my house and now I'm insulting you and your culture. That's unspeakably rude. I don't know what's the matter with me tonight.'

'I don't care. Just keep talking. I like listening to your voice.'

She glanced at him sharply.

'You mustn't fall in love with me, you know.'

'Why not?'

'Because you're homeward bound, Tommaso.'

'I am home.'

'Don't start that again! It's just expatriate sentimentality, and sentiments are of no importance here. All that matters is power. Sex may matter. Pregnancy and marriage certainly do, because those things have consequences. But don't imagine for a moment that anyone gives a damn about your feelings. Or mine, for that matter. The pasta's ready, let's eat.'

They ate in almost complete silence. Tom felt totally exhilarated and utterly crushed. He'd never been talked down like that in his life. Mirella said nothing more, and he was afraid that anything he said would sound stupid. But he couldn't take his eyes off her. He remembered now something that had been submerged by the shock of what had happened in that alley, when she was taking his attacker down with her feet and threw her hands up to maintain her balance and he'd seen the tufts of hair in her armpits and realised that she wasn't a brunette but a redhead who dyed her hair to blend in on the street. An Albanian redhead, at that. The prospect was challenging, but he couldn't take his eyes off her, couldn't wait for her to speak to him again, couldn't wait to suck the sweat off those hairs, to lick the tender hollow beneath and inhale the sweet, gamy essence of her flesh.

When the meal was over, Mirella brusquely rejected Tom's offer to help with the dirty dishes.

'That's woman's work. Go and lie down. You need rest.'

'So do you.'

'It's quicker and easier if I do it myself. After that I'm going to watch TV. Later on, I'll come and check the dressing on your wound.'

'Are you a doctor as well?'

'No, but I've got excellent first-aid skills. We have to take basic training and then refreshers every year. Don't worry. I know what I'm doing and it won't hurt.'

She piled up a stack of plates and dishes and set them in the sink.

'And then, if you're not too tired, we might fuck.'

Clatter, bang went the pots and pans.

'I don't know if I'll be able to move much,' Tom said.

'That's all right, we'll work something out. It'll help you sleep.'

'And you?'

She shrugged.

'I like being manhandled once in a while, and opportunities for casual sex don't come along often in Calabria. Besides, since you're staying here everyone will assume we've done it anyway, so I'd be a fool not to take advantage. But if you don't want me . . .'

'Are you crazy? Of course I want you!'

'Then there's nothing more to say. Go and lie down.'

Tom stood there uselessly, taking up space in the tiny kitchen, getting in Mirella's way. He had no idea what to say or do, so he asked the question that was uppermost in his mind.

'May I kiss you, Mirella?'

'No, that's too intimate.'

Once again he was tongue-tied and ended up speaking the truth.

'You're the most extraordinary person I've ever met.'

Mirella laughed dismissively.

'Nonsense, I'm very normal and boring. But I'll try not to bore you tonight, and tomorrow I'll take you to the hospital for your final check-up and then pack you off on the plane home to your American beauties with their stainless-steel teeth.'

Tom met her eyes.

'You can't get rid of me that easily, Mirella. I do have to go now, but I'll be back. I may not qualify as a Calabrian in your eyes but even you can't deny that

I'm an American. We don't quit just because the going gets tough.'

Mirella held up her right hand and extended the little finger and thumb.

'What's that?' demanded Tom angrily. 'Some superstitious gesture against that thing you believe in here . . .'

She flashed him a mischievous smile.

'*Cuntru l'affascinu?* No, I'm not that fascinated by you. Not yet, at least. Anyway, that sign is made with the forefinger, not the thumb. All I meant is that I want you to phone me while you're away. Now go to bed and get some rest, because that's not the only thing I want.'

The trap was set. There had been no phone calls to any of Nicola Mantega's numbers, but piecing together the previous evidence, including the recent delivery and return of the genuine Roman gold artefacts, Aurelio Zen had concluded that Giorgio was now on red alert and communicating only in writing. The team watching Mantega had therefore been instructed to keep a close eye on possible maildrops.

Shortly after six that evening, a roughly shaven individual of about thirty with the piercing gaze and rolling gait of the mountain folk had walked down the block of Corso Mazzini where Mantega's office was situated, entered the building and emerged precisely six seconds later. He was followed back to his car and at a hastily improvised road-block near Camigliatello he was pulled over by the Polizia Stradale and arrested for drunk driving, even though his blood alcohol level was in fact zero. Long before that, Nicola Mantega's compartment in the letter boxes mounted on the wall just inside the entrance of the office block had been opened and the plain brown envelope inside extracted. This was rushed to forensics for tests, then opened, the contents copied and replaced, the envelope resealed and replaced in Mantega's letter box.

The allegedly drunk driver had meanwhile used the one telephone call he had been allowed to make to contact the house in San Giovanni in Fiore which was the incoming conduit for Giorgio's communications network. Shortly afterwards, Dionisio Carduzzi was observed leaving his house and walking up the long, twisting main street of the town to Via del Serpente, part of the slum area of apartment blocks built illegally in the 1970s, many of them unfinished and unoccupied and all lacking double glazing and insulation and improperly positioned to face the full blast of the Siberian winds that dragged the temperature far below zero for much of the winter. Dionisio had entered the unit that contained Silvia Fardella's address of official record, but his visit was a short one. No sooner had he stepped back on to the street than Nicola Mantega's mobile in Cosenza rang and a woman's voice said, 'Check your mailbox.' The yob who had apparently passed out in a shady corner of the entrance hall, clutching an empty bottle of limoncello, confirmed a moment later on his encrypted mobile that Mantega had done so. What *il notaio* didn't do was inform the police of these interesting developments, but Aurelio Zen already had a copy of the missive in question in his hands. Stripped of its many orthographical errors, it read as follows:

I KNOW WHERE YOU LIVE NICOLETTA
BUT IT'S TOO RISKY COME TO THE DAM
ON THE MUCONE RIVER AT EIGHT THIS IS
URGENT AND I KNOW WHERE YOU LIVE

Zen smiled unpleasantly as he put the note down on his desk. Right now Nicola Mantega must be wondering how in the name of God it had come to this, running his mind back over each of the steps which had brought him to where he stood now, on the brink of a precipice, yet unable to fault himself for a single one of them. It had all made complete sense at the time, so how on earth had he ended up having to drive off after dark to a rendezvous on a remote country road up in the Sila mountains with a drug-addicted psychotic who would slit his throat if he found out what Mantega had been up to in his collaborations with the chief of police and the late Martin Nguyen, and for that matter might very well slit his throat anyway? But Mantega would go nevertheless, because he knew that if he didn't then sooner or later Giorgio would come to him. Better to calm him down now, deny Rocco Battista's absurd allegations and press a large bundle of banknotes into Giorgio's hand with the promise of more to come.

So the trap was set. Springing it, though, would be a delicate and complex operation, and Zen knew that he would only get one chance. He had therefore assembled a small group of hand-picked officials. Six of them, comprising Zen himself, Natale Arnone and four of the Digos agents, who had access to high-tech kit such as night-vision goggles, were to form the unit which tailed Mantega from the rendezvous point to wherever Giorgio was in hiding. In two separate but simultaneous operations, the residences of Dionisio Carduzzi and Silvia Fardella in San Giovanni in Fiore would be raided and searched and all persons present taken into custody.

Meticulous and detailed planning was the key to a successful outcome. The raids on the two homes in San Giovanni were relatively routine interventions straight out of the standard operating manual, needing only to be co-ordinated in time with each other and whatever events occurred after Mantega's meeting with Giorgio. It was the latter event that was the wild card in the pack. Zen spent almost an hour poring over a large-scale military map of the area with Natale Arnone and the Digos agents, working out various scenarios and planning an appropriate response, but he knew that Giorgio was both canny and crazy, an impossible combination to finesse against with any certainty of success.

Mantega had been told to come to the dam on the Mucone river at eight o'clock that evening. This dam had been constructed shortly after the war to create an artificial lake beneath the heavily wooded slopes of Monte Pettinascura, one of the tallest peaks in the Sila range at 1,700 metres, and one of the most remote. Zen's first step was to send one of the Digos men to the spot dressed like a hiker, to be dropped off by one of his colleagues as though he had thumbed a lift. He would not be part of the operation itself. His job was to walk up on to the foothills overlooking the Lago di Cecita, observe any activity at the scene and report back by radio. It was entirely possible that Giorgio might decide to arrive early and conceal himself until Mantega got there, or that one of his associates had been told to monitor any suspicious comings and goings in that isolated zone and warn his boss off if necessary.

The convoy of vehicles that would form a box around Mantega's Alfa were scattered around Via Piave, Viale Trieste and Piazza Matteotti by six o'clock. A Digos agent on the roof of an adjacent building was watching the private courtyard where the car was parked. The air was oppressively close and muggy down in the valley, while over the mountain range that was their destination stacked thunderheads loured and scoured the sky. A bad silence, against which the squeals and grunts and yelps of the traffic were powerless, had saturated the streets. Zen felt his energy drained and his will sapped, but there was nothing to do but wait.

In the end, Mantega did not leave the building until shortly after seven. This meant he would have to drive fast, which was good news. The vehicles and drivers at Zen's disposal could easily keep up with anything that wasn't airborne, and if Mantega had to keep his hands on the wheel and his eyes on the road he was that much less likely to notice that his supposedly lonely pilgrimage up into the mountains actually had more in common with the convoy enveloping the Popemobile when the Supreme Pontiff, in his infallible way, decides to pay a visit to the shrine where the cult of a miracle-working saint is celebrated. The lead man astride the MotoGuzzi played a classic hand of hiding in plain view, aggressively harrying the Alfa on the many tight bends and spectacular viaducts of the *superstrada* leading up from the river valley to the heights above, tailgating the luxury saloon with his headlamp blazing and making little darting movements that were blatantly obvious in both of Mantega's rear-view mirrors before roaring out to overtake and vanish in the manner of motorcyclists the world over, only to slacken speed as his machine demonstrated that it had more zip than stamina on the long, steep gradients, and eventually be passed himself in turn, at which point the whole game started again.

The sweeper on the team was in the modified Ape van. His job was to ensure that the Popemobile didn't have an alternative escort provided by Giorgio, and to take care of them in a suitably convincing manner if it did. The filling in the sandwich was provided by a vehicle that even Zen found interesting, despite not giving a toss about cars for the simple reason that the city in which he had grown up was one of the very few civilised niches on earth where they didn't exist, any more than horses had before them. Back then, if you wanted to go riding, you had to row over to the Lido. Even now, if you wanted to go motoring you had to go to Mestre. And no one in his right mind would ever go to Mestre.

But this item of Digos equipment had caught Zen's attention. As they proceeded up into the mountains, he elicited from the driver and his colleague, who were seated in the front, that the chassis was the military version of the Ferrari Laforza all-terrain vehicle and the engine – ironically enough, given their quarry – a specially tuned Alfa Romeo V6. There were six seats inside, as well as ample space for any extra gear, but the exterior bodywork was as near as makes no difference an exact replica of the cheap Fiat vans used by provincial tradesmen and wholesalers all over the country, to which no one ever paid the slightest attention. At the moment it was painted bright blue with yellow lettering which proclaimed that it belonged to Scatamacchia Formaggi e Salumi.

There was only one logical route for Nicola Mantega to get to his destination in time, so when they were past the summit a few kilometres from the Camigliatello exit, the MotoGuzzi put on a surprising turn of speed on the downward gradient, overtaking with some panache and surging ahead so far that it was able to take the turn-off while the Alfa was out of sight around the long bend behind. The driver swerved left and then right under the slender stone viaduct that carried the abandoned railway line across the ravine, turned off his lights, donned night-vision glasses and waited in the straggling outskirts of Camigliatello for Nicola Mantega to catch up, reporting in the meanwhile via the mouthpiece attached to his helmet.

Things almost went wrong when Mantega turned the opposite way, up into the village, to buy a packet of cigarettes and knock back a coffee. But Natale Arnone had been tracking the relative distance and direction of the transmitter attached to the Alfa, and the Laforza was able to park unobtrusively opposite a mini-market and wait for Mantega to proceed, at which point the convoy reformed. Because of this delay, it was now sixteen minutes to eight, of which it took *il notaio* another fourteen to cover the remaining stretch of twisty country road in the rapidly failing light. By the time he reached the dam, the motorcyclist had cut the power and noise of the MotoGuzzi's engine to the absolute minimum, then turned it off and free-wheeled down a path leading to the lake which Zen had identified from the map earlier. He then ran back along the shoreline to the dam, climbed up near to the roadside and reported in when Mantega's car came to a halt in a lay-by on the other side of the road. Once again, there was nothing to do but wait.

Two cars passed in the ensuing period of time, during which the darkness became absolute. The registration numbers of both were noted and checked against records at the Questura, but they appeared to belong to harmless local residents. No one will ever know what Mantega thought as their headlights appeared in the distance, swept across the vehicle where he sat listening to the radio and smoking cigarette after cigarette, but time in Calabria has its own rhythms which cannot be hurried. In the end he was rewarded when a black Jeep pulled up alongside the Alfa Romeo. According to the Digos agents watching the scene, the driver was a woman in her thirties or early forties, later identified as Silvia Fardella. After a brief parley, Nicola Mantega got into the Jeep, which turned right on to a steep minor road leading up into the mountains and disappeared.

This was the crunch, and it could hardly have been worse from an operational point of view. Zen had to make an instant decision which might prove disastrous.

He finally ordered the motorcyclist to remount and track the Jeep as best he could. It was a risk, but Mantega might well have other preoccupations at this point and ballsy bikers were two a penny up here in the Sila high pastures. He then called off the other Digos officer on the ground and the Ape van behind and told the driver of the Laforza to proceed slowly and with due caution. Eight minutes passed before lightning freeze-framed the thickly wooded landscape and a thundercrack shook heaven and earth, followed immediately by rain that broke on the windscreen like surf, overwhelming the wipers. Aurelio Zen finally relaxed. Now, he knew, everything would go well.

Next the man on the MotoGuzzi called in to say that the Jeep had turned off the paved road and taken a dirt track leading up still more steeply into the forest. Giorgio was presumably waiting at some spot high in the wilderness above, just as Maria had predicted, and there was nothing for it but to go after him, hoping that the deafening violence of the torrential rain would force any watchers to take shelter and also cover the sound of the Laforza's engine. The headlights could be dispensed with, thanks to the high-tech Digos toys – or so Zen assumed until on one particularly tight reverse curve of the precipitous, contorted and now seriously flooded track they unaccountably started moving sideways rather than forwards.

'Shit!' yelled the driver. 'Landslip's washed out half the road.'

The vehicle slid gently downhill for some distance before coming to rest.

'Can you get it back on the track?' asked Zen.

'Maybe,' the Digos agent replied. 'But I'd have to use full revs and they'd be bound to hear. I say we continue on foot and hope it's not too much further.'

Zen was aware that this was an attempt to democratise the decision-making process, but he couldn't fault the man's thinking.

'*Andiamo!*' he said decisively.

The rain had diminished slightly for the moment, but there was little comfort once outside the vehicle. One of the Digos men produced a hooded torch whose pinched beam was the only point of reference in the darkness, and the other three followed him up what was now to all intents and purposes a river-bed. It rapidly became clear to Zen that he was falling behind, and eventually he came to a halt. The others had disappeared, leaving him in the dark. He was also ludicrously dressed for the occasion, in his office clothes and smooth-soled leather shoes that were already drenched and spouting water with every step. He found his key-ring and switched on the brilliant stiletto of light attached to it. The trees to either side looked monstrous, the trunks twenty metres or more in circumference, the last remnants of the primeval forest which had covered the area for hundreds of thousands of years. There were still wild cats here, he had heard, and wolves.

Not unlike the man who had been baptised Pietro Ottavio Calopezzati, Zen started up the cruelly steep and rutted track and all things considered was making good speed when a flash of inconceivable intensity imprinted the entire surrounding landscape on his retina and the sky squealed and drummed its feet like a gutted animal. An instant later the downpour began again in the form of pebbles of hail pockmarking the molten mud ahead. Zen began running, slipped on a sheet of exposed rock and tumbled over what seemed a cliff, landing on a steep slope where he rolled over and over again before coming to rest against the trunk of one of those giant trees. The hail continued to fall deafeningly on the foliage all around, but where Zen lay the ground was covered with a deep bed of pine needles that remained dry. He heard distant gunfire – one shot, then two almost together – and got to his feet, but immediately tripped over a varicose cluster of roots. His key-ring went flying, and the miniature torch with it. There was nothing to be seen except the glittering array of stars above, each one hard, determinate and precise, but his nostrils were full of ancient odours, dense and strange, familiar and benign.

Jake dreamt he was flying. At first it was awesome, the scenery scrolling away like on Google Earth, mountains and fields and rivers and roads and towns. Some flyover state. He longed to nuke something, but he couldn't figure out which game it was, who the bad guys were or even the basic scenario. The only thing he knew for sure was that on an earlier level his character had spawned in the shining city upon a hill. That meant his game status was Exceptional and he had unlimited powers, which was way cool except he hadn't a clue what to do with them.

Maybe it was these doubts that triggered off what happened next, one of those dream things where everything goes bad just because it does, no reason given. There was this coffin on the floor he was trying to push out of the open doorway of the plane, only it was super heavy and wouldn't budge until suddenly the rollers kicked in and they both went flying, flipping over slowly down to the sea beneath and then into it, still tumbling. He ended up in a kind of desert with huge cracks in the ground and these giant spiders, except they were more like cockroaches, a gazillion of them coming at him, more and more all the time. It was a classic run 'n' gun, first-person shooter death match with randomised portals, only the software was way over-specified for his game controller, a dumb brick on a string with two buttons and a D-pad dating back to the eight-bit Nintendo games of the 1980s. He was getting killed here! This wasn't a game, it was a fucking cartoon. Loony Tunes Two. That's all, folks.

'Hate to wake you, but we've only got about an hour to run. Care for an eye-opener?'

Jake rolled over in bed and tried to focus on the babe who was shaking his shoulder. She totally wasn't Madrona, but he got there in the end.

'Sure.'

'Coffee, tea or me?'

Huh? thought Jake, but then he caught the look on her face and realised she'd been doing that thing that was big with the kids these days and gave him a headache, where you say one thing but mean something way different, ironing or something.

'I'll take a Diet Rockstar and some RapSnacks YoungBloodz Southern Crunk BBQ.'

'You want ice with that?'

He got out of bed and glanced out of the window. Mountains, fields, rivers, roads, towns, like on Google Earth. Some flyover state. He turned on ESPN and watched a bunch of ads. Black guys dunking big balls, white guys hurling oval balls, brown guys hitting white balls, all in sexy slow-mo. Ball games, celebrating designer sportswear and racial diversity. Cool. He sucked down his energy drink and tooled around the net a little till he found this site with a world map showing the area of darkness – kind of like a huge cock

– over the places where it was night. Right now Madrona was in the light zone, but the edge of darkness was creeping towards her all the time. The image updated automatically every minute, so you could just sit there and watch the shadow line jerk forward a notch as the sun sank slowly in the west. You learn something every day, thought Jake. Like he'd never realised that the sun went round the earth, although it was kind of obvious once you thought about it.

Then Madrona rang.

'Yo.'

'Where are you, hon?'

'Beats me. I get in in like an hour?'

'Bummer. I got a bikini wax at four or I'd come meet you.'

'Eeeh.'

'Are you okay, hon?'

'I had this weird dream? Kind of creeped me out.'

'Really? You know Crystl?'

'I totally know her.'

'She's just awesome with dreams. She talked me through a whole bunch of mine and showed how they like foretell the future and stuff.'

'Plus the movie thing tanked.'

'You're saying *Apocalypse!* isn't going to happen?'

'Not any time soon.'

'How come?'

'That's gaming.'

He barked a laugh.

'Chill, babe. It's not the end of the world. Life is good!'

There is a unique flavour of melancholy to remote railway stations during the long intervals between the arrival and departure of trains. And when the station is a modernistic monstrosity constructed a few decades ago on the scale befitting a provincial capital such as Cosenza, that flavour can become almost intolerably intense.

The platform stretched away like a desolate beach at the edge of the world. Opposite, a grandiose diagram of sidings was occupied by a few rusted wagons, surplus to requirements and awaiting the scrap man. The clock ticked off precise divisions of a time without meaning anywhere else in the world. Within the cavernous vestibule behind, three uniformed employees yelled insults at each other across the resonant space with the insolence of those secure in the knowledge that under the *statale* 'you pretend to work and we'll pretend to pay you' system, their jobs were not only guaranteed for life but left them enough free time to make some serious money in the black economy on the side.

Like mine, thought Zen. Italy was indeed the *bel paese*, inexplicably blessed, just as some people seemed to be. Everything went wrong all the time, but somehow it didn't matter, while in other countries even if everything went perfectly, life was still a misery.

'Il treno regionale 22485 proveniente da Paola viaggia con un ritardo di circa trenta minuti.'

No, he wouldn't lose his job. The delay to the connecting train from Cosenza to the coastal main line almost certainly meant that he would lose the seat he had reserved on the Intercity express to Rome, and therefore any hope of getting home to Lucca that night, but his job was safe. True, the powers that be had ruled that 'the tragic and disastrous outcome' of last night's events had been due to Zen's 'precipitate actions in a complex situation demanding the greatest sensitivity and local knowledge'. Suggestions had even been made that it might be in everyone's best interest, including his own, if he were to be offered early retirement.

On the other hand, he hadn't been termed 'grossly incompetent', which was just about the only way of winkling a government employee out of his comfy shell. If those railwaymen merely treated their customers with arrogant contempt, flaunted framed portraits of Che Guavara in their offices and fiddled the petty cash from time to time, no one could touch them. If they failed to align the points correctly or signalled one train into the path of another, that would be another matter. Zen hadn't done that. Two men were dead, but this had been deemed not to be 'as a direct result' of his 'regrettable initiative'. In short, he'd been a bit naughty but all would be forgiven. The Mummy State had merely scolded her son, not disowned him.

The night before, he had eventually crawled back to the track, where he was intercepted by the Digos agent on the MotoGuzzi, who had been called in by his colleagues. Zen had ridden behind him up to the crime scene. This was a level area which served as a trysting place for the young people of the locality, judging by the beer bottles, syringes and used condoms picked out by the headlights of the black Jeep. Nicola Mantega was groaning, trying to say something and occasionally vomiting blood. Near him, Giorgio lay still. His sister, handcuffed to the grille of the Jeep, was screaming hysterically.

Accounts of what had happened varied. Natale Arnone claimed that Giorgio had fired first, he had returned fire, and the others had then shot both Giorgio and then, in error, Mantega. The Digos men agreed that Giorgio had fired shots in their general direction, 'classic supersonic incoming whine and then the plonk of the discharge catching up, but nowhere near us', that Arnone had fired back, hitting Mantega, and when Giorgio ignored their orders to drop his gun they had killed him. The clearing was too small and overhung by the huge pines to bring in a medivac helicopter. An hour later, an army ambulance managed to negotiate the treacherous dirt track leading to the spot, by which time Nicola Mantega was dead.

'Il treno regionale 22485 proveniente da Paola viaggia con un ritardo di circa venti minuti.'

Aurelio Zen gazed up at the ring of mountains that hemmed Cosenza in on every side. It was not until the 1960s and 1970s that the *autostrada* and high-speed rail link to the national network had been constructed, but the character of cities and of their inhabitants are formed over centuries, not decades. Cosenza still viewed itself, and was viewed by others, as a backwater notable mainly for the fact that Alaric had been buried here. And he had done well, thought Zen. Whatever its shortcomings, Cosenza was an excellent place to be buried in, which is effectively what had happened to him that morning when Gaetano Monaco appeared at the Questura, bursting with confidence, energy and wisdom and eager to assume his duties and responsibilities as police chief of the province, the first of which was to show Zen the door.

'I'm sure you did your best, but we're not in the lagoons of Venice here!' Monaco proclaimed. 'No indeed! Calabria – or rather the Calabrias, as I prefer to think of this unique region, so diverse yet so cohesive, at once an infinite enigma and an endless delight – is a very special part of the world, *veramente molto particulare. Molto, molto, molto!* I sympathise with you, dear colleague. Your failure must pain you deeply, but I doubt whether any other outsider would have performed much better, if that is any consolation. The task you took on was simply beyond your powers. The fact is that only someone who had the good fortune to be born and to grow up here can ever hope to understand this extraordinary land and its even more extraordinary people, and know instinctively how to deal with them.'

Zen had been tempted to retort that he at least hadn't shot himself in the foot, but in the end he'd just walked out, leaving Monaco in triumphant possession of the field. True, the raids on the two houses in San Giovanni in Fiore had gone off without a hitch, and netted a wealth of evidence as well as five of Giorgio's suspected accomplices. True, Zen had stayed up all night interrogating the latter, and had bluffed one of them into admitting that Peter Newman had indeed been seized in a normal kidnapping-for-cash operation, but that when Mantega passed on the information that the victim's real name was Calopezzati, Giorgio had worked himself up into a fit of rage and sworn that he must die. Pietro Ottavio was denied food and water for three days, then told that he must do penance for his family's sins by making an arduous and humiliating pilgrimage on foot to their former stronghold in Altomonte to pray for forgiveness, following which he would be free to go.

In different circumstances, all this might have been regarded as a significant achievement. As it was, Zen had been subjected to a dressing-down by the *prefetto*, the magistrate investigating the case and an assortment of high officials at the Ministry in Rome, besides having to dodge a pack of newspaper and television reporters all day. Even Giovanni Sforza assiduously evaded him as though he were the carrier of some fatal virus. In the end, there had been nothing to do but leave.

'Il treno regionale 22485 proveniente da Paola viaggia con un ritardo di circa dieci minuti.'

A gust of wind stroked the platform with idle violence. Zen tried to visualise Lucca, and his life there

413

with Gemma, but he couldn't. Only this cradle-shaped tomb seemed real, all else an illusion.

'*Buona sera, signore.*'

An old lady and a boy of about fifteen stood looking at him.

'*Signora Maria, buona sera.*'

'Allow me to present my grandson. We're here to meet my sister. Go to the shop inside the station, Sabatino, and buy me a roll of mints. Here are five euros. You may spend the change on anything you like.'

The boy ran off.

'Thank you,' Maria said to Zen, once he was out of earshot.

Zen looked at her in astonishment.

'For what?'

'For killing that brute.'

'But I –'

'It needed to be done. Now we can all rest easy.'

'*Signora,* I –'

'You're a real man, the kind they don't make any more. Your wife is a lucky woman. May God bless and keep you always.'

'Look, I think you –'

But Maria was no longer attending to him. Her face was averted and full of joyful expectation.

'Ah, here comes the train!' she said.

Acknowledgements

I am indebted to Maurizio and Mirella Barracco for their help and hospitality. Fiction is a demanding mistress, geography a hard taskmaster. As a result, I have been forced to appropriate the former Barracco baronial estates and hand them over to a dysfunctional clan who do not resemble the original owners of the property in any way whatsoever and are purely a product of my imagination.

Like Communism, the *latifondo* system has virtually vanished, but it determined the economic, social and political destiny of Calabria for an even longer period and left scars just as deep. My guide to this eroded enigma was Marta Petrusewicz, who was generous with her time and whose study *Latifundium* is a scholarly but highly readable account of the Barracco empire and a way of life that now seems as remote in time as the slave estates in pre-Civil War America, but in fact survived until the 1950s.

This book is dedicated to the *cumpagni* who meet at a hut in the hills near Cosenza for long evenings fuelled by food, wine, conversation and haunting songs where everyone joins in the chorus, even the English novelist who was once invited there, and then invited back. I owe them more than I can say. Ar'amici da Caseddra:

Sabatino u Patruni, Giuvanni i Cacaprajeddra, Emanuele nonno Cariati, Ziju Micuzzu i Gangiulinu i Scarpaleggia, Damianu i Pacciarottu, Piatru i Pittirussu, Brunu u Sonaturu, Pippo Ardrizzo e Saverio.